WHISPER to me

NICK LAKE

BLOOMSBURY

NEW YORK LONDON OXFORD NEW DELHI SYDNEY

First published in the United States of America in May 2016
by Bloomsbury Children's Books
www.bloomsbury.com

Bloomsbury is a registered trademark of Bloomsbury Publishing Plc

For information about permission to reproduce selections from this book, write to
Permissions, Bloomsbury Children's Books, 1385 Broadway, New York, New York 10018
Bloomsbury books may be purchased for business or promotional use. For information on bulk
purchases please contact Macmillan Corporate and Premium Sales Department at
specialmarkets@macmillan.com

Library of Congress Cataloging-in-Publication Data
Names: Lake, Nick, author.
Title: Whisper to me/by Nick Lake.
Description: New York : Bloomsbury Children's Books, 2016.
Summary: Told through letter-writing flashbacks, Cassie is a New Jersey shore teen who over the
course of one summer experiences the exhilarating highs of new love, the frightening free-falls of
personal demons and family tragedy, and the bumps along the way to forgiveness, acceptance, and
self-discovery.
Identifiers: LCCN 2015022934
ISBN 978-1-61963-456-5 (hardcover) • ISBN 978-1-61963-457-2 (e-book)
Subjects: | CYAC: Letters—Fiction. | Love—Fiction. | Self-realization—Fiction. | BISAC: JUVENILE
FICTION/Love & Romance. | JUVENILE FICTION/Social Issues/General (see also headings under
Family). | JUVENILE FICTION/Family/General (see also headings under Social Issues).
Classification: LCC PZ7.L15857 Wh 2016 | DDC [Fic]—dc23
LC record available at http://lccn.loc.gov/2015022934

Book design by Colleen Andrews
Typeset by RefineCatch Limited, Bungay, Suffolk, UK
Printed and bound in USA by Berryville Graphics Inc., Berryville, Virginia
2 4 6 8 10 9 7 5 3 1

All papers used by Bloomsbury Publishing, Inc., are natural, recyclable products
made from wood grown in well-managed forests. The manufacturing processes
conform to the environmental regulations of the country of origin.

For Hannah, who probably deserves a cowriter credit as much as a dedication, but is only getting a dedication. Sorry.

inde latet silvis nulloque in monte videtur,
omnibus auditur: sonus est, qui vivit in illa.

She stays hidden in the woods.
No one sees her in the mountains,
But everyone hears her; it is sound that lives in her.

—Ovid, *Metamorphoses*

Monsters are real, and ghosts are real, too.
They live inside us, and sometimes they win.

—Stephen King, from the 2001
introduction to *The Shining*

These are the things that you need to know:

1. I hear voices.
2. I miss you.
3. I wish I could take back what I did to you.
4. What they said in the news, what they said I did. It's not true. You don't have to worry about that.
5. I'm going to write it all down, all about Paris and why I broke your heart, and then I'm going to e-mail it to you. It will take you, I don't know, a couple of days to read. So I will be waiting for you at **5:00 p.m. Friday** by the windmill hole of Pirate Golf on Pier One, where we played that one time.

If you forgive me, when you're done reading this, come and get me. Okay? Think of this as the most screwed-up love letter ever.

I hope you come. That isn't a thing you need to know, it's just true. I hope you do. I hope that when you've read this, you'll understand why I did what I did.

One of the things on the previous page was not true.

I don't, precisely, hear voices.

I hear only one voice.

But please know:

1. It's the same thing, whether you hear one voice or several. I mean, "hearing voices" is just what people say, isn't it? It's the common terminology. It doesn't matter *how many* voices there are.
2. Please don't worry. I'm not doing this to lie to you. In fact just the opposite. I'm going to tell you the truth, right from the beginning. All the things I left out, all the things I deceived you about, everything that happened after you left. *My* side of the story, not what you saw on the news. I'm setting it all down in front of you, once and for all.
3. Like my heart.
4. Like all that I am.

Yeah, okay, that was gross and hyperbolic; I can just see Paris miming putting her fingers in her throat and barfing. Sorry. I get carried away.

And I don't know. Maybe the Ovid quote right at the beginning was too much. But you do love the classics, and Ovid in particular. You said to me once, "Ovid knew more about body horror than any B-movie director"; it was when we were standing between mountains of plush toys, SpongeBobs and Tweety Birds looming over us.

And I wanted to kick this off with something you love, because I figure at this point you don't like me very much anymore.

Maybe I can change that.

I don't know.

1.

THE PART BEFORE

You know what this place—

I was—

Okay.
Okay.
Okay, so it's not like you need me to introduce you to Oakwood, New Jersey, or to the boardwalk or the amusement park. I mean, you weren't born here like me, but you know every street in this town.

The day it all began was a Sunday. I spent most of the day in my room, reading. Me and my dad never used to hang out or anything, even on the days when he wasn't at the restaurant.

You've never been in my room. It's not very interesting: there's a bed, clothes on the floor, old posters on the wall from when I used to be into horses. I've never taken them down. All along two walls are bookshelves my dad built for me. There are piles of books on the floor too.

Late afternoon, I felt like getting out of the house. When I came down, Dad was in his den at the back, next to the kitchen—I could hear him moving around in there, feeding his pets, or something.

"Where are you going?"

That was Dad, calling to me as I passed.

I leaned in the door. "Beach, maybe," I said. I had my sketch pad, and I felt like finding something to draw down there.

In Dad's room, glass tanks ran along the wall, glowing with yellow and blue light. Twigs and branches in them, moss. And if you got too close—which I didn't like to do—you could see creepy things. A praying mantis. Centipedes.

Dad was in the corner, at his computer, peering at the screen. Hunched over, his muscled shoulders tight. He's spreading a bit in the middle now, but he's still strong, still tough. Once I saw him pick up a full trash can—one of the big wheeled ones—and move it, without thinking, so that he could mow a patch of our yard. I don't think it even occurred to him to roll it.

"Don't be late," he said. "Not with that guy around."

"What guy?"

"The guy. The Houdini Killer."

"Dad," I said. "It's still light out."

He shrugged. "Don't be late."

"What are you doing anyway?" I asked.

"There's a guy on the forum got some beautiful *Tonkinbolus* from Koh Chang, Thailand—he went there and collected them himself, you believe that? Anyway, he's selling them, fifty bucks a piece. Blue-and-reds, fire-legs. Amazing."

Oh: this is something you need to know.

There are *forums for people who collect bugs*. I know. It's unbelievable, isn't it? And these people have little avatars that say whether they're newbies or Grand Master Bug Collectors or whatever, and signatures every time they post that tell you how many different bugs they have, and the names of them all, and sometimes some kind of generic inspirational quote that has nothing to do with bugs as far as I can see. My dad's list has a *lot* of bugs on it.

"What's a *Tonk*—whatever you said?"

He shook his head at me, like my ignorance on the topic of bugs was a great disappointment to him. "Millipede."

"Right," I said. "Anyway, see you later."

"Millipedes are ancient creatures," he said. "They're survivors. When threatened, they roll into a ball, protect themselves, you know that?"

"Yeah," I said. "You told me."

"Okay. So don't be late."

I nodded and turned to leave—he was already facing the screen again, typing something on the keyboard. Then he smacked his fist down on the table.

"And clean your ******** room, Cass. I'm not going to ********* tell you a-*******-gain."

This is living with my dad:

He says nothing nothing nothing nothing all day long

and then sometimes he says millipedes blah centipedes blah stick insects blah blah blah

and then

flash

like a camera going off, he hits you with something like that.

The only good thing is he doesn't *actually* hit me. Like, with his fists. Just with his words.

It isn't like he doesn't have excuses, for his anger. I have to admit. His wounds, I'm talking about: the ones you can see and the ones you can't. He didn't have armor, like a millipede; he couldn't roll himself into a ball. We'll get to that later.

Also, he curses a *lot*. And I don't really feel comfortable with writing down those words so I'm using stars, which I like, because it means when he's really, really pissed—and that will happen later in this story—the page will be filled with stars, like a constellation.

I got out of there quickly, left him with his stupid forum. I went out into the little front yard with its grass brown already, even though it was only May, and over a month of school still to go. It was shaping up to be a hot summer, the air sticky and close, though the ocean was still cool—I knew that because I had gone for a swim the previous day and nearly froze my fingers off. Not that it was stopping the vacationers: I had seen the buses unloading blinking college kids into the sunlight, and the boardwalk filling up with people in T-shirts, crackling with the energy of being released, from work, from normality.

Only this place *is* the reality for me.

And there were still fewer vacationers than the year before, a continuation of an ongoing trend that was the source of pretty much all of Oakwood's problems. Who knows? Maybe the local psycho was killing women because he worked in one of the strip malls that closed down and he's pissed that he lost his job.

Anyway.

Our house, as you know, is in what the locals call the "town." Which is to distinguish it from "the walk," i.e., the strip that runs along the beach lined with arcades, slot machines, stores selling BURGERS PIZZA HOAGIES, fortune-tellers, games, tattoo studios. And of course the amusement park on the piers, on which more later.

I don't know how you saw our house, when you first came. How it made you feel. Me, it always makes me feel sad. It's like you've stepped from VACATIONLAND! into the clapboard shored-up, scaffolded reality behind it, as if you've gone behind the film-set veneer. You can still hear the ocean—we're three blocks back from it, and the sound of the waves, the constant *tssschhh*, pervades the air for maybe four blocks. And as I stepped out into the yard that morning, I could smell the ocean and hear the calling of the seagulls.

The walk is all neon and lights—me, I lived backstage. Among the trash.

Sorry! This is super not-cheerful already.

What I mean: all the houses on our street are the same—little, cheap identical white blocks. Porches that, if we were facing the water like in Green Harbor down the coast, would be charming.

But ours are usually covered in car tires and broken furniture and other junk, some of it human.

A yard out front, a garage to the side of it, with an apartment above it. That part you know very well, but we'll come to you later.

I think it would be bad enough to live in a place that looks like every other place on your street, the suburban nightmare of America. But add to that the squalor and the pretending to be something it isn't, and to me it's everything that's wrong with Oakwood, New Jersey.

Or it was anyway. I guess maybe I feel kind of different about it now, after everything that's happened.

The part I love is the walk to the beach, because you go down Ocean Boulevard and as you get closer to the water, you start to pass those old historic motels that you love too. "Doo-wop architecture," they call it. Or "New Jersey vernacular." Like Vegas with more modest ambitions: strange space-age structures like interstellar ships that landed in the wrong place, and Egyptian pyramids and Hawaiian palaces. Neon signs, fifties' angles.

The Honolulu.

The Sphinx.

The Flamingo—with its flamingo-shaped pool out front.

Hardly anyone stays in these places anymore, but a few years back the town bought a bunch of them, to preserve them, which is about the best thing Oakwood ever did.

That's layer five of the town, because you think of Oakwood, if you grew up here, like something made of levels, like those cutaway diagrams of the ground, striations of different materials, loam and humus and igneous rock and whatever. There are seven, from land to sea, and they go like this:

- Mall land.
- Crushing, miserable poverty, boarded-up buildings, broken houses, broken people. (Keeping it cheerful!) The rhythm of the waves a background hiss.
- The residential layer. Houses. People live in them. Garages, gardens. Which merges with:
- Two blocks from the ocean: A sudden air of affluence. Vacationing joggers, running past their own parked cars. The ocean louder now, a soundtrack, whispering *fun*, saying *escape*. Even locals start to feel the pull at this point, which is why a lot of them stay in the town and never go near the walk—it's too painful.
- One block: those crazy pop-art motels, with their art-deco lines and neon. [To complicate matters this layer also includes some crushing poverty, just like layer two, so that the touristy part of town is bracketed by rundown buildings, like this sentence is bracketed by . . . well, brackets.]
- The boardwalk: pizza slices, girls gone wild, and people with facial tattoos.
- The beach: swimmers, lifeguards, seagulls stealing fries.

And of course there are layers of time too—the ghost town of winter, the crowded madness of summer. This story, since it's the story of you and me, happens in the summer. But you know that already. It's weird, telling you what happened, when you know so much of it.

But there is so much you don't know.

So much.

So, I walked past the crazy motels until I came to the start of the

11

boardwalk, where the wooden struts of it collapse into tufted sand dunes. The way my route goes, I join the walk on the south side, right at the end, so when you come to the sand you have the whole sweep of the bay to your left, the long, wide wooden boards lined with little shops and restaurants, one of which is Dad's restaurant of course, my restaurant too, I suppose you could say, the family restaurant, where . . . well, we'll get to that later; and jutting from the boardwalk, the enormous piers with their roller-coaster rides rising up like the backs of sea monsters, the expanse of gray-yellow sand. The fairground atmosphere.

From that vantage point, it's beautiful. Which is why I have never tried to draw it.

I scanned the sand until I saw something that looked more promising. Then I walked out onto the beach, checking it out, taking my time. Yeah, it looked good. I went out farther, toward the ocean.

Now I was just past Pier One and a little south, so I could see the curve of the old Accelerator, like a wooden dinosaur's back, and the slowly turning wheel of the Elevator taking people in their little seats high up into the sky, for a bird's-eye view of the worst town on the Eastern Seaboard.

What I was doing, I was planning to draw a dead seagull. That was my thing: I don't think you ever knew that. I don't remember mentioning it. The thing being: to find the ugly things, the things people don't usually notice, and draw them in my sketch pad. Like:

Electricity poles.
Trash cans.
Broken windows.
And, in this case, dead seagulls. The bird was just where

the water and sand met, way beyond the end of Pier One. I
don't know why the ocean has receded so much here, I—

Oh my God.

I just realized something. My dad with his gross insects. Me
drawing the ugly things. We were both collecting stuff other people
discounted as unattractive. *We were doing the same thing.* Mom
always said we were more alike than I realized, he and I.

So, right here on page 13, I want you to make a mental note of this:
me and my dad, we're not too different. We both got threatened,
and we both reacted in the only way we knew how, by instinct, like
millipedes rolling into balls. He's not as bad as you might think, you
know, from him throwing you out and all. He's like me—he just
faced his anger outward instead of inward.

Of course, when I say he's like me, you may view that as a bad thing,
I don't know. I guess I'll see on Friday, from whether you turn up
or not.

Where was I?

The beach. I don't know why the ocean has receded so much and
left such an enormous strip of sand—three hundred yards at least.
I mean, I read almost anything but definitely not geology or whatever the right -ology would be. Mom said the ocean was scared of
the white trash who come here in the summer, so it retreated. That
day, there weren't too many people to retreat from: it was happy
hour and the vacationers were already in the bars, apart from a few

I could see posing for photos in the just-abandoned lifeguard stands, holding each other, kissing.

That's a tradition: to sit in the stands and watch the sunset, with a boy or a girl. It's like our version of the overlook in those movies where people drive up to the vantage point above the town, and make out on car hoods.

Something else you already know, I remind myself, and the thought of it, of you and me pressed against each other in that deep, wooden lifeguard's seat, the warmth of you . . . it makes me almost come undone, slide into loose disarray, like untied laces.

Deep breath.

Another.

Apart from that, the only people on the beach were a couple of runners and a kid flying a kite shaped like Olaf from *Frozen*.

Whatever the reason for the ocean pulling away, it's one of my favorite things, the way the long piers with the amusement park on them have gotten stranded on the wide, wide beach, barnacled struts resting on dry land—the way you can walk around them and under them, into the dark spaces.

The shadow of Pier One was behind and to the left of me; it was almost like I could feel the cool of it. I walked toward the gull with my sketchbook under my arm, two HB pencils in my pocket.

If you didn't know already, which you do, you would guess from this that I was not the most popular kid at Oakwood High School. I mean, sketching dead birds is not what gets you voted homecoming queen. And of course there was the piñata thing. I might tell you about that later.

Anyway, I'm delaying.

Here's what started everything:

I was getting closer to the seagull now, and I could see that there were crabs eating it. Hermit crabs, some of them. People think hermit crabs are cute, but I can't think of anything creepier. Some dead thing's shell, with legs poking out of it. Scuttling. Feeding on corpses. Living in a borrowed skin of death.

When you see them eating a bird, it gives you a whole different idea of them.

Then, I saw movement a little farther out, where you get that sheen of thin water between the surf and the dry sand. I realized there were more crabs down there, and one or two were making their way from the gull to something else. As if it was more tempting.

You know when someone has left a door open and you feel the draft? I felt something like that, only inside. I knew whatever it was the crabs were interested in, half-submerged, washed up on shore, could not be anything good.

The water was making a soft sound, like it was hushing me because it had something important to say.

I turned and squinted at the sun. A cloud was just passing over it, and it was turning orange already, low above the buildings of town, nearly sunset. Then I walked a little closer. It sounds stupid, but I remember having a very conscious thought, which was, *oh, so this is what people mean when they use the word "dread."*

But it wasn't so bad—I saw as I approached that it was just a sneaker, one of those ankle-high basketball shoes. It was standing upright in the shallow, foamy water.

I took another step.

Gulls swooped in the air above me, calling, calling my name it almost seemed, *Cassie, Cassie, Cassie.*

I saw bone, glowing white, inside the shoe.

There was a foot in there.

An actual, severed foot. I could see a glimpse of flesh, purple as canned cat food, the bone protruding from it. You heard about the foot, of course, everyone did, but I don't think I ever told you it was me who found it.

In a movie, I would have gagged or shrieked. I don't think I did either of those things: I just stood there, staring.

And at first, I didn't even think about the Houdini Killer, I didn't see that it might be connected. The truth is that the first word that crossed my mind was an ancient Greek one:

Sparagmos.

It means: the act of tearing a person or an animal to pieces, usually for sacrificial purposes. The followers of Dionysus were big on it. The reason this word crossed my mind is that I am a weirdo and a freak and the public library is like my second home. But then, knowing you, I didn't need to tell you any of that.

So I looked at the man's foot, in the shoe, on the beach, and I thought of sparagmos. I was remembering Orpheus, being ripped to shreds by furious Thracian women.

You know the story, probably. Orpheus could charm all creatures and even objects with his music, and because of this and his beauty, he was much desired by almost all women he encountered. Yet after his wife, Eurydice, died, he forswore all others, and this so incensed the women who surrounded him that they began to throw rocks and stones at him. But the rocks and stones loved Orpheus's music, and they would not harm him; they turned away at the last. And so the women took him with their hands, and tore his body apart.

That's the version I like best anyway.

I looked at the foot in the sneaker, thinking of that story, like, here was the Chuck Taylor shoe of a vacationer who was just *too* good at karaoke and his friends had ripped him apart. I figured it was very unlikely that whoever it came from had been torn to pieces by Thracian women. I was thinking lucidly and crazily at the same time, and the weird thing was that I knew it—it was like there was a part of me standing outside myself, observing me.

I took out my cell phone, and I dialed 911. I said, "There's a human foot on the beach and I don't think it belongs to Orpheus." At least, that's what they told me I said, later. I don't remember doing it.

Then I guess I must have fainted—which is exactly what would happen in a movie—because the next thing I can remember I was in a squad car. They took me to the station and asked me questions and gave me very sweet coffee with lots of sugar and cream in it, and I'll get to all that later because it's important. But, for now, two observations:

1. Looking back, I think maybe seeing the severed foot, plus some associated memories to do with blood and bone, caused some kind of psychotic break pretty much straight away. The clue is that I was looking at a body part and all I could think about was Greek myth. Which probably partly explains all the really terrible things that happened soon after.

2. I assumed it was a man's foot in the sneaker. Because of the style, because it was relatively large, I don't know. That was why I was thinking about Orpheus. But perhaps if it had crossed my mind it might be a woman's, then I would have thought about that other famous victim of sparagmos: Echo, and the way she was

17

torn to pieces by Pan's followers, leaving only her voice in the rocks and trees. And if I'd thought about her, then maybe I'd have gotten to voices sooner, and the idea of a murdered woman. And maybe things would have turned out differently, or at least I would have been more prepared for what happened afterward.

But then again, maybe not.

Like I said, they took me to the police station and we sat in what looked surprisingly like a normal office. They asked me a bunch of questions, what I'd been doing, whether I'd moved the foot, how long I'd been there, that kind of thing. They gave me sweet coffee, I already said that didn't I? I was there an hour or more.

There were two guys, one in a suit and one in uniform. Agent Horowitz, who was clearly some kind of Fed, and Sergeant Kennedy or Officer Kennedy or something, I don't know, I don't remember. Kennedy was big and fitted badly into his blue shirt; Horowitz was skinny and young, with wire-framed glasses and a smile that actually seemed genuine. Though he was younger, he was clearly the one in charge—you would have known even if he weren't in plain clothes.

Eventually, my dad turned up.

He came into the room and said, "Do you really need to keep my daughter here?"

"We're not detaining her," said Kennedy. "We're just asking some questions."

Horowitz nodded. "But I think we're done here. You can take Cassandra home. She's had a shock—I'd prescribe sugar if I were a doctor. Ben & Jerry's, M&M'S. You know, chocolate."

"She has a peanut allergy," said Dad. "A severe one. Most chocolate could kill her."

Kennedy slapped the side of his head. "Oh yeah. The guys from the squad car saw the bracelet when they were reviving her. Almost dosed her with epinephrine before they realized she'd just fainted. Candy, then."

"My daughter found a human foot on the beach and you're suggesting candy?" said Dad.

Horowitz shrugged and gave that slight smile. I noticed his cheeks dimpled and fine lines appeared around his eyes; it made me like him even more. "It works," he said. He turned to me. "Also, we can offer counseling. Put you in touch with someone. Something to think about."

"I don't think so," said Dad. He hated counselors—he said the ones in the Navy were worse than the people shooting at you, that they just wanted you to write down what happened to you over and over again so that you were always reliving it, always scared, always in pain. Yeah, I sometimes felt like saying. Because pushing it all down and basically going around with untreated PTSD is working *so* well for you.

"Well, Cassie, you call me if you'd like to talk to someone," said Horowitz, gliding over Dad's death stare, which made me think there was steel underneath his smiles.

Dad blinked and took my hand to lead me out of there.

Kennedy passed Dad a card with his pudgy fingers. "Call us if she thinks of anything else."

I thought: *I'm right here.*

As I was thinking it, Horowitz caught my eye and rolled his, mocking his colleague, it seemed like. I laughed.

"What?" said Dad.

"Nothing," I said.

"Shock," said Horowitz, straight-faced. "A tub of Ben & Jerry's. Helps every time. Take it from me."

I've just realized I never told you my real name is Cassandra. You probably figured I was just Cassie.

It's kind of a screwed-up name, isn't it? I mean, if you know your Greek myths, which of course you do.

Cassandra: doomed to give true prophecies about the future but have no one ever believe her.

It's not a name, it's a curse.

Me, I have never been able to see the future. If I could, I would have left Oakwood that day, for sure.

Deep breath.

So this is when something really important happened, and I need you to bear with me with all this stuff because, not to sound over-dramatic or anything, but what we're getting to now is pretty much the whole reason I hurt you and the whole reason I'm having to write this e-mail to explain what I did.

To explain what I am.

I was alone in the police station bathroom, the stall doors all open. I looked at myself in the mirror, hating my freckles and dinky nose.

That was when I heard the voice.

It was a woman with a New Jersey accent, and this is what she said:

"You're disgusting. You leave the house like that?"

This time I *did* do exactly what a person in a film would do: I whirled around to see who was behind me. There was no one. Nor beside me, nor in the stalls—I checked. No one standing on the toilets or hiding behind the main door or anything.

"I'm talking to you, ugly ****," said the voice. "You ever think of coordinating? Or brushing your hair?"

"What? Who are you? *Where* are you?"

Silence.

In the mirror, my eyes were liquid with fear. "Your little prank isn't funny," I said. "Wherever you are."

Still nothing. My heartbeat started to slow again. I figured there was a camera or something, one with a speaker that enabled someone in another location to speak to me.

"Hello?" I said.

No voice.

I glanced at the mirror again before leaving the bathroom. Here's the thing: the voice wasn't wrong. I'd left the house without thinking about what I was wearing; I had on old, saggy sweatpants and one of my dad's T-shirts, the green of which really did not go with the pink of the pants. I hadn't brushed my hair.

Stupid kids, I said to myself. Though right at the back of my mind was the thought, already, that it was weird they had somehow managed to get a woman to join in with the prank. I mean, it was definitely a woman's voice, not a girl's. Anyway, I didn't want to give them any satisfaction, whoever they were, so I smiled at myself and walked out, trying to make my gait casual, though of course that's impossible to do when you're thinking about it.

That was the first time I heard the voice, but even though it made me angry, it didn't scare me. That came afterward in the car with my dad.

We were in the black Dodge Ram, Dad's pride and joy. I had been almost surprised to see that it was dark out when I left the station through the revolving doors. The lights on the instrument panel were glowing as Dad drove, and there were goose bumps on my skin. I wished I had a sweater.

Thinking about that brought back an echo, not the voice, but the memory of it. "*You ever think of coordinating?*"

I shivered, and tried to think of something else. I don't think I was aware of how badly my mind had been—and this is the proper word—*disturbed* by finding the foot. Tilted, like a spinning top, gyrating wildly, wobbling from side to side.

"You should be at the restaurant," I said to Dad. Everything, the inside of the car, the signs—24/7 LIQUOR ASK ABOUT OUR WINE BOXES—seemed so *there*, so present, that it shimmered. A white seagull flashed past in the dark sky, like a comet.

23

"I get a call saying my daughter's with the cops, I'm gonna come."

"I'm okay," I said.

He didn't answer that. "You shouldn't have gone out," he said, his eyes on the road over the steering wheel, driving past what seemed like the same streetlights we had already passed a block back, this faceless chain-store sprawl on the outskirts of town like a cartoon background the animators were recycling, using the same frames again and again. "I can't keep you safe out there."

"It's the beach," I said. "In daytime."

"Dusk."

"Daytime, dusk, whatever. It's safe."

"It's a murdered young woman is what it is."

"What is?" I asked.

"The foot, genius."

"They said that?" I was surprised. Like I said, I assumed it was a man's foot.

"Those guys? No. But I spoke to Mastrangelo." This is a cop who eats in our pizza place all the time. "One of the victims was wearing Air Jordans when she went missing."

I had been watching the wide road going past, as we crossed from the copied-and-pasted strip-mall wasteland into the first layer of "real" Oakwood, the poor part, apartment blocks and smaller stores, the closed-down entertainment places, BASEBALL LANES 24/7 over shuttered-up windows, endless stop signs. "Someone cut her up? Ugh."

He shook his head. "I don't think so. I think she was whole when she was dumped out at sea."

"What?"

"Thing about shoes that come up over the ankle—they protect the foot inside. The ocean's violent. It throws the body around, takes it to pieces. At the joints, you know. Knee, ankle, elbow. Like pulling apart a chicken."

"Dad . . ."

"Yeah, sorry. Anyway, the ankle separates and other parts disintegrate, or whatever. Clothes don't help at all. But the foot in the shoe, it's kept intact, and eventually it washes up."

"How do you know this?"

He looked at me, then tapped his shoulder.

Oh.

His shoulder is where he has a shiny, puckered scar—a bullet went through from one side to the other, in the caves at Zhawar Kili, fired from a Taliban AK-47 when I was three years old. Dad was a Navy SEAL, until he got shot anyway. The other bullet pretty much vaporized his knee. They rebuilt it—the Navy has good doctors—but he wasn't going to be jumping off a landing vessel again, or diving from a Zodiac to check for mines, so he was discharged.

But his tapping his shoulder, that was also code for the Marines. As in: *I know that when people drown at sea their feet often wash up in their shoes because I have seen it in the Navy.*

Weirdly, it made me feel close to him that we had both seen the same thing. Even if that same thing was a rotting foot in a shoe. I know, it's not exactly a sitcom bonding moment.

"You told them?" I said. "The cops, I mean?"

"Yup," he said. "Told Officer Fat and Agent Thin when you were in the bathroom. I think they knew already though. Oh, this is hush-hush, by the way. They don't want publicity yet. Till now they've never had a body; all the women have just disappeared."

I was silent for a moment.

Then . . .

I mean, we take what we can, right? Life is not a sitcom; life is not a movie.

"So . . . Dad . . . You've seen . . . what I saw?" *A foot in a shoe, washed up on shore.*

"I've seen a lot worse than that."

He didn't say this proudly or anything. Just straight. Ex-military guys can be jerks, I've met plenty of them, but he wasn't like that.

He didn't speak much about the things he saw, or the things he did. I only knew the name Zhawar Kili because Mom mentioned it once, when he wasn't around. And since she died, I don't have any way of knowing more about it.

"Were you scared?" I asked.

"Back then? Yeah. I was scared a lot."

"Dad—" I started, but then I stopped.

"Yeah?"

I wanted to ask him, *Did you kill people*? It was something I was always wanting to ask him. But how do you ask a person something like that?

And also: What would be the point?

Because I knew the answer already.

The answer was:

Yes. A lot.

So instead I just shut up. We were turning onto our street, cruising past the lights from the front windows, all of them identical. Slowing as we reached the drive into the garage. Turning, our headlights briefly illuminated the mobile home in the front yard of the neighbor's house, on its cinder blocks, rusting. It takes up the whole space and has been there forever; you would think the garden had been planted around it.

That was when the voice spoke again. The voice of the woman I couldn't see. It said:

"Ask me if *I* was scared."

I must have jumped in my seat because Dad hit the brakes and grabbed my arm, hard. "What the ****?" he said.

"N-nothing," I managed to stammer out. It was like the voice was *in the car with me*. "Just the shock, I think." I sensed it right away: that this wasn't something I could tell him about. Dad frowned and eased the car into motion again.

"There's Coke in the garage," he said. "Bad for your teeth, but I guess you need it."

I nodded.

"Ask me if I was scared when he killed me."

That was the voice again, not Dad.

I tried to control myself so Dad wouldn't freak out. Kept myself very still. But inside it was like I was falling from a building, gravity lifting my organs into my mouth.

I gripped the door handle very tightly as Dad pulled up. *There is no woman in this car*, I told myself. *There is no woman in this car.* I even took a peek at the backseats, and it was true: there was no woman in the car.

"I'm dead and you did nothing. Are you happy now?"

Take deep breaths, I told myself.

Take deep breaths.

The world narrowed, became something looked at through the wrong end of a telescope.

Please, I told the voice silently. *Please, leave me alone.*

Dad was standing outside the car, opening the door for me. I hadn't even noticed him getting out.

"Inside," he said. He took my arm and led me to the house. "Jesus, I thought I'd die with worry," he said as we crossed the porch. His fingers were biting into my forearm, bone deep. "You know there's someone killing women in this town, or did that not occur to you? Seriously, Cass. Never ****** do that to me again. And clean your ******* room."

I told you: 0–60 anger in four seconds flat, my dad.

IMPORTANT CAPS-LOCK SPOILER:

THE VOICE DID NOT LEAVE ME ALONE.

But I did clean my room.

Next day was a school day. Sunlight woke me, slanting through the venetian blinds in my bedroom. I lay there, thinking I must have imagined what happened the previous day. Not the foot—that was undeniable. But the voice.

I got up, pulled on Levi's and leather motorcycle boots. I don't have a motorcycle, but I liked the boots when I saw them in a magazine someone had left at the library, so I saved up and got them on eBay. Vintage. In the photos in the magazine they went well with jeans and a loose, plain white T-shirt, which is what I put on next, yanking it over my head.

Of course, when I looked in the mirror it didn't quite work on me. The T-shirt wasn't fitting right, and it was creased. The boots and jeans, which had looked so good on the model, somehow didn't click, somehow made me seem less like a fashionista slumming it and more like white trash on a break from busing tables in a late-night dive.

This is what always happens: I try to put clothes together and something is invariably missing, I get some detail wrong, I don't know how. Even when I buy the exact same things that I see on TV or in a mag or whatever. Even when I put on the same eyeliner, the same bracelets. Something about me, some combination of my face and body, ruins it.

"You get a job as a day laborer?" said the voice as I regarded myself in the mirror.

I felt a tight, cold sensation in my chest. So the voice was still there. Fear twisted inside me, coiling around anger.

"Shut up," I replied. I left the room, with a backward glance in the mirror at my terrible ensemble, and went downstairs.

Dad grunted at me when I reached the kitchen. He was holding a mug of coffee and eating a bagel. I waved to him. "See you after school," I said.

He looked up. "You okay?"

"Sure."

He nodded. "Take the bus. Safer."

"Yeah, yeah," I said.

That was it. The extent of our conversation.

Of course I had no intention of taking the bus, even if there was a murderer in town. I mean, I didn't fit the victim profile. So far, the killer had targeted what the media called "sex workers." Prostitutes, a girl from a massage parlor, a stripper. And it was morning—not really a time of day conducive to serial killings.

I grabbed a bagel and went out the front door. It was still early— in the east, out over the ocean, bundles of pink clouds were gathered, achingly beautiful against the blue sky. I barely noticed.

Jagging right and then left onto Fourth, I headed toward school. I started eating the bagel and imagined I was on an interstellar transport and it was a space-age snack, designed to fuel my body and provide all my nutrients, the old-fashioned mess of a meal crammed into something convenient and tasteless.

I walked through layer three, the long strip of suburban houses between the boardwalk and the empty lots, the faceless wide streets of malls. I passed a couple of people getting little kids into cars, someone pulling a suitcase on wheels, just back from a business trip maybe. I wasn't really concentrating, but then something made every detail snap into focus, and I was standing by an orange Chevy Camaro, on the back a Calvin-pissing-on-a-Ford logo.

The something was the voice, and it said:

"I'm dead, and you didn't do anything to stop it. It's all your fault."

It goes without saying by this point that there was no one around me. Just another fake-clapboard house, that orange Chevy, a bike

31

lying on its side in a brown yard. I wish I could describe what the voice sounded like. A real person, but not someone I knew. About forty, maybe? It's also impossible to convey the tone. When you write words down there are gaps between them, spaces, but spoken they run like liquid, merge together. It was a middle-aged woman with a New Jersey accent, that's pretty much all I can tell you.

One thing though: the voice was angry. Very, very angry.

I didn't think; I was tired. I just talked back. I don't know why.

"It's my fault you're dead?" I said. "Who the hell are you?" I was kind of aggressive. This will become relevant.

The voice didn't say anything. I held tight to my bag and kept on going to school. I was shaking, my heart racing. I don't think it crossed my mind then that something was wrong with me. I just thought: *It's a dead person. Or an angel, or something.*

A strange angel, yes. But I don't know. I just assumed it was supernatural, a phantasm of some kind. Which frankly scared me a hell of a lot. I was shaking as I continued the walk to school, past the long-dead FRANKIE'S GO KARTS with its vast cracked parking lot, furred with weeds, its broken neon sign pointing to the ticket office and its fading painted race courses.

At school I was distracted. That didn't make a big difference from usual. I was pretty much coasting through my junior year. It drove my dad mad. He kept saying, "You're a smart girl, Cass. You spend half your life in the library. Why are you wasting your abilities?" I told him once that using my abilities at school would be the biggest waste of them, and he dragged me to a kitchen chair and made me sit there till my assignments were done, so I never said that again.

Anyway, when I arrived at school, a few people turned and spoke low to each other when they saw me. I saw others glance at me and kind of raise their eyebrows. I figured the news was circulating about the foot on the beach, and me being the one who found it.

And underneath the buzz of curiosity, something else. *Fear.* I sensed it as I walked up the stairs, especially from the girls. That anxiety that had been there in the town, silent but present, like a tumor, since the killings began. That anxiety that said, *So far it has been sex workers, but what if he starts on other girls?*

Even as I walked, I saw people pulling away from me. Like I was a bad-luck charm. Like getting too close to me might get you killed.

Great. Another reason to be ostracized. It *had* to be me who found it. Just had to be.

Weirdly, though, I could swear a couple of kids looked at me enviously, hesitating, almost like they wanted the scoop, wanted to know if I *knew* anything. I mean, it was national at this point. How fourteen young women had disappeared in the last couple of years, never to be seen again. How the cops supposedly didn't care enough to solve it because the victims were in the sex industry, and if it were ordinary girls then the murderer would have been apprehended long ago.

I don't know how "Houdini Killer" got started. But by then it was already being used by news anchors, commentators in the *New York Times*, everyone. Because of the way that the bodies never turned up, like the killer was a magician.

Except that now, part of one had. And it had been me who found it, me who hit the jackpot with a severed foot. Even so, I was surprised by the speed with which it had gotten around, my discovery. Dad had told me it was hush-hush. I guess the officers, at least one of whom was FBI or something, didn't know how small New Jersey towns operate. Someone at the station would have told his wife, who told their neighbor, who told Marjorie the school secretary, and that was it. Someone has probably written an equation for the speed of gossip.

I walked up to the main doors, and that was when someone tripped me. I felt the foot hook my leg, and I went sprawling. I put my hands out and landed on them, hard, the jolt fizzing electric up my arms and into my shoulders. I cried out, involuntarily.

And heard a laugh, somewhere behind me.

I eased myself into a sitting position, started picking up the books that had spilled from my bag. My hands were grazed, and now there were blood smudges on my calculus.

Mr. Nakomoto held out his hand and lifted me up. "Did you see who did it?" he asked kindly. He had a round face and round glasses; circles suited him. He was like someone with no edges, you know? No sharpness about him.

"No," I said.

"Shame," he said. "These bullies." He shook his head. "I don't like to see them getting away with it."

"They always get away with it," I said.

"Not always." But even he didn't look convinced.

I shrugged. I could have said, *People who hurt other people always get away with it*, because it was the truth or at least the truth as I saw it then, but hey. What would have been the point?

I picked up one more book, and he picked up one and handed it to me, and then he coughed and walked away.

Later, I was in English class with Ms. Gilbert. I always felt kind of sorry for Ms. Gilbert. I mean, she knew I'd read most of the novels in the library, let alone the ones we were studying, so she was forever firing questions at me, trying to draw me into the discussion.

"Why do you think Fitzgerald tells us that Gatsby hasn't cut open the pages in his books, Cassie?"

That kind of thing. And I would shrug and not answer, which I could see really disappointed her. I hated disappointing her. I mean, I wasn't being a brat, I just couldn't do it. I hated to speak in front of other people. Even if I was on a bus, and someone called me on my cell, I wouldn't answer. I didn't want anyone nearby to hear my voice.

When I say "someone called me on my cell": don't get the wrong idea of my social life; I mean Mom, before she died, or Dad. Most of the class was there when the piñata incident happened, or they'd heard about it, and the few friends I'd made since then dropped away after the whole thing with Mom. I think I made it pretty hard for them to be friends with me; I don't blame them.

I should explain about the piñata:

It was my seventh birthday. Mom and Dad went big on the theme, which for some reason was Mexican. I don't think I asked for it, I don't know. And Dad is like tenth-generation Italian American, and Mom's family came from Holland, originally, so I really don't get it. But that's what it was.

The whole front yard was decorated with hay bales, flags, plastic cactuses. Cacti?

Google says cacti.

Okay, yes, and they had little ponchos for all the kids who came, and there was a table with tacos and cheese and guacamole. The thing I loved most: they had a donkey they'd hired from somewhere, and there was an old wizened guy who was giving kids rides on it. I think I asked for the donkey—in fact, maybe that's why the whole Mexican theme. They got the donkey, and then they figured they could turn it into a thing.

I rode that donkey maybe five times; I loved animals back then. I was so happy.

It's not like I remember every detail. All I know is that at a certain point, Dad produced the piñata and tied it to the apple tree. The piñata was a donkey too, every color patchworked onto it in a coat of ribbons. A big fat one. Dad bent down and grabbed a branch that had fallen from the tree, snapped a stick from it.

And here's the thing: It wasn't even me. It wasn't me who did it.

This is what happened:

They blindfolded me, and I tried and tried to smash open that donkey. I really did. But I wasn't a real coordinated kid, and I only gave it a couple of glancing blows.

Dad was going, "Come on, Cassie! You can do it! You can do it, Cassie!"

He was more excited than I was, I think. I just wanted to ride the real donkey, not smash up this fake one.

And I *couldn't* do it.

Dad shouted louder and louder. In my memory, his words are colored red. "Cassie, IT'S EASY. JUST SWING."

I sat down, and I started to cry.

According to Mom, Dane Armstrong kind of volunteered. He wasn't pushy about it. Dane was my best friend—he loved animals too and his family had tons of them, rabbits in the yard, dogs, cats, even a goat. I used to hang out with him all the time, when my parents let me. After what happened next, his parents left town though.

Anyway, Dane apparently stepped forward and said, "Hey, I'll do it for her." Dad wasn't happy about it, but Mom calmed him down. She was always good at that, which is one of the thousand terrible things about her dying, and pretty soon Dane had the stick and the cloth over his eyes.

I don't remember how long he swung at the piñata for—I know he broke it open a little and candy started spilling out, because in my mind is an image of the little packs on the grass like jewels, shining, all colors and foils, golden and silver, and that of course was what made the kids run to try to grab them, which was when Dane, who was still swinging wildly with the stick, brought it around in a wide arc and smashed the somehow-now-sharp end of it into Molly Van Buren's face, spearing her eye.

If you ever want to know what it's like to be a pariah, to be so far outside the social circle you're not even bullied, just ignored, it's easy: arrange for everyone you know to come to a party, then make them watch as a kid gets her eye gouged out. They couldn't rescue Molly's—she wore a glass eye after that. She still does. She wants to go into the Peace Corps. I don't know that from her; I overheard it somewhere. She doesn't speak to me anymore.

Memory plays tricks, but I think I actually kept a couple of friends, even after that. So if you *really* want to be alone, what you must also contrive to happen is this:

One day, in the school dining hall, get some meat loaf with peanuts in it. At this point you don't know you're allergic—your parents are not into PB&J sandwiches, so you've never had any, or maybe you did once and your parents dismissed the redness around your mouth, thinking you'd scratched yourself. I don't know.

The important thing is: you should eat the meat loaf, then very quickly suffer a massive anaphylaxis that swells your throat and bronchioles, fills you with a sense of black dread bearing down upon you like the grill of a massive truck, stops the air to your lungs, meaning that everyone in the dining hall panics as you lie twitching on the floor, until the school nurse finally gets there and takes the EpiPen from her bag and stabs it into your thigh, flooding your system with adrenaline and probably saving your life since the paramedics don't get there for another twenty minutes.

After this, you will truly have no friends.

BUT BE WARNED!

Some new kids might turn up once you're in high school, and they don't know about the piñata, or the time Nurse Kelly did a Pulp Fiction on you. They don't care about the stories either and they're into books too, just like you, so you start to hang out. They may or may not be called Scott and Trish.

In this scenario, as I have already intimated, there is only one thing to do: make sure that your mother dies horribly, so that you are forever cursed, forever doomed like Cassandra of myth—the girl who leaves a trail of violence in her wake. That should be enough to see off fair-weather friends like, oh, Scott, or—for the sake of argument—Trish.

Got that?

The recipe for being totally and utterly alone:

Accidental eye surgery

+

Major medical incident on school grounds

+

Unpleasant tragedy

=

No friends for Cassandra.

Which is a very long explanation for why I didn't like to speak in class, but thanks for bearing with me. The point is: I probably should have been more *consciously* shocked by the foot on the beach. It maybe seems odd that I wasn't more shaken by it, but I think in the waking part of my mind I just saw it as the latest install-ment in the curse of Cassie.

Unconsciously was a different story, of course. I think you can probably guess that already.

For instance:

How it was thanks to the voice that things started to go wrong at school. See, later on that very first day, I was in math class. The teacher, Mr. Fortey, was doing matrices. Afternoon sunlight was hazy through the windows, a distant view of the ocean and the piers visible beyond oceans of prefabricated buildings. We get seagulls in the schoolyard—they take your fries, if you're not careful, and they're not gentle about it.

Mr. Fortey had written five problems on the whiteboard, and we were supposed to be solving them. They weren't so hard. I was working on the third one when the voice said,

"Don't finish them."

"What?" I said, under my breath. By this point I knew something truly screwed up was happening to me. It wasn't a prank—it couldn't be. I mean, the voice had been in my room, on the street, in the classroom. In the bathroom at the police station. It was like my mind was a house and the voice was an intruder, stalking the corridors.

"Don't finish the problems," repeated the voice. "You do them, and I'll hurt you."

I looked around as if someone was going to explain to me what was going on.

"Shut up," I whispered. "Go away."

Silence. Daisy Merkel glanced over at me from the neighboring desk like I was a freak, though that was normal.

"Do what I say or I will make you suffer," said the voice, its tone as cold as dark night air.

I ignored it. I pressed my pen very deliberately down on the paper and filled in the missing numbers in the third matrix problem.

Now.

What happened next, I know it now, was a coincidence. There's no way it was anything more. But you cannot imagine how much it freaked me out.

First, the tip of the pen snapped from the pressure I'd exerted on it. Blue ink splattered the page and I cursed, putting the pen aside and reaching into my bag for another one.

My movement was abrupt, quick. My index finger, therefore, impaled itself quite deep on the pair of compasses that I had left open inside—we'd been doing a lot of work on geometry. Maybe half an inch of the sharp steel point was embedded in the soft pad of the finger.

I yanked my hand out of the case, yelping, like a spider had bitten me, which for a stupid moment was even what I thought had happened. Red blood pattered onto the paper, mixing with the ink, sounding really loud somehow. I thought: *Do what I say or I will make you suffer.*

Mr. Fortey rushed over. "Cassie, you all right?" he asked.

I was staring at my finger.

"You feel that, *****?" said the voice. "That's what happens when you disobey me."

"Leave me *alone*," I said.

Mr. Fortey stared at me. "Now, Cassie, you've been hurt. Let's get you to—"

Simultaneously, the voice said:

"Tell him to **** off, or I take the whole finger next time."

I put my hands over my ears. My palm was tacky with blood; I could feel it sticking to my hair. I hated cursing. Cursing was what my dad did.

I looked up.

"**** off," I said to Mr. Fortey.

"What the ******** ******** ******* **** were you thinking? Are you ******* insane?"

That was Dad, when he got home that evening. I told you he would fill the page with stars. He was wearing his restaurant apron, stained with pizza sauce. He never actually *made* pizza; he always sat with the regulars, being the "face of the place," as he said. But he had some theory that people liked to see him in the apron, like it made the joint unpretentious.

I didn't say anything. I had no idea what to say.

"You coast at school when you're smarter than most of the teachers. You won't work at the restaurant anymore. You think your mother would be proud of you?"

"You think she'd be proud of you?" I asked.

"Get upstairs to your room," he said. "No dinner for you."

I did. What else could I do?

In my room, lying on the bed, I listened for the voice. Nothing.

"Are you there?" I asked.

No answer, but I sensed something. A coiled presence.

"Please, whoever you are, don't do this," I said. "Don't make me . . . don't make me get hurt."

Silence, and I was just turning to look out the window, I don't know why, just for something to do, when it said—

"It was necessary to ensure your obedience," said the voice. "You will be punished when you do not do as you are told."

"Why? Why are you—"

"You are not worthy even to eat the crumbs that are left after others have dined. You are nothing. Do you understand that?"

I didn't say anything.

"DO YOU UNDERSTAND THAT?"

When the voice shouted, I can't describe it. It was like a demon,

42

right in my ear. Like every horror film you have ever seen, rolled up and squeezed into sound, and piped into your head. I would like to say that I resisted for a few days, that I stood up to it, but I broke straightaway. I thought the devil had possessed me. I really did.

"Yes," I said. "Yes. But . . . what do you want from me?"

"Right now," said the voice, "I want you to clean your room."

"What?"

"You heard me. Clean it. It's filthy. Pick up all this ****. These clothes, these books."

What could I do? I tidied my room. The place was a mess; I will give that to the voice. It was mean, but it wasn't in that case strictly inaccurate. I cleared the floor, hung up clothes in my closet, put books back on shelves, threw some stuff in the laundry basket.

"Now get the vacuum cleaner."

"Dad will hear."

"So? He knows you're a dirty *****. He'll be happy you're cleaning."

This, actually, might just have been true. I went downstairs quietly all the same and snagged the vacuum cleaner from the space under the stairs. I dragged it back up to my room and sucked up all the dust and dirt, maybe three years' worth. I found a Tamagotchi under my bed that must have been there for ten years. More, maybe. I wondered for a moment if the little digital creature was still alive, trapped in its little plastic case, desperate for food. For water.

I looked at it: no, the screen was black.

I continued to clean.

The last person to do this, I thought, *was probably Mom.*

I shook away the thought, like a wasp in my hair.

The voice said something, then, but I couldn't hear properly over the roar. I pulled the plug on the vacuum cleaner.

"What?" I said.

"Enough," said the voice. And did I file away even then that the voice hadn't been able to speak over the noise? I guess maybe I did.

Just then Dad's voice came from downstairs. "Cassie, what the **** are you doing?"

"Cleaning," I shouted.

He didn't seem to have anything to say to that because he went quiet. Later I heard the front door open and close and I guessed he'd gone out to the restaurant. It was weird; he spent so much time in a place I hadn't even been to since Mom died.

"Now the bathroom," said the voice. "Scrub your face."

I went to the bathroom; I scrubbed my face. The voice had me do it with a nail brush.

"Again," said the voice.

And:

"Again."

And:

"Again."

Until my skin was raw and red. I cleaned my teeth—the voice made me do it three times—and then I went back into my room and fell on the bed.

"See?" said the voice. "It's easier when you obey."

"Please," I said. "Please don't . . . get me into trouble at school again. My dad . . . He'll kill me." I think, right at that moment, I considered this a real possibility, not just an expression. Things between me and Dad had not been good for a long time. I'll get to why, later.

"Promise to obey me," said the voice.

"I promise."

"Promise again."

"I promise."

"You will speak to no one outside school. Only me. And your father."

I blinked. "I don't speak to anyone anyway."

"Good. Then we will see about school."

I reached for the book I was reading, *For Whom the Bell Tolls*.

"No," said the voice.

"No reading?"

"No reading stories."

I think I shed a tear then.

"Please," I said.

"No," said the voice. And then it stopped talking and I closed my eyes and the redness of my eyelid capillaries was bursts of blood and horror in all directions and then at some point I fell asleep.

NOTE:

For the purposes of this account, you can go ahead and assume, even if I don't write it down, that the last exchange between me and the voice before I fell asleep that night—me saying "please," the voice saying "no"—happened again and again over the days and weeks that followed.

In fact, you can mentally insert the following between almost every paragraph of the rest of this:

ME: "Please."
THE VOICE: "No."

You.

It's funny, even just typing "you" gives me tingles.

But you don't appear, not quite yet. Nearly, though. You're waiting in the wings, ready to come onto the stage, ready to walk into the apartment above our garage, and my life.

It feels weird, thinking about you, before I knew you existed. I wonder what you were doing.

I think I like picturing you standing in the wings.

A hero, listening for his line, his cue to enter.

But a tragic hero. A hero betrayed by me.

The voice let me go to school the next day. In fact it was silent all through my walk there, and all through my classes. I apologized to Mr. Fortey. He said, "That's okay, Cassie. To be honest it was good to hear your voice in class, for once."

Huh.

As usual, no one else spoke to me, and neither did the voice. I ate my lunch in the cafeteria alone, at a small table.

Everything almost seemed normal.

The voice didn't come back till I was walking to the library after school. I think I already had half an idea that I was going to do some reading about the Houdini Killer.

I took the ocean-view route, but avoided the part of the board-walk where Dad's restaurant was. The day was warm but there was a very light rain, so light that it seemed not to be falling vertically. It was more a mist that hung everywhere, thick with the smell of the ocean. I was hungry—I'd skipped breakfast to avoid Dad, and the food in the cafeteria sucked. I ducked into a bodega on the corner near the house and grabbed some Skittles. I don't even really like Skittles, but they're not produced in a factory that handles nuts. Most chocolate bars, even if they don't have peanuts in them, could kill me.

There was a guy in the store, an insurance salesman or some-thing, I don't know. Cheap suit, Pulsar watch. A backpack with the suit, which made me think he was staying in a motel while doing whatever business he was doing. Thin; pasty skin, acne scars.

Anyway, when I left the store, he followed not that far behind, having bought a pack of menthol Newports. He lit up as soon as he was on the street. I turned right onto Ocean and he turned right too; I could hear his leather shoes slapping the sidewalk.

That was when the voice came back.

48

"That man is following you," it said.

Behind me, the footsteps sped up. I could almost hear traveling-salesman guy's breath, could almost feel his fingers around my neck.

"He wants to hurt you."

I picked up the pace, nerves dancing now despite myself. Looking for anything to distract me: the license plates of cars, their models, whether they were out-of-towners or not. That's a game I used to play with my dad—guess without looking at the state tags whether a car belonged to tourists or not. It's not hard, though my dad made me figure it out rather than just telling me: the towns-people's cars are nearly always rusting, from the bottom, because of the ocean air.

"He's just a guy," I said to the voice, under my breath, as I passed a Toyota Corolla that by the red stains around its wheel arches belonged to a townie.

"He wants to **** you and then dump your body at sea, for the crabs and fishes to eat."

"Please stop," I whispered.

Then I felt a touch on my arm and I swear my heart nearly stopped. I spun around, arms up.

"Whoa, hey," said the guy. He sounded like a surfer dude, his vowels long and lazy. "Easy there."

"Say a word to him and I'll make you pay."

That was the voice, of course—so I just stood there, looking around me to see if there was anyone passing, anyone who could help me if he did want to hurt me. But there was no one; the street was empty.

The guy peered at me, puzzled. He had washed-out eyes; there was something sad about his whole appearance. He didn't look like a killer. "I just need directions," he said. He took a crumpled piece of paper from his jacket. "West Construction, on Fourteenth. The guy in the store didn't know."

I did know where that was, and opened my mouth—

"Speak and I'll make your dad bleed. You speak to no one."

I shut my mouth again. I turned and started trying to walk away, hoping and hoping he wouldn't follow, but I was so scared my legs wouldn't work properly. Then a big guy in a Giants shirt turned the corner and started walking toward me, laughing loudly into his phone. It was as if I'd been in a twilight zone thing where the whole world had stilled and turned into an empty film set, and then he'd come and broken the spell.

Relief shot through me like antifreeze, thawing my limbs, and I hurried off.

I heard Mr. Suit behind me say, "Hey! What's the deal?"

But I didn't stop; I kept on walking. I didn't even feel that guilty. I mean, if you're a man, you have to figure that stopping a teenage girl for directions on an empty street is stupid, right?

As I kept on walking toward the library, I checked there was no one near me and then said, "Why can't I speak to people?"

I could *feel* the voice considering. "You deserve no human contact. You are poison."

I think I actually gasped. Rivets of pain and horror pinned me to the sidewalk, and I stopped still again. You have to understand, when you've felt for a long time that you are dangerous to people, that you are a stain, and then someone else says it, it's a shock.

"Remember?" said the voice. "Remember what you did?"

"Shut up," I said. "Just ****** shut up."

The voice laughed. "Nice way to talk," it said. "Slap yourself."

"What?"

"Hard. On the face. So it stings."

"But—"

"Do it. Now."

I did it.

My mind floated away from my body, a balloon with its string cut. I was in the sky, with the clouds and the seagulls. *Cass, Cass, Cass*, they called, and I thought of Procne, her soul put into the body of a nightingale to save her from Tereus, and I wished right then that my soul could turn into a seagull, could fly away into the wet sky, full of hanging raindrops, a screen of shimmering water that was in all places at once.

Then, after I don't know how long, my breathing started to slow. The world came into focus again, slowly. I started walking. The voice didn't say anything.

I passed the baseball cages, where Dad and I used to go sometimes when I was young. Mom would come too, but she'd go for coffee at the diner on the corner. She said she didn't want to be there to see it if a ball gave me a black eye.

Now, the place was boarded shut—a lot of stuff was boarded shut. There'd been the financial crash, in 2008. I was young then, but of course I'd seen how the number of tourists went down every year, how the businesses closed one after another, enough that I had spent most of my life worrying about my dad and the restaurant, even before what happened with my mom. And then there'd been the killings. A lot of people said the town wouldn't recover until the murderer was stopped. Families with teenage girls didn't want to come here on vacation, just in case.

That was the theory anyway, to explain why the town was dying.

I kept going. Came to a construction site where a row of old condemned houses had been. This was the other thing, along with stuff being boarded up: a load of projects had been abandoned. There were empty lots up and down the boardwalk and the avenues behind, like the sockets of pulled teeth, the closing bracket of decline. Scaffolding that never came down.

The only new businesses you ever saw: gambling shops, bars, discount stores. The town had a lot of gamblers and drinkers now.

"Are you a ghost?" I asked as we passed a rusting crane, towering above us. "Are you dead?"

The voice didn't answer.

"Am I going mad? Answer me. Please."

"No," said the voice.

(NOTE: Remember me saying this exchange happened a lot?)

"What do you want?" I asked. "What do you want from me?"

"I want justice," said the voice.

"Justice?"

But the voice was gone; I sensed it withdrawing, the dispassionate eye of some great predator wheeling away, distracted, for now.

Justice? I thought. *Justice for what?*

Unless . . . I thought of the foot on the beach.

But no. It was a crazy thought.

I kept walking to the library. This was another piece of vernacular architecture—white and blue, art-deco curves, on a street just one block back from the ocean. In any other town it would have been a tourist destination; it was beautiful. But people just walked past it.

Not me.

I went in, and Jane raised a hand. "Hey, Cass."

I nodded. The voice had said not to speak to anyone. But Jane didn't seem to mind; she smiled. I liked her. She wasn't much older than me, maybe twenty-two. Her hair had a streak of purple in it, and she had a tattoo curling all around and down her arm that she said came from a standard introduction to Russian fairy tales: WHAT WERE THE FAIRY TALES, THEY WILL COME TRUE.

I paused, looking at the tattoo, thinking of fairy tales, and how I wished they would stay that way, just stories. I mean, a voice from nowhere was speaking to me, punishing me. I felt a twinge of sickness, deep in my belly. The fairy tales were coming true. The curse of Cassandra.

I felt, at that moment, truly cursed. Like there was a spell on me, an evil one, and the worst thing was I knew that I deserved it.

"You okay, Cass?" asked Jane.

Cassie, get a grip on yourself, I thought. I nodded again and did my best approximation of a smile. Jane smiled back. "Well, you need anything, you call me," she said.

I nodded. I did a lot of nodding in those days. Then I was about to look at the fiction shelves when I remembered what the voice had said—no stories. I shook my head, thinking *what am I supposed to—*

And then I saw a display Jane had made, a freestanding shelf with books on it about murders, most of them relating to the

Houdini Killer. In my memory, a shaft of sunshine came through the window at that moment, breaking through the clouds outside, illuminating the books, trapping motes of dust suspended in light.

I went over and took down a slim book called *Murder on the Jersey Shore* that Jane had put a *staff recommended* label next to. I carried it over to a table and started reading. It was pretty interesting. There wasn't much detail about the murders; I mean, with no bodies it would be hard to give any. The focus was mainly on the girls—most of them under twenty—who had been killed. The author was disgusted at the lack of police progress; his whole thing was basically that it was a huge stain of shame on them and on the state of New Jersey and the entire country that these women had been murdered and that because of their profession no one cared.

I care, I thought, half-surprised to realize this.

I looked at my watch. I needed to get home or Dad would be angry, and I didn't want Dad angry. I put the book back and got ready to leave. As I picked up my thin summer jacket—looked great online; looked awful on me—Jane glanced up. And as I passed her station, she leaned over the counter and pressed a book at me.

"Might cheer you up," she said.

I glanced at the cover. Haruki Murakami, *The Wind-Up Bird Chronicle.*

"It'll take you to another world," said Jane. "I don't think I've got you hooked on Murakami yet, have I?"

I shook my head.

"God, I sound like a pusher," she said. "Like I'm handing out meth." She laughed.

LOOPHOLE!

I laughed too. I mean, laughing is not speaking, right?

Jane seemed pleased to see me laugh. She tapped the book, nodded, like, this is the answer right here to all your problems, and sat down again. She was nice—she was always nice to me.

Which is why it's especially painful that it was Jane, later, who ruined everything.

Out on the street, the sky was overcast and I could smell the ocean, brought in by a breeze, the air freighted with salt water and molecules of sea life—ground down by the years into mist—fish scales, shells, anemone.

I breathed in deeply, loving that smell, even if I hated Oakwood.

"You laughed," said the voice, and suddenly my nostrils were full only of decay, the rotting of dead sea creatures.

"When you get home, you will slap yourself. Hard. Twice."

And you know what?

I did.

These are the times when I didn't hear the voice:

1. When I was sleeping.
2. When I was playing loud music. I used to listen to a lot of hip-hop. But rap is basically guys talking, and if you hear a voice that isn't there, already, then it's too much. So I switched to IDM, R&B instrumentals, anything with echo and reverb and bass and no one talking, ever. *Never* heavy metal. I tried that once. If you ever hear a voice and think you might be cursed or possessed or haunted, *do not listen to heavy metal.* It is a VERY BAD IDEA.

And:

3. When you were there.

I got into a routine. It sounds stupid, but I did. People cope, I guess.

There's a convention: If someone has cancer, they're "brave" and "fighting." If someone is having problems with their mind, that person is only ever "struggling." This is, on one level, stupid and offensive. I mean, the people who die of cancer—what, they didn't fight hard enough? They weren't brave enough?

But on another level, when it comes to the mind breaking down, it's not wrong that you struggle. I struggled. Everything was hard. Getting up. Getting dressed. Going to school.

The voice would say:

"Change into something prettier. You look like a ******** bum."

It would say:

"Walk up and down the stairs fifty times. You're getting a fat ass."

It would say:

"You're so ******** pathetic, that's why you have no friends."

It would say:

"Open your mouth to reply to that cute boy who has ACTU-ALLY STOPPED AND SPOKEN TO YOU IN THE CAFETERIA AS IF YOU'RE A REAL, VISIBLE PERSON, AND ACTUALLY SEEMS INTERESTED IN YOU, and I will make your dad die in an accident."

I'm paraphrasing—not the dying-in-an-accident bit, the boy bit.

And I kept my mouth shut. It didn't make much difference at school. I never had any friends anyway. I was a freak and a weirdo. I sat alone, I worked alone. The voice let me speak to teachers if they asked a direct question, and if I obeyed it in all other things. It even let me finish *King Lear* and write a short assignment on it. I guess the voice considered Shakespeare un-fun enough that it was not verboten.

At home, I noticed that the voice was always loudest in my room. So I moved out—I mean, not out entirely, but to the little apartment above the garage, the one Dad would rent to kids working summer jobs at the amusement park.

Your apartment.

But back then it was mine. I laid out all the books I'd borrowed from the library in the little sitting room and kept the bedroom tidy; the voice made sure of that. I even cooked a couple of times in the kitchen when Dad was at Donato's. Simple stuff: pasta, steak.

Like I said, when I was reading, as long as it wasn't something fun, the voice left me alone. And especially when I was in the apartment. I don't know why; I guess I would speculate that it was because my own room held more memories of my mother in it, invisible but there, like dust in dark air.

But anyway, reading in the apartment was the safest activity. Which meant no TV, no sketching in my sketchbook, no reading for pleasure. But nonfiction was fine, the drier and more boring the better.

So I read a lot. I'd stock up on books at the library and bring them back to my fortress above the garage, and I'd work my way through them: stuff on Greek myth, Native American legends, the history of the Spice Routes, technical textbooks on coding in Linux. Anything, so long as it wasn't a story.

But mostly, anything I could find about the Houdini Killer.

I remember the exact day when I worked out what was happening with the voice, or thought I did. It was June now, near the end of the school year. It was seventy degrees out. Dad was introducing a new millipede to a tank in the house; we didn't hang out much back then, but I'd seen the box arrive by FedEx, the holes cut in it. Old Mr. Grant next door was mowing his lawn; the drone of the rotor blade was coming through the open window and I could smell cut grass, mingling with ocean air. Mr. Grant lives on the side that does not have the mobile home filling the yard.

Obviously.

I was reading about Echo; what the voice was interested in was *educational value*. Not that it said so, but I got the point quickly after I turned on the TV and caught a few seconds of *My Super Sweet Sixteen* before the voice forced me to run up and down the block fifty times or it would cut out my dad's tongue, which in itself was very Ovid, but more Procne than Echo.

Anyway.

You know the Ovid version of the Echo story, of course:

Echo has been helping Zeus to sleep around, distracting his wife, Hera, with her beautiful singing voice while Zeus schtups every shepherdess and naiad he can get his divine hands on. Hera finds out, and takes away Echo's voice, her greatest asset, so she can only repeat the ends of other people's phrases. Echo sees Narcissus in the forest, this unbelievably beautiful boy, and falls in love. But she can only say what he says back to him, which sometimes distorts his words in comic ways and besides anything weirds him out, and anyway he's too, well, narcissistic to reciprocate, so he rejects her totally.

He says, "May I die before my body is yours."

And she says, "My body is yours."

Which obviously mystifies him and only makes him angry so he runs away. It's all pretty funny and tragic and she wastes away and dies and blah blah blah, you know the rest.

But *did you know there's another story*?

It's in Longus, in his *Daphnis and Chloe*. Which, incidentally, is one of the very first novels. Long, long before *Don Quixote*. You thought I was a geek before? Ha.

Anyway. In this one, there's no Zeus and Hera. There's just Echo, who is a nymph. Again, she has a beautiful voice—one she can use to imitate any sound, the song of any mortal, the call of any beast, the liquid babble of a stream. Then along comes Pan, the goat-god of chaos and hedonism. Pan is worshipped by followers who enjoy going into frenzies, and who tear animals to pieces in his honor.

Yes:

We're back on sparagmos, the act of tearing people to pieces. And the foot in the shoe. I don't say anything by accident, you know that. Or you will anyway.

So. Pan sees Echo in the woods, and hears her, and he wants to possess her beauty. But he's also a musician, a great one—the term "Pan pipes" comes from that fact, of course—and he is admiring and jealous at the same time of the way she can sing back any sound, the way she can even re-create perfectly the supposedly inimitable beauty of his own playing.

So, naturally, he tries to sleep with her.

But this time it's Echo who does the rejecting. She guards her maidenhead, the usual nymph stuff. Runs from him in the time-honored fashion, refuses his advances. The way nymphs are always trying to do with Zeus, though usually he turns into a bull or a swan or something and tricks them into coming close and then rapes them.

The ancient Greeks: a weird people.

I got offtrack there. Pan tries to sleep with Echo, and she says no, so he goes mad, and being a Greek god and therefore mental, he whips his followers up into one of their frenzies—the word "panic" comes from this—and they tear Echo into little bits with their bare hands, and scatter her and her blood all over the woods.

But the earth. The earth loves Echo's music, so the stones and the trees and the plants take her into themselves, and they preserve her voice inside them, so that anytime anyone shouts or sings, Echo imitates their voice perfectly, calls back to them.

And this way Pan is thwarted, because he can still never possess this girl or her amazing voice. Every time he plays his pipes, she pipes them back at him from the rocks and the trees and the caves, echoing his beautiful music, taunting him.

Do you see?

The whole world preserves her voice, so she can accuse her destroyer over and over again.

I read this, and I thought:

Oh.

I remembered the voice saying, "I want justice." I thought about how the voice had appeared to me first at the police station, after I found the foot. I thought of Echo's voice left behind after her death, to punish Pan. My own suspicion, which I had pushed down inside myself.

What if the voice . . .

I took a breath. I didn't know how to ask the question indirectly. "Are you . . . are you one of the murdered women?"

Silence—but mixed with interest. Focused interest. The eye of that giant predator turning slowly to look at me.

"He killed me and you did nothing."

The voice's voice was laced with venom. The voice of a snake, almost, all whisper and serious hatred. And this is how stupid I was: I took that "you" as collective, like an indictment of the whole town, the police, the justice system, whatever.

It didn't occur to me the voice was talking to *me*. Singular. Saying that *I* had done nothing. Like I said, I was stupid. You'll see.

Back then I just said: "Someone killed you. Is that right? And now you're just . . . a voice. Like a kind of ghost, but one that only speaks."

Silence.

"You want me to find out who did this to you? You want revenge?"

Silence.

"I think I'll just turn the TV on, watch a movie." I held my breath. Usually if I said something like this, the voice would tell me to slap myself or walk into a wall. I had done that a few times, walked into the wall, for considering anything that might be construed as entertainment.

Silence, still.

I sat there in wonder. The voice was a ghost, murdered by the Houdini Killer, and she wanted me to make it right. That was why she appeared after the foot, that was why she was so angry, that was why she'd picked me. Hell, I guessed it was probably *her* foot.

I knew what I had to do now.

I had to find the Houdini Killer. If the police couldn't do it, maybe I could. People who hurt other people always get away with it, don't they? That was what I'd wanted to tell Mr. Nakomoto.

Well.

Maybe not.

IMPORTANT CAPS-LOCK SPOILER:

I was not right thinking that the voice was a ghost.

I was very, very wrong.

I'd already read a lot about the Houdini Killer and what it amounted to was:

0.

Absolutely nothing.

No one knew anything because there were no bodies, only a foot—thanks to me—and nothing to link the girls, except their work.

Since the foot, of course, there were some more conjectures: most of the stuff online—the voice was cool with me researching online as long as I didn't go on Facebook or whatever—agreed that the killer must have dumped the bodies at sea, and that was how come the foot ended up on the beach. Just like Dad said.

So they cross-referenced the dead women's client lists and the membership lists of the strip clubs, where they could, with people who owned boats. But they didn't find anything.

I know this because:

I was in the kitchen with Dad one morning, and I asked him, as casual as I could, if his buddies at the police station knew anything about the foot and the whole maritime-burial theory.

"You want to know what the cops are doing about finding this guy?"

"Uh . . . yeah."

He looked at me with uncharacteristic concern. "You afraid?"

"Of the killer?"

"Yes."

"I guess," I said.

He nodded. "Thing like that, finding a foot. That'll screw you up. Make you . . . struggle."

NOTICE THE CODE WORD? The one people use about people with mental problems, as previously discussed? I didn't, at the time. I wish I had. It meant that he had spotted that something was up with me. It should have been blinking with red lights, that word, flashing.

"Hmm," I said, instead of noticing.

"I'll ask at the restaurant," he said. "See what the latest is."

"Oh, okay, thanks, Dad," I said.

"Don't let it get to you so much, Cass," he said.

ANOTHER WARNING SIGN I MISSED. People were already talking.

"I won't, Dad."

"Just, you know, keep safe," he said. "Keep sensible. Don't go out after dark. Keep dressing sensibly."

"Dressing sensibly?" I asked.

"Yeah. You know. Like, not provocative."

"Provocative?" I probably shouldn't have been getting into an argument, but I couldn't help it.

He blinked. "You see the photo in the paper of the last girl who went missing? See what she was wearing in that photo, taken just before she left the club? Looking like that, I'm not surprised that—"

"That someone decided to kill her?"

"That's not what I'm saying. I'm—"

"Dad," I said. "This is called victim blaming. Girls don't ask to be attacked. Everyone should be able to wear what they want without creepy guys going after them."

"I know that, but—"

"And men are not animals. I mean, shouldn't we expect them to control themselves if they see a girl in a short skirt?"

"Yes, Cassie," he said with a sigh. "You're right. But I'm not victim blaming. I'm protecting my daughter."

"Really?" I said. "Because mostly I thought you just played with bugs."

Silence.

A long silence.

But he didn't leave. Just stood there outside the door, on the top step, the garage below us, a motion-activated light above us that gave harsh halogen light and always came on automatically. Moths circling. The sound of a distant car engine, and way under it, ever present, the hushing noise of the sea.

"Cass, I—"

"What?"

He swallowed. "Nothing. I'll see you tomorrow. Don't be late for school."

Of course, he never did find out anything at the restaurant. If he even asked.

"Slap yourself again."

I slapped my face; it stung.

"Again."

"Please. Please, no more."

"Oh, okay, don't. Let's go play on the slot machines instead."

JUST KIDDING.

Can you guess what the voice actually said? Yes! One hundred points to you. It said: "No. Do it."

So I did.

I was in my bedroom in the apartment, sitting on the bed. Sunday before the last week of school. Outside it was getting hot, bright sun in the blue sky. A few scraps of cloud. The town was getting busier already. The workers for the piers had started arriving too. I even recognized a couple of them when I saw them walking down the street. Men and women who had been running concession stands since I was a kid. What they did in the winter, I didn't know.

I went across to the main house. Dad was in his insect room, standing over a tank filled with tree bark and leaf mulch. He beckoned me in. I went over and stood by him. Shirtsleeves pushed up, he lifted a box. The tattoo of the seal on his arm seemed to swim as he moved. It was weird—he'd spent his whole life in the ocean, diving, and he lived in a town by the Atlantic, but he never went down to the beach anymore, not since he'd taught me to swim. Just played with his bugs in his study.

"I called your cell," he said.

"Yeah? I must have missed it." This was not true. I had taken the battery out and hidden the thing under the seat in the apartment. When you hear a voice that isn't there, a disembodied voice, a cell phone becomes an unsettling object.

He sighed. "Okay." He opened the lid of the box, which had holes punched in the side of it, and used tweezers to gently lift out a wriggling millipede. The thing was the length of his finger, bright pinkish red with spikes on its back, huge, like something out of a horror movie.

"What's that?" I asked.

"*Desmoxytes purpurosea,*" said Dad. "People call this one the dragon. Because of the red. From Uthai Thani province." He deposited it on a branch, then reached into the box and took out two more.

"It's gross," I said.

"It's beautiful," he said.

This was a script we followed. But then I went off-script because I realized he was holding his arm kind of funny. His hand and wrist were swollen. Then I saw the purple bloom around his eye. "You get in a fight?" I asked.

He grunted.

"At a bar?" This would have been bad. There had been a time after Mom died. A time with bars. And fights. Now there was a sponsor on the other end of Dad's cell phone, and a disk in his pocket with ONE YEAR CLEAN written on it.

"Cass! No."

"The restaurant?" I frowned.

"Yeah. Guy was making out he was a SEAL. Bragging, you know. Had a bunch of people with him, girls."

"And he wasn't?"

"Wasn't what?"

"A SEAL."

"Oh. Yeah, no."

"How did you know?"

Dad looked at me. "He was bragging."

I waited, just looking back at him.

"You see the shit we saw, you do the shit we did, you don't brag about it."

"So what did you do?"

"I said, 'What team were you in, team twelve?' And he said, 'Yeah,' and then I told him to get out of my restaurant. There are only ten SEAL teams. Guy didn't want to lose face in front of his friends—so it got a little physical."

"And you got a black eye."

"Less than him."

This I believed. "You in trouble?"

"Come on, Cass. Half the guys in the place are police."

I had no comeback to this. "You want an ice pack?" I asked. "I'm going to the library, but I can grab one for you before I go."

Dad shook his head. "School's nearly out. You need a job," he said. "You can't be hanging around in the library all summer."

"I don't just hang out there."

"Yeah, you hang out in the apartment above the garage too."

"Exactly."

"Yeah, Cass. About that . . ."

You know the cliché "I had a sinking feeling"? It's a cliché for a reason, because you do feel like you're sinking, down into the ground. "What?" I asked.

"I'm renting it. A couple of kids from up north. Lifeguard and a concessions' stock boy."

"No," I said.

"What do you mean, no?" He took a step forward.

"No, no, no."

"Cass, you're shaking."

I didn't know that. Panic had cut all the connections between my mind and my body. I kept opening my mouth, but nothing was coming out except for *no*. I was like a goldfish spewing the word no instead of bubbles.

"Jesus, Cass, stop it, you're scaring me."

I took a deep breath. "I need the apartment."

"So do I. I don't know if you've noticed but there's a recession, and someone's snatching women, which isn't exactly the world's greatest tourist advertisement. People aren't lining up for bottles of Chianti at the restaurant. The boardwalk is almost empty."

"That's an exaggeration."

"Maybe. But it's not like it was. And the overheads have not gone down."

"School's not out yet."

"Cass."

"I'll get a job."

"Good. We need all the money we can get."

"So you can buy more insects?"

His eyes went cold. "Come work at the restaurant. The customers like you. They ask about you."

I couldn't believe he was suggesting it. "You know I can't do that."

He deflated a little. "Yeah, yeah. Something else then. Two Piers has jobs going. You could work one of the stands—hand out plush toys to kids who get a ring on the bottle. Or run one of the rides. Maybe take your old basketball-game job. You know they'd let you have it."

"Hmm," I said.

"And get out of the apartment. It's not good for you, all this staying inside."

"But I'm *safe* there."

"You're safe here in the house. I'm here."

I stared at him a moment too long, and I saw the skin of his face flush, the shame rising, with its anger chaser.

"*****, Cass, I wouldn't hurt you."

Again, I didn't reply quickly enough, and I saw the red spreading.

"I get angry sometimes, I know that, but I'm trying to—"

He stopped.

Threw the box across the room—it was stapled wood; it exploded when it hit the wall, pieces raining down on the computer monitor. A millipede landed, twitching, on the keyboard. It scuttled across the letters, as if typing a Mayday message.

"You're out of the apartment by the end of the week," he said. "And you get a ********* job or you're working at the restaurant, even if I have to drag you there."

I should back up and explain the whole Navy SEAL thing: Dad was a SEAL twice, so it was doubly important to him. The first time was when he was young—he fought in the first Gulf War, was stationed on a destroyer in the Persian Gulf. When I was small, he used to tell me stories about the dolphins they worked with, which would patrol the ships, trained to look for mines. As a kid, my whole image of the Gulf War was like a SeaWorld show. I just imagined guys like my dad playing with dolphins, in warm, glittering seas out of the *Arabian Nights.*

Like I said before, he didn't talk about it much. The only real story he ever told was about during his second stint as a SEAL in Afghanistan with Mike Osborne, a British guy. Mike was in the same unit. He and Dad both loved bugs—they would collect spiders and beetles and stuff when they were out in the mountains and fields. So they became friends.

Then Dad's SEAL team got a call one day. A load of Taliban who had surrendered had been taken to an old nineteenth-century fort in the desert, to be interrogated. Dad said the place was beautiful— sandstone walls rising out of the plain, all scrub and goats and the occasional tree, like something from an adventure story.

But then it turned out that the whole thing was maybe a Trojan horse, because these Taliban prisoners—and there were hundreds of them—suddenly rose up and killed their guards and seized the fort.

So now there was a heavily armed group of Taliban in a fortress, basically, with rockets and guns and mortars, and Dad and the SEALs were sent in to take control. Dad was put in a small team with Mike Osborne. Their job was to get as close as they could to the part of the fort that was most strongly defended, and to use GPS tracking to call in air strikes.

So they snuck up to the walls, and managed to get into the main compound through some sort of side door—I think they killed some people to do this, but Dad glosses over that part. From their position, hidden by a low wall, they could see Taliban fighters up on the north side of the fort, embedded with their guns.

They got on the radio and called in a strike.

And someone on the support team got one of the coordinates wrong, just a decimal place, but it was enough.

So when the plane came over and dropped the JDAM smart bomb that was supposed to destroy most of the Taliban resistance, it actually fell closer to where Dad, Mike, and two other SEALs were hiding. The explosion ripped out a whole section of the fort's exterior wall, deafened Dad for a week, and threw Mike Osborne fifteen feet through the air to an exposed part of the fort's interior. Dad meanwhile was smashed into a rock or something, and lay there dazed. He said it was like the whole world had tuned to static.

Dust hung in the air, blurring everything. His ears registered only white noise. It was terribly hot too—he was baking in his helmet and uniform like he was in an oven. He could smell fireworks, and it weirdly made him feel like he was a kid back in Jersey.

Immediately Mike Osborne, who Dad could see through the hole in the wall, was surrounded by enemy fighters. In the middle of all the fuzz that had fallen over everything, the dirt in the air and the buzzing—

%%
%%%%%%%%%%%%%%%%%%%%%%%%%%%%%%%%%%%%%%

—Dad watched Mike get on one knee, and shoulder his assault rifle. He was bleeding from his arm—it would turn out later that it was very badly broken. He emptied the assault rifle, holding off the guys trying to kill him, and when that was gone he took his sidearm and kept firing.

Dad says he didn't think about what he did next. His legs and arms did it for him. But whatever he says, there's still a medal upstairs in his nightstand that he doesn't think I know about. A medal for conspicuous bravery that they don't hand out very often.

Anyway, whether he thought about it or not, Dad managed to get up and he ran through a silent storm of bullets to where Mike was kneeling. He didn't know where the other two guys in the unit were—they might have been dead, or just thrown out of sight by the blast. As he got close, he saw that Mike was out of ammo.

Mike saw him coming, and Dad drew his sidearm and threw it to him—Mike caught it out of the air, spun, and kept firing. Dad opened up with his assault rifle at the same time, suppressing the fire that was coming at them from the ramparts all around.

PLEASE NOTE: This story came to me in fits and starts over the years. I am stitching it together.

PLEASE ALSO NOTE: This next part I mostly heard from Mom, not Dad. Or at least, when Dad tells it, he leaves out key details. Key details like his own courage.

So Dad said, "I'm covering you. Go."

Mike Osborne tried to say something, but Dad shrugged and pointed to his ear to show that he couldn't hear, what with the fact that someone had carelessly dropped a bomb on them.

"Go," he said again. And whether Mike could hear or not, GO is a pretty obvious word to lip-read.

So Mike Osborne nodded and ran for the exterior wall. Dad kept on firing every time he saw a head pop up or the flash of sunlight on a muzzle. Something smacked his head, and he saw only later that two bullets had hit his helmet.

AND TO CUT A LONG STORY SHORT: He managed to stop the enemy from killing Mike Osborne, and then another bomb landed in the right place this time, and that gave him the chance to run. He said it was the closest he ever came to dying, apart from when he was in a cave complex sweeping for ammunition and a teenager with an AK shot him through the shoulder and leg.

And the point is: They gave him a medal for saving Mike Osborne. For throwing himself into danger with no thought for his own safety. And I wanted to tell you this, because I wanted you to know one positive thing about my dad at least.

Also: his experience in the war, and then Mom dying . . . they kind of made him who he is today. He's an *******, it's true. But there's a reason why he's an *******.

And Mike Osborne?

Mike Osborne was out on patrol a couple of months later when his team found a wounded kid. They'd gone to check on him, but the kid was rigged with grenades, and Mike Osborne was leaning right over him, about to give him CPR, when they went off. Mike Osborne was scattered over half a poppy field.

It's weird. I'm writing this to you, and you haven't walked into my life yet. But I guess you already know when you first saw me.

It's like a wood in ancient Greece, a leafy glade. I'm here, and the voice is here—the echo—and we're just waiting for you, for the real action to start.

Which is soon.

Things are going to go fast from here.

Are you ready?

Me, I held it together, just, for the next week. I kept going to the library, hiding out in the apartment. I read up on serial killers.

Meanwhile the voice was bad, but in a way I could handle. Since I had decided to try to find the Houdini Killer, it had let up on me a bit. I figured this was because it was the voice of the woman with the severed foot. I also knew the rules now. Sometimes I would get something wrong—I would forget myself, and go to sit on the couch or whatever, do something comfortable.

Then the voice would say:

"Give me a hundred or your dad will lose his legs in a car accident."

And I would get down on the ground and do push-ups, like Dad made me do when he was teaching me to swim as a kid. Or I'd have to run to the beach and back, or up and down the stairs. I didn't think Dad was noticing any of this stuff, but I guess, looking back, he was more perceptive than I realized.

It was when I had to leave the apartment that things really fell apart. You summer-renter boys weren't moving in for a couple of days, but Dad wanted to clean the place, get it ready. I didn't tell him the apartment was already sparkling. The voice loved to make me clean, over and over again. I figured he'd see that when he came in.

Last day of school was that Friday. It wasn't a big celebration day for me. I moved back to my bedroom Saturday morning. Literally as soon as I did, the voice got worse, just like I'd thought it would. I walked into my room and it said,

"Look at this ******** place. Get a brush and dustpan and then get down on your hands and knees."

"What?"

"Get a brush and dustpan and clean up the floor."

"I can get the vacuum—"

"No."

So I swept the floor. The whole floor. I wasn't even allowed to use a broom. Dad was over in the apartment, changing the sheets or whatever. He and I weren't speaking much. There's this idea that there are optimistic people and pessimistic people. But the factor everyone ignores is that when these tendencies encounter the real world, are tested against experience, they can be dispelled or calcified. Take my dad: I'd say he's naturally a glass-half-empty kind of guy. He always expects bad stuff to happen; my mom says he's always been like that.

But then he was in the Navy and he got shot. He left, joined civilian life again, and lost his wife. So he's *naturally* pessimistic to begin with. But now, because of his experiences, he's also just *miserable*. Miserable and angry.

It took me like two hours to clean the floor, and then the voice wanted me to hurt myself, so I did.

That night, Dad brought pizza back from the restaurant, tried to get me to laugh, but I wouldn't say anything to him. I just ate my pepperoni slice and left the plate for him to clear up, left him sitting at the table alone. Just like a bratty teenager, but in my defense I was being tortured by a voice I couldn't see. I could have acted worse.

I only managed to hold on for a couple of days after that.

There were still some times even in those two days that were okay. When I was outside, for example. I ended up spending more time in our yard than I ever had before. I could tell Dad found it weird. I would sit in one of the old mildew-covered deck chairs and zone out.

A couple of times, Dad came out and tried to get me interested in bugs that were in the garden too, beetles and things that he brought to me proudly in the palm of his hand. That's exactly what he was doing in fact when you arrived.

So this is the first scene that you were there for too.

EXT. A FRONT YARD ON A LOWER-MIDDLE-
CLASS NEW JERSEY STREET. MORNING. OCEAN
MIST IN THE AIR.
A TEENAGE GIRL SITS IN A MOLDY DECK CHAIR.
SHE IS PALLID, HER HAIR AND CLOTHES IN
DISARRAY, BECAUSE SHE IS BEING HAUNTED BY
A GHOST AND DOESN'T KNOW HOW TO DEAL
WITH IT.
THE SUN IS HIGH IN THE SKY. THE TIDE IS UP.

DAD: (crouched next to me) "Look at this."
     (proffering an insect that he has taken out
     of a FedEx box) "Australian spiny stick.
     Simple but fascinating."
THE VOICE: That's disgusting. Tell him to go away.

On the street, a bus rolls past, but I don't really register it.

ME: Nothing.

Because . . .

. . . I opened my mouth to do as the voice said, to tell Dad to go away, and that was when you and Shane appeared. I guess you had gotten off the bus, but it was as if you materialized, out of nothing, out of sea vapor maybe, carried up our street from the waves. You both stood there on the sidewalk, looking at the house number and then at us, you and Shane, with big duffel bags at your feet.

I think Dad had forgotten that was the day you were arriving. You raised your hand in a half wave.

Dad stood and nodded. "Uh, hi, boys," he said. "The apartment, right?"

"Yes, sir," you said, and I could tell Dad liked that.

"We can come back?" Shane said. "If you're busy?"

Dad looked down at the bug still in his hand. "No, no," he said. "Just showing Cassie this stick insect. You like bugs?"

"Um," you said. "Sure?"

"Great," said Dad. "I'll show you some stuff later that will blow your mind. But look at this guy. Look at those spines." He stepped forward and reached out his hand and you made polite noises that only Dad would fail to notice were only for show.

What he *did* finally notice was that he was introducing a bug before he introduced his one and only daughter, so he turned. "This is my daughter, Cassie," he said.

"Hi," said Shane to me. "Nice to meet you."

"Hey," you said.

I said nothing, even though I wanted to. But I couldn't antagonize the voice, not even for you. Not then. I got up to head back to my room.

Dad glared at me, like, *make nice.* I ignored him. I must have seemed, and looked, terrible. I'm sure I was pale and thin, and I was wearing sweatpants and an old T-shirt. No makeup, hair in a scrunchie. The voice was always telling me I looked bad, but it also didn't like me dressing up or putting on mascara or anything like that because it said I looked like a slut. It was very contradictory.

Anyway, focus, Cassie, focus on the main thing, which is not me but you, and to you, I must have made an awful first impression.

What were my first impressions of *you*? I can't remember. I think I noticed Shane more—his size, his muscles. I don't mean I was attracted to him; I just mean he was more noticeable. He clearly worked out a *lot* and he had messed up his hair with wax.

His Abercrombie & Fitch hoodie looked new and expensive. He had that square-jawed thing going on.

You . . . You looked like the kind of guy you never see in a movie. Good looking, but not ostentatiously so. Sorry. Slim, but not one of those skinny quirky kids in films about outsiders who win everyone over in the end. And not the jock either. The clothes you were wearing looked old, but well looked after.

Okay, I lied. I noticed Shane, but I *noticed* you. I mean, you bothered me, right from the start. I wanted to know more about you. It was your eyes, I think. I mean, they didn't shine or any of those clichés. What they did was to *look* at things, all the time. Like you were interested in everything, curious about everything. Which, knowing you a bit better now, I think is probably true.

But you didn't look directly at me. Thinking about it now, I guess you were probably shy.

Back then I felt like I wasn't worth your attention. I felt like it made sense that you didn't look at me.

You hung back and let Shane do the talking. He told Dad how he'd come from New York and you'd come from Stonebridge, twenty miles inland, to work for the summer. You'd met each other at the bus station—you'd both been checking out the ad Dad had posted on the cork bulletin board. Shane was going to be a lifeguard for the summer, and you were going to work the concessions.

"Gutting shrimp," said Dad.

"Excuse me?" you said.

Dad smiled. "It's what they get the out-of-town kids to do. There's a big shrimp restaurant on Pier One. It's kind of their thing. Buckets of shrimp, you know. The kids pull **** out of shrimps, all day long, six days a week. They keep the cushy jobs for the townies—running the stands, that kind of thing."

"Oh," you said, frowning.

"Shane here has the right idea," said Dad. "Lifeguard certificate. Smart. Sit on your ass all day long, watching the girls go— Oh, sorry, honey."

I shrugged. I wanted to be alone.

"You were a lifeguard, sir?" you asked Dad, breaking my fantasy, picking up on the tone of nostalgia in his voice.

"Yep," said Dad. "You don't swim? You couldn't have gotten a certificate like your buddy here?"

You and Shane exchanged a look. I didn't know, then, what it meant. "I swim," you said. "But the hours are longer on the Pier. Beach shuts at sunset."

"You need the cash, huh?" said Dad.

You nodded.

"I feel that," said Dad. "Well, I should show you two the apartment. You've got everything—washing machine, if you know how to use one, bath, kitchen. Though I don't guess you'll want to be cooking after shelling shrimp all day."

You gave a weak smile. But even that crinkled the skin around your green eyes and dimpled your cheeks. A half-formed thought crossed my mind that I wanted to make you smile at me.

I want to be as accurate as possible, you know? It's not like you were haloed by sunlight, or anything, that moment in the yard. I didn't know then who you were going to be.

Dad walked you up the stairs by the garage, you and Shane. I noticed something else then. Shane bounded up the steps, muscles moving under his sweatshirt. He had both your bags in his hands, showing off for me, I think. You walked up slowly behind him, looking around you, like you always did.

I watched you, and I thought about ballet dancers. Not because you moved with grace, because you didn't. It was like . . . You know how you watch a ballet dancer pirouetting or extending their leg or whatever, and you think what they're doing seems smooth and effortless? But then you try it yourself—I did some ballet as a kid—and you realize that it takes just an unbelievable amount of strength to hold your body like that. Watching you climb the steps, that was the impression I had. That Shane might be the one with the muscles, but you were the strong one. It was something in the way you moved. A control.

But I'm making it seem like this was a big deal in my mind, and it really wasn't, sorry to offend you. I just want to try to record the things that went through my head when we first met.

Mainly, I was thinking about how it was going to be way harder now to be alone, that's the honest truth. As soon as you disappeared into the apartment you disappeared from my mind. It's so hard, when you fall for someone—the temptation is to look back on the past and rewrite things so they seem more significant. There's a part of me going: Did I know? Did I know the first time we met that you would change everything? That you would change me?

But I didn't. I'm sure I didn't. The absolute reality is that I probably had a mental image of making out with Shane, just for a second. I mean, he was the *obviously* attractive one.

Given what I did to you later, or what you think I did, I know this will not be easy for you to read. And I know this is not helping you to forgive me. But bear with me, please. I promise you, things are more complicated than you realize.

Well, you know that already, now.

But there's more.

Oh, there's so much more.

More:

The day after you arrived, I went to the library. I walked, as usual. Mist had rolled in from the Atlantic: the ocean invading the town, sending smoke ahead of it to hide its troop movements. The street was full of cars now, and almost none of them were rusted. Tourists.

I waited until someone was talking to Jane, but just as I walked past, the woman turned and walked away.

Jane waved. "Cassie!" She'd redyed her hair; it was green now. Her nails looked like she'd painted them with Wite-Out. She was wearing a T-shirt with an old *Moby-Dick* cover on it.

I tried to keep walking.

"Cassie!" she called again, waving even more.

****, I thought.

I turned and smiled at her. I felt like I was stepping in front of a bus. I went closer.

"Hi," I said.

Waited, tense.

No voice.

Not yet.

Jane beamed. "*Hi!* I haven't wanted to disturb you. You've seemed like you wanted privacy. But you were passing and, well, I've missed you." I could hear tinny music coming from the iPod buds hooked around her neck. It sounded like the Smiths.

"You too," I said truthfully. "Sorry, I've been . . . I don't know."

"Okay," she said. "You like the Murakami?"

"Oh, yeah. Yeah, it was great." I hadn't read it of course.

"The Manchuria part is dark, right?"

"Hmm."

"And school's out for the summer, that's cool, huh?"

"Yeah, cool."

All the time we were speaking I was wondering what the voice was going to do to me.

"So what have you been researching? Murder? You planning to commit the perfect one or something?"

I smiled, but I don't think it looked right; I think it looked fake. "Watch out," I said. "I'm kind of an expert now."

She laughed softly. "Just warn me if you're going to go Jeffrey Dahmer on my ass, okay?"

Even at the time this didn't sound totally like a joke, but I kind of did one of those "ha" laughs that isn't really a laugh.

"Anyway, it's good to see you," she said. "I mean, properly."

"Yeah, you too."

"You'll be here more now school's out?"

"I think so, yes."

"Good. I look forward to seeing even more of you."

A man with glasses and a loosely tied tie was walking up to ask her something, so I smiled and walked over to my usual seat, hidden in the corner, beneath a READING OPENS DOORS poster.

I opened my bag. It was the same bag I used for school and right at the top, in its own little pocket, was my EpiPen. The world contracted around it, a pupil narrowing in bright light. Fuzzed at the edges.

"Take it out," said the voice. "Take it out and inject yourself with it."

"I can't," I said. "It's for an emergency. For anaphylaxis."

"You think it might hurt you if you inject it when you are not suffering an allergic reaction?"

"Yes."

"Good. So do it."

You know this part.

Me: "Please."

The voice: "No."

Me: "Please. Don't make me."

"You ignored me. You ignored me and spoke to that girl with the stupid hair. You remember what happened to your mom? That was because you didn't listen to me."

"What?" I said, under my breath. "I didn't hear you back then."

"Yes, you did. See? You're so ******* pathetic, you don't even remember **** like that. I was there."

Confusion seemed to blur the edges of everything. "No . . . you came . . . after the foot. On the beach."

"Wrong. Take the EpiPen."

"It could kill me. Give me a heart attack."

The silence of thought.

"Well," said the voice. "Let's take the risk. Or this time, I will *kill* your father. I will make the guy he had a fight with come back with a knife when the restaurant is closed."

"You can't do that."

"Try me."

What could I do? I picked up the casing, took off the outer plastic box. Removed the gray safety catch. It actually doesn't look much like a pen—it's thicker, more like a pregnancy test.

Anyway, I stabbed the black end into my thigh and felt the sharp sting and heard it give a *click*. You have to hold it there for ten seconds; that's something some people don't know about epinephrine. To give it time to get right into the muscle. Maybe the voice wouldn't know that. I started to pull it out—

"Uh-uh," said the voice. "Ten seconds."

I counted.

One.

Two.

Three.

Four.

Five—

I had to stop counting. My breath was rushing. My heart was filling my body. It was in my neck and my eyes, pulsing, getting faster and faster. The library was spinning the way the world spins when you've been swimming in the ocean all day—the way I used to with Dad, before Mom died—and then you're lying in bed with your eyes closed.

I put my head between my knees. Sweat was beading on my forehead, drops of it hitting the cheap concrete floor with a sound so loud I thought Jane would hear. I actually felt my heart

—stop—

for the longest

moment.

And start again with a jolt that hurt. I think, and I'm embarrassed to say this, I was actually disappointed for a second. I wanted to be gone, to not have to deal with this voice anymore, this angry murdered person in my head all day long.

I must have dropped the EpiPen because I heard it clatter on the ground. There was no universe beyond the blackness of my closed eyes. There was no time apart from the fast beating of my heart.

Gradually, gradually, the world started to come back. My heart slowed—it was still going terribly fast, and I felt like it was going to burst at any moment. I gasped, and put my hands over my mouth, trying to breathe in my own carbon dioxide, to wind myself down.

"Oh," said the voice, in the tone I imagine boys use when discussing the bees whose wings they have torn off. "You didn't die."

Then a dark shape loomed in front of me. I looked up. Jane was standing there, looking down at me with solicitude turning her face into one big frown. "You need help?"

"Outside," I said quietly. The voice would want to punish me, but what could it do that would be worse?

Jane got one hand under my arm and levered me to my feet, then escorted me out the front door and onto the sidewalk. I sank down against the side of the building.

"What happened?" she asked. "You have low blood pressure?"

I knew she was going to find the injector. "I . . . had some cake. From a bakery that supposedly is nut free. But I felt my throat swelling. I used my EpiPen."

"Jesus. I should call the paramedics."

"No, no. I'm fine."

"Really, I'm going to call an ambulance. You need to go to the hospital. Get checked out."

I looked into her eyes. "I'll go. I'll go, I promise. But not right now. Not an ambulance. My . . ." I searched for inspiration. "My dad will be pissed. I'm not supposed to eat out."

Something in her wavered. "I'll call a cab, go with you."

"No, I'm fine on my own, honestly. See?" I stood up straighter. It was an effort. "Anyway, you need to stay here, right?"

She glanced at the library. Past the peeling paint on the concrete wall, softened by ocean air, and through the grimy windows to the two people already waiting at the information desk. She was on her own, and I could sense her hesitating. "I'll pay," she said. "You go straight to the hospital, okay? You have insurance?"

"Yes, yes."

She nodded and pulled the cell from her pocket.

Five minutes later I eased myself into a cab. There was a little statue of Ganesh that wobbled as we drove and a prayer in Sanskrit taped to the dash. Colored glass beads hung from the rearview mirror. Once we pulled away, I told the driver not to go to the hospital, to drop me off at home.

"You sure?" he asked.

"Yes," I said, and he just nodded and turned up the Indian dance music on the stereo. He was a young guy with a big oversized watch on his wrist; he couldn't care less where I went.

When he dropped me off I hauled ass upstairs and lay down on my bed. I reached for my stereo, but my iPod wasn't docked. I didn't know where it was. The whole time the voice was keeping up a monologue—

"You're nothing. You're a ***** ******. You deserve nothing. You will amount to nothing. You should just kill yourself. Your dad would be happy if you killed yourself. I don't even hate you, you're so pathetic. You are to be pitied. You are not worthy of . . ."

I fumbled with the controls. I managed to get the radio on, and loud rock filled the room, but I could still hear the voice.

"You will never be anyone. You are the ghost, not me. You have no one and nothing. You will . . ."

My fingers kept turning, and the radio station disappeared into crackle, a phantom retreating into nothingness, fragmenting.

Then I was in the space between stations, electromagnetic desert, blankness between the oases of music and talk.

And the voice was gone.

All that was there was white noise.

Blissful white noise.

%%%%%%%%%%%%%%%%%%%%%%%%%%%%%%%%%%%%%%%
%%%%%%%%%%%%%%%%%%%%%%%%%%%%%%%%%%%%%%%
%%%%%%%%%%%%%%%%%%%%%%%%%%%%%%%%%%%%%%%

%%%%%%%%%%%%%%%%%%%%%%%%%%%%%%%%%%%
%%%
%%%%%%%%%%%%%%%%%%%%%%%%%%%%%%%%%%%%%
%%%%%%%%%%%%%%%%%%%%%%%%%%%%%%%%%%%%%
%%%%%%%%%%%%%%%%%%%%%%%%%%%%%%%%%%%%%
%%%
%%%%%%%%%%%%%%%%%%%%%%%%%%%%%%%%%%%%%
%%%%%%%%%%%%%%%%%%%%%%%%%%%%%%%%%%%%%
%%%%%%%%%%%%%%%%%%%%%%%%%%%%%%%%%%%%%
%%%
%%%%%%%%%%%%%%%%%%%%%%%%%%%%%%%%%%%%%
%%%%%%%%%%%%%%%%%%%%%%%%%%%%%%%%%%%%%
%%%%%%%%%%%%%%%%%%%%%%%%%%%%%%%%%%%%%
%%%%%%%%%%%%%%%%%%%%%%%%%%%%%%%%%%%%%
%%%%%%%%%%%%%%%%%%%%%%%%%%%%%%%%%%%%%
%%%%%%%%%%%%%%%%%%%%%%%%%%%%%%%%%%%%%
%%%%%%%%%%%%%%%%%%%%%%%%%%%%%%%%%%%%%
%%%%%%%%%%%%%%%%%%%%%%%%%%%%%%%%%%%%%
%%%%%%%%%%%%%%%%%%%%%%%%%%%%%%%%%%%%%
%%%%%%%%
%%%%%%%%%%%%%%%%%%%%%%%%%%%%%%%%%%%%%
%%%%%%%%%%%%%%%%%%%%%%%%%%%%%%%%%%%%%
%%%%%%%%%%%%%%%%%%%%%%%%%%%%%%%%%%%%%
%%%%%%%%%%%%%%%%%%%%%%%%%%%%%%%%%%%%%
%%%%%%%%%%%%%%%%%%%%%%%%%%%%%%%%%%%%%
%%%%%%%%%%%%%%%%%%%%%%%%%%%%%%%%%%%%%
%%%%%%

I floated on a sea of static. It made me think of my dad, his ears ringing after the bomb nearly killed him, the atmosphere filled with dust. I remembered he said once that the weirdest thing about it, about the explosion and then running to help Mike Osborne, was how peaceful it felt. The hiss in his ears, the stillness of the motes of dust and metal and blood hanging in the air.

Until then, I never understood what he meant—how could it be peaceful when people were shooting at you? But now I kind of got it. I closed my eyes, and let the white noise wash over me.
%%%%%%%%%%%%%%%%%%%%%%%%%%%%%%%%%%%%
%%%%%%%%%%%%%%%%%%%%%%%%%%%%%%%%%%%%%
%%

Until I heard the door to my room open, and my dad came in followed by two guys in green suits with medical logos on them.

"That's her," my dad said. "Cass, turn that **** off."

I turned off the radio. The voice only I could hear said:

"Who are those people?"

"Who are those people?" I asked, pointing to the men in green.

"People who have come to help," said Dad. He walked over to me, grabbed my arm, and pulled up my sleeve. He let out a fast breath when he saw marks on my skin, where the voice had made me pinch myself, or worse. He nodded to the two guys, like this confirmed something.

"Dad!" I yanked at my sleeve. "What the hell?"

He didn't answer me, but I saw his eyes were red. Had he been *crying*? He turned to the paramedics or whatever they were. "She needs help," he said.

The two guys stepped forward. The first one was big, his arms like slabs of pork. One of those arms had a tribal tattoo around it. His hair was shaved close. The other was young, with a friendly face and curly hair. He looked like a boy playing dress-up.

The muscle-builder took my finger and put a clip on it, which glowed red and had a cable running to a handheld reader. He looked at the monitor.

"One hundred thirty," he said to the kid. "Saturation one hundred."

"What's happening, Dad?" I asked. "What are these guys doing?"

He turned to me, and looked at me sadly. "Ms. Austin called me," he said.

"Ms. Austin?"

"The public librarian."

I stared at him. "How do you spell that?"

"Cass . . ."

"How's it spelled?!"

"P-U-B—"

"No. Her name."

"Oh. A-U-S-T-I-N. I think. I knew her mom—used to teach at Fairview. She was still there when you were young, but—"

"She's named Jane Austin?"

"The librarian?"

"Yes."

"Oh," said Dad. "Yeah, I guess. Why?"

"*Why*? Jesus, Dad."

"What? What's this Jesus Dad?"

I shook my head to clear it. "Whatever. So you want me to go get checked out? Okay. Let's go. We need a new EpiPen too."

He sat down on my bed. "No, honey."

"No, you don't want me to get checked out?"

"Yes, but not in that way."

"In what way?"

Dad turned to the paramedics, but they were examining the ceiling and the walls like there was a Michelangelo mural there.

"She told me you've been talking to yourself," he said. "Your teachers too. They called me last week."

I felt the bottom falling out of the world. At the same time, I was glad. Or part of me was. That it was out of my hands now. But I still didn't want to go to the hospital.

The voice didn't either.

"Make him stop," it said. "Make him stop or you'll suffer."

"Please, Dad, I don't want to go anywhere."

He couldn't meet my eyes. "I'm sorry, Cass. I don't know how else to help you."

"*Help* me? You never help me. You've never been there for me."

He took a step back. "Maybe I . . . I don't know. But this is what I'm doing now. I'm getting you some help."

I pointed to the two men. "*This* is help?"

He made a *what can I do?* gesture. Then tipped his head to the guys, to say, *take her.*

"YOU CANNOT LET THIS HAPPEN," said the voice, and in that moment I was so afraid, so unable to deal with what would happen if these men took me someplace where I would have to talk about the voice, so freaked out by the thought of how much it would punish me, that I grabbed onto Dad, onto the front of his shirt, and I think I started to cry then, and I said, "Please, please, please, Dad, please, please, please, please . . ."

You get the idea. I said please a lot.

I begged, I'm ashamed to say.

I cried, and I begged.

AND THEN . . .

AND THEN:

Dad literally put his fingers in his ears, like he was a kid and I was saying something he didn't want to hear. "Don't, Cass. Don't make this harder," he said.

"I'm not making this hard," I said, through my sobs. "You're making this hard."

Dad turned to the two guys. "Come on, let's get this over with," he said. He *was* crying. I could see it now, his eyes overflowing. He turned to me. "They're going to take you someplace you can get some help."

In my head I thought, *If you see aliens, you get taken away by the men in black; if you hear a voice, you get taken away by the men in green,* because one of the things I do is to think of lame jokes in really incredibly serious situations.

97

"Please, Dad," I said, one last time.

"No."

And, oh, what an echo that was, that little exchange.

The muscle-bound paramedic looked at him. "Let's be clear here, sir," he said. "You're saying she's a danger to herself?"

Dad indicated my arms. "What do you think? Plus she had an allergic episode at the library and injected herself with adrenaline, but she didn't go to the hospital. I don't even know if she *had* an episode. Maybe she just injected herself for whatever reason. I don't know."

"And her behavior up till then?"

"Erratic. Private. She's been holed up in the apartment above our garage. Her teachers are worried about her. She's been cutting herself in her room and talking to herself and God knows what else and I just can't—"

To my surprise, he burst legitimately into tears.

He took a breath.

"She's been withdrawn since her mom died. But since she found the foot on the beach . . . "

"That was her?" asked the young paramedic, the kid.

"Yes."

The older one nodded slowly. "Okay, sir," he said. "Sign here." He held out a clipboard to Dad. Then he and the other guy lifted me up.

"You going to struggle?" he asked. It was almost kind, his tone.

"Oh yes," I said. "But not with you."

He looked at me strangely, then shrugged.

And they took me to the ambulance. They didn't exactly carry me, but it wasn't far off. I mean, it was clear I had no choice in the matter.

On the way, we crossed the yard, and I saw you, just for a second.

You were in the space under the stairs where the shared washing machine and dryer are; I guess you were doing laundry.

You didn't turn around, thank God.

But even then, even being escorted to an ambulance, I noted the elegance of your stance, the lines of your shoulders. You were working your way into my heart already, I think. Like people say that splinters do, slowly easing through the bloodstream until they hit the chambers of your—

Although I think that's an urban legend, so this is a bad analogy on a number of levels.

It was just a glimpse, and then you were gone. Or I was gone, more accurately speaking.

%%%%%%%%%%%%%%%%%%%%%%%%%%%%%%%%%%%%%
%%%%%%%%%%%%%%%%%%%%%%%%%%%%%%%%%%%%%
%%%%%%%%%%%%%%%%%%%%%%%%%%%%%%%%%%%%%
%%%%%%%%%%%%%%%%%%%%%%%%%%%%%%%%%%%%%
%%%%%%%%%%%%%%%%%%%%%%%%%%%%%%%%%%%%%
%%%%%%%%%%%%%%%%%%%%%%%%%%%%%%%%%%%%%
%%%%%%%%%%%%%%%%%%%%%%%%%%%%%%%%%%%%%
%%%%%%%%%%%%%%%%%%%%%%%%%%%%%%%%%%%%%
%%%%%%%%%%%%%%%%%%%%%%%%%%%%%%%%%%%%%
%%%%%%%%%%%%%%%%%%%%%%%%%%%%%%%%%%%%%
%%%%%%%%%%%%%%%%%%%%%%%%%%%%%%%%%%%%%
%%%%%%%%%%%%%%%%%%%%%%%%%%%%%%%%%%%%%
%%%%%%%%%%%%%%%%%%%%%%%%%%%%%%%%%%%%%
%%%%%%%%%%%%%%%%%%%%%%%%%%%%%%%%%%%%%
%%%%%%%%%%%%%%%%%%%%%%%%%%%%%%%%%%%%%
%%%%%%%%%%%%%%%%%%%%%%%%%%%%%%%%%%%%%
%%%%%%%%%%%%%%%%%%%%%%%%%%%%%%%%%%%%%
%%%%%%%%%%%%%%%%%%%%%%%%%%%%%%%%%%%%%

%%%%%%%%%%%%%%%%%%%%%%%%%%%%%%%%%%%%
%%%%%%%%%%%%%%%%%%%%%%%%%%%%%%%%%%%%
%%%%%%%%%%%%%%%%%%%%%%%%%%%%%%%%%%%%
%%%%%%%%%%%%%%%%%%%%%%%%%%%%%%%%%%%%
%%%%%%%%%%%%%%%%%%%%%%%%%%%%%%%%%%%%
%%%%%%%%%%%%%%%%%%%%%%%%%%%%%%%%%%%%
%%%%%%%%%%%%%%%%%%%%%%%%%%%%%%%%%%%%
%%%%%%%%%%%%%%%%%%%%%%%%%%%%%%%%%%%%
%%%%%%%%%%%%%%%%%%%%%%%%%%%%%%%%%%%%
%%%%%%%%%%%%%%%%%%%%%%%%%%%%%%%%%%%%
%%%%%%%%%%%%%%%%%%%%%%%%%%%%%%%%%%%%
%%%%%%%%%%%%%%%%%%%%%%%%%%%%%%%%%%%%
%%%%%%%%%%%%%%%%%%%%%%%%%%%%%%%%%%%%
%%%%%%%%%%%%%%%%%%%%%%%%%%%%%%%%%%%%
%%%%%%%%%%%%%%%%%%%%%%%%%%%%%%%%%%%%
%%%%%%%%%%%%%%%%%%%%%%%%%%%%%%%

There's a whole load of static in my memory after the trip in the ambulance.

I know I walked into the hospital, and it was raining, a damp warm smell rising from the asphalt. People smudged into ghosts. There was a low glass-walled restaurant taking up a whole city block by the hospital parking lot with the words EARLY BIRD SPECIAL $4.99 5–6 P.M. FILLS YOU UP ALL NITE frosted into the glass.

I know I was in room 314A on ward PP2. It was small and square, with beige walls, and had a small bathroom adjoining it, with an emergency pull cord, bright red, hanging from the ceiling by the toilet. The bed frame was made of metal, and there is something that immediately sickens the soul about a bed made of metal.

I remember all of that. But a lot of the sequence isn't there. It's like someone took a film and cut it into pieces, then stitched it back together in any order.

I *don't* know how many days I was in that place. That's because of the sedation. Have you ever been sedated? There are so many things we have never talked about. So many things I still want to learn about you.

If you will let me.

The thing about being sedated: You don't remember what happened when the drugs were in your system. But you remember *being conscious*. So you knew what was going on; you just can't recall it.

It's really hard to explain.

Anyway, the reason for the sedation is that apparently when I first arrived I tried to hurt myself quite a lot, I assume because the voice told me to, but like I say, it's a bit foggy to me.

So, the first thing that stands out clearly, like an island in the sea, is when I first met Dr. Rezwari. She was the psychiatrist. They must have dialed down my sedatives so that I would be able to talk to her.

I met her in her office. There was a window that looked out over the ocean, and over the older end of the boardwalk where there aren't any stands or restaurants or gift shops, just old warped boards with grassy mounds of sand sticking through them. I watched seagulls wheeling in a pale blue sky, puffs of pink cloud scattered across it. From that I figured it was dawn or dusk, the time that Mom always called the gloaming.

We must have been three stories up. There was a collection of bonsai trees in the corner, like a little bonsai woods.

Dr. Rezwari saw me looking at them. "Someone gave me one as a gift once," she said. "Now everyone does it. I don't even like them. They strike me as unnatural. You know?"

I blinked at her.

She smiled. She had long eyelashes and black hair and the grayest eyes I had ever seen. Aqueous, like looking into a stream running over pebbles. Her face was small and delicate. Her desk was immaculate: some sort of antique, I thought, like something you would have seen in a lawyer's office in the nineteenth century. There was a single pad of paper on it and an expensive-looking pen next to the pad. No computer—just a single silver plaque on a little wooden stand.

Not much *stuff* in the room in fact—no certificates on the wall, no photos, no personal effects that I could see. It was less like a doctor's office and more like some person's memory of a doctor's office, the details elided by time.

The only exception, the only sign of personality at all, was a whole wall lined with books on shelves, behind me.

Out of habit, I turned and glanced at them. I was surprised to see that they weren't textbooks, not psychiatric journals or whatever. They were nearly all fiction—Margaret Atwood, Philip Roth, Don DeLillo, Alice Munro story collections, a set of Dickenses, Mark Helprin—

"You like reading?" asked Dr. Rezwari. Her voice was soft.

Almost reflexively, the voice said,

"Speak and I remove your feet."

So I didn't say anything.

Instead I looked at the plaque on the desk. On it was written: A CLUTTERED DESK IS A SIGN OF GENIUS.

I did not know what to make of it. I looked at the desk. It literally could not have been tidier. There were only three objects on it, not counting Dr. Rezwari's elbows, which were propped there, her hands under her chin.

Was it a joke? Was it supposed to be ironic? Or was the desk usually a mess, and so someone had gotten her the plaque, and then she cleaned it? It bothered me and so I opened my mouth to ask—

"Your feet," said the voice. "And your father goes under a bus."

So I closed my mouth again.

Dr. Rezwari was studying me, but she made it seem friendly and curious, not detached and scientific. She picked up the pen and spun it around her thumb. That surprised me. It's usually guys who do that.

"I like reading," she said. "I think *Middlemarch* is my favorite novel. Don't you just love it? It's like she created a whole world, totally real and believable. I don't think I have ever loved fictional characters more."

I very much wanted to reply to this. I wanted to say that *Middlemarch* was my favorite novel too, but I couldn't. Dr. Rezwari must have seen something in my eyes though, because she smiled.

"Of course I love Stephen King too," she said. "I'm not snobbish. *Bag of Bones*, that's an amazing book."

YES! said my mind.

My mouth said: .

She kept spinning the pen. "Your father seems to think you have been speaking to people who aren't there." It was a statement, not a question.

She waited, then when I didn't say anything, nodded.

"I'm here to help, you know," she said. "I would dearly like to help you. I can see that you have been through some very traumatic times. You must borrow any of my books, anytime you like. I know from your father that reading is a great hobby of yours."

She paused. Then she said something totally unconnected—I learned that this was one of her tricks. "Tell me, Cassandra, do you ever hear voices?" she asked.

The voice said,

"I'm warning you. Do not speak to her about me. I will make sure you burn in hell."

I closed my eyes.

"You can answer yes or no, Cassandra," said Dr. Rezwari. "You can even just nod or shake your head. I'm only trying to ascertain what we're dealing with here. But we're good, and we have good drugs. *I'm* good. I can help you. It occurs to me, from things your father has said, that perhaps you may be afflicted by this voice-hearing, which is what we call it."

I wasn't listening now, I was focusing on those words: NOD OR SHAKE YOUR HEAD. I opened my eyes again.

Did the voice have access to my thoughts? Would it know if I tried to use this loophole?

I waited. Nothing from the voice. I remembered how I had

waved at Jane, and the voice had not punished me. Perhaps it only knew what I said and did, not what I was thinking?

Dr. Rezwari just went on spinning that pen. "Sometimes," she said, as if it was a passing thing that had come into her mind, "sometimes, people hear voices that tell them to hurt themselves. It's important to know that these voices are not real. They don't exist. They are fictions, created by the mind. Of course this may not apply to you. Although you could nod if it does. We would protect you. We would not let anyone hurt you. Or anything."

I was trembling with fear and hope. I wanted to nod, I so desperately wanted to nod, but I was terrified of what the voice might do to me. Truly, I don't know when I have ever been more scared. I felt as though my heart might burst and splatter Dr. Rezwari with blood and fragments of rib.

Please let this be over, I thought.

"These drugs," said Dr. Rezwari in that way of hers, that way she would go silent for ages and then say something as if it were some incidental piece of information she was passing on because it might, just might, be of interest. "They make the voices go away. Always. I can guarantee that."

I looked at her. The twirling of her pen seemed to slow, the room seemed suspended in time, as if we were held in an invisible, viscous fluid.

I took a deep breath.

And I nodded.

Dr. Rezwari took a breath too. "Okay," she said. "Okay, thank you. That is helpful. We will start you on risperidone right away, while we try to establish a diagnosis. I am thinking psychotic dissociation, perhaps brought on by . . . what happened with your mother. But this is not a worry. You will be fine, we will help you. And you must borrow any book you like."

"What did you do?" said the voice.

I sat there, a mouse between two cats. "What did you do? She will take me away. She will take me away, and you will be defenseless. You know how ****** pathetic you are. You ****** idiot. Take it back. Take it back and I won't rip out your nails; take it back, you

******* *********** *************** **************** *************** **** ******* ***** ******."

I put my hands over my ears, but it didn't stop. The language—I have never heard anything like it, before or since. There was something strange, though: the voice sounded afraid.

Dr. Rezwari frowned. "Are you well?" she asked. "Is the voice talking to you now? Does it want you to hurt me?"

"PUT YOUR HANDS AROUND THAT ****** ******'S NECK AND CHOKE HER. DO IT NOW. KILL HER BEFORE—"

"Drugs," I said quietly, as loudly as I could manage.

"I'm sorry?"

"Drugs," I said. "Please. Now."   ,

They started giving me risperidone.

This is the good thing about risperidone: it stops you hearing voices, most of the time.

This is the bad thing about risperidone: everything else.

You start sleeping all the time, you can't remember things, the walls of your mind become slippery as if oiled. You feel tired every second of every day, perceive the world through frosted glass.

Anyway, I was outside looking at the roses—because what else is there to do when you're in a mental institution—when I felt the presence of someone behind me. I turned around and there was this preposterously beautiful girl standing there. She sort of flicked a cigarette into her mouth from a packet of Lucky Strikes in a move that seemed almost magical, and lit it with a match. She took a deep drag and blew smoke over the roses.

"What's wrong with you?" she asked.

I blinked at her.

She gestured at the walls of the hospital encircling us. She was too thin—her wrists were rails—and she had dark bags under her eyes, but those eyes were fat almonds and her lips were a bow. She looked like a model doing an old-school heroin-chic photo shoot.

"Not a talker, huh?" she said. She was maybe five years older than me, twenty-two, something like that. She blew a perfect ring of smoke that rippled over a red rose.

I shrugged.

"That's okay," she said. "I talk enough for two anyways." She stuck out her hand to shake mine, like a businesswoman or something. I was surprised so I took it without thinking.

"My name's Paris," she said as she pumped my hand up and down. "But really I'm more of a Delaware. An Atlantic City at best."

"What?" I said. I couldn't help it. I was living in a fog, but this girl was like a wind machine; she blew the fog away. I don't know, she just had this energy. You wanted her attention on you as soon as you met her; it was like sunshine. Which was surprising because everything about her was dark—black hair, almost-black eyes, black clothes.

She smiled, and I realized there had been a thin cloud over the sun all that time; now she was blasting rays at me, beaming, in the real sense of the word, and it was like being floodlit. "A lame joke," she said. "Commenting wryly on the hyperbolic romanticism of my name. And shit."

I laughed. I didn't know anyone who used words like "hyperbolic." "Cassie," I said. "Short for Cassandra. My parents weren't romantics. Or big readers of Greek myth, evidently."

"Ha," she said. "Cassandra of the disbelieved prophecies. Okay. You predict ending up in here?"

"No," I said.

"Figures. What's the deal? Depression? Self harm?"

"I don't know. Psychotic dissociation. Schizophrenia, maybe."

She raised her eyebrows. "Impressive."

"You?" I asked.

"Bipolar. A bunch of shit."

"Bipolar?"

"It's what they used to call manic depression. Doesn't matter. Just know that it sucks. Well, sometimes it doesn't. Sometimes you feel great. That's kind of the whole entire problem."

"Sorry," I said.

"Not your fault," she said with perfect equanimity.

"Of course," I said. "We're always alone with our inner voices, we Cassandras."

Paris laughed and stubbed out her cigarette on a low wooden

wall that was holding in the earth and the roses. "You're cool," she said. "Most people in here can only talk about the Kardashians and *Jersey Shore.* Hopefully I'll see you around."

"Yeah," I said. "You too."

She turned and started to walk away. Then she stopped. She came back to me, hugged me tight, and automatically I hugged her back, as if someone putting their arms around you is a switch that flicks you into doing the same thing; she felt delicate under my hands, like she might float away, like she had the bones of a bird.

She pulled back and out of the hug.

I stared at her. Not offended, just surprised.

"Sorry," she said. "I have boundary issues. Apparently."

Then she really did walk away. Her jeans were designer, I noticed, and she was wearing the kind of jewelry that you just know isn't fake. Rich dad, I figured. I was right about that, as it turned out. But I was wrong about where the expensive jewelry came from.

With her going, the fog rushed back in, and I was enveloped in grayness again. I did a couple more laps of the rose garden, but my eyelids were drooping and pretty soon I went back in to lie motionless on my bed.

Repeat.

Repeat.

Repeat.

Weird thing though:

Often, when I was looking at the blank white ceiling of my hospital room, one of those ceilings made of square panels of thin board, as if the whole building was made to be disassembled quickly if necessary, often, at those times, counting the white panels or watching a fly buzzing across them, what I would be thinking about was . . .

You.

You, climbing the stairs to the apartment. You, smiling.

I didn't really get it at the time, though I let it happen because when I was seeing you, strangely, I tended to feel calmer, more in control, more like some hand wasn't going to reach down and take apart all those panels and the bricks of the walls, like children's building blocks, and leave me defenseless on a bed propped up only by air and teetering scaffolding.

It puzzled me though, because, like I said, you didn't make a big impression on me when we met.

Yeah. Right.

DR. REZWARI:	You understand now that the voice is not real?
THE VOICE:	(dim, like a person speaking in another room) Don't listen to this *****. Don't—
ME:	I don't know.
DR. REZWARI:	It's a hallucination. A product of your brain.
ME:	(crying) But I hear it from *outside*. Like any other voice.
DR. REZWARI:	I know. It's difficult. But, like I said, I can help you. Are you still hearing it?
THE VOICE:	Cut her. Slash her face. Slash her ******* face, cut out her—
DR. REZWARI:	Cassie?
ME:	You could say that.

Dad visited, a couple of days later, and I couldn't even muster the energy to speak to him at first. He sat in the plastic chair in the corner of my room. There was a copy of a Graham Greene novel on my bed. Dr. Rezwari had given it to me, but even though I didn't hear the voice anymore, I didn't have the energy to read it.

I was lying on my bed, which was what I did much of the time. There wasn't even a view of the ocean out my window—just a redbrick wall.

Dad handed me a local newspaper, like, I don't know, he thought I had been really missing out on all the news about traffic zoning and the plan to build more community housing in Linklater Heights, and really needed to stock up on coupons for 99¢ BURGERS.

"I'll read it later," I said.

"The regulars have been asking about you," said Dad. "Fat Joe. The Greek. Marty. They send their regards."

There was not even an echo of a thought in my mind about this information. Fat Joe, who liked to sit at the bar by the wood-fired oven of the restaurant and drink grappa, was no longer a part of my world.

"Dad," I managed. "I just want to sleep."

He nodded. It looked like there were more lines around his eyes and mouth than I remembered. "Okay, honey," he said. "Okay." He came over and lifted the sheets at the bottom of the bed and laid them over me, like I was a little kid. Then he reached out his hand to stroke my hair.

"I'm sorry, Cass," he said.

"Sorry for what?"

"I don't know. For whatever I did wrong. For whatever . . . has made you like this."

"Nothing made me like this," I said.

Silence.

"I just . . ." He paused. "You're my life. I would sell my soul if it would make you better."

A wheel came off the mechanism of my breathing; it rasped and scraped in my chest, loose, broken. I hugged myself.

I wanted to cry, but the risperidone wouldn't let me.

Okay, so that's basically the bad stuff out of the way. I mean, apart from me trampling all over your heart but . . . Okay, that's not all the bad stuff out of the way.

I mean more: that's the important bad stuff from *before* you. And I'm going to have to start summarizing a bit now; otherwise I'm never going to get this finished before Wednesday, and I figure I have to give you two days to read it. Your dad said you were going to college Saturday, so Friday is my last chance.

So . . .

Hmm . . .

JUST SKIP TO WHEN YOU WENT HOME, CASSIE.

That was the voice, speaking to me right at this moment, as I type this. I hear the voice again these days, but she's my friend now. I know, I know. I'll explain. Honestly, this will all make sense.

Anyway, she's right.

So:

I went home from the hospital some number of days later. Maybe ten days. I had a prescription for risperidone and another for paroxetine, which is an antidepressant that has a super-high incidence of suicide in those trying to come off it—a fun little fact the doctor didn't tell me at the time. You can just assume that I met with Dr. Rezwari quite a few times when I was in the hospital but we didn't really talk about anything. She just gave me risperidone and referred me to a counselor in the town to talk about my mother, when I was ready to.

And that was it. They discharged me.

Luckily, when I came back from the hospital, you and Shane weren't there. It would have been amazingly awkward if you had been. You were out somewhere, working on the piers, I guess. I don't know what my dad told you about where I had been; maybe he didn't tell you anything, I mean, it's not like he is accountable to the people he rents the apartment to.

Anyway, I was glad you weren't there.

No offense.

From the side window in my room, I could see a small corner of the beach. Just a sliver—between the roofs of two houses, crisscrossed by telephone wires. A V-shaped fragment of ocean. I sometimes used to focus on it and pretend I was on a ship floating over an endless ocean. It was something Mom taught me to do, when I was worried about something.

I tried it, that first day home, but I didn't have the energy.

That day and the next, I just lay on my bed and stared at the ceiling. I also tried reading—there was no voice to tell me not to, or at least the voice was quiet now; muffled—but I couldn't get past page one of any book I tried.

I heard Shane come home at sunset. Dad was still at Donato's. I looked out the front window of my room. Shane set himself up in the yard—he unfolded a lawn chair, sat down, and cracked open a beer. There was a six-pack by his feet. He didn't do anything; he didn't read or listen to music or call anyone. He just sat there and slowly drank the beers. Shane has the kind of mind that people who have had a mental illness envy.

A couple of hours later, a white Ford F-150 with the Piers branding on it pulled up to the sidewalk. I saw you get out of it and walk over to Shane. He stood up, walked over to the pickup, and spoke to you for a bit. Then he gave you a high five. You joined him—he pulled up another lawn chair—and he handed you a beer. You were wearing a Piers uniform—khaki chinos, a pale denim shirt with the logo showing the two piers on the pocket. A CB radio was clipped to your collar.

He's not gutting shrimp, I thought. Because you wouldn't have been driving that branded pickup truck if you were. I wondered what job you had gotten at the piers. I was interested. I watched you and Shane, drinking your beers, chatting. It was calming, somehow. But then you saw me at the window, and I ducked down, ashamed.

You must have thought I was such a weirdo.

The next morning I had my first outpatient appointment at the hospital. Dad was coming back from the restaurant to drive me at eleven. I went downstairs and out onto the porch. Five minutes later, I got a call from Dad on my cell. He'd insisted on getting me a new one to make sure he could contact me when he needed to. I didn't mind so much—I wasn't hearing the voice as often since taking the drugs, so the idea of invisible people speaking in my ear wasn't as scary as it had been. It was a cheap cell; it didn't even have the Internet. But I didn't care.

I pressed the Answer button.

"Honey," said Dad. "Chef has cut himself bad. There's no one else here; I've got to take him to get it sutured."

"You're kidding."

"No, sorry. Can you ride the bus?"

I closed my eyes. "Um, yes. I guess."

"There's five dollars on the hall table. Sorry again, honey."

"He hates you," said the voice, matter-of-factly. It was quiet now, the voice, and I hardly ever heard it, but occasionally I would get these bursts, like a radio catching fragments of speech from the ether. "He wishes you were dead, like your mother."

"Shut up," I said.

"Huh?" said Dad.

"Nothing, Dad. Nothing."

I hung up. Then I started walking to the street. I'd have to take two buses, I thought. The 9 and the 3. I wasn't sure if I was going to make my appointment at eleven thirty.

I turned left on the sidewalk and walked to the bus shelter. I leaned against it to wait. No one else was there. I could see joggers and Roller Bladers passing, one block closer to the ocean, but here in the residential layer, layer three, nothing moved. There was a time I would have listened to music or something, but I didn't. It was weird: there were moments, like then, when I almost missed the voice talking to me. I mean, it had made me do terrible things, mostly to myself. But it had been company, you know?

Now I had no one, and I was living in permanent mist, obscuring everything, making it woolly and still.

I was just thinking that when I saw a gleam of white, and then you were there, sitting in the driver's seat of your Ford pickup truck.

"Hey," you said.

I nodded. I didn't know what else to do. I noticed, close up, that your eyes were a shade of green I had never seen before: river green. But flecked with gold. A slow river, dotted with ocher leaves.

Sorry. But it's true. You have amazing eyes.

"You need a ride?" You made a face. "Sorry, that sounds creepy. I mean, it's not a pickup line. It's just, you looked kind of down. I thought you might need a lift." You swallowed. "I'm on break. I have till—"

"It's okay," I said. "I don't need a lift."

A pause.

"Uh, but, thank you," I added.

"S'cool," you said.

You didn't drive away, and admittedly I had just been thinking about how I was lonely, so even through the fog I was living in, some glimmer of desire for human contact obviously shone. At the same time I was kind of surprised that the voice, even though it was mostly gone, didn't say anything about you. Usually the voice hated if I spoke to someone.

So . . .

I figured I would speak to you.

When I say it like that it sounds ridiculous, makes it sound like such a radical decision, but it was. But also, I'm telling you this for a reason, because I think you thought I was being standoffish, and I wasn't, not deliberately.

"What's with the truck?" I asked in a lame attempt to make human contact.

You smiled. Then you opened the door and got out. You stood by the Ford and did a little bow, kind of showing off but mocking yourself at the same time. When you straightened up, I watched the muscles in your neck move. "You're looking at the Assistant Plush Manager for Two Piers," you said.

"What?" I said. I flashed back to meeting Paris at the hospital, how I had said the same thing. It was like a tic with me.

Suddenly you looked self-conscious. You straightened up. "Oh, uh, it's stupid," you said. "I just . . . I'm delivering plush."

I looked at you blankly; at least I assume I did, because you had an uncomfortable expression on your face.

"Stuffed toys, you know? For the stands. Prizes. I get them from a warehouse in town, and I drive down onto the beach. Throw them up to the guys on the piers. To restock." You gestured with your thumb toward the open back of the pickup truck.

I looked: there was a plastic bag in there, the size of a person, full of Angry Birds.

"After my break, I'm taking those to Pier Two," you said, filling the silence nervously.

"They have an assistant manager for that?" I asked.

You shrugged. "Like I said, it's stupid. Really, I'm just the plush delivery guy, but they gave me that title. You wouldn't believe how quick the stands run out of prizes. And there are a lot of stands."

I wasn't really interested in the stuffed toys, which is sucky of me, I know. I was still amazed that the voice had said nothing about you. I hadn't even had my risperidone that morning; it made me too tired to do anything, so I'd skipped it, which I knew Dr. Rezwari would bust a gut about if she knew. The voice had stopped with the threats. It didn't seem to tell me to hurt myself anymore or that it would kill Dad or whatever—I don't know if that was the drugs—but it would still sometimes insult me, sometimes curse about stuff.

I thought for sure it was going to say something like, "He knows you're ugly," or whatever. That would have been its style.

But that's the thing about you—you're an insulator. A muffler. You silence the voice.

Then the little mike on your shirt buzzed.

"714, come in," said a crackly voice, sounding reedy through the small speaker.

You reached up and pressed a button. "714."

"What's your 20?"

"On my break for another half hour," you said. "Then I've got a delivery to Pier Two."

"Okay," said the voice on the other end of the radio. "I need five medium Tweety Birds and ten large SpongeBobs to Pier One, when you're done."

"10-4," you said, and signed off.

"10-4?" I said. "Seriously?"

You held up your hands defensively. "I think all the guys on the piers wish they were cops. They believe they're characters in an Elmore Leonard book or something."

"A lot of them eat in my dad's restaurant," I said. "The real cops too. I'd say they're more Carl Hiaasen than Elmore Leonard. They're the kind of guys who wear novelty socks."

You leaned your head to one side, intrigued. "You like books?"

I shook my head. "Used to."

I could see the curiosity on your face, but you didn't press. I think you heard something in my tone. "Well, okay," you said, backing away.

Me: repelling people since seven years old.

I saw the 9 bus then and jerked my head at it. "That's my bus," I said.

"You sure I can't drive you? In a noncreepy way?"

"I'm sure. Thanks."

You smiled a tentative smile. That was one of the things that impressed me about you: another guy faced with what I'm sure was a pretty frosty demeanor from me might have felt hurt, rejected. But you stayed nice. I think you really did just want to help. "Catch you later," you said.

"Yeah," I said.

I KNOW: It's like Romeo and Juliet all over again, isn't it? Dialogue FOR THE AGES.

Of course, I didn't feel anything though. I didn't have, for instance, butterflies in my stomach. I *couldn't* feel anything, because of the drugs.

No. No, that's not true. I think I did feel something for you, even then, but it's like when I was sedated—I know I felt it, but I can't remember it. Which sucks in a whole other way, as if my memory is taking you away from me, erasing you. When I look back on myself in those days I see a dead person walking around, dressed up in new skin. Even then, standing at the bus shelter, in the light, with you by your truck, it was as if everything was a little too shiny and unmoving, like everything was behind glass, even the sun.

Then you drove off and I got on the bus and went to my appointment, where Dr. Rezwari asked me if I was hearing the voice anymore and when I said no, not really, she pretty much just shoved me out of her office right away. She'd given up even on offering me books by this point.

Here is the thing: if you hear a voice, it is very important to those like Dr. Rezwari to make it stop, and keep it stopped. This is because they are afraid the voice will tell you to hurt other people. And yourself, of course. So they load you up with risperidone until you're nothing but your own shadow, and they call it a day.

I don't blame them for this. I get it.

It's just—if she had, only once, asked me *when* the voice started. Or why I thought I heard it, or anything about it. What it sounded like. Who it sounded like.

If she'd asked those questions, then maybe I would have gotten better sooner. Would have been spared a trip to the ER.

Anyway.

You probably remember that whole conversation at your car differently, of course. I am quite sure you were confused and maybe even a little hurt by my flatness, I mean; in those days I could barely motivate the muscles of my mouth to smile. That's the thing. Our versions of reality always differ, even when we're supposedly sane.

But I thought you were cool, even right then at the start. I want you to know that.

I think it was maybe a week later that I saw Paris again. I hadn't really seen you in that time. I mean, I'd passed you and Shane on the lawn a couple of times, drinking your beers, and I'd seen you drive past in your truck, sometimes laden with bags full of Elmos or Beanie Babies. We'd said hello and stuff. Had some epically awkward interactions in the laundry area—Dad and I used the same machines—some painful false starts.

"Oh, you wear T-shirts too!"

That kind of thing.

Awful.

Anyway, I was on my way out of the hospital from seeing Dr. Rezwari and Paris was standing there smoking by the revolving door. It was hot, and she was wearing a string vest. I mean like an old man's mesh tank top; you could see *everything*.

"Hey, Fortune Teller," she said.

"Hey," I said.

She was leaning against the wall right by the door, in the cool blast from the air-conditioning inside; the air in town was muggy, full of rain that needed to fall. "Appointment?" she said.

"Yeah. You still here?"

"No. Outpatient too now."

"Good," I said. When they let you out it means they don't think you're in imminent danger of doing something stupid. "You got an appointment too?"

"Done. Now I'm waiting for a ride." She examined me. "You look ******* terrible, BTW."

"What?"

It really was a tic, see?

"Your skin, your eyes, everything. Diazepam? Valium?" She peered at my eyes. "No. Haldol. Wait, no, that's kind of a big gun,

123

you'd be drooling more. Risperidone. Yep. Risperidone. I'm right, yeah?"

I stammered. "Y-yes."

"You feel like you're wrapped in cotton?"

Fog was how I thought of it, but, yes, close enough. "Uh, yeah."

"Me too. You have to stop that shit, seriously."

I shook my head.

Paris flicked her cigarette; it exploded on the concrete, sparking. "Afraid of the voices?"

I nodded. Then I shook my head. "Just one voice."

"Same thing. Anyway, I stopped it. You can too. 'Course, the docs go ape if they find out. But the docs think drugs are the answer to everything."

"You . . . heard voices too?"

She made an equivocal motion of her head. "Kind of. Visual phenomena. Apparitions. Which would sometimes speak as well."

"Like ghosts?"

"Like ghosts."

"And you still see them?"

"There's a woman standing behind you right now. Half her face is missing."

I whipped around, heart jumping.

"Kidding," she said. She gave a wicked smile. "But yeah, I still see shit."

"I don't want to hear my voice. It . . . It wasn't nice."

She waved a hand, dismissing this. "You have to learn to deal with it, is all," she said. "Dr. Lewis can help with that." Then she leaned closer. Suddenly she was conspiratorial, serious. "Here," she said. She handed me a card. On it was printed:

NEW JERSEY VOICE SUPPORT GROUP

Under it was a number and an e-mail address.

"Thursdays, at the bowling alley on Elm," she said. "There's a room at the back. If I'm not there, tell them Paris sent you."

I looked at the card. "Is it . . . safe?"

She laughed. "It's not a *cult*. It's run by a super-respected guy. Dr. Lewis. It's just . . . they're psychologists, mostly. The docs aren't on the same page as them. Though there are a couple who are coming over to the light." She paused. "Who are you seeing? Rezwari? Yeah, she's not one of them."

"And the people in this group . . . don't believe in drugs?"

"They begin with the principle that the voices are real, and are created by trauma, and must be accommodated, not silenced." It sounded like she was reciting something.

"My voice scares me," I said. Admitting this out loud seemed major.

Paris glossed over it though. She waved a hand. "Thursdays, seven p.m. You don't have to go. But give it a chance. Those drugs they're giving you are just putting a lid on things. They're not turning the heat down on the range."

I glanced at the paper bag she was holding, which obviously contained prescription drugs.

"These are antidepressants," she said. "Different ball game. Without these, my life isn't worth living, seriously. I'm not, like, antipsychiatry. Just the way they deal with people like you."

"Which is?"

"Tell you you're schizophrenic, or whatever. They did that, right?"

I nodded. It was one of my three possible diagnoses.

"Fill you with drugs. Treat the symptom, not the problem. Most people who hear voices, they're not mentally ill. They've just suffered something. Lived through something really bad. And it manifests itself as a voice that seems to come from outside."

My legs suddenly shook. There was an image in my head: blood pooling around a head, small white tiles. A baseball bat.

I put out a hand and grabbed her wrist.

"You okay?"

I gasped. "Yeah, yeah. Sorry."

She looked at me, and her eyes were lit with intelligence. "I would hazard a guess"—she talked like that sometimes—"that something bad may have happened to *you* when you were younger. Am I wrong?"

"No. I mean, yes, you're wrong."

My veins and arteries were alive, thin snakes writhing within me. I was so freaked out I didn't even think to ask the obvious question.

Can you see what the obvious question would have been?

Take a moment.

Yes.

The obvious question would have been:

If that's true, if it comes from trauma, then what happened to *you*?

"Okay, then," she said. "Fine. You just remember what I said." She thought for a second, then she flicked some invisible hair from her ear and looked right at me. She was wearing no makeup at all and was pale and skinny, but I still almost had to look away from her; it was painful, her beauty, like looking at the sun without those weird shades that have a slit in them that people wear for eclipses. "Pop quiz," she said.

"Huh?"

"Obamacare: Pro or con?"

I closed my eyes. "I'm tired. I can't—"

"Oh please," she said. "I aced an Anthropology midterm at Rutgers on Xanax and methadone. On which note: Marcel Mauss."

"What?"

"*Marcel Mauss,*" she said, stressing it this time.

I thought for a second. My brain was so slow. "Uh, magic. Or sacrifice?"

"Both, actually." She gave a soft clapping mime. "Back to the start. Obamacare: Pro or con?"

"Pro?"

"Good. Word association. Pro."

"What?"

"What word do you associate with the word 'pro'?"

"Choice."

"Good answer. 'Life' would also have sufficed. Next one: leather."

I hesitated for a moment. "Notebook."

"Martin."

"Amis."

"Eleanor," she said.

"Rigby."

"Good. I would also have accepted 'Roosevelt.'"

"I think you might be crazy," I said.

"Wiser minds than yours would agree," she said. "Next one: procrustean."

"Bed."

"Pan."

"Echo."

She frowned. "Echo?"

"In one version, Pan wanted her, and she said no, and so he had his followers tear her apart. But the earth loved her, so it kept

127

her voice in the stones and the trees and the caves. To cut a long story short."

"Wow," she said. "You taught me something. Doesn't happen often. I was going for pipes, or Dionysus." She looked at me funny.

"What is it?"

"I *knew* I recognized you, that first time. You go the library, right?"

"Ye-e-e-s. You?"

She did a comical big-eyes thing. "Are you serious? No. But I pick up books for school sometimes. Books are expensive shit. Anyway, you're a big reader, huh?"

"Yes. I mean, I was."

"Risperidone stop you reading?"

I nodded.

"Told you, you have to get off that stuff. Yeah, I saw you, I remember now, you had a load of books . . . about murder or something?"

"Yeah."

"Light reading."

"It was . . . you know what, forget it." It had made so much sense at the time—the idea that the voice was a victim of the Houdini Killer, a remnant left behind. If I said it now it would just sound *insane.*

"Well, anyway, I like you," she said. "You're okay."

"Okay?"

"Yeah." She reached into a front pocket of her skinny jeans and handed me another card. Her dark eyes were warm on mine, like black asphalt heated by the sun. "E-mail me if you want to hang out."

I glanced down at the card. It had a silhouette of a girl sitting on a chair, legs wide. Under her, embraced by her legs, was:

CAM GIRL. GLAMOUR. PRIVATE PARTIES.

INSTA: @jerseygirl95

There was no phone number, just an e-mail address: jerseygirl95@_____.com

I looked up at her.

"She's a ******* whore," said the voice, but not loud, as if it were coming from the other side of the parking lot, by the Dumpster and the trees, shimmering in the heat.

"Oh yeah," she said. "I forgot to mention, I'm a glamour model. Or, you know, aspiring. It would drive my dad *crazy* if he knew. Which is a big part of why I do it."

DR. REZWARI	(making notes on her pad) Do you ever hear the voice now?
ME:	(lying) No.
DR. REZWARI:	You're sure?
ME:	(lying) Yes.

So, you see, it wasn't just you I lied to.

I checked out Paris's Instagram feed—I know how to do that; I'm not a total Luddite. It was basically photos of her in bikinis and underwear, sometimes modeling things that had obviously been sent to her free, and I was surprised to see that she had 39K followers.

Paris liked to take her clothes off, clearly, but she was smart. Or maybe I should say, *and* she was smart. To avoid any implication of contradiction.

She loved books. She loved knowing stuff. She was a college student.

I liked her.

The voice did *not* like her. It called her "that ******* whore" and other stuff that was even worse. But it didn't say much when she was around, and it didn't threaten me about seeing her; it didn't say much ever those days, and when it did it was kind of dulled, as if coming from the other side of a window. Looking back, I think that was not just the risperidone working, it was also because the voice knew that Paris was offering a different way of dealing with things, one that didn't involve drugs. The voice *hated* the drugs, because they muffled it, suffocated it, a pillow over a mouth.

EDIT: *I* hated them. The voice is me. I understand that now. Even you probably do, just from reading this. But I didn't then of course.

I guess it was maybe a week after I saw her at the hospital that I e-mailed Paris. I hadn't seen you much—even though Dr. Rezwari kept telling me to get to know you. It wasn't easy. You were working most of the time, or you were hanging out with Shane. You would wave to me, but I didn't feel like you were interested in me or anything; in fact I was convinced I had offended you by being cold when we spoke, and not accepting your offer of a ride.

So I just lay in bed or sat in the kitchen or whatever. I'd just spent a whole day sitting in Dad's study watching millipedes crawl all over a log, and my brain was mush. I had the impression that I was locked out of my own body, floating somewhere above it.

I wanted to *feel* stuff again.

I set up an address: echo@_____.com

And I e-mailed Paris one word:

HELP.

It was a Thursday. The day when the voice support group met. I think unconsciously I knew that. Paris e-mailed me back exactly fifty-seven minutes later. When you are watching millipedes crawl, you are very conscious of the passage of time. Her e-mail said:

CALL ME. 800-555-5555

I took out my cell and dialed the number.

"Jerseygirl95 here, I'm wet and in front of my camera and—"

"It's me, Cass."

"I know. I was just ****** with you."

"Oh."

"Sorry. Tell me. What's up?"

"The drugs."

"Yeah, I thought so." The kindness in her voice made me almost want to cry. Dr. Rezwari wasn't kind. I mean, she wasn't some kind of monster. But she didn't really *care*. You could tell. I could tell.

"You said there was a guy, a—"

"Already done. Dr. Lewis doesn't think you're ready for group, but he'll meet you before. Massey Bowling Alley, six p.m."

I looked at my watch. Two hours. "Okay," I said. I must have sounded pretty bummed because Paris said:

"Come see me now. I'm close to there." She gave me the address of her condo.

133

"You're sure?"

"Yes! Come hang out. Meet my roomie."

I wrote a note for Dad. It took me a while to think what to put in it. I couldn't say I was meeting a friend; he knew I didn't have any friends, and I didn't think he would be cool with me hanging out with someone I'd met at the mental hospital. He and I had been living together like two people made of bone china, scared to bump into each other.

In the end I wrote:

Gone to see a movie. Love you. Cass.

Most likely he wouldn't be back from the restaurant before me anyway. I left the house. I passed your apartment, but of course you and Shane were working. I walked the whole way—Oakwood is a small place, as you know, and Paris didn't live far away.

Her condo was just back from the boardwalk; a fifties building like a pink iced cake, with white balconies like wings. I rang the bell, and she buzzed me up.

When I got to the door, another girl opened it. She had red hair, but I thought it was probably dyed—it was a really bright color. There was a tattoo on her arm of a kind of pinup woman from the forties or something, and she was wearing a vintage dress and her hair was swept up with bobby pins.

"I'm Julie," she said. "Paris is in the kitchen, making cookies."

I must have looked surprised.

"She bakes," said Julie. "I know. Go figure."

"I'm Cass," I said. "Um, hi."

"Nice to meet you, Cass. Go on through—I'm heading out. I

have a team meet." She picked up a pair of roller skates by the door and slung them over her shoulder.

"You do roller derby?" I asked.

"Yep."

I'd watched a movie about roller derby with Mom once. So I knew a tiny bit about it. "What's your, like, player name?"

"Player name?" She raised an eyebrow.

I felt stupid then. "I don't know what you call it . . . but don't you have, like, crazy names that you put on your shirts and stuff?"

"I was messing with you. I knew what you meant. And, yes, I do. One Thousand Mega Joules. 'Cause I'm Julie, and I study—"

"Physics?"

Julie smiled. She wasn't pretty—her face was a little blunt—but her smile was like the sun when it hits the ocean on a gray still day, and even though the water is flat, matte, it flashes. "Close. Chemistry." She turned to face back into the apartment. "Hey, Par, this one is smart."

"I told you," said Paris's voice, from an unseen corner of the condo.

"Kitchen's on the left," said Julie. "See you soon, I hope." Then she whisked out. She was someone with her dial always turned to full, Julie. She still is.

I followed the sound of Paris's voice, across a smooth wood floor. There was a small hall that went straight into the main living room. Floor-to-ceiling windows looked over the beach and ocean, like you were sailing over it. Just to the left, I could see the first pier jutting out over the wide expanse of sand, the Ferris wheel slowly turning. There were a couple of armchairs like you see in magazines—curved metal bases, leather stretched over them. A coffee table made of polished driftwood. It did *not* look like a student's condo.

I turned left and into the small kitchen. Paris banged the oven door shut. "I'm baking cookies," she said. "For the occasion. They'll be ready in a half hour."

"Wow," I said. I was worried about cookies and my allergy, but I didn't want to put a downer on things.

"I know. I will make someone a fine wife one day."

I smiled. "Someone eligible, I hope," I said.

"Oh, Mother!" she exclaimed, in a surprisingly good British accent. "He hath two hundred a year, and a good house." She did a curtsy. "I ****** love those old books. Austen and stuff."

"Me too." I would have said more. I would have said that I *had* loved Austen anyway, or I would have asked her if she knew that Jane from the library was actually Jane Austin, but I was wiped out from the walk. I just waved vaguely at the living room and reached out for the countertop to stabilize myself, and Paris looked stricken.

"Sorry! Sorry! Go sit down." She ushered me ahead of her.

I sat on one of the armchairs. It kind of cradled me.

Paris sat opposite me; hooked her leg over the side of her chair. She fidgeted for a second, then leaned over and grabbed a piece of purple paper from a pile on the end table. She started folding it— some kind of origami.

When it was done, she held it up in front of her, and it obviously passed inspection because she smiled.

"What's that?" I said. My best guess was some kind of bird— pointed head, arched wings.

"Crane," said Paris.

"Cool. You like origami?"

She shook her head. "Not really."

"So . . ."

"Oh," she said. "It's this thing. The thousand cranes? You have to

136

make a thousand of them, and when you do, you get one wish. It's like this old Japanese—I don't know what you would call it—folk tale or belief or meditation or some kind of mix of all of them."

"A *thousand*?"

"Yeah. If it were easy, it wouldn't be worth a wish."

"I guess not. So how many have you made?"

"Two hundred and sixty," she said. She glanced at the purple crane in her hand. "Two hundred and sixty-one." Abruptly, she got up from the chair—a motion like a spring uncoiling, quick and elastic. "Come look," she said.

Paris led the way to a door at the other end of the room. She opened it and flicked a switch—bright electric light burst into being, illuminating a room that was obviously hers. Mess of clothes on the floor, a king-size bed nearly disappearing under books and magazines and plates of food—just a kind of tunnel to climb under the covers like a rabbit.

And all over the shelves on the walls, in among the beer glasses and photos and teddy bears, standing on every available surface: cranes. Paris pointed up and I looked; there was a string from the light shade to the wall, and on it more cranes were hanging. It seemed like more than two hundred and sixty. They were all colors— mostly white, but also red and green and blue and silver and gold.

"Whenever I get the chance, I make one," she said. "Should hit a thousand in . . . I don't know. A year, maybe?"

"Serious commitment."

"I know. Worthy of an Austen heroine, isn't it?"

"Yeah."

I imagined a thousand cranes, in all colors, filling the room. It was going to be beautiful. I could understand why someone would want to do that.

She picked up a small white crane and pressed it into my hands. "This was the first one I made," she said. "See how it's not folded so crisply?"

I looked down at it. I nodded. It was a little misshapen.

She took it back and put it down, gently, on the bookshelf where it had been.

"What will you do with your wish?" I asked.

"If I said, it wouldn't come true," she said seriously.

"Oh. Yeah, of course."

She smiled, and for a second I was dazzled by her smile: it was so warm, so beautiful, so totally unguarded, as if it for no single second occurred to her to think about what anyone else thought of her; very few people smile like that. "A lot of people would have laughed at me there. Probably even Julie, even though she would feel bad about it afterward. But not you."

"Why would I laugh?"

"Because it's stupid, believing in wishes. Childish. Crazy, even."

"I hear a voice that isn't there," I said.

She laughed. "Touché."

A pause.

"Are you okay, Cassie?"

"Huh?" I said. I felt like the world had blinked—a fraction of a second gone, some gap in the film, a shudder. It was disconcerting. I was leaning against the wall of the room now, and I felt light-headed. What happened?

"You look pale," said Paris.

I closed my eyes. And when I did I saw a bowling alley, a bowling alley of my imagination, yawning open in front of me, front wall peeling up, to reveal the lanes stretching back like tongues into darkness, the pins standing up like teeth.

"Uh . . . I think I'm just nervous," I said, when I opened my eyes. "About the . . . you know. The meeting." My heart was beating wildly.

Her eyes grew.

I mean, of course they didn't grow. But they seemed to. "Oh, ****," she said. "Of course you are." She reached into a cupboard and took out a bottle with a white label—vodka. She handed it to me. "Here. Take a gulp of that. Liquid courage."

I held the bottle in my hand. "I can't. I don't—"

"You're worried about the risperidone? Because—"

"No. I'm just . . . well. Underage."

She rolled her eyes. "Drink. You need to calm down a little."

"Don't even think about it," said the voice. "I will make you whine like a dog."

I hesitated.

"Yes. Give it back," said the voice. "And then go home. Or you will pay."

*Oh, **** it,* I thought. I'm going to pay anyway, for going to this group thing.

I tilted the bottle back; swallowed. It was like swallowing fire: it seared down my throat and warmed my stomach. A beeping came from the kitchen.

"Time is up for you, *****," said the voice. "I swear I'm going to—"

"Ah!" said Paris. "Cookies."

Paris put the vodka back in the cupboard, took my hand, and dragged me back to the kitchen. She opened the oven, slipped on a flowery mitt that I never would have pictured in her apartment, and took out a tray of huge chocolate cookies, perfectly browned.

"Ta-da!" she said.

I mimed clapping.

Paris expertly slid the cookies onto a plate and then led the way back into the living room. She indicated for me to sit down again.

Right. The moment I'd been putting off. The awkwardness.

"Eat," said Paris. She pushed the plate at me. They looked good—soft in the middle, the chocolate still molten.

I swallowed. "Um. Sorry . . . I should have said before . . . I'm allergic," I said. "Peanuts. I'm really sorry. They look amazing."

"No peanuts in these."

I gave a half smile, embarrassed. I hated this, I always had. "It's more complicated than that. What about the flour?"

"What about it?"

"Is it made in a facility that handles nuts? The chocolate?"

Her eyes widened. "Really? It's that serious?"

"Yep." I held up the bag I always carried with me, the one my mother had embroidered my name onto, and showed her the two EpiPens inside, the bronchodilating inhaler. "The smallest trace, and I could die."

She went to the kitchen and came back with a bag of chocolate chips. I turned it over, showed her the label: MAY CONTAIN NUTS.

"Sorry," I said.

She shrugged. "Don't be. Next time I'll get the right stuff. Can't have you dying on me."

I smiled.

She started carrying the plate of cookies back to the kitchen.

"You're not having one?" I asked.

"Carbs? Are you kidding me?"

I frowned. "But you baked them."

"Yeah. I like the distraction. It's therapeutic."

"Oh. Okay."

Paris was wearing a long bodycon dress with vivid neon flowers all over it. Her hair was piled up, secured with chopsticks. She looked much better than she had at the hospital. She threw herself down on the chair opposite me, splayed herself—she had a way of sitting down like a cat; her limbs didn't seem to have the same bones as most people.

"Your condo is beautiful," I said.

"Thanks."

"Is it . . . um . . . do you . . ."

"Do I pay for it with the ill-gotten gains from taking my clothes off on a webcam?"

THE VOICE: ******* slut whore.

"Uh, yeah."

"Partly. But my dad pays too. Sends a check in the mail. His signature on those checks is pretty much the only communication I ever have from him."

"You're not close?"

She smiled. "You could say that."

"Does he live in Oakwood?"

She shook her head. "New York. Mom too. But, I mean, in separate apartments. They can't stand each other. I went to high school there, but as soon as I could I got out."

"Headed to the glamorous Jersey Shore," I said.

"Yeah," said Paris, grinning. "But with the checks from my dad, and my work too, I got this sweet pad. So I'm happy."

"Do your parents know about . . . you know. The cam stuff?"

"No, thank God. They don't check up on me, which is good, because they have some serious problems with my lifestyle choices as it is. We are, what would you say? We are somewhat estranged."

"Sorry."

"Sorry what?"

"That you're, I don't know, estranged."

She waved this away. "Only one of my *many* issues."

"How does it work?" I asked. "The modeling. I mean . . . do you have, like, an agency?"

Paris laughed. "Cass! It's the twenty-first century. I have Instagram for promotion, and then I have a website. People subscribe, and they can watch me when I decide to stream a video. Or book me for an event or whatever."

"People? You mean men?"

"Well, yeah. I guess."

I remembered her card. "And the bachelor parties?"

"Stripping, basically," she said. "Private parties. Way more lucrative than the clubs. Five hundred bucks a pop. Julie hates it."

"Because . . ."

"Because she thinks it's not safe. But these are birthday parties, you know? College graduations, bachelor parties."

"But . . . what about . . . safety? Don't you get scared?"

"I have a no-touching policy," said Paris. "That puts off the worst creeps, I figure. And Julie drives me if I go to a party. Plus, there's kind of a network, you know? Someone gets a bit rough, one of the other girls will e-mail about it. Post it on one of the forums—his e-mail address, that kind of thing. We watch out for one another."

"Wow." I seemed to keep saying that.

She looked at her watch. It was a men's Rolex—I recognized it because it was like the one my dad got from the Navy stores, but much newer. A black-bezeled Submariner. A diving watch.

"You dive?" I asked.

"What?"

I pointed at her watch. She laughed again. "No. I just like shiny things. Like a magpie." That was Paris—always a bird. Light bones, mind flitting from place to place, acquiring things. Something tailored from wind, unanchored in the sky. She walked over to a big flat-screen TV. "Anyway, we have forty minutes. Just enough time for *Project Runway* before we go. I DVRed it."

We walked to the bowling alley. The place was kind of run-down. There was an empty lot next to it, full of weeds, cordoned off by a wire fence. I guessed it had been built when Oakwood was still a tourism boomtown, before people started flying to Mexico. A long, flat edifice, warehouse-like, squat.

There was a neon sign out front, still lit, one of those ones with three images kind of overlapping so it looks animated—a guy holding up a ball, then kneeling, then releasing it. Except the third batch of tubes was busted, so the guy was just standing and then kneeling, standing and then kneeling, like he was proposing or something.

Or having a stroke.

Inside, we walked past an empty reception area. The place was closed; I mean, it was closed for bowling. Behind the desks were rows of compartments holding white-soled sneakers in different sizes. We cut right and went past the lanes; the lights above them were off, but screen savers cycled on the computers above them, showing cartoons of shocked-looking pins tumbling end over end, creating flickering shadows. It felt like an introductory scene in a horror movie.

"Spooky, isn't it?" said Paris.

"Uh-huh."

The balls gleamed in their racks. Green and blue and black and red, the colors pearlescent, swirling like gasoline in a puddle. They gave me a sick feeling. They reminded me of bruises. I could smell stale popcorn.

"In here," said Paris. She opened a utilitarian fire door with a letter-sized piece of paper taped to it, saying PRIVATE MEETING IN SESSION VSG SOUTH JERSEY BRANCH.

I followed her in. There was an oldish-looking guy sitting on a cheap plastic chair with steel legs; ten or so empty chairs were arranged in a circle in front of him. The room was bare—against one wall was a table with a paper cloth over it, and a coffeepot and cups.

"I'm hoping someone's going to bring cookies," he said. He had gray hair, twinkling eyes. Kind of handsome, in a scruffy, old-guy kind of way. He was wearing Nike sneakers with jeans and a polo shirt. He looked like the antidoctor. He looked like, I don't know, an advertising executive or something. Not that I know what an advertising executive looks like.

"****," said Paris. "I baked some. I swear. Then we were watching *Project Runway*."

"A valuable use of your time, no doubt," said the old guy. But he was smiling as he said it. He turned to me. "Dr. Lewis," he said. "But you can call me Mike. And you must be . . . what do you prefer? Cassandra? Cass? Cassie?"

I shrugged. "Whatever."

The voice said,

"Manners, Cass. For ****'s sake."

"I mean, I don't mind," I said. This was weird. The voice wanted me to be polite to this guy? Suddenly I felt scared. I mean, this was the thing that had made me slap myself and inject myself with epinephrine, and it wanted me to play nice with the doctor?

Anything the voice *wanted* had to be bad, didn't it?

But I squashed this thought down, jumped on it, like Daffy Duck jumping on Bugs Bunny when he's trying to get out of his hole. I didn't want to be taking the drugs either; I didn't want to be a zombie all my life.

"Cass?" said Paris. "Earth to Cass?"

"Sorry," I said. "I'm here."

"That you are," said Dr. Lewis. Mike. "And it's an important first step. So. Why don't you take a seat and tell me about it. Paris, you mind giving us the room?"

A nervous voice inside me spoke up then, not *the* voice, but an instinct voice. It said,

You want to be alone in here with this guy you don't know?

Then the actual voice said,

"Shut the **** up, *****. Stop being so pathetic." It was quiet from the risperidone, but it was still pretty forceful.

I closed my eyes as my inner voices argued. "Can she . . . can she stay?" I said.

Paris looked at the doctor.

"Why don't we leave the door open?" he said. "Paris can wait in the main hall. She could even bowl a few rounds."

"Bowl?" said Paris, like he was suggesting necrophilia or something.

He shrugged. "The balls are there. Might as well use them."

Paris smiled. "The philosophy of every male," she said. "Okay, fine. You need me, Cass, you call for me."

And then she swept out the room, long legs tick-tocking. I watched her go, amazed as I always was by her, by her self-possession and her grace, despite her illness. She was like a machine in tight-fitting clothes, engineered to hold the eye, but she had charisma too, blazing out of every pore.

"She shines like a star, doesn't she?" said Dr. Lewis, more succinctly. "I just hope she doesn't turn out to be meteor."

"Why?" I said.

He looked sad all of a sudden, thoughtful. "Because they fall to the earth. And they burn."

DR. LEWIS: Take a seat. Sorry about the plastic chairs.

ME: That's okay.

DR. LEWIS: Paris has told me a little about you. But why don't you tell me something.

ME: Like what?

DR. LEWIS: I don't know. How about your favorite music.

ME: Oh. Uh, I used to like hip-hop stuff. But now I mostly listen to, I don't know what you would call it; electronica. Stuff without voices. Just . . . beats and bass, you know?

DR. LEWIS: (Rolls up his sleeve. There is a tattoo reading COME AS YOU ARE in gothic script down his forearm and an anarchy symbol.) I listen to a whole load of stuff. When Kurt Cobain died, that was the day I decided to be a psychologist. Sounds stupid, but it's completely true. I was, what, seventeen?

ME: (inside my head) *Oh, he's not as old as I thought. It's the gray hair, I guess.*

DR. LEWIS: I just thought, what a waste, you know? I thought if I could stop one person from doing what he did, then my life would be worthwhile. It's like . . . a world ending, every time. Do you know what I mean?

ME: (thinking of my mother, her likes and dislikes, her opinions, her favorite foods and movies and her jokes and smiles and angry days, the songs she liked to sing, reduced to a red puddle of blood on a tiled floor) Yes.

DR. LEWIS: The loud music helps?

ME: With?

DR. LEWIS: Your voice.

ME: Oh. Yes. It does.

DR. LEWIS: This voice, do you have any idea who it might be?

ME: (puzzled) I don't . . . I don't think I . . .

DR. LEWIS: I mean, is it someone you know? Someone you knew?

ME: It's a voice. It's not real.

DR. LEWIS: The shrinks told you that, right?

ME: (nods)

DR. LEWIS: (sighs) The voice is real to you, is it not? I mean, you hear it, like any other voice? With your ears?

ME: Uh, yes.

DR. LEWIS: So it's real. It's a real phenomenon. It doesn't matter if you can see it or not. It's real *to you.*

ME: I guess.

DR. LEWIS: It's possible to do scans, you know. Functional MRI. Electrical signals. What we know is that a person who hears voices, when they do hear them, the exact same brain areas light up as when they hear real speech. It is, for the purposes of the brain, *exactly the same experience as hearing an actual person speaking.*

ME: Okay.

DR. LEWIS: Anyway. Your voice, it isn't someone you know.

ME: (suddenly too hot, suddenly itchy all over)
                 I don't think so.

DR. LEWIS: History of mental illness? Other
                 hallucinations?

ME: No.

DR. LEWIS: And what does it say, the voice?

ME: Horrible things.

DR. LEWIS: Like?

ME: To hurt myself. To not talk to people or it
                 will punish me. Stuff like that. But not so
                 much now.

DR. LEWIS: Drugs?

ME: Yes.

DR. LEWIS: Hmm. And when did the voice first speak
                 to you?

ME: The police precinct. I'd just found a foot
                 on the beach.

DR. LEWIS: That was you?

ME: Yes.

DR. LEWIS: Wow. And what precise words did it use?

ME: I think . . . it said, "You're disgusting." I think.

DR. LEWIS: Interesting. Did you agree?

ME: Um, with what?

DR. LEWIS: Did you agree with the voice that you were
                 disgusting?

ME: (Thinking how weird this is, how Dr.
                 Rezwari never wanted to know anything
                 about what the voice *said*. Only that it
                 threatened stuff, and that meant it had to
                 be stopped.) Um. Yeah. I guess so.

DR. LEWIS:	Gender? Age?
ME:	The voice?
DR. LEWIS:	Yes.
ME:	A woman. I don't know how old. Forty? Not young.
DR. LEWIS:	Hmm.
ME:	Does that mean anything?
DR. LEWIS:	Do you think it means anything?
ME:	I thought . . . it's dumb, but I thought maybe the voice was a ghost. Of one of the dead prostitutes, you know? And that it wanted me to solve the murder.
DR. LEWIS:	Imaginative. But I doubt it.
ME:	You said the voice was real.
DR. LEWIS:	Real *to you*. Because it is you. On some level. Often, the people I talk to, their voices say things that deep down they think about themselves. The voice says they're dressed like ****, or whatever, and the person looks in the mirror and thinks, yeah, I've become a bit of a slob. Or the voice bans contact with other people, but actually the sufferer really, unconsciously maybe, believes that they don't deserve contact with other people.
ME:	(blank mind)
DR. LEWIS:	It's a lot to deal with. We have to take it step-by-step.
ME:	You think I'm . . . doing this to myself?

THE VOICE:	Who is this man? What are you doing? You ******* worthless piece of ****. When you get home you're going to bleed. I'm going to—
ME:	(screams)
DR. LEWIS:	I'm sorry. I don't mean to distress you.
THE VOICE:	******** ***** this ******* ******.
ME:	(puts hands over ears)
DR. LEWIS:	The voice is speaking to you now?
ME:	(nods)
DR. LEWIS:	Okay, okay. Let's leave it there. Listen. I don't know if I can help you. But I would like to try. Would you accept that?
ME:	(nods)
DR. LEWIS:	I'd like to think we can get you off the meds too. They're not necessary, if you can cope with the voice. Control it.
ME:	(looking up, feeling the voice recede into quietness) You think?
DR. LEWIS:	Oh, I know it. There are many in this group who take no drugs at all, yet their voices, if they still hear them, are managed. They come when the person wishes it, and not otherwise. They are no longer aggressive.
ME:	(inside: *This sounds too good to be true.*)
DR. LEWIS:	I promise it's true. If you're willing to try. And to talk through some things. Wherever this voice comes from, it is most likely in your past. Some recent studies say that in somewhere around sixty percent of voice hearers, it's triggered by a past

trauma. Usually childhood. Not an underlying mental illness. You might be in the other forty percent of course, those who really are schizophrenic, or what have you. But I suspect not. And then, some of my colleagues would argue that even those who are ill are often made so by abuse. Or neglect. Or whatever. Sorry. I am rambling. It's a tendency of mine. What I mean is: you can help yourself. I assure you of that.

ME: So what do I do?

DR. LEWIS: Come here. Once a week. You can talk or you can listen or you can do both. That's it.

ME: And that's going to help? Just talking?

DR. LEWIS: It's a support group. It will support you.

ME: Like . . . therapy?

DR. LEWIS: No. This isn't a treatment. It's a circle of survivors. The source of therapeutic change is the social contact itself. The talking about the problem. A problem shared, et cetera.

ME: Right.

DR. LEWIS: I'd also like you to come fifty minutes before the group starts for the first few weeks. So we can get a handle on your particular voice experience.

ME: We'd . . . we'd have, like, one-on-one sessions?

DR. LEWIS: Yes. To begin with.

ME: And . . . what would that cost?

DR. LEWIS: Cost?

ME:	What would you charge?
DR. LEWIS:	(laughing) I don't charge.
ME:	Seriously?
DR. LEWIS:	Seriously.
ME:	Oh. Okay. Why not?
DR. LEWIS:	Well, for one, as I said, this isn't a treatment group. It's a support group. And I am a support facilitator, not a clinical psychologist. Or rather, I am. But not in this context.
ME:	Oh now I'm clear.
DR. LEWIS:	(laughing) It's just talking. And some guidelines for dealing with voices, which we have found to be helpful.
ME:	And for two?
DR. LEWIS:	Pardon?
ME:	You said, "For one, as I said, this isn't a treatment group." So what's for two?
DR. LEWIS:	I think . . . I think I was probably going to say that the other reason I don't charge is that I'm not here for money. I want to help people.
ME:	(staring blankly, unable to compute)
DR. LEWIS:	Turn up, we talk, that's it. (pause) Oh, and tell your doctor you're talking to me. You're seeing . . . ?
ME:	Dr. Rezwari.
DR. LEWIS:	Inform her you've joined the group. She knows about us. She might not absolutely *agree* with us, but she can't deny the data. The recoveries.

ME:	But you think she's wrong to prescribe drugs?
DR. LEWIS:	Whoa! I didn't say that. I think the overriding prerogative of the health care system is to protect the public and the patient. Which they do well. Just sometimes . . . the cost is . . . a certain quality of life.
ME:	(thinking of my constant need to sleep, my loss of appetite, my inability to read) Uh-huh.
DR. LEWIS:	So, tell her, and stick to whatever she tells you when it comes to drugs. She knows her business. If we make some real progress, you can discuss it with her again. Oh, I'll also need to speak to your parents. Get their permission for you to come. It's boring, I know. Sorry.
ME:	(inside: ****.) Um . . . It's just my dad. My mom is . . . That is . . . It's just me and him. And you can't talk to him.
DR. LEWIS:	I can't?
ME:	I don't . . . I don't really want him to know if I . . . if I come. Here.
DR. LEWIS:	I'm afraid it's not an opt-in, opt-out kind of situation. If we're talking, he needs to know about it. (shrugs apologetically) It's the law.
ME:	(shaking my head) No. He'd . . . he'd freak out. He'd be angry.
DR. LEWIS:	Your father gets angry often?
ME:	Yeah.

DR. LEWIS:	Any particular reason?
ME:	He was a SEAL. In Afghanistan. He got hurt. And . . . And he hates me. I mean (**** *Cassie why did you say that?*) he doesn't *hate* me. But he's always ****ed with me. I have to be super careful, or he kind of explodes. Even little things set him off. If I told him about this . . .
DR. LEWIS:	He seeing anyone about that—his anger I mean?
ME:	No. He used to have some kind of therapist, in the Navy, but he didn't like it.
DR. LEWIS:	Let me get this straight. It sounds like you're telling me that your father has untreated post-traumatic stress disorder from his time in the Navy, that he has a temper that is triggered by even small things, and that if he knew you were pursuing this treatment, he may harm you or jeopardize your recovery. Is that a correct summation?
ME:	I don't know about harm. He wouldn't . . . hasn't . . . hurt me. But yeah. Apart from that.
DR. LEWIS:	Apart from that, you'd agree with my statement? This is important.
ME:	Yes.
DR. LEWIS:	In that case my view is that it is in your best interests that he should not know.
ME:	Mine too.

DR. LEWIS: Okay then.

ME: Okay? Seriously?

DR. LEWIS: (nods)

ME: You called it a treatment though. I thought
                 it wasn't a treatment.

DR. LEWIS: (smiling) You're right. I can see that these
                 are going to be interesting sessions.

ME: I—

But then a guy comes in the door, trailing Paris behind him. He's skinny, nervous looking. Maybe thirty. He's wearing Dockers and Timberland boots, a denim shirt. My first thought is, *construction*. I am wrong about this. I am wrong about so many things.

"Hey," says the guy.

"Sorry, Doc," says Paris. "It's five after."

"Really?"

"Yep."

"Well. Time flies. Cass, this is Dwight. He comes every week."

Dwight nods at me. "Nice to meet you, Cass," he says. He still has a little acne on his cheeks. I'm thinking now more like twenty-two.

"Uh, you too."

"I think," says Dr. Lewis, "that the group may be a little much for your first day, Cassie. Come back next week?"

"I . . . Yeah, I think so."

He smiles. "Good. Welcome to the group."

Dwight winks at me. "It's like a family, but better."

"Nothing that's like a family is good," says Paris.

"You know what I mean."

"I do."

Dr. Lewis turns to Paris. "Are you joining us?"

Paris shakes her head. "I'll walk Cassandra home. Like a gentleman."

"Of course. Well, we're always here. Should you need us."

"Thanks, Doc," says Paris. "But I think I have it under control."

"Excellent. You're knocking them dead at Rutgers, I hear. Professor Jenkins told me they're thinking of recommending you for a grad program at Harvard."

Paris shrugs.

"Well, go with my blessing. And bring that girl back next week. You're going to do amazing things, Paris French."

MOST WRONG STATEMENT EVER.

I gave Paris a little curtsy when we got out the door.

"Thanks for escorting me home," I said. "Thanks for being my gentleman."

She bowed, twirling her hand. "You're welcome."

"But seriously," I said, "you don't have to. I mean, I'm grateful. I am. But you don't have to walk me home. You probably have better stuff to do."

Paris frowned. "There's a serial killer on the loose," she said. "You think I'm letting you walk home alone in the dark?"

Oh yeah. That.

"Anyway," she added. "I have *nothing* better to do."

It was when we were nearly back to my house that it finally clicked. We were passing a slushie machine outside a corner store, blue and red ice churning, glowing in the half dark of sunset. Already you could hear the shushing of the ocean, as if it were trying to quiet our voices. I think it was her saying that thing about families that made it fall into place.

"Your trauma," I said. "What was it?"

She looked at me.

"He said it comes from trauma. Usually."

The slushie machine turned and turned. I thought how weird it was that people were happy to drink it. After it had been in there for who knew how long, just spinning over and over, the color bright like a chemical solution, radioactive.

"Nosy all of a sudden, aren't you?" said Paris eventually.

"Sorry. It doesn't matter."

I started walking again.

"Someone . . . did stuff to me. When I was a kid."

"Someone?"

She paused. "My dad."

I stopped. There were wide cracks in the sidewalk; grass was growing through. Above us, tattered clouds were lit bloodred as the sun set somewhere over the great landmass of America.

"It stopped when I was twelve. When I finally spoke to my mother about it, she left. Not immediately. But she packed her bags the next day. Said I was a liar and a whore and she couldn't stay in the same house as me. Moved to an apartment in the West Village."

I turned around, very slowly. Like there was a baby deer behind me, and I might startle it off into the dusk.

"Jesus, Paris," I said. "I'm so sorry."

She shrugged. "I still speak to my mom sometimes. On Skype actually. Sometimes I worry that I might get mixed up and, like, send her one of my cam videos instead. 'Hey, Mom, like my ass in these panties?'"

Paris winked. I half laughed, shocked.

"Sorry," said Paris. "Humor is my defense mechanism. Apparently. Anyway . . . if I try to mention it now, when I'm speaking to my mom, she just goes blank. A laptop going into sleep mode, you know? That on its own is enough to drive a person crazy."

"She never . . . confronted your dad?"

She laughed. "No. As far as she's concerned it never happened and he never happened."

"Oh my God."

"Yeah. It's ****ed up."

"And your dad?"

"He and I are not on speaking terms," said Paris. "That's why I want to stop taking his checks as soon as I can. I mean, he's paying my tuition and allowing me to learn, and I don't have to see him. That's almost acceptable. But not really."

"Hence . . ."

"Hence, yes, the side work."

I took a step forward, and she flinched when I put my arms around her; her body was thin and hard against me, barely any flesh there to clothe her, to protect her. Then a kind of shiver went through her and she hugged me tight, before letting go.

"I will never speak about this again," she said. "Just so you know."

"That's cool," I said. An impulse overtook me. "Who cares about your sob stories anyway?"

She stared at me for a second. Then she burst out laughing. "I knew you were friend material," she said.

I put my hand in the air, solemnly. "I swear never to speak to Paris again about her childhood."

"Or my dad."

"Agreed."

I thought. "Paris. I'm scared."

"Of what?" she asked. Her face was serious again now.

"Me."

"Oh, baby," she said. "Yeah. That's normal." She took my hand and began walking briskly. "I'm not even going to ask about your trauma because I doubt you know yet. But the Doc will help you, I do know *that*. And I'll be there to support you. I'll be looking out for you. Always."

NO.

THAT WAS THE MOST WRONG STATEMENT EVER.

Paris left me on the sidewalk outside the house. I stood there for the longest time, looking at it. I'd never noticed its squat malignance before; the way the windows seemed like eyes glaring at me. The lights were out, so I figured Dad was still at the restaurant.

After a while, I sat down on the sidewalk. It was still warm from the sun of the day, though it was dark now and the crickets were chirping. There was a moon, and in the eastern sky I could see a gleam from where it was reflecting on the ocean.

I heard a car and turned, and there was your F-150, pulling up by the curb. You killed the engine and got out.

"Going inside?" you said.

"No," I said. You were wearing a short-sleeved shirt; I noticed that your arms had got more muscular already. Lifting those bags of plush. There was a scent of flowers on the air.

"Argument with your dad?"

I shook my head. "Just don't want to."

You came and stood next to me. "Houses look kind of malignant when they're unlit, at night, don't they?"

I turned to you, surprised. "Yes," I said. "I was just thinking that." Silence.

Or rather: crickets far-off engines music people shouting.

But silence between me and you. Comfortable silence.

"So what's your plan?" you said. "You just going to sit out on the sidewalk all night?"

I shrugged. "You have a better plan?"

You looked up at the moon. "Yes," you said.

You were driving.

You crossed the last intersection, and then we were a block from the ocean, the houses falling away, replaced by dirty dunes. At the end of the block, there was a turn that you could take, but if you did you'd have to turn around again pretty quickly—it became the boardwalk.

But at the corner, where the road curved, there was a track between the dunes, and it led onto the beach.

You drove toward it, not showing any signs of steering. A sign said NO VEHICULAR ACCESS TO THE BEACH OFFENDERS WILL BE PROSECUTED.

I said: "Are you going to—"

And . . .

It appeared so. You drove right off the road, onto the track, and we bumped over tufts of grass for a few dozen yards, and then we were on the beach. You stopped. We were on the far south side—to our right, an expanse of sand and dunes, followed by houses on stilts, small from here, looking like shacks but I knew they were worth like a million dollars each. To our left, the wide strip of sand that runs the length of the town, the lights of the city and boardwalk fringing it, bright and garish against the gunmetal shine of the moonlit ocean. The piers two dark stripes connecting city and ocean, bristling with the odd shapes of fairground rides.

And that flat, smooth beach . . . empty, apart from a couple of groups huddled around coolers, not wanting to say good-bye to the day.

"Beautiful, isn't it?" you said.

"You get used to it," I said.

Why did everything that came out of my mouth have to come out rude? I didn't mean it. That's what I'm telling you now.

"Is this allowed?" I asked. "The truck?"

"For me, yes. Because of the deliveries."

I nodded. "Cool."

"You want to drive?" you said.

"Drive . . . this?"

"This truck, yes. Do you want to drive it?"

I stared at you. "My dad doesn't like me to drive."

"But you have your license, right?"

"Yeah."

"Then why not? This beach is three hundred yards wide, easy. And there's no one around. Almost no one. What are you going to do, crash into a pier? They're pretty big. I find it easy to avoid them."

Smart-ass, I wanted to say. But I wasn't in that kind of place. I wasn't ready to be joking around with you. I just sighed. "Okay."

"Hey, don't be so enthusiastic," you said.

"Sorry."

"You don't have to be . . . Look, just switch with me."

You got out and we switched places. The engine was still running—all I had to do was slide the lever from *P* to *D* and we were rolling, over that hard-packed sand, and a gull that had been picking at some leftover food went clattering into the sky, screeching at us, *Cass, Cass, Cass, what are you doing driving this boy you hardly know on the beach, Cass, Cass, Cass.*

But the voice—*my* voice—was gone.

I was with you, and the voice was gone, so right then I wanted to stay in that truck forever, to never have to go home.

I pressed the accelerator. The truck lurched forward, and soon we were, well, it's something people always say but it really was like we were flying over the beach, not like driving on a road at all, the sand so smooth below the wheels, and I turned in a long arc to avoid

164

the first gaggle of people and then we were cruising again, between the city and the ocean, the wheel seeming to connect me right to the ground-up sea creatures beneath, to the rock under them.

I don't know if I have described the beach and the town properly, but I mean the beach runs the *whole* length of the town. It's hard to think of a comparison for how big it is, how wide, how long. We're not talking in football fields, as a unit of measurement, we're talking in airport runways, and even then we're talking about many of them, lain end to end.

What I mean is: I wanted this to last forever, and it was like it did last forever. I rolled down my window and you rolled down yours, and the cool night air came whipping in, bringing with it fine sea spray, and I rested my left elbow on the door frame and put my hand out the window and curved it, concave, let it ride on the wind, undulating, like a bird, feeling the resistance of the air, sculpting it, and it was like one small part of me was free and flying away.

And the moon was shining, and the ocean was bright, and we could hear the music from the stalls on the boardwalk, and far-off laughter, and yada yada yada.

You were there too, I know, I know.

Anyway I drove up and down the beach, I don't know, three times, and then I realized my dad was going to be home soon probably and I said I had better get back.

I slowed, passing a lifeguard stand. There were two silhouettes sitting in it, close together, merging almost.

"Kids go up there to make out," you said. "Watching the water."

"I know," I said.

Then I wished I hadn't. I felt myself blushing. I coughed. I saw your hand tense on the coat-hanger holder thing (to use the technical term). "You should take over," I said.

165

I stopped the truck, and we switched back. I don't really understand how, but some kind of frostiness had settled into the space inside the truck; I was almost expecting to see steam from our breath. Maybe it was just the downer that always comes when something magical ends; maybe I was reading too much into it, I don't know. But I don't want you to think that I wasn't . . . feeling stuff, I guess.

"Thanks," I said, inadequately.

You nodded. You drove back toward the road.

Silence.

Not so comfortable now.

WHAT I MEANT: *thank you so much, that was a beautiful experience I loved the wind and the feel of the beach thrumming, resonating through the whole body of the truck and through my skin, and my hand buoyed up by the air, and the lights of the city and the glimmering of the ocean, like dancing jewels all around us, like stars surrounding the black space of the beach, galaxies, towers of interstellar dust.*

But all of that is a lot to say if you've been in the hospital, and then put on drugs, and then you've been talking to girls who tell you their fathers molested them and you're supposed to process all of that.

You drove the truck carefully over the small mounds leading to the path onto the road again. "What kind of music do you like?" you said, a little nervously.

"I don't like music," I said.

****, I thought.

You flinched a little. "Right."

WHAT I MEANT: *I don't "like" music. I need music. I use music, to keep the voice quiet, at least for a moment. The same way I'm using you, right now, sitting in your truck.* But it came out all wrong. It always does with me.

Silence for a block. The pickup halted at a stop sign, the last stop sign before the house.

"I swim," you said suddenly. "Swam. In high school. But I'm on a swim scholarship to college too. You swim?"

Someone help me someone make the earth rise up and swallow me. "I did," I said. It was all I could say, it was like there was a rock on my tongue, like I had forgotten how to speak to someone.

"O . . . kay . . . then," you said, drawing it out, like, why is this girl so weird, and honestly I was impressed you had even tried again given my TOTAL LACK OF CONVERSATIONAL SKILLS OR EVEN BASIC TOOL KIT OF SPOKEN POLITENESS.

So again, for your benefit now:

WHAT I MEANT: *I used to swim, with my dad, who after all is a Navy SEAL, so actually swimming has always been a major part of my life, or always was up to a certain point anyway, and that's so cool that we have something that we share, because, yes, being in the ocean, held up by it, my strong arms knifing through it, I love that.*

You pulled up to the house. The windows were still dark. "There you go," you said. "I mean, me too, of course." Because, as you said, OF COURSE you had to live in the apartment above our garage, just in case the whole thing wasn't awkward enough.

I got out without saying anything. I couldn't think of anything to say, even though I knew, of course I knew, that it was rude. I don't know if you've ever been in that situation.

Behind me I heard the engine cut out. Heard the truck door slam, and then your steps on the stairs up to the apartment.

I kept walking and didn't turn.

Well, I'm telling you stuff now.

Maybe too much stuff.

Only time will tell.

Even writing this is making me cringe.

You must have thought I was *such* a weirdo.

Okay, I'm not going to finish this in time if I don't start summarizing.

I went to the group the next week, and the week after that. I barely saw you; you were always working. Probably you didn't have any interest in seeing me anyway. You were probably hurt by how I totally failed to talk to you in any meaningful way. At group, I listened to people talking about their voices. There was a woman named Marie, who heard a devil and an angel, or that was what she called them. The devil told her to hurt herself, like my voice, called her names. The angel would help her, though—tell her where she had left her keys, stuff like that.

There was a guy called Rasheed who had what he called the Red Voice and the White Voice. The Red Voice sounded terrifying. Way more extreme than mine. Rasheed said the Red Voice was the voice of a guy who had tortured him in Syria. He lifted his shirt once and—

It was bad.

Dwight turned out to be a cop. His voice was his father's, he thought. It would punish him. Shout at him. In real life, his father had beaten him "like a dog" since he was a toddler. When he was three, his dad threw him down the stairs and he broke fourteen bones. His dad said it was an accident, and the paramedics believed him.

Dwight told a psychiatrist about this when he was a teenager, and the psychiatrist told him he had invented the memories. Dwight gripped the sides of his chair, hard, when he told us that.

But.

But the Doc was *helping* all these people. They'd all gotten to the point where they rarely heard their voices anymore, where they had it under control. The only bummer for me was that he said it took months or years, in most cases, to get to that point.

What I'm going to do is, I'm going to give you what the Doc told me, over the next weeks, as if it was all one thing, okay? Just to save time.

This was what the Doc taught, or *recommended* is maybe a better word. I mean, he kept stressing how these weren't "rules"; they were just "guidelines," and it was about finding what worked for each individual and yadda yadda yadda. Anyway these were basically the steps. The group's philosophy, their approach to hearing voices:

1. SAFETY. Ensure that your psychiatrist and the people close to you know what you're doing. Continue to follow your doctor's instructions in addition to pursuing the following precepts. Notice that I had already failed at this.

2. ACCEPTANCE. Acknowledge your voice as real, both a real part of yourself and a manifestation of your feelings about yourself.

3. DIALOGUE AND CONCILIATION. Welcome the voice, instead of ignoring it or telling it to shut up. Encourage more positive interaction and negotiation.

4. SCHEDULE. Allot a regular time at which the voice can speak to you. Refuse to engage if the voice tries to speak at any other time.

5. FREEDOM. Challenge the power of the voice and establish dominance over it.

Looks simple like that, doesn't it?

Of course, an easier philosophy, an easier alternative plan, would have been:

1. Spend all my time with you.

Since you always silenced the voice, always muted it, just by being around. But that would not have been realistic then. And is most likely not realistic now.

1. SAFETY. Ensure that your psychiatrist and the people close to you know what you're doing.

I did not do this.

There is no simpler way of putting it.

I don't even know why, really. I think it was the drugs. It's like . . . You know when you're walking in a swimming pool? And in some sense it's analogous to walking on normal ground, the same motions are involved, the same mechanics, but you're slower; the resistance is higher.

With the drugs I was on, it was the same. It was as if all the air in the world had been substituted with water, making every movement harder. I hated the drugs, and I didn't want to take them. And I knew that Dr. Rezwari would tell me to take them, so I just . . . didn't say anything to her.

I started stacking the unopened blister packs in my nightstand, piles of them. When I saw the doctor, I told her how much better I was feeling, how I never heard the voice anymore.

Which was a lie.

When the drugs went, the voice came back. It wasn't there all the time, but enough, and louder now—telling me to run up and down the stairs, to keep my head down when passing anyone in the street, to clean my teeth fifteen times before bed, to slap myself, all kinds of things. But the voice was better than the walking in water.

Meanwhile, Dad started coming home early from the restaurant.

"You could come over to Donato's, you know," he said. "It's still nut free." Dad had eliminated nuts from the restaurant after my anaphylaxis at school. They weren't allowed in the kitchen—the staff wasn't even allowed to bring snacks with nuts in them to work.

"No, thanks," I said.

"Figures," said Dad.

Instead, he would come back at seven o'clock and we'd eat together. Dad was a pretty good cook. I don't think he was really interested in it, but he was a smart guy, and he'd spent the last decade running a restaurant. He'd make penne amatriciana, gnocchi con panna e prosciutto, veal marinara, prawns with garlic.

"*************** . ******** stupid ******** ***** of a *****."

That was Dad, working in the kitchen. He made good food, but he was always cutting himself and burning himself. His hands were covered in Band-Aids and scars, like he lived with a tiger cub.

After dinner, we would sit and talk. Dad didn't know how to talk about feelings, that kind of thing. So he would tell the funny stuff that had happened at the restaurant. The lady who kept asking for more garlic bread, which is free, and they realized she was putting it in her purse, stashing it, to take home. The guy who didn't realize the chili oil had chili in it, and covered his pizza with it.

"Your father is very boring, isn't he?" said the voice. "I see where you get it from."

"Shut up," I said, under my breath.

"Honey?"

"Nothing. Nothing."

Dad nodded, nervously. "You know I'm here if you want to, ah, talk."

"Yeah."

"Good."

But of course he wasn't; he just wanted to be.

There's a gulf between those two things.

Then there was you. I barely saw you at all, except from a distance. We did cross each other once in the yard. You were getting even more muscles. Plush toys don't sound heavy, but I guess when

173

they're in big bags and you're throwing them up, I don't know, ten feet onto a pier, they're heavy enough.

Anyway, you were in your short-sleeved work shirt with the logo on it and I could see the new angles in your arms. You were tan, your skin full of sunshine, walking to your truck. In one hand was a book, I couldn't see what it was, and the bend in your elbow and the outline of your bicep were the most incidental details on one sunny day in New Jersey, couldn't matter to anyone ever, but also seemed to me like the fulcrum on which all existence was balanced.

"Hey," you said.

"Hey."

SHAKESPEARE WOULD HAVE BEEN PROUD.

"How are the stuffed toys?" I asked.

"Plentiful," you said, shrugging. We walked together to the truck; I was heading to the library, I imagine.

"Well," I said.

"Well," you said. "Hey, listen, I dreamed about you the other night. The weirdest thing."

I thought: *He's dreaming about me?*

I was staring at you blankly, and you looked uncomfortable. "Yeah," you said. "I was in the yard here, and you were at your window, watching me. Or . . . waiting for me, I guess. Like, beckoning me. But there was no door into the house; it was all bricked up. So I knew I had to climb up to the window. Except there were no handholds, nothing. And then my mom showed up with a ladder, which is weird because my mom hasn't been around for . . . Well. Anyway. I put the ladder up against the wall and started climbing and . . . that was it. I woke up."

Just like when we were driving on the beach, I literally couldn't think of a single thing to say. I was thinking, *I'm in his dreams? What does that mean?* And I was so much in my head and not in the actual yard with you that the moment stretched and stretched, like taffy.

AWKWARD.

"Well I guess I'll . . ." Your voice trailed off as you turned and walked to the truck. I half followed you, half walked with you. I needed to get to the street anyhow.

"*Beckoning*?" I said eventually.

You flushed. "Uh . . . yeah."

"I don't think I've ever heard anyone say that word out loud before," I said.

You said nothing.

DOUBLE AWKWARD.

What I meant, of course, given the pretty obvious hint you had just dropped was: *What happened to your mom? Oh God, I'm so sorry. I lost mine too. I'm so, so sorry.*

I didn't mean to come across like such an *******.

We were standing by the pickup now, not precisely standing together and not precisely separate either; the sun was bright in my eyes. I was conscious of your chest under your shirt. You rocked on your heels. Your eyes caught the sun and flashed. "I should—" you started.

"How did you get that job anyway?" I blurted out.

"Excuse me?"

"The plush. How come you're not gutting shrimp?" I knew that my dad had not been kidding about that.

You raised your hands in a *beats me* gesture and leaned against the pickup. "Guy named Bill does the orientation," you said. "He took us down under the shrimp restaurant, in among the pillars of the pier. He explained the job—said it was ten hours a day, in a kitchen topping out at eighty degrees, literally just pulling **** out of prawns all day long. Maybe a short break to fry them, then back to it. He said we were going to be sweating, that we'd lose twenty pounds easy over the summer."

"Sounds great."

"Yeah. Then he said: put your hands up if you don't think that sounds like fun. If you'd rather do something else."

"And you did?"

"I did. After a moment anyway. The others, I think they figured it was a trick question, like they'd get fired. I thought that was a possibility too, but I came here to work the boardwalk, not broil in a kitchen. I thought, *What do I have to lose?* So I put my hand up and Bill said—he's a really big guy, Bill, a bull of a guy, but kind— anyway, Bill said, 'Can you drive a car? Have you got your license?'" You indicated the pickup. "And I said yes, and here I am."

"Delivering stuffed toys."

"Beats unstuffing prawns."

"True."

Another pause.

"You should come see the warehouse sometime," you said. "It's crazy. Plush animals stacked to the ceiling."

"Hmm," I said, in that polite way people do when they know it's not a real offer. I was trying to work out if you were flirting with me. I didn't have a lot of experience with boys. Still don't. Maybe you were wondering the same thing; I have no idea.

But you were not to be deterred. "No, really," you said. "I'll drive you one day. When I'm off. Monday?"

"Um. Okay."

You smiled and beamed out some of the sunshine that had

gotten trapped in your skin. "You look good," you said. Then you blushed, your cheeks going red. I thought that was awesome. I don't think I had ever seen anyone blush before. "I mean . . . you look better." You closed your eyes and sighed. "God, that's worse."

"It's okay."

"What I mean is, you looked kind of sick before. Now you look better." You clapped a hand to your head. "Ugh. Now it's like I'm prying. I mean, I don't know what the deal was with you and it doesn't matter. I'm going, before I screw anything else up."

You unlocked the pickup and started to open the door.

"Thanks," I said. "Really."

You stopped, and smiled. "You're welcome."

"What's the book?"

"*Metamorphoses*," you said. "Ovid." You held it up—an old Penguin classic.

"Ah. 'My mind is moved to sing of forms changed into new bodies.'"

You nodded. "I was . . . this is going to sound so lame."

"Try me."

"I was getting kind of into the metaphysical poets, you know? Donne, Marvell. Then Jane at the library said I should read Ovid, that it was sort of the source of so much stuff. The metaphysicals, Shakespeare."

"T.S. Eliot."

"Yes! Totally."

Your smile lifted the dimples to your cheeks, but I frowned. It was your mentioning Jane, and the memory of how she had sold me out, ratted on me to my dad, and started all the trouble. "You know Jane?" I asked.

"Oh yeah. I go to the library all the time. Get books to read on my breaks at the plush warehouse. I kind of make a throne of stuffed toys and sit in there with a book. And Jane—she's amazing, isn't she? So smart."

"Uh-huh."

"And beautiful. She's one of those girls, she doesn't know how beautiful she is. I always thought that was crap. The beautiful girls I've met, they *always* know it. But then I came here."

I felt some structure move inside my stomach, like there was a part of my anatomy mounted on a gimbal I hadn't even known about, able to revolve. Of course you would be attracted to Jane. Why wouldn't you? She was super intelligent and interesting, and hot, with her dyed hair and her tattoos and her ironic T-shirts.

I half expected that the voice would say something then. Something about me being nothing, me being beneath his attention, pathetic, a ****** disgrace, all the things the voice so often said. But it said nothing.

And then I remembered: the voice didn't speak when you were there. It seemed like it was really true.

"Hmm," I said, which along with "what?" was becoming something of a catchphrase for me.

You could see I was upset, I think. I don't know what it was—just the mere idea of Jane, who had betrayed me, or the fact that you called her beautiful. You lifted the book again. The awkwardness surfaced between us, smooth gray back of a whale breaching the water. "Anyway . . . back to Pygmalion," you said.

"Yeah," I said.

"See you around," you said.

"Uh-huh."

Then you got into your pickup and drove away.

I am only telling you this, from my side, because I get it now.

I do.

Jane didn't betray me. She helped me.

And you weren't talking about Jane, were you? I have always been good at reading, but I have never been good at reading between the lines. When you said that thing, about her being one of those girls who doesn't know how beautiful they are. You were talking about me, weren't you? I think, maybe, you were. And I was thinking how you were crushing on Jane, and meanwhile you were probably thinking *I'm really obviously flirting with Cass and she's just constantly knocking me back.*

Sorry.

I wish I'd been more perspicacious.

I wish I could reach into time, to its secret levers and wheels, and turn it back to that afternoon, so that I would get it, what you were saying, and not hurt you. Because it must have hurt you, when I seemed so standoffish at the end, didn't it?

Of course, I hurt you much worse than that, later.

DR. LEWIS:	Cookie?
ME:	No, thanks. (I show him my EpiPens.)
DR. LEWIS:	Ah.
ME:	The voice is still hurting me. Telling me to hurt myself, I mean.
DR. LEWIS:	And you? Are you hurting it?
ME:	Huh?
DR. LEWIS:	Try to remember for me what happened when the voice came to you for the first time. It said you were disgusting, right?
ME:	Yes.

DR. LEWIS:	And you. What did you say in return?
ME:	I said . . . I think I said, "Shut up."
THE VOICE:	You did. You ****. You ******** did.
DR. LEWIS:	The voice is speaking now?
ME:	Yeah. How did you know?
DR. LEWIS:	You get a look in your eyes. What did it say?
ME:	She.
DR. LEWIS:	She. Yes. What did she say?
ME:	She agreed with me.
DR. LEWIS:	Interesting. One of the theories we work with is that the hearers of voices are damaged, yes, but *they also damage their voices.* Because they are scared, because they are freaked out. They set the tone early on, by reacting aggressively.
ME:	But the voice started—
DR. LEWIS:	It's not a schoolyard. I am not establishing blame. I'm merely saying that you may need to recalibrate the tenor of your relationship with the voice.
ME:	Meaning?
DR. LEWIS:	Meaning be nicer to it.
ME:	Hmm.
DR. LEWIS:	Tell me about your mother.
ME:	(blinking) What?
DR. LEWIS:	She died, yes? Three years ago.
ME:	(silence)
DR. LEWIS:	That must have been hard for you.
ME:	(quietly) What do you think?

DR. LEWIS: How did it happen?

ME: She . . . There was a robbery at our pizza
               restaurant. She was killed.

DR. LEWIS: I'm sorry.

ME: (silence)

DR. LEWIS: I don't mean to pry. I am interested in the
               idea that this event may have been the
               trigger. For your voice.

ME: It was years ago.

DR. LEWIS: This is often the case.

ME: (silence)

DR. LEWIS: Were you there?

ME: Excuse me?

DR. LEWIS: When your mother was killed. Were you
               present?

ME: (silence)

ME: (silence)

ME: (silence)

ME: Yes.

DR. LEWIS: I see. That must have been very upsetting.

ME: (silence)

DR. LEWIS: (looking at watch) Okay. Well, we'll leave it
               there for the moment. The others are due.

**2. ACCEPTANCE. Acknowledge your voice as real,
both a real part of yourself and a manifestation of
your feelings about yourself.**

This was not easy, but I tried, and it did make a kind of sense to me.

For example: when I got back to my room after talking to you about Ovid, about Jane. The voice said,

"He doesn't see you. Just as you deserve."

"Who?"

The voice laughed. "Like you don't know. You are invisible to him. You are worthless. He sees only Jane."

I cried then. I wish I could say I was strong and always stood up to the voice, but I didn't.

"He invited me to go see the plush warehouse," I said.

"He is being polite," said the voice. "You are a piece of nothing shaped like a person. You are Echo, after she dies, speaking only the words of Narcissus back to him. You may as well be dead."

"No."

"Yes."

"Please. Don't say that."

"I will say what I please."

"I can make you go away, you know," I said.

"Oh yes? How?"

I flicked on the radio, turned the dial to find static. But I wasn't fast enough. I caught a snippet of conversation—*the Houdini Killer appears to have struck yet again, with local prostitute Shayna Jennings reported missing two nights ago, only a week after—*

I kept turning the dial, let the words sink into:

%%%%%%%%%%%%%%%%%%%%%%%%%%%%%%%%%%%
%%%%%%%%%%%%%%%%%%%%%%%%%%%%%%%%%%%
%%%%%%%%%%%%%%%%%%%%%%%%%%%%%%%%%%%
%%%%%%%%%%%%%%%%%%%%%%%%%%%%%%%%%%
%%%%%%%%%%%%%%%%%%%%%%%%%%%%%%%%%%%
%%%%%%%%%%%%%%%%%%%%%%%%%%%%%%%%%%%
%%%%%%%%%%%%%%%%%%%%%%%%%%%%%%%%%%%
%%%

%%%%%%%%%%%%%%%%%%%%%%%%%%%%%%%%%%%
%%%%%%%%%%%%%%%%%%%%%%%%%%%%%%%%%%%
%%%%%%%%%%%%%%%%%%%%%%%%%%%%%%%%%%%
%%%

But I couldn't keep it up forever. Eventually I had to turn it off, and the voice was waiting. The voice was always waiting.

"See what you did?"

"What?"

"You let another girl die. You failed. You were supposed to be finding him, right? The Houdini Killer? But what have you done? You've done NOTHING."

"What am I supposed to do? How am I supposed to—"

"You're supposed to TRY."

"I . . ." I shook my head. I felt like I really was going crazy. "Why me? Who do I have to—"

"BECAUSE YOU'RE LETTING THEM DIE. BECAUSE OTHERWISE HE GETS AWAY WITH IT. Don't you see? Just like the guy who killed your—"

"SHUT UP SHUT UP SHUT UP SHUT UP."

Silence.

Then, a voice like a gust of cold arctic air, frost hanging in it, crystals, capable of getting into the lungs, into the ears and freezing you from the inside out.

"Wash your face," it said. "Ten times. Maybe if you deal with those zits he will be more interested. Maybe it will make you less disgusting."

Yeah.

At times like those, I thought maybe Dr. Lewis was right. I mean, I looked in the mirror, in my bathroom—the en suite that Dad had made for me when we moved in—and I saw two pimples, one on my cheek and one on my chin.

And I felt disgusted by myself when I saw them.

So even though there was a part of me that still thought the voice might be supernatural, might be some kind of ghost or something, I could see the logic of the Doc's position.

I.e.: everything the voice was saying was really what *I* was saying. My own hatred of myself, my own desire to punish myself, to make myself pay—

And then my thoughts would stop, would come to a brick wall that didn't let them go any further, a barricade in my memories. I know what it is, now, that barricade.

But I didn't then. I genuinely didn't.

Anyway, yes, I could see that maybe the voice was me. I mean, I could understand it intellectually, as an abstract concept.

It was the concrete aspect I had difficulty with.

That is: the voice *was not my voice.* It was someone else's voice, a woman's, and I heard it through my ears. You have *no idea* what that feels like, when you hear a real voice that seems to be from outside you, and it hates you too.

At least, I hope you don't.

"Wash your face again."

"You said ten times."

"Again."

I looked at myself in the mirror. The dark circles were gone from beneath my eyes, but the pimples were like the size of the moon, blotting out my whole face, they were so enormous.

Disgusting, I thought.

But Dr. Lewis had made me believe I could control this thing, at least. Even if it was hard. So at the same time I was thinking about the next precept, the one about dialogue and conciliation. "If I do, can I read a bit of a book?"

"What book?"

"I don't know. The one Jane gave me."

"That *****? You want to read her book?"

"It's not hers. It's the library's. It's by Haruki Murakami. He's Japanese."

"The ***** called your dad, and he took you to the hospital, and that's where they killed me again with those pills. I already died once and you did NOTHING to stop it. Then she killed me again."

I closed my eyes. "Please," I said.

ALL TOGETHER NOW:

"No," said the voice.

3. DIALOGUE AND CONCILIATION. Welcome the voice, instead of ignoring it or telling it to shut up. Encourage more positive interaction and negotiation.

I've touched on this already. And the weird thing is, it *did* kind of work. Not right away, but it did.

So:

I was sitting on my bed, the room full of red morning light. The room was spotless. Here's something freaky: I really liked that. I mean, it was the voice that had me always cleaning up after myself, but I had come to realize I enjoyed the feeling of space and order.

This, essentially, is what the Doc meant about the voice being part of me.

Anyway. I was sitting there feeling half-awake. This must have been a week and a half after I started seeing the Doc? Maybe. I was in my SEAL TEAM 5 EATS SHARKS FOR BREAKFAST T-shirt of Dad's that I always slept in.

From downstairs, the smell of bacon came creeping up, I visualized it like tendrils of vapor, reaching out for me, luring me. Dad, cooking for me. It was how he showed his love. He'd also been very noticeably keeping his temper under control, never lashing out like he used to, never hitting things. That must have taken a lot of effort because Dad was an *angry* person.

Mom's . . . Mom's death made him that way.

The voice said,

"No bacon for you if you don't clean your ******* room."

"It's clean!"

"Clean it again. And then clean your bathroom."

I took a deep breath and thought about the steps. "Hello," I said. "I'm sorry I didn't greet you properly. How are you?"

Silence.

"Are you okay? I didn't hear you last night, and I worried about you."

Silence.

"It's good to hear you again anyway."

Silence. But a pregnant one. I could *sense* the voice there, invisibly breathing.

"Clean," it said finally.

"With pleasure," I said.

Then I thought: *negotiation.*

"If I clean extra well, can I read some of my book?"

"What book?"

"The novel."

"The one the ***** gave you."

I held my tongue. "She is a *****, we have established that. But if I clean, can I read a chapter?"

Silence.

"Can I?"

"No."

"It's just a book."

"Yeah, and that boy in the apartment *just* broke your heart when he turned his sights on that ****** ***** ******."

"He didn't *break my heart.* Please. I'm not some princess in a story. I'm not, like, in love with him or anything. I barely know him." Though even then, another voice in my head, not *the* voice but a little, quiet fantasizing voice, said, *He dreamed about you.*

"Yes. You are. I saw you looking at his arms. It's pathetic."

I tried to keep calm. "I'm not talking about him. I'm talking about the book. You want me to clean the bathroom. Fine. But then I want a chapter of my book."

"No."

"Please."

And then . . .

And then I WOULD LIKE YOU TO TAKE A MOMENT TO APPRECIATE THE MAGNITUDE OF THIS:

"Okay," said the voice. "But not a chapter. Ten pages."

"Fine," I said. "Thank you. Thank you so much."

THE VOICE: silence.

Unimportant lowercase spoiler:

Dad's bacon was awesome. So were his pancakes. His bacon and pancakes are *always* awesome. This is, to be honest, a good reason on its own to forgive me, and to forgive him.

You do *not* want to miss out on his breakfasts.

4. SCHEDULE. Allot a regular time at which the voice can speak to you. Refuse to engage if the voice tries to speak at any other time.

I was surprised by how well this one worked.

This is what I did:

Every time the voice came to me, I followed a script in my head, like a telesales operative.

Here's an example from the shore:

EXT. DAY. A SOUTH NEW JERSEY BEACH. THE SUN IS HIGH IN THE SKY. THERE IS THE BARNACLED AND SEAWEED-FESTOONED PILLAR OF A PIER TO THE LEFT OF OUR HEROINE, WHO IS STRIPPING OFF HER T-SHIRT AND JEANS TO REVEAL A SWIMSUIT. IT IS THE FIRST TIME SHE HAS BEEN DOWN TO THE BEACH SINCE SHE FOUND A HUMAN FOOT THERE. IT IS ANOTHER WARM DAY, THOUGH THERE ARE CLOUDS GATHERING IN THE SKY, AND LATER IT WILL RAIN. THE SEAGULLS ARE CALLING, CALLING, CALLING THE GIRL'S NAME.

TAUNTING HER.

SHE IS IGNORING THEM. WHAT SHE FINDS HARDER TO IGNORE IS THE VOICE. THE VOICE BELONGS TO A MIDDLE-AGED WOMAN WITH AN INDETERMINATE NEW JERSEY ACCENT. A DOG RACES PAST, CHASING A FRISBEE; A SMALL YAPPY DOG, IT THROWS ITSELF INTO

THE AIR, SPARKLING WATER FALLING FROM IT,
AND TIME SEEMS TO STAND STILL, THE DOG
HANGING AT THE TOP OF ITS LEAP, JAWS
CLOSING ON THE FRISBEE.

THE VOICE:	You even think about swimming in that ocean and I'll—
ME:	Oh, hi! How are you?
THE VOICE:	(silence)
ME:	I was wondering where you were. It's nice to hear from you.
THE VOICE:	Swimming is enjoyment. You are not allowed to enjoy yourself.
ME:	I'm sorry you feel that way.
THE VOICE:	(silence)
ME:	(checking the G-Shock Dad gave me for my sixteenth) It's two o'clock. I would prefer you to speak to me only after six p.m.
THE VOICE:	You dare to—
ME:	After six p.m., please.
THE VOICE:	Put your clothes back on. Go home. People can see your *body*. Your ******* fat body.
ME:	Okay. Okay, boss.
	I pull on my Levis and T-shirt. Then I turn away from the ocean, which keeps whispering to me when my back is turned, the surf hissing onto the sand, a Greek chorus behind the calling of the gulls.
THE VOICE:	Good. Now you're not making anyone sick with your flab.

ME:	Thank you. But please, don't speak to me again till six p.m.
THE VOICE:	(silence)

I never meant to swim, of course. It was a tactic. Not something the Doc taught me either.

But hey: if your father runs a restaurant, one thing you learn is how to negotiate.

So:

Same script, on repeat. My lines, every time the voice said anything to me:

Oh, hi!

Every time:

I would prefer you to speak to me only after six p.m.

And it must have worked, because a few days after that, Dad came home for dinner and it was only then I realized I hadn't heard the voice all day. In fact, I had read like ten chapters of *The Wind-Up Bird Chronicle* and I hadn't even thought about it.

"Hey, honey," said Dad. "Why are you smiling?"

"No reason," I said.

"Well, it's good to see." He held up a bag. "I'm making meatballs. And . . ." He hesitated. Then he held up another bag, this one clear and blue. "And . . . I got a movie. I mean, if you want. It's no big deal. The girl at the store said you would like it. I mean, she thought you might—"

"Yeah," I said. "Yeah, maybe."

Dad blinked at me for a second. Almost every night he was suggesting TV or a movie or going out somewhere, and every night I said no. "Oh. Oh, that's great, honey." He turned around and headed to the kitchen, and a very small part of me noticed him wiping his eye with his sleeve like he had shed a tear, and *all the rest of me* refused to notice this at all because it would mean consciously realizing how much he loved me, and that was something so painful it might create a supernova right here on a New Jersey street, suck the whole solar system into it, turn it to atoms.

Even now, my fingers are white as I type.

But where was I?

Oh yes, the DVDs.

See, before the voice, box sets used to be a big part of our lives, mine and Dad's. We didn't talk about much, me and my dad, but we did talk about Tony Soprano and Walter White.

After the voice: there was basically nothing. I mean, Dad was into collecting millipedes. I liked books. There was really nothing we shared. We lived in different parts of the house.

But that night, we shared the meatballs that Dad made—they were awesome; please bear this in mind along with the bacon and the pancakes—and then some nut-free chocolate ice cream. Dad told me stories about work, and I told him how I had started a book that day, and he wiped his eye again so I shut up.

But then he told a joke, a lame joke about one of his regulars and I . . .

I . . .

I *smirked*.

Everything about that night is bright lacquered in my memory; I could almost reach out and touch it all. It was a crappy old plastic-covered table in a small kitchen in New Jersey with green cabinets from, like, the seventies, but I felt like I was in a palace. The halogen strip light in the ceiling was bathing us. I felt like the whole world was full of light.

I reached out for more ice cream.

"Seriously?" said the voice. "With your ass?"

I lowered the spoon very slowly. I checked my G-Shock. 8:10 p.m.

"I've missed you," I said. I chose my words very carefully, knowing they would go for the voice and Dad both.

Dad smiled. "I've missed you too, Cassington." That was an old nickname he hardly ever used anymore.

THE VOICE: silence.

"I've been looking forward to speaking to you all day," I said.

Dad got all embarrassed then and gruff and alpha male. "Yeah," he said. "Yeah, me too."

THE VOICE: "No more ice cream. You barely fit into your jeans. You could be pretty, if you looked after yourself better. If you weren't so—"

"Thank you," I said.

THE VOICE: silence.

DAD: silence.

I started clearing away the dinner stuff. "Can we watch a movie tonight?" I asked.

Dad looked puzzled. "I told you I got one, Cass. So, yeah."

But of course I wasn't asking him. I kept listening as I washed the dishes. We didn't have a dishwasher. Mom used to say, we do have a dishwasher, and it's me. But it wasn't her anymore. It was me.

THE VOICE: silence.

"Can we have popcorn too?" I asked.

"Sure, honey."

THE VOICE: "No popcorn. Just the movie. And don't enjoy it too much. I'll be watching."

"I'm okay actually, thanks, Dad. Just realized I'm too full."

"Sure."

We went into the living room. Dad slotted the DVD into the player. The girl in the store was right; it was pretty good. I curled up on the sofa and Dad put his arm out and I leaned against him.

It was nice.

Then, like an hour into it, something happened in the movie that made me laugh.

"Bite your tongue," said the voice.

"I'm sorry," I said.

Dad peered at me. "You don't have to apologize for laughing, Cass."

"Bite it," said the voice.

And I did it; I mean, I was negotiating, I was scheduling and being polite and all that stuff, but the voice still scared me. And it had let me have this time with Dad.

I bit my tongue.

"Harder."

I tasted salt blood, rushing into my mouth.

"Enough," said the voice.

"Can we watch the rest?" I asked.

"Of course," said Dad. "It's like ten. It's not late."

"No," said the voice.

I sighed. "I'm super tired actually, Dad. Tomorrow night?"

"Sure," said Dad.

"Maybe," said the voice.

Hell, that was a victory in my book. We got up and turned out the lights and powered down the TV. Dad went into the bug room, and I followed him in. He lifted the first lid and started taking little pots of food from a drawer beneath the wooden workbench. Artificial light glowed all around us; blue UV.

"Here," he said, when he saw that I was there too. He handed me a stick insect.

I held up my hand and looked at the thing. It was trembling, I swear, its long body very stiff. I wanted to stroke it and tell it I wasn't going to hurt it, but it was an insect; what would the point have been? I turned my hand to get a better look at it.

The stick insect fell—tumbled to the ground.

Dad whirled. "For ****'s sake, Cass!" he shouted. He bent down and picked up the stick insect carefully. He examined it and then reached out with his other hand and gripped my arm, tight enough to hurt.

"How can you be so ******* clumsy?" he said. "How come everything you touch turns to—"

He stopped himself, like he'd been taken over by some possessing spirit and had just gotten control of his mouth again. That was what Dad's tempers were always like—like he was under the influence of something that needed to be exorcised.

He stared at me.

He saw the tears running down my cheeks.

"Oh Jesus, Cass, oh, I didn't mean . . ."

I twisted out of his grip and ran for the stairs.

"Cass, I wasn't talking about—"

"Wow," said the voice as my foot hit the first step. "Your dad really hates you, huh?"

So.

A half victory, I guess.

5. FREEDOM. Challenge the power of the voice and establish dominance over it.

This did *not* work very well.

Actually, you were there for part of this one.

Paris called; she wanted to hang out. We'd spoken on the phone a few times but hadn't seen much of each other since she took me to meet Dr. Lewis. Dad was going to be home soon so I told her I couldn't go to her condo, but she could come over to the house.

When she turned up, I was waiting on the porch. Paris was wearing torn fishnet tights with a fifties flowered summer dress. She looked crazy and beautiful. As she walked across the yard, you were just parking your pickup—she turned and looked at you as you went to the apartment stairs.

"Who's the hot guy?" she asked, when she joined me on the porch.

I glanced at the apartment. "Him?" I had not thought of you as someone who would be conventionally thought of as hot. I also, at this point, was maybe not quite aware of my own interest in you. Although maybe that's a lie; maybe I was. Because I remember thinking something very strange when Paris asked about you.

I mean, hearing a voice is extreme. But often, even when we're supposedly sane, our own thoughts can be foreign to us.

The alien, strange thought that went through my mind at that moment, and I wish I could say it was the voice but it wasn't, was:

He's mine, bitch. Like . . . like we were she-lions or something. Weird how quickly we revert to being animals.

But I waved a hand in what I hoped was a casual manner as we went up the stairs to my room. "He's one of the summer workers," I said. "From the piers. Dad rents the apartment over the garage."

"Sweet," said Paris. "So you get to check out Mr. Guns there whenever you like."

I shrugged, trying to appear more relaxed than I really was. "They're usually working."

"There's more than one of them?"

"Two."

She licked her lips. "Hmm. And is the other one hot too?"

"I guess."

"Then I shall be a frequent visitor to this abode, methinks."

"******," said the voice. "Filthy ******."

I flushed. "After six p.m.," I said.

"I can come after six p.m.?" said Paris.

I'd been talking to the voice. "Oh. Uh, yeah. Any day."

"Cool."

I sat down on the bed.

Paris was a bit freaked out by my room, I think. She gazed around at the shelves and the walls.

"It's very . . . clean," she said finally.

"Yeah. The voice makes me do that."

"Really?"

"Uh-huh."

"Tell the voice my condo could use a good housekeeper."

"Very funny."

She picked up a shell from the chest of drawers; it was one that I'd found with Mom, on one of our walks on the beach. "How's it going with the Doc?"

"Good, I think."

"You're reconciling with the voice? Making schedules, all that ****?"

"Yep."

"And what about the source? Any progress there?" she asked.

"The source?"

"Yeah. The ... What did you call it when you asked me? The trauma?"

I knew what she was doing. She was reminding me that she'd told, hinting at reciprocity. Basically saying that I should tell her, in turn.

"No, nothing," I lied. "There's nothing."

"Hmm," said Paris.

We hung out for a while—I played her some music; we ate some nut-free brownies that Dad had made. "Wow," said Paris. "These are amazing. Your dad's single, right?"

"Don't even think about it."

"Joking, Cass, joking."

I showed her Dad's bug room, and her eyes went wide as she looked at all the brightly colored millipedes and stick insects and beetles. "They're gross, but they're kind of beautiful at the same time," she said.

"Yeah."

"A bit like you," she said.

I punched her arm.

"Come on," she said. "Let's have another brownie."

Later she looked at her watch. "Your dad gets back at seven, right?"

"Usually."

"Okay, I'd better split." She walked to the door, and I opened it for her.

"See you," I said.

She smiled. "Not if I see you first."

"What does that mean?"

A frown. "Actually," she said, "I don't really know. I just say stuff sometimes." A pause. "Speaking of. I didn't see any photos of your mom in the house. What happened to her, Cass?"

(*Why does everything you touch have to turn to—*)

That wasn't the voice, just to be clear; that was Dad's voice, in my head.

"Nothing," I said.

Paris looked at me. "Nothing happened to her."

"No," I said.

She raised her hands. "Okay. Okay. Leaving it." She turned and started across the yard. "Oh, Cass!" she exclaimed. "You lucky girl."

"Huh?"

"Bare abs. Just *lying around.*"

I followed her out. She strode to the street, still giggling. Asleep on the lawn, next to a couple of open cans of Bud, was Shane. He had taken his top off—I guess because it was hot and he wanted to sunbathe a little. Then he'd obviously fallen asleep. He was wearing loose red lifeguard shorts. I could see the ridges of his stomach muscles.

Paris was gone; there was just me standing there, and Shane lying on the ground like a Greek statue lain out in the grass.

"Look away," said the voice.

But I kept looking. I was fascinated—I'd seen boys' bodies on the beach, but never one this close. I mean, apart from my dad, and he didn't count. I couldn't turn away from that hard chest, the V that ran down from his—

"You're enjoying this," said the voice. "Stop it, or I will punish you."

"After six p.m.," I said automatically. "No talking before six p.m."

"Look away, now. Or you will pay."

201

I didn't look away. I know I should have. Aside from anything else, it felt like a betrayal, of you. That sounds stupid. I mean all we had done was drive on the beach and talk a couple of times. But that's how it felt. Sometimes the things we feel are not rational.

Often, in fact.

Then Shane stirred. He kind of snuffled and said a name—Linda—I still don't know why—and rolled to the side a little. I thought, *Oh no, he's going to wake up and see me looking.* I couldn't move; I was stuck there like a woman turned to stone.

But then something worse happened.

As Shane turned, his hand went down and . . . well . . . scratched his crotch. Not in any sexual way, just a guy, asleep, shifting *stuff* around or whatever. And because he was wearing those baggy life-guard shorts I saw his . . . junk.

I literally could not look away. I wasn't titillated or anything, I was horrified.

Oh my God, I thought. I felt sick.

I guess I should have found it funny. But I didn't find it funny at all. I just felt nauseous and appalled, and one thought went through my mind, the one that didn't help at all with challenging the voice's power:

The voice did this. It told me to look away or it would punish me, and then when I didn't look away it made me see . . . this.

Finally I managed to make my legs work, and I turned and went back into the house. I knew the Doc would say that the voice had nothing to do with it, that it was just coincidence, but I didn't really *believe* it. I was remembering how it had made me stab my finger on the compasses at school.

I was still afraid.

But I'm not afraid anymore, I'm not afraid of anything. Not of the voice, not of my dad, nothing.

Come to the pier on Friday, and I'll show you.

Things were so much better with the voice, but it still had power. It was still the one in control.

I was leaving the house to go hang with Paris at her condo. I went to grab my keys from the monkey butler. He was a wooden monkey in a red jacket with a fez, balancing a platter that would hold my keys, Dad's, his car keys too. I don't know why we had a monkey. Mom and Dad got him from an antique store in Cape May when I was little, or something.

Anyway, I reached out for the keys and the voice said:

"No."

"Hi!" I said. "How are you?"

"Leave the keys."

"I'd really prefer if you only spoke to me aft—"

"It's six fifteen p.m.," said the voice.

I looked at my watch. Oh.

"Leave the keys," the voice repeated.

"It's a latch bolt," I said. "It automatically locks when the door closes. I won't be able to get back in."

"That's the point, yes," said the voice.

"But *why*?" Something about the voice made me sound like a whining teenager. I hated that.

"You only brushed your teeth once this morning. And you didn't wash your face. What is it, do you *want* to be revolting?"

"No."

"Good. Maybe being locked out will make you think about these things."

I withdrew my hand, leaving the keys where they were. I would have to hope Dad was home not too late, though he'd said he wouldn't be back for dinner—that was why I was going to Paris's place to begin with. He'd be pissed with me for staying out at

204

night—not that I had a formal curfew, but he didn't like me being out in the dark with the killer around—but what could I do?

I opened the door.

"Wait," said the voice. "Put on a jacket. You look like ****."

I went to the closet.

"No! Not that one! What are you, color blind?"

"Better?" I asked.

"Satisfactory," said the voice.

As I passed the monkey, I pushed my luck—I reached out my hand, thinking the voice might not be paying attention.

"You want to bleed tonight?" asked the voice.

I went out without my keys.

When I got to Paris's apartment building, I pressed the bell and heard the buzz that said the door was unlocked. I went in and rode up in the elevator to the second floor. As I neared her door, a guy in a dark suit came out—he was in his forties maybe? I glanced at his hand—there was a gold wedding ring on his ring finger.

He lowered his eyes as he passed me and hurried into the elevator. He had a belly that was stretching his white shirt, although the rest of him was skinny.

Paris was holding the door open and she looked—and if you'd told me I'd ever see this I wouldn't have believed you—she looked *embarrassed*. Or more than that, ashamed.

I didn't say anything—what could I say? I just smiled at her and she smiled back, and we went inside.

"Let's go to the piers," said Paris.

"What?"

"Let's do it. Ride the Ferris wheel."

"You're kidding?"

"No. Why?"

"I'm *town*. People from the town don't go to the piers."

"Oh please," said Paris. "Like you didn't go when you were a kid."

"That was different. I was a kid."

She shook her head sadly. She had eyeliner ticking up from the corner of each eye, bright blue; it made her look like a cat. Pinstriped pants, high heels, a shirt. Big bangles on her wrists, in all colors. She grabbed a half-full bottle of Smirnoff from the counter. "Anyway, I'm not town," she said. "I'm from New York. I'm a tourist basically. A student tourist. I'm everything you town people hate. So we're going," she said. "There's nothing you can do about it."

Story of my life.

I've just noticed that I called the bottle of vodka "half full." Whereas I told you that my dad is a glass-half-empty kind of guy.

That must make me an optimist.

Well, I guess I wouldn't be writing this otherwise.

Paris, of course, was right; we had fun.

The sun was setting over the town as we got to the end of the street by her building. We climbed up the steps onto the board-walk, joining it just between the SLOT MACHINE ARCADIA, which is decorated with spray-painted murals of satyrs and nymphs frol-icking in a dell by a stream, and VINNIE'S TATTOO STUDIO.

"You want?" said Paris, holding out the bottle of vodka.

I shook my head.

"Killjoy," said Paris.

"My allergy," I said.

"There are no peanuts in vodka, Cass."

"No."

"So have some."

"I can't."

She stopped, took another swig, and looked at the bottle, then at me. "You did before we went to the group."

"Yeah, because I was nervous. But it was only that one time. I don't drink."

Paris puzzled was a beautiful thing to see. It was not something that happened a lot. Her eyebrows stayed knitted. "Why not?" she asked.

"It's if I *do* eat peanuts. Or something with peanuts in it. Alcohol makes an anaphylaxis much worse."

"Yeah?"

"Yeah. Seventeen to twenty-seven. That's the danger zone. When most allergic people die. Because they drink and get sloppy, and then they get a reaction and their bodies are already weak from the booze."

"Huh. Who'd have thought it." She took a swig of vodka and threw the bottle, still nearly half full, into a trash can—laid it up like

208

a basketball player, hand curled over, the bottle flying in a perfect parabola before landing with a *chink*. Then we crossed the wide wooden walkway, skirting kids carrying cotton candy, and laughing groups of teenagers. Balloons in a hundred colors rose from the wrists of toddlers, like sky-jellyfish.

Then we were across the boardwalk, and in the amusement park.

We went to a booth and bought evening tickets—they gave us blue wristbands with the moon printed on them. Already the sun was low in the sky over the town, painting the rooftops orange. We were just paying the teller—a young girl working for the summer, I guessed—when a guy at the back of the booth came over and looked at me through the glass.

"Cassandra?" he said.

I nodded.

He came out a door in the side of the booth. Russian Pete, I think he was called? Short, always wore a bow tie, had eyes that puffed out, fishlike. He did a kind of measuring motion with his hands. "Jeez, you got big." He called over his shoulder. "Hey, Finn."

There was a guy in a dolphin suit just behind the booth—the Piers mascot. He ambled over and stood in front of Russian Pete. Then he took off his head. "'S'up, Pete?"

"See that?" said Pete. "That's Mike's girl."

"Cassandra?"

"Yep."

The mascot named Finn took another couple of steps forward. He leaned down. It was weird being leaned down to by a guy in a dolphin costume. His hair was all mussed from the big foam head, and there was sweat on his forehead. I recognized him—he had been a regular at the restaurant. Finny McCool, the guys called him. I had no idea why.

"You got big," he said slowly. He had a big, round face. Finny was kind of a simple guy.

"She sure did, didn't she?" Pete turned to me. "His name's Finn, and he wears the dolphin costume. Finn. Kills me every time."

"Huh?" said Finn.

"Never mind," said Pete. "Go thrill the kids with your impression of a sea mammal."

"Huh?"

"Go be a dolphin."

"Oh. Okay." He turned around, putting his head back on. I could see the sweat beading at his neck. I felt sorry for him. Even though it was evening it must have been seventy degrees, easy, and that dolphin costume had to be seriously hot. Dad always said it was the worst job on the pier.

Paris was watching all this like she'd been dropped into another reality. "How've you been?" said Pete to me. "I haven't seen you since . . . ah . . ." He swallowed. I saw the panic enter his eyes, saw him add it up. "Since . . ."

"Yeah," I said.

"Yeah," said Pete, sadly. I always liked Pete. He told stupid jokes and he did lame tricks, but he was sweet, you know? Then he brightened. "You paid!" he said. "Only out-of-towners pay."

I shrugged.

Pete sighed. "Let's see what we can do about that." He reached behind my ear, and I thought he was going to pull out the twenty bucks we had paid, but he didn't. He frowned. "Hmm. Not there. Check your pocket."

I reached into my jeans. There was a shape in there like a cigar—

two ten-dollar bills rolled up. "Hey," I said, genuinely impressed. "Your tricks got better."

"You're older now," said Pete. "Got to up my game."

"Seriously, though, we can pay," I said.

Pete looked at us both. "You girls like popcorn, right? Dippin' Dots?"

"Yeah," said Paris, smiling.

"See," said Pete to me. "Your girl is with me on this. Take the twenty, use it on the concessions. The rides are free. I absolutely insist. If you say no you will be insulting not only me but also the entire Piers staff, present, past, and future."

"Okay," I said, putting my hands up in a gesture of surrender. "Thanks, Pete."

"You're welcome."

Then he raised a hand, like, *hang on*. He went into the little booth and came back out with two lanyards with VIP cards on them. "Wear these," he said. "Skip the lines—the guys will let you on the rides first."

"Really?"

"Yeah. Go."

"Thank you, Pete," said Paris.

"Thank *you*," said Pete. "It's good to see our girl with a friend."

Jesus, Pete, I thought. *Way to make me sound like a loser.*

But Paris smiled. "She's special, this one," she said.

"She sure is," said Pete. He waved us toward the park. "Go, have fun."

And we did.

We went to the Accelerator first. It's the oldest and biggest wooden roller coaster in the United States. Did you know that? It doesn't loop the loop or go upside down or any of that stuff. But it's still a rush. You get on it and the chain pulls your car up up

up

up

into the twilit sky. You see the ocean, all the way to the horizon, stretching out, shining in the red light of dusk. The city on the other side, a million points of light. You hear laughter and shouting, carrying over the clear evening air. Then there's a moment where you're teetering, in equilibrium, and then you *tip*, and you rush down . . . so fast that it feels like you're merging with the wind.

And then *whoosh*, up again, and down, and up, and all the time screaming.

"That was wild," said Paris, after.

"Yeah. It's good for an old ride."

"No, I mean that guy. Pete? Giving us these." She held up her VIP pass on the gold lanyard.

"Cool, isn't it?" We had breezed past the line for the Accelerator, as people looked at us enviously. It felt like being famous. The park was pretty full—some parents and kids, the older ones, because it was already dark. Young guys in baseball caps; girls in short skirts and short shorts. A bunch of bros from a frat somewhere, leaning on one another and whooping. There was a smell of popcorn and beer and sweat, all mingled together, and beneath it, an under note from a perfume bottle, the ever-present scent of the sea.

"I wish I had it," said Paris.

"Wish you had what?"

Paris swept a hand over the park. "It's like . . . a whole family. As well as your dad."

I thought about that. "I don't know," I said.

"Seriously? That Pete guy? And Finn? Those guys love you; you can see it."

"Hmm."

"And what was that woman's name? The one who let us on the Accelerator?"

"Sweet Sarah?"

"You're kidding me? That's her name?"

"Yeah."

"She hugged you. She was smiling like she just won the lottery, just because you turned up at the ride."

I shrugged. "They're just people who know my dad. Who eat at the restaurant."

"The restaurant?"

Oh.

"Yeah . . . ," I said. "My dad has an Italian place. On the boardwalk—up by Pier Two."

"Donato's?"

"You know it?"

"Oh, come on. It's like the best pizza in the state. Your dad owns it?"

"Donato was my grandfather."

"Holy ****," said Paris. "You're, like, New Jersey mob. I mean, you're like a Soprano."

"It's just a restaurant. It's not a gang."

"Yeah, right. I figure there are fridges in back full of coke and heroin in big white bricks. Does your dad keep a gun under the counter? I bet he keeps a gun under the counter."

"No," I said, my voice flat; hard. I must have flinched, bodily.

"Whatever, moody," said Paris. "So your dad isn't some kind of mob boss. But, still, must have been cool growing up with your own pizza restaurant."

I shrugged. I wanted this conversation to be over. "It was okay."

She raised her eyebrows.

"It was *fine*," I said, frustrated and not totally sure why I was so frustrated. "I used to hang out there after school. Do my assignments at one of the small tables, you know? All the waiters knew me of course, and they'd help me out sometimes. Frank was good at math. I had my own pizza on the menu—it was, like, a ham and mushroom with artichoke and egg." As I spoke, I realized how much I missed the place, how much a small part of me missed it anyway. "It was . . . it was an extension of home, I guess. I'd walk in there and I was like a mascot. It was great."

Paris looked at me. "I think that's the longest thing I've ever heard you say."

"Hmm."

"That's more like you, yep." Then she touched her stomach. "I'm hungry. Let's go get pizza at your dad's place."

"No," I said, too quickly.

"Why not?"

"I . . . It was great when I was a kid. Now it's not."

"Ri-i-i-ght," said Paris, in that *there's a story here and I want to know what it is but I'm not going to pry for now* tone.

"It's my family restaurant, you know?" I said, trying to cover myself. "Boring."

"Okay. I get that. Well, I see a hot dog stand. You can eat those, right? I mean, with your peanut thing?"

"I don't think so," I said. "Processed meat. Kind of an issue."

"Just the bun, then."

"Have to be careful with bread too."

"You're that allergic?"

"I'm *oh, she's not breathing* allergic. I'm *the funeral is on*

214

Saturday, no flowers allergic." I held up my ugly purse with the insulating sides.

"Fries then?"

"The oil is often unrefined peanut oil."

"Jesus. The world is full of peril for you, huh?"

She didn't know how right she was.

We rode the Spin-Dry.

We rode the Barrel Roll.

We rode the Spraymaker, our little boat crashing into the water at the bottom, soaking us from head to waist, the drops shimmering in the neon lights of the fair on our Danny Dolphin ponchos.

The Elevator, the Ferris wheel, we left for last. It was on Pier Two so we had to cut back to the boardwalk and keep walking. We passed the stalls lined up on the ocean side of the boardwalk—the Pro Basketball Challenge, the T-Rex Ring Toss. Now, when I saw these places, I noticed the stacks of plush toys on the back walls. The prizes—all delivered by you. The thought of you gave me a strange feeling inside, something unfolding in my stomach, some delicate carapace turning to wings.

He might be close by, I thought. *Driving his truck. His arm resting on the door . . .*

"Control yourself, slut," said the voice. "You're like a ***** in heat."

"After six," I said automatically.

"It is," said the voice.

Dammit.

Paris and I kept going toward the wheel. As we walked, we could hear the patter of the kid running the basketball game.

"Come on by,

Give it a try,

We've got prizes money can't buy . . ."

Paris was looking around like someone transported from the seventeenth century.

"This is amazing," she said.

"You haven't been before?"

"No."

"Never? But you live, like, one block away."

"I know."

"Your parents never took you? In the summer or—"

She held my eyes for a moment. "No."

"Oh. Sorry. Of course. So why didn't you go on your own? Or with Julie?"

"I don't know. I think I was waiting for you to come along."

Silence. I didn't know what to say to that.

Then she grabbed my arm. "Anyway, it's awesome. The guys doing little poems, to draw in players, you know? It's like . . . Like something out of a story. But it's real. You know?"

"It's just patter," I said.

"Pat—"

"Patter. Everyone has a different one. I—"

"What?"

"Nothing."

We'd stopped now. There were people separating and streaming around us, like those illustrations of air going around a plane's wing.

"You were going to say you could do it, weren't you?"

"No."

"You *were*." Her eyes were flashing in the electric light of the stores and stands. We were right in the middle of the pier; it was like being inside a pinball machine. People and music and games all around. "You totally worked one of these things, didn't you?"

My shoulders slumped. "Basketball hoops. Two summers."

"Oh, *Cass*. You're doing it. Your patter. You're doing it for me right now."

"No."

"Yes."

"Paris, there are people."

"Pretend they're not there. I do it all the time, with clients. It's easy."

An uncomfortable moment.

"Yeah, okay, TMI," said Paris. "But you're still doing it."

"No way."

"Please. I'll be your friend."

"You're already my friend."

"Curse your fiendish intelligence. I'll buy you a pony."

"I don't want a pony."

"I'll buy you—"

"Oh, okay," I said. "If it'll shut you up."

Paris clapped her hands. She pulled me over to the side of the pier, by one of the circular stands that are dotted all over—some of them with games, shooting galleries, some of them selling ice cream and hot dogs and whatever. "Go," she said.

"I'm rusty," I said. "Wait."

I took a breath.

"Hey," I said, "don't walk on by,

Come on in and give it a try,

It's a simple game

If you've got aim,

Split a buck

To double your luck,

A quarter won't break you

But it might just make you."

I gave a little bow.

"Wow," said Paris. "My little carny."

"They're not called—"

"I know. I'm ****** with you. That was amazing. Thank you."

"Uh, yeah. Okay."

"Gracious as an Austen heroine."

"Whatever," I said.

"As Elizabeth Bennet herself declared."

"*Paris*. Let's ride the Elevator now."

"Oh, yes. Let's."

We skirted around the stand—it was a rings-on-the-jars game—and worked our way to the end of the pier. Then we passed Hook-the-Duck in its circular island. The water was bright green under neon lights; the sky above almost entirely black now. Katy Perry was blasting from the speakers hung above. Also hanging were all the toys you could win—the plush and the cheap stereos and stuff. Every color in the spectrum, just pulsing at you, and the music too.

"—this," said Paris, and I realized I'd missed the start of whatever she had said.

"What?"

"I want to play."

"You want to hook a duck?" I was kind of shouting over the music.

"Yeah."

"Why?"

"I don't know. I just feel like hooking a duck."

I did a not-real sigh and handed her one of the ten-spots. I don't know why I just wrote "ten-spots." That's not how I speak. I think it's writing about Paris. I mean, she was just so cool, you know? And she didn't even mean to be. She was just a hundred-watt bulb in a world of forty-watt bulbs. She *shone*. When she walked by, you saw people following her with their eyes, like it would hurt them to look away.

Anyway.

She got a fishing rod and she was *terrible*. Pretty soon I was laughing as she knocked the ducks together, sent them spinning, flipped their backs under the water. Eventually she hooked one sad little blue duck and yelled with triumph and the girl on the stand said, bored,

"You can have anything from the outer ring."

Paris looked up. "I'll take that red monkey thing."

"That's Elmo."

"Yeah, him."

The girl pulled down the little Elmo stuffed toy and handed it to Paris. Paris clutched it to her chest. "It's mi-i-i-ine," she said dramatically. "It's finally mi-i-i-ine."

"Hmm," I said. "Come on."

She pretended to be a chastised kid, kind of moping along behind me, pulling a moue of exaggerated sadness, lips pushed out.

"Stop that."

"Spoilsport."

Then I saw something from the corner of my eye. We were near the side of the pier. It was a white F-150 truck, driving across the sand of the beach, toward us. I could see a stack of clear plastic bags in back, full of toys. You? It had to be you. "Follow me," I said, and I started walking, keeping an eye on the truck to see where it was headed.

"Where are we going?" asked Paris.

I didn't answer. I swerved past a group of women on a bachelor-ette thing, pink furry mouse ears on their heads, angel wings fluttering out behind them. Between two of the round stalls, along the side of the Sidewinder. Beyond its steel struts and riveted cross-pieces, there was a little gate, waist high. A wood-sided office was next to it. A sign said STAFF ONLY AFTER THIS POINT. It wasn't locked—I pushed it open and walked through, and then there was the side of the pier—a sheer drop to the beach below.

"Cass, what the—"

I held up a hand to cut her off. I walked right up to the edge and looked down.

"Jump," said the voice. It was only the fourth time I had heard it that day, I realized. The schedule thing was really working.

"Jump," it repeated. "Break your legs."

"Shush," I said.

"You little *****. Don't you d—"

"Not now," I said.

"Uh, Cass?" asked Paris from behind me. "Cass, are you all right? What are you doing?"

"Wait," I said. I looked down.

"Wait for what?"

I didn't say anything.

"Is this, like, some kind of bravery thing? Like Chicken? How close will you go? Okay, I'll play."

"What?" I said, turning to her. But she was already coming up beside me, shuffling her feet till her toes were over the edge of the wooden planks. Then she leaned forward, right over the edge, almost ready to topple.

I looked down. The hard gray sand was easily fifteen feet below us.

"Jesus," I said. "Don't do that."

"Just because I'm winning," she said. She leaned right out now, ten degrees or something. I don't know degrees. I don't even know why I'm making that analogy. Let's say instead: she leaned out till she looked like the woman on the prow of an old ship, her hair stirring in the breeze.

"It's not a *game*," I said.

"Not if you're losing," she said. Leaned more.

I backed away from the edge. "Seriously, I'm not competing with you."

She turned, looked quizzically at me. And that's when she lost balance, her arms wheeling as she began to fall. Her eyes went comic-book wide, and I lunged without thinking and caught her wrists. I then did a beautiful move where I just kind of sat down, all my weight at once, to pull her back onto the pier.

She collapsed on top of me. "Thanks," she said, with a grin, the fear already gone from her eyes, as if it had never been there.

"You're welcome."

We stood up.

"So what were you doing at the edge?" she said.

I pointed down. "Waiting for him," I said. You had just pulled up in your truck and were climbing out of it; you hadn't looked up yet, and consequently had not noticed us standing there.

"*Oh*," said Paris. "That makes much more sense."

Below us, you closed the door of the truck and walked around to the back. Then you leaped up onto the tailgate.

"Hey," I said.

You looked up. You raised your eyebrows and smiled. "Hey, yourself," you said. "What are you doing there? Where's Pedro?"

"I don't know who Pedro is."

You sighed. "Always late."

"It's him!" said Paris, moving to stand next to me. "Hello, cute boy who lives at Cass's place."

You blinked at her. "Uh, hello, um . . ."

"Paris."

"Hello, Paris."

I looked down at the bags of toys. "So you just throw them up on the pier?"

"Yeah," you said. "Then Pedro carries them to the stalls that need them. When he's around anyway." You saw the toy in Paris's hand. "You won that?"

"Hook-the-Duck," said Paris. "I sucked ****."

"Hang on," you said. You moved a couple of the bags. Then you made a little rip in one of them and pulled out a big Elmo, like half the size of me. "Catch," you said, and tossed it up to Paris.

Paris held out her hands but missed—the Elmo fell to the wooden floor of the pier.

"See?" she said. "I suck."

Was she flirting with you?

And if she was, why would I care?

"Do me a favor," you said, interrupting my thoughts.

"What?" I said.

"I need to roll. I have another delivery. So I'm going to toss these bags up. You make sure they don't fall off the side, okay? Pedro will know what to do with them."

"Just don't throw them to her," I said, pointing to Paris.

You laughed. "Seriously, though, don't try to catch them. They're heavy."

"Okay."

You picked up the first bag and kind of pitched it up onto the pier. It landed with a dull thud and a flat flopping motion that made me think queasily of a body.

Blood.

A tiled floor.

No.

I pushed it under again.

You grabbed another bag, threw it up. Then another and another. No wonder your arms had gotten ripped. Then you jumped back down and opened the cab door. "Me and Shane are going to Pirate Golf on Pier One after work, if you want to come," you said. "Both of you."

"That would be wonderful," said Paris, before I could say anything. "We most humbly accept your gracious invitation. We shall see you upon the Pirate Golf course. At what hour should we convene?"

You looked at me. "Your friend is weird."

"I know," I said.

"He's talking about you," said Paris.

"No, he's not."

"No, I'm not," you said.

"Now you're just ganging up," said Paris. "What time?"

"Nine thirty?" you said.

"See you there," I said. It was like a small creature with unknown motivations had taken over my brain and my mouth.

"It's a date," said Paris, with a mischievous smile.

"Paris!"

"Laters, cute boy," said Paris. She turned, and I gave you a *what can you do?* gesture with my hands; I could feel the heat of the blood in my cheeks. You smiled and slid behind the wheel of the truck; then I heard the engine roar as I caught up with Paris.

Huh. Was it a date? Did it count as a date? We were meeting you later anyway. That creature in my stomach spread its wings, took flight.

"And when will you tell him about me?" said the voice. "I mean, this is all very romantic and all but have you forgotten you're crazy?"

"Quiet," I said.

We walked back onto the pier proper. As we approached the gate, a guy opened it from the other side—Hispanic, with wire-rimmed glasses. Young looking, skinny, more like a chess-club kid than a fairground worker.

"You're . . . ," he said. "You shouldn't be back here."

"Oh, sorry, Pedro," said Paris. She flashed her VIP pass at him.

His mouth opened and closed like a fish's. "How did you . . ."

Paris blew him a kiss. "The bags are there," said Paris. "Elmos and . . . some other ****. Bunnies and ****. I suggest you hurry up, Pedro."

"Who are you? How do you know my—"

"Laters, Pedro," said Paris. Then she put a hand on the fence and tried to vault it, but her foot caught and she tumbled to the ground on the other side, did an ungainly roll and came to her feet again. She walked off without a backward glance.

I gave Pedro an apologetic look and ran to catch up to her.

"You're beautiful," I said to Paris, "but you are *not* graceful, are you? I mean, what were you even thinking, putting your feet over the edge of the pier like that? A clumsy person like you."

She shrugged. "I thought it was a game."

"And if you'd fallen?"

Another shrug. "Then I guess I would have gotten hurt."

That was Paris: she was fun, but she didn't really know where the line between fun and danger was. That was Paris's whole entire problem.

We were walking toward the Elevator—the Ferris wheel at the piers—when Paris's cell rang. She fished it out of her pocket and answered it.

"Hey! You win? (Pause.) Aw. Sucks. Where are you? (Pause.) We're at the piers. Well, yes, *on* the piers. A pier, actually. (Pause.) We're going to ride the Ferris wheel. (Pause.) Seriously, yeah. (Pause.) Yeah, with Cassie. Look, come down. Get a ticket. Ride it with us. Oh, come on. It'll be fun! (Pause.) Great, cool. See you there."

She flicked it off and put it away. "Julie," she said.

"She's coming?"

"Yep. They lost their roller derby game. She's in a bad mood. Figure the Ferris wheel will help."

Weirdly, I felt a little jealous. I just . . . I was enjoying spending this time with her, just her. It was awesome, and I felt like Julie coming along was going to ruin it.

Although when we got to the base of the wheel and the queue, and Julie waved and then walked over, I felt kind of stupid because Julie was smiling and holding out three sticks of cotton candy and being super nice.

I held up my hands when she proffered mine. "Sorry. I—"

"Cass here is allergic to basically everything," said Paris. "Including heights. Chances are she's going to barf on you."

"Just peanuts," I said hurriedly when Julie frowned at me. "It's really boring. I just have to be really careful."

Julie shrugged. "More for me," she said, and kept hold of two of the cotton candies, giving the other to Paris. Paris plunged her face into hers, started making gross noises like a T. rex eating another dinosaur's stomach. She lifted her eyes to us, pink shreds hanging from her chin.

"*Roar*," she said.

"T. rex?" said Julie.

"Yeah."

"I got the same thing," I said.

"Psychic connection," said Paris. "Look at us! BFFs."

"No one says BFFs," said Julie. "Except in stupid TV shows."

"Nuh-huh," said Paris. "I just said it. Anyway. What was I *eating*?"

"Diplodocus?" I said.

Paris sighed. "Stegosaurus. I thought that would have been perfectly obvious."

"Is she always like this?" I asked Julie.

"Always," said Julie, with a strange little smile.

Then there was a buzz from Paris's phone and she checked the screen. "Bachelor party," she said. "Tomorrow night. You drive me, Julie?"

Julie gave an awkward glance at me. "You know I don't think you should—"

"Oh, I know, *Mom*," said Paris.

Julie sighed. "Where is it?"

"Goose Heights." This was a nice part of town.

"If I can come in with you," said Julie.

"Julie, do we have to have this conversation every time? If you want to watch me strip you're welcome to subscribe to my cam site. No. You can wait in the car. I have my phone. I have you on speed dial. I'll call if I need you."

Julie pursed her lips.

"And I'll give you a hundred dollars," said Paris. "You're the best, Julie, for doing this, for helping me to earn my own money, get out from under my dad and—"

"Okay, okay, fine," said Julie. "Fine."

"Right," said Paris, putting away her phone. She flashed a grin at me; a shark's grin, full of joy and danger. "Let's get high."

We looked at her blankly.

"On the *Ferris wheel*."

We flashed our passes and skipped the line. Well, Paris and I did, but Julie didn't have a VIP pass. Not that it held us up for long—Paris did this eyelash-batting thing at the kid managing the line and he let all three of us through.

It was nine, full dark, a slight chill in the air. Purple clouds covered the moon, over the black ocean. The Elevator was almost as old as the roller coaster. A lot of its supports were still wooden. Each of the cars was done up like an elevator, and the joke was that there was a single button inside, which said,

UP AND DOWN AND ALL AROUND.

"The last time I went on this I was eight," I said.

"All the more reason to ride it now," said Paris.

"Is it a bad time to say that I'm a little afraid of heights?" said Julie.

"Please," said Paris. "You do roller derby. Your biceps are bigger than my personal trainer's."

"You have a personal trainer?" I asked.

"No," said Paris. "But that's beside the point."

We climbed into our elevator car; it rocked slightly. There were seats, which kind of ruined the illusion, and the whole side was open, secured by a thin metal bar that the kid running the ride dropped into place. Paris and Julie sat on one side, me on the other.

"You get two go-arounds," he said, in a bored drawl. He was my age, with the broken nose and big shoulders of a football player. "Then we fill the cars again." He stepped out, leaned on a lever.

We shuddered up into the air, then stopped while people got into the next car—a family with one laughing kid and one crying kid.

We jerked into the sky in increments as the ride filled.

Finally we reached the top.

"Oh, wow," said Paris.

"Yeah."

"Huh," said Julie. She had her hand on Paris's arm. She'd obviously been only half-joking—she looked a little white. "Suddenly it's so *beautiful*."

I knew what she meant; I was feeling the same surprise, even though I'd been up here when I was a kid. It still struck me.

I mean.

Oakwood was a dump—the old-people's homes, the slot machines, the white trash on vacation. The used-car lots, the Early Bird Specials, the motels, the broken-down lots where go-kart rides used to be, the demolished blocks like pulled teeth, the wire fences. But from up here, at night, it was as if a witch had put an enchantment on the town, a prince/frog kind of deal, and only when you rode up on the Elevator would you see the true beauty. The boardwalk curved below us like a broad sickle. Pale sand extended from it to the ocean, which glittered like a vast black jewel.

And everywhere was light.

Streetlights, running in ribbons, connecting houses that, too, spilled yellow light into the darkness. A giant phosphorescent creature, throwing out tendrils in every direction. And below us, the constant glow of the theme park, flashing bulbs, floodlights, flickering neon lights. The rides coiling over and around themselves like silver snakes.

It's stupid, I mean, it's not the Taj Mahal—it's Oakwood. But it was so beautiful I can't describe it.

"I never knew," Paris said.

"Yeah," said Julie. "Me neither."

"Jump," said the voice.

I must have flinched. "What's wrong?" said Paris.

"Nothing."

"Jump. It would be so easy."

I shook my head.

"Heights?" said Paris. "You too?"

I nodded.

"Suit yourself," said the voice. "Coward." But it sounded flat, uninterested. Like if it had the opportunity, it was going to say something, but it wasn't as committed as it used to be.

It's nice to hear from you, I said inside my head. *It's beautiful up here, isn't it?*

Nothing. The voice had withdrawn.

". . . totally with you," Julie was saying.

"Excuse me?"

"I'm with you. It's beautiful, but those houses are just too small down there. It's not natural." She smiled at me, and I wondered what I had done to deserve these new people in my life.

"Jump," said the voice.

Oh Jesus. When were we getting off this thing? A cool breeze moved over my skin, bringing up goose bumps on my arms. The ocean was a long way down, so far I couldn't hear it, and the beach too, the dark silhouettes of the lifeguard stands. I noticed that our car hadn't moved for a while. I looked down—the guy had walked a few steps away from the wheel and leaned against the small shack where people handed in their tickets. He reached into it and pressed something, I guess.

Loud music started. That song, "Got to turn aro-o-o-o-ound," I don't know what it's called. Paris would have known. The wheel began to revolve smoothly, and *oh thank God*, I thought, taking us down into the lights, the glow and the colors rushing up to meet us, so it seemed like we would become light ourselves, dissolve into a million points of brightness.

"This is lame," said the crying kid in the car behind us.

Paris shook her head, sadly.

We reached the bottom. *Oh good*, I thought. Finally. But then the wheel started to rise again.

You get two goes, I remembered.

Outstanding.

Julie looked a little queasy too. When we got close to the top, Paris pointed down. "Look how tiny everyone is," she said.

"I'm trying to ignore that," said Julie.

I looked, though. I had been focusing on the lights, but now I saw the tiny figures, the thousands of people walking around the piers.

"Have you seen *The Third Man*?" asked Paris.

"No. What's that?"

"It's a movie," said Julie. "Old. Graham Greene wrote the script."

"*Our Man in Havana*?"

"Yeah," said Julie. "Same guy."

"Look at Miss Film Studies here," said Paris, amiably elbowing Julie. "Anyway, the point is, in the movie there's a spy who's gone bad or something. The guy who has been sent to bring him back in from the cold meets him in Vienna, and they ride the Ferris wheel. The rogue agent, Harry I think his name is, basically won't acknowledge that he's done anything wrong, even though he has gotten people killed. He points down. He says—and I'm paraphrasing—he says, 'Would you feel guilty if any of those dots stopped moving? What if I gave you twenty thousand for every dot that stopped?'"

"Um. Okay," I said.

Paris leaned forward, took my hand, and pointed to the little people below. "His point being, when you zoom out your perspective, when you look at people from a distance, they're small and insignificant. It doesn't matter if they die. What do you think?"

I looked at the people. The wheel was turning slowly; we were just reaching the peak of the arc. "I think they matter," I said.

"Me too," said Julie. I noticed that her eyes were closed.

"And me," said Paris. "That's what I'm saying. For me, it's the opposite of the guy in the film. I look down, and I see those tiny people, and I want to wrap my arms around them all, around the whole town, keep them safe, you know?" She put her arms out wide, and we were so high they encircled the town, she was big enough to hold it, the whole place, all the people, all the lights.

"Yeah," I said. "I know."

Julie's eyes opened momentarily, and she looked around her with a hooded, half-attentive gaze. "You know what I think when I see those little people?" she said. Red light flashed off the piercing in her nose. "I think I want to get off this ******ing ride."

A conversation that signifies a lot, and also means nothing at all:

We were walking down the pier, Julie and me. Paris was up ahead, basically skipping instead of walking, like we were in a musical.

Julie was going more slowly, her gait a little unsteady. I realized she hadn't been joking *at all* about the fear of heights. But she'd gone on the ride anyway. That registered somewhere, resonated on some taut string in my mind. What she was willing to do for Paris.

I glanced over at Julie. There was a tattoo of the Little Prince on her arm, standing on his little planet, with his rose at his feet.

"'That which is essential is invisible to the eye,'" I said.

"What?"

"The fox says it, in *The Little Prince*," I said.

Julie smiled. "Oh, yeah. My tattoo. Yep, I love that book. It's sad, but it's amazing too. I have the snake on my other arm."

"Yeah?"

She turned and showed me—the snake swallowing the elephant, making it look like a hat from the side. Saint-Exupéry's example of how children see things differently than adults, see the magic that adults can no longer see.

"You think it's true?" I said. "That when we grow up, we see things differently?"

Julie thought about this for a moment. "Maybe for some people. Not for Paris. Look at her."

I looked. Paris was doing cartwheels down the middle of the pier, people scattering to either side of her, waves.

"Ha," I said. "Yeah. When we were on the wheel . . . I felt it. The magic."

"That's what she does," said Julie. "I mean . . . she has bad times too. She calls them the Black Days. When she can't leave her room. But living with her ... you almost start to believe in magic, you know?"

"I do," I said. I remembered the crane, how it had seemed to tremble in my hand. "She said *you* didn't believe in magic though."

"What? Really?"

"Yeah, she was talking about her cranes and the wish you get when you've made a thousand and she said that you would laugh at her."

"Oh. Well, she's probably right. Wishes don't come true. Everyone knows that."

I remembered all the times I had wished for my mom not to be dead. "Hmm," I said. "I guess."

"Abso-*******-lutely right," said the voice.

"The thing about Paris ... ," said Julie. "She trusts people too much. She gets hurt. All the time."

Had she glanced at me there? Shot me a warning?

"Uh, okay," I said.

"Sorry," said Julie, with a cough. "I just ..."

She trailed off.

I thought:

— Riding the Ferris wheel when you're afraid of heights.
— That strange smile when she said that Paris was "always like this."
— That weird line about wishes not coming true.

"You love her," I said, without thinking.

Julie nodded. "She's my best friend."

"No. I mean, you *love* her. I just figured it out."

Side note: I said this proudly. Like, I was proud that I had guessed. Can you imagine? The arrogance? The stupidity?

Julie turned to look at me. She was walking quicker now; we were passing the Walk the Plank game. "What?"

"It's cool. I'm not judging . . ."

Julie narrowed her eyes.

"And I mean . . . ," I said, less confident now. "I'm not . . . You don't have to worry about me, with Paris. I'm not . . . I mean . . ."

Julie laughed, a hollow laugh. "I'm not worried about you," she said. "Not in *that way* anyway. You're pretty obviously straight. As is Paris, incidentally."

"Then what—"

"You heard her," said Julie. "She'd hug the whole town if she could. Fold it in her arms. The thing about Paris: she loves *everyone*. She even loves her dad. And she hates her dad."

"Right . . . ," I said.

"She loves everyone. So, like I said, she gets hurt."

"By?"

"By people leaving. Coming into her life, and then going."

"And you think I'm going to do that?" I said.

Julie sighed. "I don't think anything. You brought this up."

Oh. That was right. I did.

"Sorry," I said. "I speak before I think. But anyway, I'm not going to do that. I'm not going to just come into her life and then leave."

"Good," said Julie. "Paris . . . she sometimes makes bad choices, you know?"

"Like what?"

She looked at me, puzzled—that *duh* face that we all used to do as kids. "You know. What she does?"

"Oh. Yeah."

"It's like the stupidest thing ever," said Julie. "And all because she doesn't want her dad's money. I told her she could get a job in a bar, but that's not Paris—not enough money, not quick enough, not exciting enough. I don't mind the cam stuff but the parties . . . she has *no idea* who's going to be there. What's she going to do if a bunch of frat guys decide they want more than she's offering?"

I hadn't really thought about it till now—had just thought it seemed edgy and dangerous and exciting and cool, which gave me a flush of shame at Julie using basically those words, in a sarcastic way. Now I actually imagined it: going into a room with strange men, taking their money. Doing . . . stuff. "It sounds pretty dangerous," I said.

"It's *very* dangerous."

"So why don't you tell her how worried you are?" It had crossed my mind to bring it up myself, but I didn't know Paris that well, and I didn't want to upset her.

"I do, constantly," said Julie. "It doesn't make any difference. Now I just try to minimize the risk."

Silence.

"Anyway," said Julie, faux-bright. "Where are we going?"

"Pirate Golf," I said. "We're meeting some boys."

"Oh good," said Julie, with an ironic wink. "*Boys.*"

To get to Pirate Golf, we had to leave the pier we were on and go around to Pier One.

Which meant passing the restaurant.

Paris bought a beer and sucked on it like a thirsty builder as we walked the boardwalk. It takes—what, five minutes?—to walk from one pier to the other.

I went ahead, through the crowds of people, and turned onto Pier One, ignoring what was behind me.

"Hey," said Paris.

I pretended not to hear her.

"Hey, Cass."

I turned. Paris was poking her beer bottle at the businesses lined up on the street side of the boardwalk. And there was Donato's, the red-and-white-striped awning, the little tables on the sidewalk that had gotten popular since the smoking ban—but not popular enough to reverse the damage of the crash; people sitting out there and eating pizzas, chatting.

Inside, I knew, was a mural covering one whole wall, the bay of Naples, a sunny day, boats drifting on the blue waves. A donkey in the foreground, pulling a cart, its legs anatomically incorrect. The land of my ancestors.

Also white tiles.

Also blood.

Also the pizza oven, decorated with broken pottery, red and white, the—

Also blood.

My stomach contracted like a fist.

"You want to go see your dad?" said Paris. "I mean, we're here, right?"

"No," I said. "No."

"Where's her dad?" said Julie.

"He owns that pizza restaurant," said Paris. She turned to me and frowned. "He doesn't know you're out?"

"Uh, no, he doesn't," I said, grateful for the excuse. My insides were still tight, still clenched.

"You were ******* weak then and you are ******* weak now," said the voice.

I didn't have the energy to reply, didn't have the strength to follow my welcome script. And it was past six, so it was a free-for-all on the voice front anyway.

Paris shrugged. She looked at her watch. "Time to go meet your hot crush anyway," she said.

"He's not my—"

"Yeah, yeah."

We walked away from the restaurant, people moving all around us, molecules in a test tube, walking in all directions, somehow not crashing into one another. As we did, the tightness in my stomach eased, like the restaurant was exerting some kind of gravitational force.

"At some point, you ******* *****, you're going to have to face up to what you did," said the voice.

"Please, leave me alone," I whispered.

"No."

We made our way down the pier. Pirate Golf where we were meeting you was past all the rides and concessions, right at the end. The voice cursed at me the whole way, kept up a barrage of insults, like:

******** *********** you ********* ******** yourself ******* ****** ********* ******* die ******* ******* ******** such a ******* ******** ***** ******** ********* ********

I tried to concentrate on what I was passing:

The basketball stand where I had worked.

The Haunted Hovel.

A Dippin' Dots concession.

A mom and dad swinging their toddler between them.

The Twister.

A guy smoking a cigarette and talking loudly into a cell phone.

The Hurricane.

You, playing a little old-fashioned electric organ, while a mechanical monkey on top of it danced.

A knock-down-the-tin-cans game.

The entrance to the—

Wait.

I stopped, grabbed Paris's arm and turned around. People had gathered around you, watching attentively. You were playing that Adele song, I think, the one about finding someone new. A guy in a football jersey called out, "'Hey Jude,'" and you nodded, then segued into the Beatles song. Laughing and clapping from the audience.

Someone else, a girl, shouted, "'Roar.'"

"What, the Katy Perry song?" you asked.

"Yes!"

You smiled, and your fingers tripped from "Hey Jude" to the opening verse of "Roar" before building up to the big chorus, the song sounding weird in the piped tones of the organ.

I took a step forward. You hadn't seen me; you were looking down at the keys. Your playing was amazing—you were riffing on the tune, improvising, every note perfect. My mom made me take piano lessons twice a week till I was eleven, and I knew how hard it was to play like that.

"'Smells Like Teen Spirit,'" I said.

You looked up and grinned. Then you crashed into the opening chords, deliberately abrupt, breaking off the Katy Perry song. You played the whole thing, people swaying and linking arms, then raised your hands. The clockwork monkey stopped dancing instantly. He was dressed in a red suit, a hat on his head, like the one in our hall at home.

"I'm out," you said. An old guy stepped up behind you. He was dressed in coattails and a bow tie, with a neat vest, a gold watch hanging from his pocket. He looked like a carny from a hundred years ago, totally out of place among the roller coasters and concessions stands. You nodded to him, leaving the organ.

The old guy sat down carefully on the little stool. I could sense the disappointment in the crowd. A couple of people started to shift away.

"Sorry, y'all," said the old man in a Deep South accent. "Back to the classics now."

He flexed his fingers above the keyboard. Then he brought them slamming down, the ancient organ blasting out the intro to "Born in the U.S.A." by Bruce Springsteen. Laughter rippled through the crowd, and those who had been leaving turned around to watch again.

"Hey," you said, joining us.

"Hey," said Paris. "This is Julie."

"Hi, Julie," you said.

"Hi," said Julie.

"Hi," I said, IN SCINTILLATING DIALOGUE REMINIS-CENT OF THE CLASSIC MOVIE *CASABLANCA*.

"This is surreal," said Paris. Behind us, the old guy was playing Kanye West.

"That's Cletus," you said. "I don't know if that's his real name. He lets me play when he's on break. He's like eighty years old, and he smokes forty a day." You glanced at our passes, mine and Paris's. "VIPs, huh?" you said.

"On account of her dad," said Paris.

"'Cause of the restaurant?"

"Yeah. They treat Cass like she's royalty."

You looked at me with a faint smile. "Really?" you said. I couldn't tell if you were teasing or not. Like, implying that it was strange anyone would do such a thing.

"Seriously. Roll with Cass in this place, and you're *money*."

"Why are you talking like that?"

"I don't know," said Paris. "I literally don't know what I'm saying half the time."

I was feeling left out; but then you turned to me and smiled. "Your friend is not getting any less weird."

"No."

"Will she?"

"No," said Julie. "Never."

"Oh well."

"I'm right here, guys," said Paris. "Jeez."

"That's not going to stop us," said Julie.

Paris made a face. "Come. Follow me to the golf course. I can see it over yonder." She put a hand to her forehead like an old-time ship captain. "'Tis either a long way off or uncommon small. Perhaps both."

She strode off toward the miniature golf course, humming Nirvana, Julie at her side. Paris said something to Julie and they both laughed, loud. I felt a pang of left-outness.

But then, I was walking with you. And that gave me a good, fizzy feeling in my stomach. Which was nice.

"You're good," I said, and then immediately felt like an ass. "At the piano, I mean. The organ. Whatever."

"Thanks."

"Are you in a band?" I asked.

Something crossed your face, a shadow, or a flock of birds, and then it was gone. "No," you said.

"You should be."

You smiled, but I thought there was something fake about it. "It's just a party trick," you said. "Anyway, let's go. Shane's waiting at the mini golf. I mean, he's supposed to be. For all I know he's drunk a six-pack already and passed out at home again. The lifeguards get off earlier. In both senses of the term."

"Ha," I said. It came out too sarcastic, and you frowned.

Dammit, Cass.

That was me. The voice was silent as ever when you were around.

As we walked, you nudged me with your elbow. "You on Facebook?" you said. "I looked you up, but I couldn't find you."

He looked me up on Facebook?

"No," I said. There is no point in social media when you don't socialize.

"Twitter? Instagram?"

"No." Twitter? Too much like voices in your head. So many people's voices, never shutting up.

That's what I was thinking, but all I *said* was no. It probably came out too abrupt. You went silent.

Pirate Golf was close. We caught up with Paris and walked over there, and Shane waved from the entrance. "Hey!" he said. "Cassandra. How's it going?"

"Okay, thanks," I said.

"I'm Shane," said Shane, to Paris.

"I'm Paris," said Paris, to Shane.

"Ah," said Shane. "The City of Romance." He pronounced it like that, with the capital *C* and the capital *R*. He was looking at Paris with a slightly stunned expression, at her long legs and her wide eyes.

"Nope," said Paris. "Wrong name. Easy mistake. I'm Paris as in Texas. The City of SUVs. And fat people."

"Huh," said Shane. He struggled for a riposte. "Bummer," he said eventually.

Paris winked at me and laughed.

"I'm Julie, by the way," said Julie, in a sarcastic tone.

"Oh, hey, Julie," said Shane, but you could tell he wasn't really interested.

"Hey, Shane," said Julie, flatly.

Paris clapped her hands. "Let's play," she said.

"I get the feeling she's always playing," you whispered to me.

"Yep," I said. "Me too."

Paris and I showed our VIP passes, and you and Shane showed your employee IDs, which was kind of unnecessary given you were in your denim-shirt uniform with the radio clipped to the V where your chest— And I looked at your chest and you saw and oh the *embarrassment* of it—and Shane was in his red lifeguard shorts and a white T-shirt with the Piers logo on it, and Julie just kind of said, "I'm with them," and the kid behind the counter gave us sticks and a ball, a different color for each of us. "There's a family on hole one," he said. "Just wait two minutes and you can go."

Is it sticks? I'm hopeless with sports, even mini golf.

I'm going to look it up. I'm on my dad's computer, by the way. I never said that. I'm in the study, surrounded by bugs, the tanks glowing. It's kind of peaceful. The keyboard is old though and heavy and the keys make an annoyingly loud clicking sound. Then that sometimes gets the bugs going, and they click back at me. I don't know which ones click—the beetles, maybe.

This room used to be where my mom would sew. I haven't told you that either. She was a dressmaker—she had mannequins in here, measuring tapes, an old Singer sewing machine. Patterns and scissors; fabrics on rolls; it was like a treasure shop. Mostly she didn't make stuff outright—women would bring her expensive dresses though, which they'd bought from Bergdorf Goodman in New York or whatever, and she would alter them so they fitted *perfectly*. Those women loved her for that: I could see it in their eyes, the joy when they saw themselves in the long mirror Mom had hung on the wall.

Dad kept it all for two years, after she died. The mannequins, everything. Then one day I came downstairs and it was all gone, and his bugs, which had been in the basement, were all along the walls. He also put in a safe, and bought a handgun—for protection, he said. After Mom died, he was obsessed with protection. With keeping us safe. Only I never felt very protected; I felt mostly the opposite, like his anger was the biggest threat. It was like living with a black bear.

Anyway.

I didn't like his redecorating the room and filling it with insects and a gun, but I never said anything. It was like she was finally gone, even from the house. Like, before that, if the house had a mouth, the house would have said it missed her too, because it was still filled with objects that belonged to her, like memories in a mind. You know?

Anyway.

I did look it up. It's not a stick, it's a club. A golf club.

Okay, so we got the clubs and went around the course, but of course you were there, you know all this already. We laughed; we had fun. We chipped our balls up into a pirate ship, along the rigging, off a plank and into shark-infested waters. We tapped them up spiral slides and over ramps to clear rivers. We made clocks chime and windmills turn.

Shane tried desperately to hook up with Paris, and she gave weird answers to his questions until he gave up and just started acting normal instead, which was much less annoying. After a while he even tried to hit on Julie for a bit, but he dropped that pretty fast when it was obvious it was going nowhere.

You spoke to me. You spoke to me about the town you grew up in, twenty miles away, and how there was nothing to do there, no way to make money in the summer—just a general store and a gas station and a bunch of farmland that no one could earn a living from.

You spoke to me about how you wanted to go to college; the

books you loved. Which were mostly the books *I* loved, and that was cool. I had noticed you, the very first time I saw you. But the more I spoke to you, the more I realized *why* I had noticed you. Does that make any sense?

"I'm on an old-texts kick," you said. "Now that I've finished the Ovid. I'm on the *Epic of Gilgamesh*. It's Babylonian, the oldest written work in—"

"It's Sumerian, actually," I said.

You rolled your eyes. "Geek," you said.

"Hey," I said. "You're reading it. I'm just correcting your elementary errors. There are Babylonian versions, but the Sumerian came first."

You made a face. "Speaking of which," you said, "I don't think the ball is supposed to go in the *actual* water. You aim for that painted ocean there; see the track up the octopus's tentacle?" My ball had gone flying over the fence ringing the course, and presumably had landed on the beach below.

"Bite me," I said.

"Don't worry," you said. "It's a complex game."

I stuck out my tongue at you.

We talked for hours, it felt like. The voice said nothing at all; the voice couldn't get past the force field that was you.

It was nice.

I know, I know, that's the lamest thing I could possibly say, but you have to understand, for me it was major. I mean, hanging with Paris was weird, and fun, but the voice was always there, somewhere—hanging on the edge of things like a dark bat—and it took a lot of energy, being with her, even when the voice was silent.

Being with you though . . . being with you was nice. And not just because the voice wasn't there. I want you to know that.

As we walked back down the boardwalk, we passed another basketball stall—the racks of plush toys, the little hoops and child-sized balls. People think the whole thing is gamed, that the hoops are too small for the ball, or that the stallman bends them or something to make the angle impossible. But they don't. It's just hard.

Paris stopped. "Competition," she said.

"What?" said Shane.

The stall was being run by a pimply kid in the same blue shirt that you wore to work, with a leather jacket over it two sizes too big. "You playing?" he said. "Five dollars, three shots."

"Yes," said Paris. She reached into her purse.

"We are?" you said.

"Yep," said Paris. "All of us. Best shot wins . . . I don't know. Pride, or something."

"You get a toy," said the kid behind the counter. He held out a ball to Paris.

"What size?" said Paris.

"Make one shot, get a small one. Two shots, medium; three shots—"

"Large?" said Paris.

"Yeah."

"Shocker," said Paris.

The kid rolled his eyes.

"I work in the plush warehouse," you said. "I can get a stuffed toy whenever I want."

"Winning one is different," said Paris.

"Tell me about it," said Julie. "I've never won anything in my life."

"Don't be defeatist," said Paris.

"Well, I'm up for it," said Shane. He was kind of bouncing on his toes. He wanted to impress Paris. She wasn't even looking at him.

She lined up her ball and threw it; it bounced off the rim and the kid caught it. Smoothly, I have to say. He didn't look sporty, but he'd been behind that counter for a month maybe. I knew the feeling.

Paris missed her next two shots too, and then Shane stepped forward and sank his first ball beautifully, straight down through the hoop. He missed the next two though and chose a bunny rabbit Beanie Baby. He handed it to Paris, and she clutched it to her chest, with her two Elmos. "My hero," she said.

"Uh, okay," said Shane, like he didn't know if she was insulting him or not. It was sometimes hard to tell with Paris.

You took your first ball. "I suck at ball games," you said.

"Excuses," said Paris.

"Sucking is not an excuse. It's just sucking. I'm not trying to hide anything."

Paris frowned. "Yeah, acknowledged. I take it back."

"Good," you said, and Paris laughed, and I laughed, because I was glad, I was glad you and her were clicking, even if somewhere deep down I had a worry that went, *What if he likes her more than he likes you?*

You shot: missed.

Missed again.

Missed again.

"Said I sucked," you said.

"You were not lying," said Paris. "Cass. You're up."

Maybe it was the kid who made me do it. I don't know. The way he patronized me. I mean, he handed me the ball and he said, "You might want to come a bit closer. The hoops are higher than they look."

I raised my eyebrows. He had a month on that stall; I had two whole summers. I got the ball up on my palm, rolled it off my fingers as I laid it up, and it back-spun in an arc that just happened to send it sailing over the kid's head, and it fell through the hoop with a *hush*.

Nothing but net.

"You done this before?" said the kid.

"Yep."

I spun the next ball on my finger and then let it settle in my hand.

Hush.

Two.

Hush.

Three.

"So . . . ah . . . you get to choose a big one," said the kid.

Paris started to say something, behind me, some innuendo, but Julie got in quick, said, "Nuh-uh. Don't even think about it."

"Spoilsport," said Paris.

"What do you want?" asked the kid. He gestured at the big toys on the top shelf.

"I don't know," I said. "What do you recommend?"

"What do I recommend? Out of the plush kiddies' toys?"

"Yes."

He shrugged. "Cookie Monster, I guess."

"I like cookies," you said.

"Perfect," I said. I reached out, took the Cookie Monster the kid handed me. It was surprisingly heavy, and furry. It's funny how holding a toy like that gives you a momentary feeling of warmth, of comfort, even though you're not small anymore. I handed it to you.

"For me?" you said.

"You like cookies. There you go."

"Oh wow," said Paris. "Now it's Jersey Official."

"What?" said Julie.

"She's from out of town," said Paris.

"So are you," I said.

Paris waved this away like it was an unimportant detail; small print.

"*What?*" said Julie.

"When a guy wins a toy for a girl on the boardwalk, that's like the sign that they're, you know, together," said Shane.

"Shut up, it's not," I said, feeling myself going red. Even though I knew it totally was.

Awkward.

"Anyway, she's not a guy," you said. "She's . . . a girl." But you had hesitated too long—Paris caught it. Hell, even I caught it, and I'm not exactly experienced with this stuff. The pause. The inflection on "girl."

"She certainly is," said Paris. "You've noticed that, huh?"

Double awkward.

"Shut up," I said again. I was waiting for the voice to chime in, to tell me that I was imagining this vibe anyway, this idea that you might be interested in me, but then I remembered that you were there, so the voice wouldn't speak.

You lifted the Cookie Monster, pushed it between me and Paris. "Excuse me," you said, in the Cookie Monster's voice. "I'm hungry. I want cookies."

Paris smiled. "No cookies. This is Jersey, land of the funnel cake."

You nodded. "Funnel cake it is, oh courageous leader."

"I should think so," said Paris. "But first, Julie's turn."

"No, no," said Julie. "I told you, I never—"

"—win anything, I know," said Paris. "Still." Julie sighed and stepped up. She took the balls and she barely tried, she just threw them kind of randomly. She didn't win anything. I have to say, she didn't look at home there, competing for a plush toy at a concession stand in an amusement park. I felt a flash of irritation at Paris for humiliating her like this. I mean, Julie had tattoos all down her arms and was wearing a pleated fifties skirt with a Replacements T-shirt. This was *not* her scene.

"See?" said Julie, as the last ball pinged off the board and went flying. "It's like a curse."

"What is?" you said. You'd been chasing Shane with the Cookie Monster a moment before, growling; you'd missed the part before.

"I never win anything," said Julie. "Like, not even scratch cards. *Never.*"

"That sucks," you said.

Julie did an eye-shrug. "Whatever." She started walking, and we followed.

Your cell rang and you looked at it, then at us. "My dad," you said. "Save some funnel cake for me." You answered the phone. "Hi, Dad. Yeah, I'm at work. Yeah, I've been practicing. Yeah, listen . . ."

You walked off a little distance, head down, talking low and intently into the phone.

"Funnel cake, yes?" Julie said. There was a funnel stall a bit farther down—we could see it.

"Yep," said Paris.

You put your hand over the bottom of your phone. "Save some for—"

"You, I know," I shouted back.

You nodded, pleased, and turned away again. "Yeah, Dad, I know, I'm—"

I stopped eavesdropping, and walked on.

Fell into step beside Julie.

"Not even a spelling bee?" I asked, as we walked.

"Huh?"

"You said you didn't ever win anything."

Julie shook her head. "I am a born loser," she said.

"What about you, Shane?" Paris asked. "Won anything?"

"Well, yeah," he said. "Like, football trophies."

"And him?" she gestured back to you, still on your phone.

"Oh yeah," said Shane. "He has a shelf of the things."

"My brother's the same," said Julie. We were in line for funnel cakes now. The smell was amazing. "Growing up, he was always winning that stuff. You know, those little pedestal things with statues of guys on them, swinging a baseball bat or diving or whatever. His room was full of them. I always . . ."

"Yeah?" said Shane. I felt like I had underestimated him. He looked genuinely interested, I mean, interested in the story.

"I don't know. I just wanted *one*, you know? Just one." She rolled her eyes. "I don't know why. They were stupid, those little statues."

"Give us all of your funnel cake," said Paris, reaching the front of the line.

"I've got like a ton," said the redheaded girl in the stall.

"Give us five of your funnel cakes."

"Five dollars," said the girl, handing over a bag.

For a long moment we just ate funnel cake. When I say "we" ate it, I mean the others, not me, because of my allergy. I miss out on all the fun. Major understatement!

Paris said it was good. I mean, you know that anyway. I don't know why I'm telling you. Funnel cake is good. Alert the President and the Joint Chiefs.

Anyway.

"But you might still win a trophy," said Paris, to Julie.

"What?" said Julie.

"Roller derby," said Paris. "You guys are in the final, no?"

"Oh. Yeah. But you get, like, a certificate."

"No trophy?" said Shane.

"No."

"Dude. That *sucks*," said Shane. He was serious. I kind of fell in love with him a bit in that moment. I mean, in a platonic way. I knew now why the two of you were friends, even though you were so different. He would never be reading Ovid, that was for sure.

Julie brushed some powdered sugar from her T-shirt. "If we win a certificate, I'll be happy," she said. "At least that's something."

"So, roller derby?" said Shane. "What are you, a jammer or a blocker?"

"You know it?"

"Yeah, my sister . . ."

The two of them strolled on, chatting about roller derby. The two unlikeliest people to be talking to each other. The jock and the punk. It was like a Benetton ad or something.

And you were still talking on the phone, like twenty feet behind, pretty intensely. Now I've met your dad, of course, and I know a bit more about you, so I get why, but at the time it seemed strange.

Which left me and Paris.

"What was that?" I said.

"What?"

"That whole deal with the basketball. You know I worked one of those stalls. You knew I'd be good."

"No. But I figured you might be."

"So?"

"So what?"

"So what was the deal?"

"With what?" she asked. She seemed truly bemused.

"With me and . . . him. Now he'll be feeling, I don't know, emasculated. He lost. I won."

Paris smiled so wide it was like her face splitting. Only nice. Okay, ignore that simile. Let's leave it at: she smiled wide. "Please," she said. "If he was feeling that, then he wouldn't be the guy for you. And now the tone has been set, you know, for your relationship. You won him a Cookie Monster. Now he's your bitch. Not the other way around. I think St. Thomas of Aquinas said that."

"Our *relationship*?"

"Come on. You're seriously crushing. Even after an hour I can see that. And the whole deal with rushing to the side of the pier when you saw his truck?"

"I'm not—" I started to say.

"Whatever," said Paris, waving a hand. "Anyway, he's cute. Not the other one, Shane. The troglodyte."

"He's actually quite—"

"Yeah, yeah, I'm sure he's an angel. But anyway, your guy? I approve."

"Oh good," I said. "What would I have done otherwise?"

"Not gone out with him, obviously," said Paris.

"You're serious, aren't you?"

"Of course," said Paris. "What, you've never had anyone look out for you before? Someone has to watch out for a person. For you, that's me. Okay. That was inelegantly phrased. I am not on fire today. If I am a fire, I am officially out. I am, what would you say? I am damp."

"*Damp*?"

"Like wood that won't catch, you know? That's how not on fire I am."

I couldn't help it, I laughed. "Well, thanks," I said. "For watching out for me."

"Of course. And now he has passed my stringent tests."

"By acting cool when I won him a Cookie Monster?"

"Indeed."

We sped up, to catch you and the others. You were off the phone now and eating your funnel cake. It left a white sugar smile around your real smile.

"Seriously, has *anyone* been looking after you?" asked Paris as we approached. "Your dad . . ."

"It's complicated," I said.

"He hurts you?"

"No! God, no. No, he just . . . it's complicated."

"You said."

"Yeah."

She linked her arm through mine. "Well, I'm here now. And I will keep you safe. I'll be, like, your tooth fairy, watching over you."

"I think you mean fairy godmother," I said.

"Yeah," said Paris, shaking her head. "I felt it even as I was saying it. Not my A game."

I smiled.

"Hey," said Paris. "You look nice when you smile."

"I don't usually smile?"

"No," said Paris.

An uncomfortable silence.

"Oh," I said.

"Well," said Paris, after a while. "We've only just met. I mean, relatively recently. We have our whole lives ahead of us. Whole lives of smiling and fun."

False statement.

I paid for the fun, it goes without saying.

We got home about eleven, and Dad wasn't home yet. There were no lights on. You and Shane said good night, then went up to your apartment. Shane was nudging you with his elbow, whispering to you, and you whispered fiercely back at him. I thought . . . I thought maybe he was telling you to make a move.

I hoped.

But you didn't make a move. You followed him up, and disappeared through the door.

I put my hand to my pocket where I usually kept my keys—

No keys.

Oh yeah.

"You're locked out," said the voice.

"Uh, yes," I said. "Because I wasn't allowed to take keys."

"You'll have to wait for your dad."

"He'll ground me. I have a curfew."

"Yes. That was the point of the exercise."

"You wanted to get me grounded?"

"I wanted to *get* you."

I sat down on the porch step and closed my eyes. "I thought . . ." I hesitated, amazed at the weirdness that had become normal in my life. "I thought we were getting along well," I said. It sounded crazy even to me.

"You're having too much fun," said the voice. "It's time you realized that I am the ****** boss around here and what I say goes. And you forgot the date."

"The date?"

"Think about it."

I did. Oh, Jesus. August 7. It was the day . . . the day . . .

"You ****** forgot, Cass. You *forgot.*"

"I didn't mean . . . I just . . ."

"You disgust me. You are a ****** disgrace. I am going to ruin your life. I am going to break you. You are nothing."

There was wetness on my cheeks; I touched them with my fingers, felt the tears. I didn't mean to, I wanted to say, I didn't even think, I didn't say anything to Dad, didn't mention it this morning at breakfast, and no wonder he was acting so weird and quiet when he was making pancakes.

I put my head in my hands, then I saw movement in the window of your apartment, and a moment later the door opened.

"Cass?" you called.

"Yeah."

"You locked out?"

"Yeah."

"Come up. We're watching a movie. Some trash about a shark fighting an octopus. It's *awesome*."

I thought for a second. At least the voice would go, if I was with you.

I climbed the steps, and you opened the door wide for me.

"You okay?" you asked.

I nodded. "I got locked out."

"But you've been crying."

"I was upset about being locked out."

You gave me a sympathetic look mingled with doubt. "Well, I'm sure your dad will be back soon," you said.

That's the problem, I thought. But I didn't say anything. You ushered me in. You'd turned it into a dump, the two of you. Pizza boxes everywhere, stacked like Jenga. Beer cans, take-out menus. Clothes hanging from furniture to dry, or maybe just to hang there, I don't know.

"It's a mess," you said. "Sorry."

I shrugged. "Not my apartment. But don't let Dad see it."

"He doesn't come up here."

"He might."

Shane, who was standing in the door to the living room, made an exaggerated scared face. "We'd better clean tomorrow," he said.

"I can do it," I said.

You frowned at me. "You want to clean our apartment?"

"I like cleaning," I said. Also I didn't like my bedroom, I mean the voice was always so *loud* there, and it had been better in the apartment. There were less memories there. *Fewer* memories. Damn autocorrect, underlining my words in green. "I can do it when you're at work, the two of you."

"Seriously, Cass, it's gross, you can't—"

"I don't mind."

"I say let her," said Shane. "We can pay you in beer."

"I don't drink."

"Pizza."

"My dad owns a pizza restaurant."

"Money."

I thought for a second. "No. Books. Bring me books from the library. I'll keep this place clean. Okay?"

You looked at me. "You can't get books from the library?"

"No."

You seemed confused by this. Of course *now* you understand why. "Uh, deal," you said.

We went into the living room and watched the movie. It was stupid and also, as you'd said, awesome. I was sitting next to you on the couch. I could feel you, feel your leg next to mine, even though there was four inches of air between our skin, and clothes. It was still like we were touching, like our bodies were magnets, held close to each other—something in our molecules vibrating; buzzing.

There was a crunch of tires on gravel.

"Oh no," I said. "Dad."

I jumped up; ran to the door and pulled it open, started down the steps. I was on the bottom one when Dad looked up, his hand on the door of the Dodge as he closed it. He looked at me silently. Then he walked toward the door of the house. I thought: *Maybe he's going to go easy on me. Maybe he's going to give me a break.*

I followed him, and he stayed silent as he held the door for me, just like you had done an hour before with the door to the apartment, but also so very differently.

"Dad—"

"No, Cass. Don't ****** even. What were you doing?"

"I forgot my key and—"

"You went out? At night? When you have a ***** mental illness and there's a ****** guy killing ****** women in this town?"

"I—"

"I don't care. And you went up there? When we've had a RULE, Cass, a goddamn RULE, since you were twelve ****** years old, that you don't go in the apartment when it's boys renting. What were you thinking?"

"I don't know," I said.

He put his hand out and clasped it around my arm, tight enough to make me gasp. "On THIS ****** day of all days? THIS day? Did you even remember it was the anniversary? You have to be ****** kidding me. You don't leave this ****** house again after sunset, do you hear me?"

"Yes."

He shook his head. "Upstairs," he said.

I started up the stairs. "Are you having fun now?" said the voice.

That night, I lay on my bed and imagined that I was a bird, flying above Oakwood. Same view as on the Ferris wheel. Looking down on the sudden small beauty of the town, embracing it with the outstretch of my wings, untethered from the ground.

Floating.

Inhuman trajectory and lift: carried higher by updraft of warm air, no effort at all, wings arched above me. The houses and streets dwindling, forming into fractal patterns, dissolving into distant abstractions of light; the dark mass of the ocean.

Floating on the air. Freed from all movement and decay, freed from the voice, blessed with a new perspective. The place where birds live: the same world but different, in the mirror of the sky, inverse to us as death is to life, hovering in the spaces where our roofs and cars and towers aren't; in the gaps; in the blue brightness; a kind of heaven.

DR. LEWIS: So things have regressed.

ME: (nods)

DR. LEWIS: But you deployed the strategies we talked about. The welcoming. Scheduling.

ME: Yes.

DR. LEWIS: And things improved?

ME: Yes.

DR. LEWIS: But now they're worse again.

ME: (nods)

DR. LEWIS: Has anything happened? Anything that might have triggered a return of the trauma?

ME: (Thinks about the restaurant. *Blood*. Dad getting home and finding me in the apartment. *Tiles*. Me forgetting Mom's day.) No.

DR. LEWIS: What does the seventh of August mean to you?

ME: (looks up sharply, breathes hard) What?

DR. LEWIS: The seventh of August. It's a date. What does it mean to you?

ME: Are you . . . What the . . . I . . .

DR. LEWIS: It's the day your mother died, I think?

ME: How do you . . .

DR. LEWIS: The Internet.

ME: Oh.

DR. LEWIS: It's also two days ago.

ME: Yes.

DR. LEWIS: Do you think that might have something to do with your regression?

ME: (cries)

DR. LEWIS: Here. (He hands over a box of tissues.)

THE VOICE: Are you crying again, you ******* pathetic
               piece of ****? All of this is your fault. You did
               it. I died, and you did nothing to—

DR. LEWIS: You said the voice was a woman's. An adult
               woman's?

ME: (nods)

DR. LEWIS: You have any theories about that?

ME: (shrugs) It might be the voice of one of the
               . . . one of the prostitutes that was killed.
               Wanting me to, you know, solve the murder.

ME: (Watches, carefully. Having said this fake-
               casually. Wanting to see what he makes of it.)

DR. LEWIS: Right.

ME: It adds up, huh? A woman. Speaking after I
               find the foot . . . wanting revenge. Wanting
               justice. Maybe that's where I come in. To . . .
               to get him. To make him pay.

DR. LEWIS: Maybe.

ME: You think I'm crazy, don't you?

DR. LEWIS: I certainly don't think that.

ME: But you think I'm deluded.

DR. LEWIS: No, I think you're . . . hiding from certain
               things.

ME: Hiding from what?

DR. LEWIS: You say your role is to find the killer. What
               have you done to further that goal?

ME: Um.

DR. LEWIS: Anything? Any progress at all?

ME:	I read some books. About him. About other serial killers.
DR. LEWIS:	(significant pause)
ME:	Okay, so I have been busy with other things.
DR. LEWIS:	Busy? Did you get a job?
ME:	(pause) No.
DR. LEWIS:	I have a theory. Do you want to know what it is?
ME:	No, but I have a feeling you're going to tell me anyway.
DR. LEWIS:	My theory is that this notion of yours, about the voice being one of the murdered women . . . it's a distraction. Pure and simple. That's why you've done nothing about it. So let's think about other adult women. Other women the voice could represent.
ME:	Like who?
DR. LEWIS:	Your mother was an adult woman.
THE VOICE:	TEAR OUT YOUR ******** EYES, YOU ******.

ME: (head reeling, roiling, a receptacle for liquid, set spinning, detached from my body and sliding around on a smooth
   tiled
   floor—my mind revolving, finding no purchase on the slippery
   tiles,
   and that's really what it feels like; like my body is gone and I'm just a head, with eyes that for some reason are seeing a static image of the Doc sitting on his chair, the blank walls, the coffee dispenser

and the cookies on the table, while my head itself is rolling uncontrollably, unstoppably, on that

tiled

floor)

THE VOICE: (SCREAMING INCOHERENTLY, A KLAXON
OF ANGER AND CURSING AND JUST, JUST, JUST
AWFULNESS)

I put my hands over my eyes and my head between my knees. I
took deep, long breaths. There is an expression—my mind was
spinning. Usually it's just an expression. But that was what was
actually happening. My mind was a whirligig; I felt sick.

DR. LEWIS: Cass?

I looked up. I wanted this feeling to stop, I wanted to never feel
like this again. "What are you . . . I mean . . . ," I said.

Dr. Lewis was looking scared, and at the same time—not
pleased, but like something he had been suspecting had been
confirmed. "The voice is very angry with you, is that right?"
he said.

"Tear out your throat," said the voice. "Tear it out, right now."

"Oh God," I said. "Help me."

"I'm trying to, Cassie," said the Doc. "It may not feel like it, but
I'm trying."

"It's not my mother!" I said. "The voice is not my mother!"

"Okay, okay. Take a deep breath." He paused while I panted,
trying to get my heartbeat under control. "We often find that people,
especially younger people, respond to trauma with anger. Perhaps
they feel angry with a person who abused them. Perhaps they feel
angry with someone for dying. But they are taught to hold that
anger in, that it is inappropriate to express it. So they turn it on
themselves. The voice begins to punish them."

"What are you saying?"

"I'm saying maybe you are angry with your mother for dying. Maybe the voice is an expression of that."

"I'm not angry with my mother."

"Not consciously, no, but it's possible that—"

THE VOICE: It's *you*. It's your fault. It's all you.

I stood up, quickly. My plastic chair fell, landed on its side, the thin metal legs sticking out like it was a wounded animal.

"It's ME," I shouted. "It's ME, okay? I'm not angry with my mom for dying. I'm angry with me. It was MY FAULT, okay? Don't you understand? I KILLED HER."

I killed her.

Me.

Stupid, disgusting me.

In my memory there's a jump cut.

One moment I'm standing there screaming, and then, without seeming to cross the intervening space, without seeming to operate as a body in a physical universe, requiring time to move from one point to another, the next moment the doctor has his arms around me and is holding me.

Holding me.

Do you know something?

It was the first time someone had held me for three years. Dad had never, Dad had never, Dad had never—

My thoughts were a storm. A maelstrom. A whirlpool. Charybdis.

My dad never—

It was me—

I KILLED HER.

My breath was hitching in my chest; I was not a body but just lungs and a mind, a pounding heart. I was broken into pieces, like Echo, like Orpheus, torn into my constituent organs and pieces.

Sparagmos.

I was all over the floor, scattered.

"It's going to be okay," said Dr. Lewis, over and over again. "This is a breakthrough. This is a breakthrough."

But it didn't feel like a breakthrough.

It felt like a break.

Like I was broken.

"I have to go," I said. My whole being felt like a slept-on hand; tingling, filled with pain.

"I don't think that's wise. I think you need—"

"*I have to go.*"

"You shouldn't be alone at this point," he said. "This is a very sensitive time. Perhaps your dad could pick you up?" He was standing back from me now, one pace, his hands on my arms. The parts of me that had fallen all over the floor had started to knit back together again.

"Are you ******* kidding me?" I asked.

"He's at work?"

"*No!* He *knows* I killed her! Don't you see? He *knows.* That's why he hates me."

"You think your father hates you?"

"No."

"Good, because—"

"I know he hates me."

"Cass . . ."

"It was *my fault.* Why are you not understanding that? He knows it, the same as me."

He shook his head. His gray hair rippled. "I know you feel like that, but—"

"But it's true. Now let me go."

He withdrew his hands, quickly, like I was burning. "At least call Paris," he said. "Have her come be with you."

I opened my mouth to say something angry, then stopped. "Yeah, okay," I said. I took out my cell and dialed. It rang for a long time, and I was about to hang up when Paris answered.

"Hey," she said flatly. Distantly. At any other time I would have wondered what was wrong.

"It's Cass."

"I know." Her voice still not quite there. Absent, somehow coming from someone or somewhere else. A ventriloquist's dummy, talking to me.

"What are you doing?" I asked.

"Nothing. Just had a bad time doing a party, that's all."

I realized I hadn't even asked her what was wrong; but she'd answered anyway; she'd assumed I'd asked. That was how much of a selfish asshole I was.

"Sorry," I said.

A sound like a shrug made of air. "It happens," she said.

"Did they hurt you?"

"No, Cass. No. Not . . . physically."

"Good. I know Julie worries that—"

"I'm fine, Cass."

"Good. That's good. But I mean, are you sure? Because you sound kind of—"

"Look just ****** leave it, okay, Cass?" Her voice had a sudden coldness in it I had never heard before, like the coldness of stone; sharp-edged, mineral, angry but distant at the same time. Somehow . . . not human. It's hard for me to describe. All the time I'd known her I'd never seen her as someone with . . . issues, you know? Despite what she said about her drugs and her therapy and whatever, she seemed so together.

That was the first time I saw another shape underneath her, the contours of a troubled mind.

A pause.

"I'm sorry," I said. "I shouldn't have called but . . . but, Paris, I need you," I said, all in a rush. "Please, I really—"

I *heard* her snap into the real world. Like a penknife closing. "Where are you, Cass?"

"At the bowling—"

"Ten minutes. I'll be there in ten minutes." She hung up.

I turned to Dr. Lewis. "She's coming. I'll wait for her outside."

Dwight the cop opened the door as I walked unsteadily toward it—he was always the first to arrive. Dr. Lewis looked torn for a moment, but then finally he nodded. I guess he had heard Paris's side of the conversation, so he knew I wasn't lying.

"Hey, Cass," said Dwight. "You joining group today?"

"Not today, Dwight," said the Doc.

"Hey, ****, you okay, Cass?"

"Yes. No. I don't know. I think I . . . realized something. About myself."

Dwight nodded slowly. His big, kind eyes were full of sympathy. "That's good, Cass," he said. He always used your name when he was talking to you. I think it was a trick he learned from the cops. "I mean, it doesn't feel good now. But it's good."

I nodded at him. I couldn't talk.

"I'll see you next week," he said. He was wearing a T-shirt that said NJPD SOFTBALL on it, under a crest.

I nodded again. Then I walked out of the hall and through the bowling alley, past the glowing lanes, the iridescent balls. And out onto the dusk-lit street. It was raining, softly, the droplets hanging in the air, almost seeming to rise up from the concrete; a cold steam, everywhere.

I started by leaning against the outside wall of the bowling alley, but my legs wouldn't hold me up.

I slumped down until I was sitting on the damp ground. It soaked through my pants, numbed my butt. I wished the mist would numb me all over.

Around me, the street shimmered. The mattress store on the other side, the 7-Eleven. The cheap hotel with the flashing sign: VACANCIES.

That was how I felt.

Like a vacancy.

At the same time, there was another scene superimposed on the street, bleeding into it. It was the restaurant, Donato's. The bar counter was over the bowling alley, the pizza oven was behind me; the tables with their red-and-white-checkered cloths were covering the street, the

tiles

were gleaming where concrete and asphalt should be. Ghost figures came and went; waiters, customers. Dad wasn't there— Dad was in New York, talking to a new tomato supplier, one who flew the tomatoes over from Tuscany. Mom and I were holding the fort, as he put it, running the Sunday night shift—I was taking orders and she was hosting, greeting people as they came in.

Dad didn't like leaving us alone. That was one of the worst things, one of the ways his fear and his foreboding ended up getting confirmed, ended up bricking him into the personality he started out with already.

He'd bought Mom a gun. A small pistol, two shots—a Derringer. I don't think it was legal, but he got it from some gun fair some-where. The idea of it was that you hid it in a sock or something.

Only she didn't like it, didn't like carrying it, and she didn't have it on her that day.

She left it in the restaurant safe, where she always left it.

Anyway. She was so beautiful. Dark hair pinned up, spilling out in wavy strands, a gray dress, no makeup. Everyone who came in was captivated by her; you could see it. I wanted to look like her one day. To move like her. To smile like her.

Then I was shaking Parmesan over a woman's amatriciana and I heard my mother gasp—you know how you recognize your parents' voices even when they don't say anything?

I turned around, and there were two guys standing just inside the door. They both wore ski masks. They were both big. One of them was holding a shotgun and the other a baseball bat. It happened so fast. Faster than your reading this. Faster than my typing it, and I type fast. I took an online course.

"Empty the register," said shotgun guy to Mom. She moved over to it, moved strangely, jerkily. She pressed the key to make it open but nothing happened; she must have gotten it wrong; her hands were shaking. She banged it with the side of her hand and the tray shot out. She started pulling out money. The guy closest to her, the one with the baseball bat, held out a bag—an ordinary plastic bag from a supermarket—and she stuffed the cash into it.

The other guy handed another bag to the diner closest to him. "Pass it around. Watches. Wallets," he said.

Everyone in the restaurant took off their watches, took out their wallets.

"And jewelry," said the guy.

Women started removing their earrings. Mom too. They were emeralds surrounded by diamonds, the only nice jewelry she owned; Dad bought them from Tiffany's for their ten-year anniversary. She nearly ripped them out of her ears and handed them over to the guy who had taken the cash.

Pretty soon the bag came back to the guys.

They turned, began to leave, took their eyes off Mom for a second.

Mom hit the button under the cash register, the panic button that Dad had insisted on installing, an alarm with a link to the local PD. I don't know why she did it.

Correction: I do know why she did it. Because times were tough, that's why. And the restaurant was barely breaking even. We couldn't afford to lose that money.

The alarm started blaring. The two men stopped, and their heads twisted to look at Mom. They didn't even say anything; they didn't shout or curse or anything like that—the one with the baseball bat just took a step toward her, and swung.

The bat struck the rear side of her head with a sound like an ax burying itself in a wooden log. She dropped instantly, as if a magician had removed her legs. She sprawled on the tiles. I started screaming then; I don't remember this, but it was in a lot of witness statements. I screamed and screamed and screamed. One of the cops we spoke to afterward said a diner had described it as the worst sound he had ever heard. Said he hadn't known a human being could make that noise.

The two guys left, running.

I moved, suddenly *able* to move.

Mom was lying on the white tiles. There was a halo of dark red blood around her head; her hair was matted. I knelt beside her— her eyes were open and staring, the eyeballs twitching, saccadic, as if she were reading something I couldn't see, something hanging in the air above her. I could see blood trickling from her nose. I couldn't see what had happened to the back of her head.

Apparently at this point I was screaming "Mom" over and over. I remember hearing someone dial 911 and ask for an ambulance.

And that's when I did it. I didn't realize. I swear I didn't realize. I just wanted to hold her, I just wanted to make her okay. I lifted her up into a hug, and I held her tight, calling in her ear, calling for her to come back to me.

I lifted her head off the ground.

Do you see?

I lifted her head off the ground.

Because I wanted to hold her.

She died of a massive subdural hematoma. That means her brain bled all over itself, drowned itself.

I know this because I looked up brain injuries, afterward.

That was where I learned that the last thing, the *last thing* you do, if someone suffers a head trauma, is to move them. It can disturb the bleed. Make it worse. Hell, I may even have *started* the bleed.

I never said anything to Dad. I mean, he knew already. He was a goddamn Navy SEAL. He knows all about injuries.

So we both knew I killed her. We just never said anything about it.

They never caught the two guys either. Dad searched for a while. He used his contacts—his cop buddies from the restaurant. But nothing ever came up.

Probably a good thing. If he'd found them, I'd have lost both my parents. He'd have ended up in prison.

There was a voice, and the street by the bowling alley began to reform itself around me, patchily. A scrap of concrete, a parking meter, the 7-Eleven, slowly reappearing out of the fog. A Polaroid, developing.

"—ambulance?" said the voice.

I looked up. There was a middle-aged woman standing over me, kind looking, with a fake Louis Vuitton purse and a long red coat. She looked like a housewife out to meet her lover. That may even have been what she was doing.

"Excuse me?" I said. I was coming to the realization that I was lying on the damp ground. It had stopped raining. But no more than a few minutes could possibly have elapsed—it was no darker than it had been when I left the bowling alley. The sky was still ablaze with the setting sun.

"Do you need an ambulance? Are you epileptic? Diabetic?"

I seized on this excuse for my weird behavior; anything is better than saying you hear a voice and someone has just pointed out that it is probably you internalizing your own mother, because you feel guilty about making her die.

"Just . . . need some sugar," I said.

I must not have looked like a meth head or a bum, because the woman nodded and ran across the road to the 7-Eleven. She came back with a candy bar, which she handed to me. "Here," she said.

At that moment I didn't think about my allergy at all; it was like it had been rinsed from my mind, washed away by the storm of memories. I just tore open the bar and ate it. Chocolate. With some kind of crunchy filling.

"Thanks," I said. I sat up, to show that I had more energy now. "Thank you so much. I'll be fine." I smiled, as best as I could.

"If you're sure . . ."

"I'm sure. Thank you though. Please, let me . . ." I started to take out my wallet. I kept it in my back pocket, with a chain to my belt loops.

"No, no," she said. "On me. I'm just glad you're okay."

I saw the crucifix around her neck now—a true Good Samaritan. "Thanks again," I said.

She nodded and walked off. I took a long breath. *Paris, where are you?* I thought.

Then my long breath caught in my chest, like my body had closed around it, vice-hard. I coughed. I coughed some more. I pursed my lips. My mouth was fizzing, tingling, electricity running through it. I *felt* my lips swelling. My tongue. My bronchioles were going to swell too, till I would no longer be able to take in any oxygen.

Till I would die.

Yep.

Just my luck.

Peanuts.

Paris parked and opened the door of her surprisingly ordinary sedan—a Prius I think—just as I was injecting myself with my EpiPen, counting down the elephants.

"What the—"

"Shh," I said. I finished counting. "—six elephants, seven elephants, eight elephants, nine elephants, ten elephants."

"Elephants?" said Paris, in a hysterical tone. Like she was freaking out but *hard*. She was fully human now, the stony tone gone from her voice, and I almost forgot about how she had been on the phone earlier; I had other stuff on my mind.

I was a terrible friend.

Anyway.

I took another deep breath. Better. No hitching in the chest. I took another.

Okay.

My airways were clearing. The epinephrine was doing its job. My mouth was still sore though.

"You count to ten," I said, as I massaged my thigh. "Because the spring keeps squeezing the drug through the needle. If you don't wait, you lose some of the injection. They teach you to count elephants, because it makes sure."

"What the **** happened?"

"A good Samaritan," I said.

"Huh?"

I shook my head. "Long story." I picked up my bag from the sidewalk—the shoulder bag I carried everywhere. It was green and had red writing embroidered onto it:

ALLERGIC TO PEANUTS!

CASSANDRA DI MATTEO

76 OCEAN DRIVE OAKWOOD

Mom had sewn it herself, and it was the lamest and least cool thing in the world, but I still carried it with me at all times and would have fought anyone who tried to take it from me, bare fists. I opened the bag and handed Paris my spare EpiPen. "Here: if I start struggling to breathe, give me that. Meanwhile, call an ambulance."

"Now?"

"Yes, now. Make sure it's a paramedic ambulance. Tell them I'm having an anaphylaxis and have injected myself with 0.3 of epinephrine. At . . ."—I checked my watch—"at about twenty past seven."

Paris made the call, then she sat down beside me. "This is why you called?"

"What? Oh. No. I called because . . . You know what, I can't . . . I can't."

"Sure," said Paris. "Sure. Let's just get you better."

"I'll be fine," I said. "But they'll want to keep me overnight."

We waited in silence for a moment.

"Want me to come with you?" asked Paris.

"Please."

"And your dad. You want me to call him?"

"Um . . . yes. Please. Wait."

"Yeah?"

"We need a story. I need a story." I thought for a moment. "Okay, so I was at your place. You made cookies. I ate one. Then we left to get sodas, and I had a delayed reaction. It can take two hours."

"I don't live very near here."

"He doesn't know that."

"And won't he be pissed with me for making you the cookies?"

"No. He'll be pissed with me for not checking. I'll say they were chocolate; that I wanted to be polite. Or something. He'll probably never let me leave the house again; he'll think I'm totally irresponsible. But hey."

"You can't tell him the truth? Whatever that is?"

"No."

Paris frowned at me. "He doesn't know about Dr. Lewis, does he?"

"No."

"Jeez, Cass. Way to set yourself up for a fall. Wait. Does your psych know?"

Silence from me.

"*Jeez*, Cass."

Paris dialed the number I gave her. It was a short conversation. What I could hear of it sounded like this:

PARIS: Hi, Mr. . . . Oh. Actually, I don't know Cass's last name. Hi, Mr. Cass's Dad.

DAD: *Kccccchhhhhh.*

PARIS: No, no! No, she's okay. I mean, she's not okay. I mean . . . ****. She's had a reaction. To nuts, you know? She stabbed herself with the thing . . .

DAD: *Kccccchhhhhh*

PARIS: (nodding) The EpiPen, yeah. Yes, she's breathing fine. No, it's totally my fault. I insisted she eat a cookie. I didn't realize.

DAD: *Kccccchhhhhh Kccccchhhhhh Kccccchhhhhh*

PARIS: Oh, no, yeah, no, she did tell me. But I didn't know how serious it was. (Raising her hands and eyebrows at me, like, *I'm trying!*)

DAD: *Kccccchhhhhh*

PARIS: Anyway, I've called an ambulance. We're going to City.

DAD: *Kccccchhhhhh Kccccchhhhhh*

PARIS: I will.

She hung up.

"Wow," she said to me. "That guy's tense. Anyone would think I was telling him that his daughter had suffered a potentially life-threatening allergic reaction."

I rolled my eyes at her, and she laughed.

"Seriously," I said, "is he pissed?"

"Hard to tell. He's jacked up though."

"Super," I said.

Paris started laughing again. I loved her for it.

Remember that:

I loved her.

Not like you, not *romantically*, but I loved her.

The ambulance came, and Paris rode in it with me all the way to the hospital. She was having the best time, now that I was clearly going to be all right. She flirted with Ben, the younger paramedic, and thought the banks of instruments were the *coolest*; she had never been in an ambulance before, she said.

Ben stuck tabs to the top of my chest and a clip to the end of my index finger. Then he watched my heartbeat on the screen. "107," he said. "Saturation 100."

"Good," said the guy I think was called Peter. He was older, with a mustache. "Looks like you won't need to be intubated," he said to me.

"Hooray," I said.

"I'm watching your heart on TV," said Paris, eyeing the jagged peaks and troughs of my pulse. "It's awesome."

"Your friend is a little strange," said Ben, smiling.

"People have commented," I said.

"Wouldn't you say that was a beautiful heartbeat?" said Paris. "Wouldn't you say Cass has a beautiful heartbeat?"

"Uh, yeah," said Ben.

Paris nodded, sagely. "She does," she said, as if it had been *his* idea, as if she was agreeing with him.

Ben started filling in a chart. "You on any medications?" he asked.

I glanced at Paris. "Yes," I lied. I knew my dad might see the chart, or someone might say something.

"Which ones?"

"Risperidone. Paroxetine."

I saw his face change. Or maybe I imagined that I did. But I think it did. I mean: I had just shifted in front of his eyes into a different person, like a movie morphing trick. I had gone from:

Reasonably cute but maybe a bit plump teenage girl → mental patient.

He wrote something down on his chart.

He didn't say anything after that. Nor did Paris. I think she sensed how he had swerved too, how his opinion of me had changed, and she was angry with him. Angry on my behalf.

And I loved her even more for that.

When we got to the hospital Dad was waiting outside and he spoke briefly to Paris, but he wasn't even looking at her, so she waved to me and kind of subtracted herself from the scene, backed away, until she was gone. And Dad and I went into the building with the paramedics.

DAD:	Are you *trying* to get yourself killed?
ME:	No!
DAD:	You know about food someone else has prepared. You *know* this stuff, Cass.
ME:	I do.
DAD:	Clearly you don't!
ME:	(silent)
DAD:	I have to work, Cass. I have to ******* work. I have to know you're going to be okay when I'm at the restaurant.
ME:	You do know that. You can know that.
THE VOICE:	You will never be okay. You will always be worthless.
ME:	Not now.
DAD:	Not *now*? Are you serious? Evidently I *can't* leave you on your own! If you're not with boys, you're having a ******* anaphylaxis, Cass! I can't ****** worry about you like this, it's ******* kill me.
PEDIATRICIAN:	Sir? This is a public ward. Could you lower your voice, sir?

So now you know.

Now you know about my mom, about how she died.

I don't . . .

I mean . . .

I guess I don't need to tell you much about how it made me feel. You know all about parents dying. You get it. I mean, I didn't know *that night* that your mom died, but I knew something had happened to her. And you told me later of course.

For a long time after the restaurant—this is even before I looked it up and found that I shouldn't have moved her head—I felt a whole range of different things, different emotions, no single feeling that could be identified as "grief."

I laughed at inappropriate ****. I laughed at the funeral, because we walked into the chapel and there was this little old lady at the back at this, like, raised mixing-desk thing, all knobs and lights and sliders to control the sound on the mikes at the front of the church, and I just started giggling hysterically because she looked like an octogenarian DJ, in a DJ booth.

My dad glared at me, then.

I felt okay for long periods, I forgot my mom was dead, and then it would hit me like a tidal wave, literally nearly knock me off my feet, the realization, the stupid simple realization, that she was gone and would never come back and we'd never make brownies again with peanut-free chocolate and lick the spoon.

I did that thing; I'm sure you did it too. That thing where I would go into my room and I'd see an album and I'd think, the last time I played that album my mom was still alive; I'd wear a T-shirt and I'd think, the last time I wore this T-shirt my mom was still alive; I'd pick up a book and—

You get the picture.

It sucked. I mean, you know all about it, right? One night I dreamed she was still alive and it was all a big mistake and she bent down low to fold me in her arms and then I woke up and—

Well. You know. I thought I might never stop crying that morning, like an ocean would come flooding out of me and I would disappear, just turn into a puddle on the floor, like some mutant in one of those comic book movies.

I dreamed about the robbers too. Daydreamed also. Fantasized about finding them and torturing them, choking the lives out of them. Making them feel a fraction of the pain I was feeling.

Every day, for like a month, I thought, *This is the day the cops will find them.*

But they didn't, and they didn't, and then . . . it was a year later, and the robbers were just gone. Like Keyser Söze, you know? Into the sea mist. Evaporated. Like they were never there.

The police kept saying they had leads, that it was only a matter of time, but I didn't believe them anymore. And time slipped by. Breakfasts, TV, books, school, assignments. All the stuff that just keeps chipping away, keeps happening to you, and that you have to engage with.

"Life goes on" would be the simpler way to say this. But I don't like those kinds of expressions; they're so old that they've gotten worn and faded, and they don't really convey what they're supposed to mean anymore. And it doesn't tell you anything. Life is always going on, for the living anyway.

Instead, what happens is that things accrete, tiny things, tiny experiences, going to the bathroom, doing makeup, getting dressed, walking places, and they end up covering the shape of the dead person, filling it in, like little bricks, tiny, until the hole is almost filled up and you realize that you're forgetting, and that makes you feel even worse.

I didn't want to feel bad anymore though.

And so . . .

Slowly . . .

Surely . . .

I just stopped myself from feeling stuff. From thinking about the killers, about justice, about revenge. I edited my memory. Deleted the part where I lifted her head, where I killed her.

Well.

I thought I had anyway.

It turns out that all I did was push this stuff way inside, tamp it down, squash it, until just like old shrimps and stuff got slicked into oil, far underground, the pain got transmuted into something black and liquid, running through the crevices of my mind.

The voice.

Four things happened after my unfortunate hospitalization with anaphylaxis:

1. Dad banned me from ever seeing Paris again.
2. Dad banned me from eating any food outside the house.
3. Dad tried to ban me from leaving the house at all, and I screamed so much he ended up backing down.
4. I remembered, when I got home, why I had taken my eye off the ball in the first place, why I had eaten the candy bar.
5. I knew why the voice had come. Because I had killed my mother and the voice was angry with me. Dr. Lewis was right. The voice *was* my mother. Or it was the part of me that hated myself, the part that I didn't want to acknowledge. *I was punishing myself.*
6. This insight did not help. The voice came back but *hard.*
7. I know I said four things.
8. Yeah, yeah.
9. Whatever.
10. It's my list.

5. FREEDOM. Challenge the power of the voice and establish dominance over it.

Round two.

It was weird.

I knew now what my trauma was: I knew, I mean consciously knew, that I had killed my mother. That it was my fault that my mother was dead.

But here's the thing: you would think that would be terrible . . . only knowing that somehow made it easier, not harder. Because now that it was out in the open—I mean, the open inside my head, if that's a thing—I could at least talk to myself about it.

I could say to myself,

"But, Cass, she would have died anyway."

I could say to myself,

"But, Cass, you saw her eyes. She was gone. The doctors said there was nothing anyone could have done."

And I didn't really believe it, but at least I could talk to myself about it.

Not out loud of course. That would have been crazy.

HAHAHAHAHAHAHA.

So . . . mentally, I was doing a bit better. I hated being basically grounded and I wanted to see Paris, and wanted more than I could even admit to myself to see you . . . but in my head, in the echo chamber of my mind, I was improving.

I realized, too, that I had been wrong—I mean, I had known there was something in Ovid, but I was looking for the wrong thing. I had been looking for Echo in the voice that I heard, when I should have been looking at *myself*. Ever since Mom died I had been

Pygmalion's statue—a girl who had been a solid object, an ivory girl—and now I had come to life, like Venus made Pygmalion's statue come to life, and it was painful and amazing at the same time.

Dr. Rezwari was pleased with my progress. I went to see her in her strange empty room, with its shelves of books, and she said I was responding very well to the drugs. This was funny because I was NOT TAKING ANY. But I was lucky: I think I looked so dopey from the anaphylaxis and being generally tired and emotional that I *looked* like someone who was taking powerful antipsychotics.

"And do you ever hear the voice these days?" she asked.

"No," I lied.

"That's excellent," said Dr. Rezwari. "Excellent." Then she sent me home. Whether I heard the voice: that was the only thing she cared about. Not what might have caused it.

The day after that I was in my room. Dad was outside, on a ladder leaning against the wall, painting the window frames. He liked to do it in summer, when it was sunny. But not too hot, because then the paint would dry too quickly and crack. He wasn't painting my window, he was doing his one, the next one along.

"Walk into the wall, *****," said the voice.

"Hello," I said. "How nice to hear—"

"Walk into the wall or your dad falls off the ladder."

Deep breath.

"It's two p.m. I'd really rather you spoke to me only after—"

"He'll break both his legs. Walk into the wall. Right now."

I don't know why I did it. I really don't. Maybe because the voice told me to eat the candy bar, and it really could have killed me? Anyway. I said,

"No."

"What?" said the voice.

"No. I won't walk into the wall."

"Are you ****** serious? Both legs, Cass. You want to hurt him like you hurt your mother?"

Rage filled me suddenly. I pictured it like redness rising up my eyes, flooding them. "Fuck you," I said.

"Last chance," said the voice.

Fear was fingers clasped tight on my body, shaking it. "No," I said. I waited.

The clock on the wall—Peter Rabbit, from when I was small—ticked and ticked, chopping up time into seconds.

I could hear Dad whistling as he painted. The Beach Boys. "God Only Knows." He and Mom had it at their wedding. I smiled a little. I listened for the sound of his ladder slipping, him falling, the scream when he hit the ground.

Nothing.

"Are you there?" I asked the voice.

Silence.

The voice was gone.

AND SUPER UNSURPRISING CAPS-LOCK SPOILER ALERT: Dad did not fall off the ladder.

DR. LEWIS:	(eating a cookie) Of course, the voice didn't threaten *you*.
ME:	Huh?
DR. LEWIS:	It threatened your father.
ME:	Yes.
DR. LEWIS:	The next test, I think, is to resist the voice when it is *you* it's threatening.
ME:	I . . . I . . .

DR. LEWIS:	You're still afraid of it, yes?
ME:	(silence)
DR. LEWIS:	You still believe it could hurt you.
ME:	I guess.
DR. LEWIS:	So what happened when your father didn't fall off the ladder?
ME:	Maybe the voice decided not to do it.
DR. LEWIS:	No. It *couldn't* do it. Because it's part of you. It has no supernatural powers.
ME:	(thinking of the compasses, of the moment when Shane rolled over and scratched himself and I saw his junk, all wrinkly and gross) Hmm.
DR. LEWIS:	What I want you to do is, next time the voice threatens you, suggests some specific punishment . . . I want you to call it. Like in a poker game. Call it, and see if it can really do it. If it can't, you start to get your life back.
ME:	You make it sound so easy.
DR. LEWIS:	Oh, no. No, it won't be easy. But what is?

It wasn't all bad though.

I didn't see you apart from a couple of glimpses out of the window, and that sucked. And I didn't hear much from Paris, and that sucked too.

But then one day she texted me like five times.

Hey hun come to the roller derby tonite it's the final & Julie is skating. It'll be fun! I promise.

I know your dad's working tonite b/c I asked in the restaurant. I pretended that I wanted a job as a server. HAHAHAHAHAHA. Once I worked in a burger joint & I got fired b/c I kept eating the burgers and I accidentally kissed the short-order cook.

Hello? OK it wasn't an accident it was totally deliberate but he was hot.

Hun? OK OK OK also I sprayed MEAT IS MURDER on the front window. I was confused, I was going through some stuff, OK?

And, okay, that made me laugh. Then the last one dropped the joke:

Roller derby. Tonite. Be there. I want you there. Please?

I wanted to reply. I wanted so badly to reply. But there was my dad, and my work with the voice and . . . and I didn't.

But Paris wasn't going to take no for an answer that easily, and maybe half an hour after my dad went out that evening, there was a ring at the door. I went to it thinking it would be Paris but it wasn't, it was you.

"Hey," you said. You looked super awkward.

"Hey," I said.

(I have just had a call from Spielberg saying he wants to option this conversation for a tentpole movie next year. I have said yes. Hope that's okay.)

"Um, Paris sent me," you said. "Is your dad here?"

"No."

"Oh good. Um . . ."

"She sent you to take me to the roller derby, right?" I asked.

"Yeah." You shuffled a bit. You looked good. You were wearing jeans and a white T-shirt, and your hair looked like you'd slept on it but still . . . you looked good. Hot, actually. God, I am curling up inside writing this. "She's totally amped up about it," you said. "She really wants you there. I'm supposed to drive you in the pickup."

I looked over at the road, where your white Ford was parked under a streetlight. I sighed, but only inside, so you wouldn't hear. "Well, I do love that pickup," I said. "But my dad . . ."

"Is out till late, right? He told me earlier."

"I'm supposed to be grounded."

"Why?" you asked. "What did you do?"

"Nothing," I said.

"Mysterious," you said.

"Yeah."

Then one of our classic awkward silences.

"Come on," you said. "How can you resist a trip in that sweet ride of mine?" You gestured at the pickup.

"It's tough, I'll give you that," I said. "It's the big Piers logo that really makes it."

You smiled. The world got a bit brighter. "Please?"

I sighed. "Well if you say *please* . . . Fine. Let me get my Vans."

"Awesome," you said, a bit too enthusiastically. Then you paused. "Um, I mean, for Paris . . ."

I saw the embarrassment on your face, and inside I smiled. I grabbed my shoes and slipped them on and then you let me into the passenger seat of the F-150. It was still clean in there; I was kind of surprised. I figured, you know, seventeen-year-old boy in a pickup.

I thought there would be McDonald's bags and whatever. Eighteen-year-old? I've just realized I don't know how old you are. But you've finished high school—so you have to be eighteen or nineteen, right?

I digress.

You drove us in your spookily clean pickup to what I thought was going to be some cool velodrome-type place but was actually a high school gym on the outer edge of town.

"It's a gym," I said, as we parked the truck and got out.

"Yeah."

"Disappointing."

"Hmm," you said. "I was picturing an arena with, like, sloping sides."

"Me too. Same exact thing."

"Oh well," you said. "It's—"

But I never knew what it was because . . .

"CASS! CASS, YOU ******** ****! CASS, I ******** LOVE YOU, YOU SPECTACULAR ******* PERSON! ****."

Paris ran over. She had been standing in the shadows outside the gym, invisible, and I guessed we were late because there was no one else out there in the parking lot but light was coming from the windows of the gym. She picked me up and spun me around.

"You came!" she said.

"Evidently," I said. But I couldn't help smiling.

"I knew you couldn't resist *him*."

"Actually," I said. "It was his sweet ride."

Paris looked over at the pickup, nodded sagely. "The iconography of the Piers has ever been potent. Once I hooked up with a guy just because he was wearing one of those mascot costumes. You know, the Piers dolphins?"

"Ha-ha," you said.

"No," said Paris. "That's actually true."

"When he was in the costume?" I asked.

"Well," said Paris, "he took the head off."

"Wow," you said.

"Follow," said Paris, gesturing to the gym. "The game is already afoot and we squander precious time." She led the way through double doors and then down a corridor with lockers running down it. She was carrying a really big purse. Prada, I think? Black leather with a gold clasp thing.

When we stepped into the hall the roar took me by surprise— the hall was flat, there was no sloping track, but there was a running track around the outside of the hall; it was big, I guess that was why it was chosen, and the bleachers were *packed* with people.

The skaters were already racing around the running track, some of them in yellow and black, like wasps, the others in bright red.

"Which is her team?" I asked.

"Places first," said Paris. She pushed past people, alternately charming and elbowing them, until we came to a good spot roughly in the middle, one bench back from the front. A rigged-up fence was between the audience and the skaters, those metal barriers that kind of slot together?

You know this already. I keep forgetting.

Anyway, so we sat down and started to watch the . . . match? Game? I don't know. I would look it up, but I'm conscious of not wasting your time. Ironic, I know. There were lots of people in the center of the gym, inside the track the skaters were skating around. More skaters, in the same uniforms but not skating. Plus coaches, I think? And also people in black-and-white-checkered tops who I took to be referees.

"See Julie?" said Paris. She pointed and, yes, I saw her. Yellow-and-black uniform, a helmet with a bright yellow stripe on it, her name emblazoned across her back: ONE THOUSAND MEGA JOULES. "They're the Oakwood Miss-Spelling Bees," she said. "Other team is the Wildwood Wild Kittens."

"She's fast," I said. Julie was behind a pack of the red skaters and closing on them quick.

"She's a jammer," said Paris. "Well, right now, she's a pivot, but—"

"Excuse me, what?"

"It means the jammer can designate her to take over as jammer, if she gets injured or whatever," you said.

I raised my eyebrows at you.

"What? I read up on it."

"Suck-up."

"Scr—"

"Children," said Paris. "No bickering."

We watched some more of the play. I couldn't really follow what was going on. After a minute or so they stopped skating and milled around, and then some of the players swapped with the ones waiting in the center space. It seemed like there were about fifteen girls on the team, but only about five of them were skating at any one time. Julie was one of the ones who stopped ... playing? Competing? Skating? Anyway, she stopped. She looked around at the bleachers, finally saw us, and waved. We waved back.

Meanwhile the skaters were skating.

"Yeah!" you shouted at one point.

"Um," I said. "What happened?"

"They scored."

"Really? How?"

Paris turned to me. "You really don't know *anything*?"

"Uh, no."

"The jammer scores by lapping the pack," you said. "The blockers from the opposing team try to stop them."

I looked at you blankly.

"The one with the stars on her helmet has to pass the other ones," said Paris. "Then she scores."

"Why didn't you just say that?" I asked you.

You rolled your eyes.

I watched them play. Now that I had a vague idea of the rules it was easier to understand and I was less bored. There was one more two-minute jam (see, I am all over this stuff now) where Julie sat out, and then she joined the team again. Almost straightaway the jammer shot past the pack and I jumped up and whooped. Okay, I got into it for a bit. I don't like sports usually, but it was exciting.

Paris and you stared at me.

"What?" I said. "They scored. Right? *Right*?"

"Yeah," you said.

"But you whooped," said Paris. "You, whooping."

"What? I whoop."

"You're not a whooper."

"Hey!" I said. "I can whoop."

"You don't strike me as a natural whooper," you said.

"Stop saying whooper, both of you!" I said.

"Maybe you could ask Julie if you could be a cheerleader," said Paris. "You could follow the team around and—"

"Shut up."

She smiled. It's a picture I have pinned on the inside of my mind, to look at.

Then the jammer seemed to lock skates with one of the blocker girls from the Wild Kittens, and went spinning on her back. The play stopped and she hobbled off, and various people talked to one another, and then Julie took off the helmet with the stripe on it and put on one with stars all over it instead.

"Julie's the jammer now," you said.

"Yeah, I got that, thanks," I said.

The previous jammer seemed to be okay. She sat on the ground cross-legged, rubbing her ankle, but didn't appear to be badly injured. There was a scoreboard up on the wall of the gym, an electronic one. It said:

BEES 42   KITTENS 50

So I could see that the other team was winning. But as we watched, even in the first two-minute jam, it was clear that Julie was making a difference. She flew past the Kittens' blockers a couple of times, and there was a big cheer when she did and Paris cheered too, so I joined in; I mean, I wasn't going to be the first to whoop. Not after the last time.

Soon after that it was 50–52 to the Kittens. Really close. There was like one more jam and then it all stopped for some reason; the skaters all went into the middle and huddled, the two teams standing far apart so as not to hear each other. Paris turned to me. "Seriously," she said, under her breath. "Are you okay? With . . ." She gave a meaningful look, knowing that you were sitting there too.

I nodded. "Surviving. Just about."

"Good," she said. "That's really good. Let's talk. Not here though."

"Okay," I said.

(We didn't. We didn't get a chance.)

Anyway, then the announcer, who was standing in the middle of the gym with a corded microphone, the track running in an oval around him, said it was time for the second period.

The skaters set off, the blockers first, Julie and the Kittens' jammer behind. Some stuff happened. It's not like I was registering every detail for later transcription. The score stayed pretty even. Julie scored some. The other blocker too. She was called Patricia Pornwell, I remember that because it was kind of a book name, and I liked that.

Even a sports illiterate like me could see that the time was running down. There were eight minutes of play left, and that's when stuff got kind of exciting.

74–75 to the Kittens.

Julie was trying desperately to get past the pack. The Kittens' blockers were all mixed up with the Bees, and then one of her team reached behind her and caught Julie's hand, linked up with another girl, and kind of pivoted and slingshotted Julie past them all.

Slingshot?

Slingshooted?

Who knows.

Instantly, I was on my feet, screaming.

"She *scores!*" shouted the announcer. "75–75!"

Julie looked right over at us as she cruised past, and she fired a salute off the side of her forehead at us. It was like the coolest thing ever.

"**** YEAH!" screamed Paris. "**** YEAH!"

Now it got kind of rough. The blockers were jostling one another, pushing. Not violent but close. It was messy. The red jammer got past the pack and scored for the other team.

"No," said Paris. "No no no."

Then Julie came flying up behind, putting on speed. She closed on the pack. Her hair was in two ponytails sticking out from her helmet, and they were flying behind her like pennants.

It happened suddenly—one of the Kittens went down. I think she caught her skate on another girl's, and she wiped out on the hard floor of the gym. She spun for what was probably a fraction of a second but felt like forever, all of us in slow motion now.

Julie was maybe four feet away when the girl fell. She couldn't turn. She couldn't stop.

Julie—

—jumped, right up in the air, and she kind of hugged her knees to her chest, literally five feet off the ground, and then she touched down on the other side and just kept skating.

The girl on the floor did a thumbs-up to show she was okay, and the skaters slowed so that she could get up. A medic-type guy went over, but she shook her head and went back onto the track.

"Holy cow!" said the guy on the loudspeaker, when they were all skating again. "We see stride jumps in this competition but a full jump—wow! Mega Joules back in play here, and she's gaining and—"

I don't even know what he said after that, because there were Bees supporters around us and they were going pretty much crazy. The noise was getting louder and louder. Actually the other team's supporters were going wild too. It was hard not to get swept up in it, even if at the back of my mind I was counting down time for another reason, glancing over at you again and again, thinking about later. About how we would be alone together when you drove me home.

I wondered what might happen when we got out of the pickup. When we stood in the warm night air, outside the house.

Then you caught me looking, and I turned away embarrassed.

I looked up at the board.

Two minutes to go. Still 75–75.

"What happens if they tie?" I asked.

"I don't know actually," you said.

"Well, ladies and gentlemen," said the announcer. "We haven't had a tie in the Eastern league before, but it might just happen tonight. If so, we'll go into extra time. Oh, oh! Patricia Pornwell almost past there, but edged out by a human chain of Bees. Still a tie, everyone!"

"There you go," you said. "Extra time."

"Sport sucks," I said. It was too tense for me. "Couldn't they just have a tie and everyone be friends?"

"Shut *up*," said Paris.

It may have been two minutes, but it felt like more. It was intense. Both of the jammers were pushing and pushing, trying to get past the group. But they couldn't. The Bees did this thing where four of them linked arms and made like a diamond, trapping the Kittens' jammer inside. It didn't seem fair to me, but you said it was legal.

It didn't help though. Julie couldn't get past the Kittens either—she was trying, but every time there'd be a girl in a red uniform there, blocking her with a hip, or dropping onto the track just in front of her, preventing her from overtaking.

On the scoreboard, the time was ticking down.

Sixty seconds.

Thirty seconds.

The diamond was still in place, and the Kittens' jammer was powerless. But it was no good because their blockers were in a chain and there was no way for Julie to dodge past them.

Fifteen seconds.

The pack was skating down the hall on the far side from us, toward the turn after the straight, and there was still no way past, and there was still no way past, and—

Eight seconds.

And—

Five seconds.

And then they came to the turn, the pack right on the inside of it, and Julie was there, suddenly, going faster than I had seen before, really powering up behind the blockers and then she leaned into the corner, leaned much too far into the corner and she kind of dived and I thought she was going to fall—

No.

She *jumped*, again, only this time with one leg and then the other, so that she kind of leaped past the blockers by cutting *across* the sharpest part of the turn in the air—without her skates ever touching down outside the track—and came down again just past them, just past the most acute angle of the turn, and we were on our feet before I even really knew what was happening.

"The Bees WIN!" the announcer screamed. "Mega Joules jumps the apex and wins the final for the Bees! 76–75! Unbelievable!"

After the end of play it was actually kind of anticlimactic. The crowd—at least the Bees' supporters anyway—kept cheering for a while, and that was fun, being caught up in that.

In the middle of the gym the announcer got both teams together. He had the mike in one hand and a framed certificate in the other. "The Oakwood Miss-Spelling Bees!" he said. "Winners of the New Jersey Eastern League!"

Applause.

He handed over the certificate to Julie. She smiled.

And that's when Paris slung her bag over her shoulder and vaulted over the bench in front of us, her bag knocking the head of a girl with red hair who turned and said, "Hey!"

Paris turned at the safety barrier. "Come *on*," she said. "Boost me."

"Wh—" I started, but you were already on your feet and jumping down beside her. I guess boys are just better at obeying commands without thinking about them at all.

You cupped your hands and crouched; Paris got one foot on them and you powered her up. Everything was happening very fast, and I wasn't really processing any of it because I had two conflicting thoughts in my mind:

— He's helping, that's so sweet, he doesn't know what she's doing or why she's doing it, *I* don't even know, but he jumped right up to help her over the fence, like a knight in shining armor.

And:

— He's helping, that's so awful, he doesn't know what she's doing or why she's doing it, but he jumped right down and he put his hands out, and they're touching oh God I'm so jealous her foot was in his hand and her hand was on his shoulder, just for a moment, and THIS MEANS HE LIKES HER DOESN'T IT? He's only here for her, he's a knight in shining armor, but he's a knight in shining armor for her.

It made me feel sick, that feeling, that envy, seeing your bodies touch, just for that moment.

And, yes, I know this is repetitive, I know it's just like when I thought you were into Jane from the library, and I apologize for that. But the thing is that minds are repetitive. They tend to get into fixed patterns.

This is something I know better than most.

Anyway. Those two thoughts were warring in my mind, but it was so much faster than I am conveying it here. It all happened in an instant.

Paris pivoted over the top of the fence, using the momentum you had provided with surprising grace, at first anyway. Then . . . then it kind of went wrong, her leading foot was over but her back one caught, and she flipped suddenly, scary-fast, like someone being hit by a bull, and for a frozen instant she was upside down on the other side of the fence.

Then she hit the ground, sprawling, her head and shoulders taking the impact, and rolled.

"****," you shouted. "Are you okay?"

Paris stood, awkwardly. She shook herself like a dog. Then she put her arms up in a V, like an Olympic gymnast, like, "TA DA!"

She turned and hurried over to where the two teams were gathered, though it was obvious she was limping.

"What's she doing?" you asked.

"I have no idea," I said.

You frowned. I must have sounded angry. Because of the touching. Because of you giving her that boost, and how *obviously* you would be more into her than me.

And then Paris was pushing a big silver trophy into Julie's hands and there was a flurry of movement and suddenly the Bees lifted Julie up into the air and the crowd went *wild*.

Click. Kodak moment.

"Um," you said, over the noise of celebration. "What was *that*?"

"I'll explain later," I said.

But I didn't.

I mean, I didn't explain later. I really wanted to, I really wanted some time alone with you, I had been looking forward to that all evening, thinking about the ride home and how we would stand in the yard together, under the night sky . . .

But sometimes life thwarts our plans. Often, in fact.

First off, we were hanging out with Paris and Julie and the team in the parking lot and then you offered them a ride and the whole way to their apartment the pickup was just filled with them, with their excitement and happiness, and Paris was so *loud*.

"My girl got her trophy!" she was shouting. "My girl is a *champion*!"

"It was a team effort," said Julie, but I could hear the bright joy in her voice, and it made me twist inside.

"She is the champion, my friends . . . ," Paris started singing. You glanced over at me and raised your eyebrows. Paris did not have a beautiful singing voice. I just wanted her to be quiet, but she was Paris. She was *never* quiet. I mean, what are you going to do? You can't ask the sun to stop shining.

So she sang the whole song, only she didn't know most of the words, not that it stopped her.

Then we dropped them off, and Paris and Julie went up, Paris still shouting stuff, mostly impossible to make out now, and Julie was holding the trophy aloft that Paris had given her, and finally they went into the apartment building and you turned to me. And then I found out that sometimes your own feelings can thwart stuff for you; you don't even need life to do it.

"Wow," you said.

"Uh-huh," I said. I must have sounded cold.

"What is it?"

"Nothing," I said.

"Did I do something wrong?"

"Absolutely not."

"But you're pissed with me. Is it because I offered them a ride?"

"No."

You sighed. "O . . . kay . . . So nothing is wrong?"

"No."

But of course I was speaking in monosyllables and it was pretty obvious I was not happy, and in the end you just raised your hands and said, "Fine. Let's just go home."

That made it sound like our home was together, like we were a couple or something, which just made me feel even worse, thinking of you rushing to help Paris, of how stupid I had been, thinking that any of this had anything to do with me. I knew that was a thing boys did—get to the beautiful one through her plain friend.

I figured that was what you were doing.

I know better now. I know you were helping Paris because you liked me, and I liked Paris, and so automatically you liked Paris. At least I assume so; just as likely you just saw that she needed help and you didn't even think about it. I'm the one who thinks about stuff too much, I'm aware of that.

Anyway, that's why I was frosty to you in the pickup, okay?

Eventually you gave up on me and a little part inside me died, and you started the engine and drove back toward the house. After a while, watching the streetlights go past, I started to think maybe I had been an idiot. Maybe I had read something into nothing. I opened my mouth to say sorry—

—and we passed Dad's car, a few blocks from the house, driving home.

****.

"Hit the gas," I said. That was another opportunity wasted to spend time with you, to talk to you alone, because you sped up to beat him and we got home like two minutes before him so I didn't even say good night to you, just ran into the house while you lay down in the pickup so he wouldn't see you. And we made it. We got away with it.

So that's why I've told you the story of the game, which you know anyway, what with being there and all.

One: because I was mean to you afterward and you didn't deserve it and I'm sorry. Two: because you saw what happened at the game, with Paris and Julie, but you didn't *understand*.

You see, you were on the phone at the pier when Julie was talking about never winning anything. You probably just thought it was Paris being crazy, as usual.

But you get it now, right? You get what I'm telling you about her?

You could call her crazy. If that was the way you saw the world. Or you could call her someone who would go to the trouble of having a trophy made, specially, and then crash a sporting event just to give it to her friend.

That's the Paris I want the world to remember. That's the Paris I want you to remember.

"Can you wash up?" said Dad. We had just finished eating—pizza from the restaurant for the third night in a row.

"Sure," I said.

"I'll be in the study."

"Sure." I was not varying my vocabulary much. I was thinking about you, and how even if you did like me, which I wasn't at all sure about, but still, even if you *did*, I had messed it all up now.

He left his plate and went to the bug room. He was still pissed with me, even though he didn't see me get back from the roller derby, luckily. I didn't blame him, really. At least he hadn't shouted for a while. Of course that didn't necessarily mean anything. Dad's anger, it surfaces unexpectedly, I've told you already. Like spray from a whale's blowhole. Stillness . . .

then . . .

whoosh.

So I was just waiting for him to blow over some tiny inconsequential thing. Like the dishes not being cleaned properly—so as a result I scrubbed them for ages before putting them in the rack to dry, trying to give him no excuses.

I stopped at the door to the study, on the way up to my room. Dad was hunched over the computer, typing. On the forum, I guessed. Dad was always on the forum, when he wasn't actually feeding the bugs or breeding them or whatever he did with them.

On the forum he was BEETLEJUICE3. It was like a lame superhero identity. I mean, in real life, he was an ex-soldier with a failing restaurant and a sick daughter. But there on the forum he was a PRO-LEVEL BUGGER. He had seventeen hundred posts or something and two thousand comments. People would ask him questions, post comments with lots of animated emojis about how awesome he was—I'd seen him answering them lots of times. He was like a legend on that site.

No wonder he didn't want to deal with real things. Like me.

"'Night, Dad," I said.

He turned. "'Night."

"Watcha doing?"

"Posting some pics of my new giant pills."

"Pills?"

"Millis. They roll into balls. Like a pill bug, you know?" He went back to the screen, typing with one finger, slowly.

"Okay, well, see you tomorrow."

He grunted and I went up the stairs. I lay on my bed, all my clothes still on. I stared at the ceiling for a long time. Then I grabbed my phone and texted Paris.

U there? xxx

I waited for, like, half an hour, but she didn't text back. I turned on the radio, and Katy Perry blasted out into the room.

"Turn that ******* **** down!"

That was Dad, shouting up from the study.

I sighed and turned it down. I got up onto my knees on the bed and looked out the window—but I couldn't see you and Shane on your deck chairs, and there was no light spilling from your apartment.

My phone buzzed. I picked it up.

Going out. Client. C U tmw?

I thought of Dad, banning me from seeing her. But he'd be at work from eleven in the morning . . .

Yeah. Wld have to be daytime tho.

The answer popped right up.

That's cool. Maston Theater? Matinee of Toy Story.

Toy Story? I replied.

Hey don't diss Pixar.

OK. What time?

1.

OK. Night, Paris.

Night, Cass.

I put the phone down. I lay down again and reached for the Haruki Murakami book on my nightstand.

"No," said the voice.

"Oh hi," I said. "Nice to hear from you. And thank you for waiting till after six p.m. to—"

"No reading."

I thought of Dr. Lewis. I thought: I have nothing to lose here. "Or what?" I asked.

"Excuse me?"

"If I read my book, what are you going to do about it?"

The voice thought for a moment—this sounded different from when it went away. I can't explain it. I mean, I could still *feel* it there. "I will make you cut off one of your toes."

My toes curled. "How?"

"What?"

"How will you make me do that?"

"I will force you to."

"No."

Then the voice screamed at me. That was new. I mean, it was always saying horrible things. But the screaming was different. "*Don't push me!*" it screamed.

"I'm not pushing you. I'm just saying no."

"Go to the kitchen *this instant*. Tell your dad you're getting a glass of water. Take a bread knife, and come back up here. Then cut off your pinky toe on your left foot. Do it right now."

"Or what?"

"What do you mean, or what?"

"I mean, if I don't cut off my toe, what are you going to do about it?"

The voice thought. "I'm going to kill your father. No more injuries. No more minor ****. You don't cut off your toe, your dad dies. Okay?"

You can't imagine how scared I was. My eyes were filling with tears. It was dark out; my room was gloomy with shadows. I flicked on my bedside lamp. But that only made it worse. Now my clothes hanging on the door handle, my posters, my shelves, cast weird shapes on the walls and floor.

"I won't do it," I said.

"Then you will wake up in the morning and your father will be dead."

I said nothing.

"*He will die.* Do you understand? *I will kill him in his sleep.* I will smother him until he stops breathing and his body is cold and dead."

I said nothing.

"Get the bread knife. *Now.*"

"No."

"Last chance, Cass."

"No."

The voice sighed. "He dies, then," it said.

And then it did go. I felt it withdraw from the room.

From my head.

The voice didn't speak then, but my mind was unquiet. You get that word in old gothic novels, don't you? Unquiet ghosts and so on.

That was my mind that night. My thoughts just raced around, like ghosts in a haunted house, unstoppable.

What if your dad dies because of you?

How selfish are you?

You really want to kill another parent?

Sometimes they were words, like that, and sometimes they were images. Scenes, flashing in and out of my consciousness.

Tiles.

Blood.

The house was mostly wood and I could hear it expanding or contracting or whatever houses do at night when they cool down. Outside, there was a strong wind coming from the ocean. I could *smell* it through the cracks of my windows, salty and holding the promise of distance and forgetting—a promise I wished it would make good on. I wished that wind would sweep into my head and rinse it clean, whistle through the cavities of my skull until there was nothing there but emptiness, and silence.

But the wind didn't do that, and the voice was still in my head. "He's going to die, he's going to die, he's going to die, he's going to die like a dog on the ground, like your mother. It's going to be your fault."

The voice was *everywhere*. It was speaking, in my ears, as a voice, but it was merging with everything else too. The creaking and clicking and ticking of the house were all consonants, the wind outside was all vowels, and together the house and the wind were saying,

Your dad is going to die.

In the end I couldn't stand it anymore, and I got some old headphones out of my nightstand—I had to dig under the piles of medication that I hadn't been taking; archaeology. I plugged them into my radio and tuned it to a dead channel again, the way I used to block out the voice.

I filled my head with white noise.

%%%%%%%%%%%%%%%%%%%%%%%%%%%%%%%%%%%%
%%%%%%%%%%%%%%%%%%%%%%%%%%%%%%%%%%%%
%%%%%%%%%%%%%%%%%%%%%%%%%%%%%%%%%%%%
%%%%%%%%%%%%%%%%%%%%%%%%%%%%%%%%%%%%
%%%%%%%%%%%%%%%%%%%%%%%%%%%%%%%%%%%%
%%%%%%%%%%%%%%%%%%%%%%%%%%%%%%%%%%%%
%%%%%%%%%%%%%%%%%%%%%%%%%%%%%%%%%%%%
%%%%%%%%%%%%%%%%%%%%%%%%%%%%%%%%%%%%
%%%%%%%%%%%%%%%%%%%%%%%%%%%%%%%%%%%%
%%%%%%%%%%%%%%%%%%%%%%%%%%%%%%%%%%%%
%%%%%%%%%%%%%%%%%%%%%%%%%%%%%%%%%%%%
%%%%%%%%%%%%%%%%%%%%%%%%%%%%%%%%%%%%
%%%%%%%%%%%%%%%%%%%%%%%%%%%%%%%%%%%%
%%%%%%%%%%%%%%%%%%%%%%%%%%%%%%%%%%%%
%%%%%%%%%%%%%%%%%%%%%%%%%%%%%%%%%%%%
%%%%%%%%%%%%%%%%%%%%%%%%%%%%%%%%%%%%
%%%%%%%%%%%%%%%%%%%%%%%%%%%%%%%%%%%%
%%%%%%%%%%%%%%%%%%%%%%%%%%%%%%%%%%%%
%%%%%%%%%%%%%%%%%%%%%%%%%%%%%%%%%%%%
%%%%%%%%%%%%%%%%%%%%%%%%%%%%%%%%%%%%
%%%%%%%%%%%%%%%%%%%%%%%%%%%%%%%%%%%%
%%%%%%%%%%%%%%%%%%%%%%%%%%%%%%%%%%%%
%%%%%%%%%%%%%%%%%%%%%%%%%%%%%%%%%%%%
%%%%%%%%%%%%%%%%%%%%%%%%%%%%%%%%%%%%
%%%%%%%%%%%%%%%%%%%%%%%%%%%%%%%%%%%%

%%
%%
%%
%%
%%
%%
%%
%%%%%%%%%%%%%%%%%%%%%%%%%%%%%%%%%

I must have fallen asleep at some point because when I opened my eyes there was sunlight flooding the room and the white noise was still blasting in my ears,
%%%%%%%%%%%%%%%%%%%%%%%%%%%%%%%%%%%%%%
%%%%%%%%%%%%%%%%%%%%%%%%%%%%%%%%%%%%%%
%%%%%%%%%%%%%%%%%%%%%%%%%%%%%%%%%%%%%%
%%%%%%%%%%%%%%%%%%%%%%%%%%%%%%%%%%%%%%
%%%%%%%%%%%%%%%%%%%%%%%%%%%%%%%%%%%%%%
%%%%%%%%%%%%%%%%%%%%%%%%%%%%%%%%%%%%%%
%%%%%%%%%%%%%%%%%%%%%%.

I pulled off the headphones and vaulted off the bed. I ran out my door and just down the hallway to Dad's.

I banged on it, hard.

No answer.

I hammered again on the door with my fist.

BANG, BANG, BANG.

Oh please oh please oh—

"Cass? What the hell?"

Relief snapped open and expanded inside me, like a parachute. "Dad?"

"Uh, yeah. It's five thirty ********* a.m., Cass. What's wrong?"

"Nothing's wrong, Dad. Nothing's wrong."

I heard him roll over in bed. "Then go back to ******* bed."

But I didn't. I bounced down the hall, elastic with happiness. I had challenged the voice and *I had won*. I had taken on step five for the second time, and I had come out victorious.

"You there?" I asked the voice.

No answer.

"Figures," I said.

I didn't know how I was going to wait till one o'clock for the *Toy*

Story matinee with Paris. I was buzzing. I had 220 volts of electricity running through me, fizzing in my veins and nerves. I was *wired*. I went to my room and tried to read some of the Murakami—the voice said not one thing about it—but I couldn't concentrate on the words.

A little later I heard Dad go downstairs and have his breakfast; then he left. He didn't make me anything to eat, or call up, or anything. I went downstairs and tried to watch some TV for an hour or so, but I still couldn't concentrate. I went back upstairs, still in my pajamas.

I pulled on my swimsuit and then faded jeans and a T-shirt with my old Converses and went outside. My phone went into my back pocket. I was going to walk to the beach, do some drawing, maybe swim in the ocean. If the voice wanted to say anything about it, well, what was it going to do? I grabbed my sketch pad and my pencil.

Thin mist hung over the town. I followed our street to where the asphalt began to break up, sand pushing through the cracks. The road just became the shore at a certain point. Then I stepped from the sidewalk down onto the scrub and dunes of the beach.

I walked the beach until I found something I wanted to draw— an old Coke can, it looked like it might have been seventies even; the font was weird, and it had washed up, faded out, on the sand. Trash. I loved to draw trash—that was my thing, remember? Neglected things. Ugly things.

I took my pencil and pressed it to the paper and—

Nothing. I couldn't draw it. I couldn't draw the ugly old squashed Coke can. It held no interest at all for me, its folds, its little holes, its faded lettering. It was just a dead, broken object, and the pencil wouldn't move.

It was like . . . like it was something I used to like to do, but now it was just gone. Like a switch had been turned off. It wasn't even the voice saying no, it was just me. Losing interest.

I shrugged and put the sketch pad and pencil in my back pocket. Then I went to the spot where Dad taught me to swim, south of Pier One. I slid off my jeans and took off my T-shirt. The late morning air was cold on my legs and arms.

For a second I thought, *Really*?

But then I smiled to myself. Yes, really.

I ran straight at the ocean, my legs crashing through the low waves, the salt water freezing, and then I dived down; my face and hands scraped the bottom and I surged up, grabbed the water in my hands and pulled myself out, stroke after stroke. I swam the crawl, only occasionally lifting my head to breathe.

Silky water embraced me, held me up, the feeling like a promise. A promise of buoyancy, of not letting me fall. A promise you never get from the air. If you lose your balance in the air, you always fall.

The taste of the ocean was in my mouth: salt, sand, small creatures. Water was all around me, containing me, shaping itself to my contours.

What I mean to say is:

It was amazing.

I swam all the way up to the first pier, then turned and swam back to the little pile my clothes made on the sand. My movements were stiff at first, forced, but got smoother as I swam, the feeling coming back to me. I felt free and I thought about nothing except the waves and timing my breathing and my strokes.

As I neared my clothes, I saw your truck. You were driving onto the sand where the road merged with the beach. The way you took me, that time. You drove a little way down the long, wide stretch of beach, toward the shore, and then you turned in the direction of Pier One.

I swung my legs down, planted my feet in the hard wet sand; it compacted around my toes. I stood and waved with both arms.

The white pickup slowed, then turned and drove toward me. You parked up by my jeans and T-shirt.

I walked slowly out of the water as you stood by the pickup, your arm on the open door. You raised a hand as I got close.

"Venus exiting the sea," you said with a smile. You were wearing Ray-Bans.

"You're letting him see your body," said the voice, because you were too far away to mute it. "You're letting him see your disgusting—"

"Yeah?" I said. "What are you going to do about it?"

"Kidding," you said, thinking I was speaking to you, raising your hands in mock defense as I neared you. "I'm not looking."

The voice disappeared. I was too close to you now; I was in your force field.

"What do you mean, you're not looking?" I asked.

You raised your sunglasses. Your eyes were closed. "See?"

I laughed. "Okay, keep them closed. I'm going to get dressed."

"You didn't bring a towel."

I looked around. "Oh."

"I have one in the truck. Hang on." You turned, put up a hand to shield your eyes, and felt around in the cab of the truck. Then you were facing me again, eyes closed, holding out a towel.

I hesitated.

"It's clean. I always have one. So I can swim after work."

"Thanks." I reached out and took it. "You swim?"

"Yeah."

"I didn't know that."

"There's a lot you don't know about me." You paused. "You looked good out there." You flushed. "I mean, your stroke. ****. I keep doing that. Your stroke looked good."

He thinks I look good? So maybe he does like me.

But how am I supposed to know?

"Dad taught me," I said, trying to ignore the thoughts racing in my head. This was true. When I was a kid, I was always in the ocean with my dad. I mean always. Every evening, every weekend. I loved it, sharing his passion with him, learning from him. My mom called me her water baby—she would come too, swim with us, though she was never as fast, would get left behind, joke-cursing us.

So many of my memories of my dad have the texture of water. And they evaporated, too, like water. Dried out, leaving the ocean behind, and him washed up in front of his bugs, and me left stranded in my room, alone.

"Oh yeah," you said. "He was a SEAL, right? That's hard-core."

"Was," I said. "He's not so hard-core these days."

You smiled, your eyes still closed. "Yeah, he showed me his bugs. Creepy. Like, literally."

I had finished drying myself now and quickly pulled on my clothes. "You can open your eyes now," I said.

You did. "Truth is, I've had them open a crack the whole time."

"You—"

"Kidding! Kidding."

He is. He's totally flirting.

"You swim a lot?" I asked, to change the subject.

You shrugged. "I was on the school team."

"Oh! You told me. Sorry. You must be good."

You shrugged again.

"But you left the team?"

"Huh?"

"You said you *were* on the school team."

"Oh. No. I'm going to college. In the fall. On a swim scholarship actually." You looked a little embarrassed.

"Then you must be really good."

"Hmm," you said. "Anyway, I'd better get going. These Angry Birds are not going to deliver themselves."

"Okay. Thanks for the towel."

"You're welcome," you said. Then, "Oh!" you added, as you put the towel away. "Hey, I forgot." You pulled a pile of books from the footwell of the truck. "I got these for you. From the library."

"But I never cleaned the apartment."

"Well, no, but still. I got them. Vonnegut, Carver, Austen. Kind of a random selection. I didn't know what you liked."

I looked at the pile. *He brought you books. Still think he likes Paris? Idiot.* That wasn't the voice, that was just me. "Thanks," I said. "Really."

"You don't have to take them now. If you don't want to carry them. I can bring them to your—"

"No," I said. "Better not. That's kind of why I never cleaned the apartment. My dad doesn't want me . . . um, hanging out with you." I reached out and took the books.

Looked away.

A long moment.

Looked back and you were watching me. A small smile on your face. Like: intrigued, and amused. "Star-crossed!" you said. "A dramatic turn." In my defense it was not always obvious that you liked me. You had a habit of making everything into a joke, if it turned too serious. I know it's hypocritical of me to say that.

"It's not funny," I said, and it came out harder than I meant.

Your face sank. "Oh. Yeah, of course. Your dad's strict?"

"Uh-huh."

"Bummer."

"Yeah."

Silence.

"Um, well, then. I guess, 'bye," you said.

"Um, yeah, 'bye."

→ OUR ROMANCE, STILL SCRIPTED BY SHAKESPEARE ←

You pulled yourself easily into the cab, kind of swung yourself. I . . .

Okay, I've been sitting here at Dad's PC in the study trying to think of how to describe you, the way you moved then, the way you always move. And I think I have it, finally. It's . . .

So, you have to start by thinking of the word "fitness." I mean, thinking of what it *really means*. We use it all the time—that person is fit, that person isn't fit, he's doing fitness training, whatever. But think about the root word. Fit. To fit. To be *fit or apt for a purpose.*

That's you. You're fit, yeah, in the obvious sense that you're healthy and have a slow resting heart rate, and all that stuff. From all the swimming. But you also *fit*, your movements fit with the world, you interlock elegantly with it.

You fit into the world like a key in a lock.

Anyway.

So you swung yourself into the cab like your body was meant to fit into that sweep of air, that motion, at precisely that moment, and then you started the engine and drove off, waving.

I thought: *I wonder if life gets any better than this. The voice has no power over me and he moves like that and . . .*

I don't know. I was happy. I reached into my pocket and took out my phone to check the time; I had left my watch at home. That was when I saw that I had a missed call, and a message. I hadn't looked at my phone in the morning. I mean, I know people do that, but I'm not people; I'm someone used to having no friends. All of which is to say that I had not looked at the thing until I saw on the screen:

Paris. MISSED. 1:24 a.m.

I dialed the number for my messages, and put the phone to my ear. There was a beep, then a click, then a hiss.

"*Kccccchhhhhhh . . . Kccccchhhhhhh . . .*—" And then a scream.

And then:

Click.

I held out the phone, held it far from my body, like it was contaminated.

Fear flooded through me; freezing water. I had been in the ocean and now the ocean was in me; rushing, merciless.

Cold.

2.

THE PART AFTER

As I walked home I dialed Paris's number.

No answer.

I dialed again.

No answer.

Come on Paris, come on Paris. Answer your phone.

But nothing.

It was eleven thirty. I paced up and down in the kitchen until twelve thirty, and then I nearly ran to the theater where *Toy Story* was showing. There were a few people waiting outside—a handful of hipsters, some parents with young kids. The theater was old, art deco, like the motels. There were old posters pasted on the walls— *Back to the Future*; *American Gigolo*. The facade was dirty, the posters peeling. It was fading, rotting, in need of investment—but with beautiful architectural lines underneath. A microcosm of the town.

I stood there for twenty minutes, hoping. The hipsters and the kids went in. A couple of old people I figured were just looking for an air-conditioned place to spend the hottest part of the day. The sun was high in the sky and sweat was trickling down the back of my neck, pooling in the small of my back.

I looked at my watch: 1:10.

No Paris.

In my mind's eye, terrible scenarios played out. A john slitting her throat, letting her bleed out. Then dumping her body at sea. Someone cutting her up in a shed. Submerging her in an acid bath. I couldn't see the man's face in my imaginings. But it was always a man.

I felt like the sky was gone from above me. I felt like everything beautiful in the world had been stabbed to death and thrown in the ocean, weighed down with concrete blocks or whatever it might be.

At one thirty I left the theater and walked to Paris's condo. It wasn't that close; it took me a while. And the whole time I was seeing these awful images. Seeing her screaming for help as a knife entered her stomach. That kind of thing.

"Just what she deserves," said the voice. "******* whore."

"Oh shut up," I said.

Amazingly, the voice did shut up.

I turned the corner onto Paris's street and what I saw there made my heart clench like an oyster closing. A cop car, pulled up at an angle to the curb, like it had been parked quickly, carelessly. I started running, then. I entered the building and took the stairs, not wanting to wait for the elevator.

I got to the front door out of breath. Julie opened it before I even knocked; she must have heard my footsteps in the hall. She was wearing a pink sweater and a short skirt, polka-dotted, a headband in her hair—like she was going to a dance in 1959. But she had been crying; her eyes were red rimmed.

"Cass," she said, and her voice was a hand desperately reaching for the side of a boat, to pull itself out of dark sucking water.

"Julie, what—"

But she launched herself forward and put her arms around me. I hugged her tight. "Julie, is she . . . is she . . ."

"We don't know."

She pulled back, straightened her hair. I looked past her and saw the young agent from after I found the foot.

"Horowitz," I said.

"Cassandra. You knew Ms. French?"

My mind was blank for a second. "Oh. Paris. Yes. I knew her."

Wait.

"You said *knew*."

Horowitz looked down. "Slip of the tongue. Agent's habit. At the moment she's just missing."

"What happened?" I asked.

It was Julie who answered. "She had a . . . a bachelor party last night. Or maybe it was a birthday party, I can't remember. I drove her. I always drive her, if she goes out to an . . . engagement. For safety, you know?" She started crying; wiped her eyes brusquely with the sleeve of her sweater. "When she started . . . I didn't want her to get into it. But she was Paris, you know? She always got her way. In the end, I said she could only do it if I drove her to every . . . appointment. I said it was the minimum safety requirement. But I . . . I . . ."

She broke down in tears.

"Go on," said Agent Horowitz gently, after a pause. "You drove her?"

"Yeah. It was a house up by the shore. On the north side of town, in Bayview, before you get to the Cape—an okay area, not a great one. A row of clapboards. There's an old rotten pier behind? Just a small one. I parked and she went in. Then . . . then I think I must have fallen asleep. But not for long. I woke up because I heard an engine—a car turned in front of me, onto the road, swept me with its headlights. Then a few minutes after that Paris called me. She was . . . she sounded . . ."

I took her hand and squeezed. "Go on."

"She sounded *terrified*, Cass. Scared for her life, you know? But it was hard to hear what she was saying—the line was really bad. Like, a kind of *shhhhhh* sound like the ocean, you know? She screamed for help, told me to come quick. I said I was calling the police. And then that was the weird part."

"Weird part?"

But Julie had her eyes closed and was choking up. She shook her head and walked quickly to the kitchen, to get some tissues, I guessed.

I looked over at Horowitz.

"Evidently Ms. French told her roommate not to call the police. Was very insistent about it. She—"

"She said it over and over," said Julie, appearing at the kitchen door. "'No, Julie! Not the cops! Don't call them!' And then the line suddenly went quiet. Then there was this heavy metal sound and then a *thunk* and then the line went dead." Her impression of Paris was eerie; it was like Paris was in the room. But of course she wasn't.

I shivered.

"Why do you think she said not to call the police?" said Agent Horowitz.

"I don't know! Because . . . because of what she was doing?"

Agent Horowitz spread his hands. "Possible," he said. "But stripping? I mean, it's not exactly illegal." His face looked like it had acquired a couple of new lines since I'd first met him. Around his eyes, his mouth. Stress?

"No, but she didn't want her dad to find out," said Julie.

I wondered if that was true. Her Instagram was pretty public. But anyway it didn't seem logical to me.

"What," I said, "she's afraid for her life and at the same time she's worried her dad's going to find out she's stripping?" I said. "Really?"

"I admit it seems implausible," said Horowitz.

"So then why would she say not to call the cops?"

"I have no idea. That is what we are going to have to try to establish."

"But you think she's gone," I said. "You think it's the Houdini Killer. Of course you do—you're FBI or whatever you are."

Julie was looking from me to him, from him to me, like a metronome. "You're not police?"

"Not precisely," said Horowitz.

"Oh Jesus," said Julie. "She's dead, isn't she? She's dead, and I didn't do anything to stop it."

A weird echo in my mind. The voice: *I'm dead, and you didn't do anything to stop it.* I put a hand out to steady myself, caught hold of the sideboard in the hall.

"Cassandra?" said Horowitz. "You okay?"

"No one is okay!" said Julie. "I went into the house," she continued; a total non sequitur, her mind jumping all over the place, to stop landing on the image of a dead Paris, I guessed. "The door was open. I ran in. The place was empty. Repossessed or something, you know? Bare walls. People had written things on the surfaces. '**** the bankers.' 'Foreclose my ass.' Stuff like that. It stank of piss and there were empty bottles everywhere, condom wrappers. But no Paris. *No Paris*! And I watched her go in there, like half an hour before."

Horowitz had taken out a notebook from his pocket. "Did you hear anything? Car engines, anything like that?"

"I don't know!"

"Did the place have a garage? A lot of those properties, they have a garage that can be accessed from the kitchen. At the side of the house."

Julie thought for a moment. "Yeah. Yeah, I think so."

"Is it possible someone had a car in there? That they left when you came in the door?"

Silence.

Then:

"Yeah. Yeah, it's possible. I mean, I was shouting. Calling for Paris, you know? I wasn't really listening. I was looking. For her. Oh

*****. Oh Jesus. You think I missed something because of that? You think I—"

"I think you were looking for your friend, to try to help her," said Horowitz softly.

Julie sat down abruptly on one of the living room chairs. Her movements, her speech, were abrupt—like someone had cut up footage of her, taken out the slow transitions, so that she jumped around the room.

"So after that, that was when you called the police?" said Horowitz.

Julie sighed. "Yeah. I mean, Paris had said not to. But I was freaked. The house being empty, you know? It was like a horror movie. So I dialed 911, and this cop car turned up like one minute later. It must have been close by, I guess."

"This was . . ." He consulted his notebook. "Officer O'Grady."

A shrug. "Maybe. He said his name was Brian. He came with his lights flashing, the siren, everything, you know? He was going fast and he braked hard; the tires squealed. It was ****** up. It was like a movie, and I couldn't turn it off. And you know the stupidest thing? You know how much of an ******* I am?"

"What?" said Horowitz. His tone pretty gentle.

"I had this song going around and around in my head! You know, the old hip-hop song? "Woop, woop, it's the sound of da police . . . woop, woop, it's the sound of da police." Someone was probably slitting my friend's throat at that very moment, and I was sitting in my car like a moron, watching this cop turn up and with a random ******* hip-hop song stuck on repeat in my head." She hung her head and sobbed.

"It's not your fault," I said. I knew all about unwanted sounds in the head.

341

"The mind responds to stress in unusual ways," said Horowitz. "I've seen people laughing uncontrollably when they find out their kid is dead."

"Mm," said Julie, noncommittal.

"And what happened after the cop, I mean Officer O'Grady, turned up?"

"He spoke to me for a while and then ran into the house. He didn't come out again, and after I'd sat there for like half an hour I figured he wasn't *coming* out, so I drove home. Which is why you came here, right?"

"Right," said Horowitz. "Like you, Officer O'Grady—Brian—found no one in the house and nothing suspicious. But we have a tech team over there now. If there are traces . . . if there's anything there, they'll find it."

"Oh God," said Julie.

I went and put my arm around her shoulder. She shook under my touch. "She didn't even get to finish her cranes," Julie said.

"What?" said Horowitz.

Julie was crying too much to explain; I filled him in about the thousand cranes.

"Oh, right," he said, like it didn't matter, when of course it did. I mean, it may not have been important for finding Paris. But it mattered *to* Paris.

She never got her wish.

"I think we need to take you in," said Horowitz to Julie. "Get a proper witness statement. Cassandra, I can give you a lift home if you like."

"Am I a *suspect*?" said Julie.

"No," said Horowitz. "And a suspect in what? At the moment we have a girl who has gone missing. Admittedly a sex worker in a town where sex workers have been disappearing, which fits a pattern. But for all we know she's run off to her parents in New York."

"She hates her parents," I said. I was thinking: *sex worker*. Hearing it like that, flat, neutral, was like a hammer blow.

"People have been known to go back to parents they hate. But for now I need to do this by the book, and that means bringing you in for a formal witness statement, Julie."

Julie closed her eyes. "Fine."

But it wasn't fine. Nothing was fine; not anymore.

Horowitz dropped me outside the house, but I didn't go in. I couldn't go in. Dad was at work anyway, so what was I going to do? Who was I going to talk to?

I waved to Julie as the car pulled away. She didn't wave back.

I took out my cell, went to call you, but then I remembered that I didn't have your number; I'd never asked for it.

Right then I wished I had.

"It's your fault," said the voice. I was standing on the sidewalk. Heat was rising from the ground in shimmers, in waves. I was blinking sweat and tears. A gull wheeled above me, crying its ugly cry, accusing me.

Cass, Cass, Cass. "You killed her," said the voice. "You were listening to your white noise and she called. She needed you. But you didn't answer."

"She called Julie," I said. "She called Julie too, and Julie was closer. But Paris told her not to call the cops. She couldn't do anything."

"She did more than you did. She went into the house."

"What could I have done?"

"You could have answered your cell. Instead of being so selfish. Instead of fighting with me."

"You said you were going to kill my dad! You told me to cut off my toe or you would murder him."

Silence.

"It's not my fault!" I shouted. "It's you! With your threats, with your cursing, with your making me block you out, with your endless—"

"You could have just cut off your toe," said the voice, sullenly.

"No, I couldn't."

Silence.

"If we had not been fighting, we would have heard the phone," said the voice.

I stood there very still for a moment. I had never heard the voice sound sad before. I had never heard it use the word "we."

"Excuse me?"

"It's us," said the voice. "It's our fault. Both of us. But . . ." And now the voice's tone went sly again. "But we're the same person, aren't we? I *am* you. That's what Dr. Lewis says, isn't it? I'm just the angry part of you. So it comes down to the same thing."

I felt sick. It *was* my fault. It was all my fault.

Like an automaton, I walked down the sidewalk, not watching where I was going. It was only when the hardness under my feet was replaced by soft sand that I realized I was at the beach.

I walked toward the ocean, drawn to it, an iron filing toward a magnet. It was high tide; the water was almost up to the piers. You wouldn't have been able to drive your truck around them. I could smell that indescribable smell of seaweed and salt and the deep.

I thought of Venus, stepping out of the sea. My feet were in the foam now, the wet sand sucking at my Converses. I took another step forward. Cold water pulled at my calves, made my jeans heavy; icy fingers. No matter how hot it gets in New Jersey the ocean always feels freezing to me. The Atlantic. It's too vast, too empty, to ever warm up.

I knew how it felt.

My feet moved forward of their own accord until I was waist deep. There were other people on the beach—I mean, it was daytime—but they were a long way away, closer to the piers.

Then, suddenly, I felt hands on my shoulders. I gasped and turned around, and there you were.

"What are you doing, Cass?" you asked.

"I don't know."

"Come in. Come in and talk to me."

You took my hand and pretty much dragged me back up onto the sand. You sat me down, then went to your truck and got a towel, put it over my legs.

"How can you drive around the piers?" I said.

"Huh?"

"High tide." I indicated the water.

"Oh. I don't need to. Just delivering to Pier One." You pointed to the truck. I couldn't see any bags of toys in it. "Dippin' Dots. I do plush and Dippin' Dots ice cream. I have no idea why. The hot dogs and stuff, they come from somewhere else. My warehouse is just stuffed animals and Dippin' Dots."

"Weird," I said.

"Yeah. So what were you doing walking into the ocean with all your clothes on?"

I looked at you. You were so *there*, so present. I can't describe it. You were just *with* me, looking at me, looking at me like I was real, and mattered. Interested in me. You and Paris, you were the first people ever to be interested in me. Even my dad wasn't, not really.

Especially since I killed his wife.

You were looking at me curiously, like you really genuinely wanted to know what was going on with me, like you *cared*. Did you care? Do you remember? I think you did. I think you care about everything. I think that's what makes you be *you*. If you came across a sea anemone that was out of the water and unable to breathe, you would throw it back in; you would save it. I don't know why I'm talking about sea anemones. It's stupid.

"You know my friend Paris?" I said.

"The weird one?"

"Yeah. She . . ."

"Cass, you're crying. What's wrong?"

So I told you. I told you everything.

"She was a prostitute, then?" you said, when I had finished.

"*No*. She was a stripper. And, what did she call it? A cam girl."

"Huh," you said. "I wouldn't have guessed. She seemed so . . ."

"Smart? Cool? Smart girls can be sexual, you know. It's her body, she can do what she wants with it." I sounded defensive; shrill. I didn't know what I was saying or why.

"I know that," you said. "I didn't mean to . . . Oh, I don't know. I'm just surprised, that's all. I'm sorry."

I looked at you for a moment, then sighed. "Julie told her it was dangerous. I should have too. But I guess I was, I don't know, I guess I thought it was glamorous, you know? I got why it was a thrill for her."

You nodded. "I see that. But, look, you are not to blame for this."

"No," I said, unconvinced.

"So I guess there's one big question," you said.

"Which is?"

"Which is what are we going to do about it?"

"What are we . . ."

"Yeah. What are we going to do? To find her?"

"I don't . . ."

"We have to try, right? We have to try to find her."

I thought back to all my research in the library. My theory that my voice was one of the dead women. And now it was like the circle had turned all the way around again, and again the Houdini Killer was in the middle of it.

"You hardly know her," I said.

"So?" you said. "She's in trouble. We have to help her."

"Why, because you like her?"

You stared at me. "What?"

"I saw you, the way you boosted her over the fence. I . . . it's fine. I don't know why I'm even mentioning it. Sorry . . . I'm . . . I'm not used to speaking to people, I'm not . . ."

"Cassie," you said gently.

I looked up.

"Yes?"

"Is this why you were weird in the pickup?"

"Uh-huh."

He smiled. A sad kind of smile. "I don't like Paris. I mean, I do, I like her a lot, she's a cool girl. But I *like* . . . you."

I blinked. "What?"

"Oh come on. You didn't pick up on it?"

Yes. Maybe. I don't know.

But I said nothing.

"****," you said. "Now I've made it super awkward. I'm sorry. I . . . look, just forget that, okay? Let's focus on Paris."

Yes, focus on Paris. Focus on Paris. Don't think about . . .

Don't think about . . .

His hands on your sides, his hands in your hair, his hands . . .

No.

You took a deep breath. "So. Paris. The cops have not done one thing to stop him so far, have they? The killer, I mean."

"You think it's the killer? Horowitz said she might have run away."

"You think that's likely?"

I looked away. "No."

"So," you said. "We need to hurry."

"This is the real world," I said. "People get away. Killers get away. It happens all the time. How are we going to stop it?"

You looked at me strangely, narrowing your eyes. "'People get away'? What are you talking about?"

"Nothing," I said.

MY MOTHER. I WAS TALKING ABOUT MY MOTHER. A GUY BRAINED HER AND RAN AND THAT WAS IT.

But I wasn't going to tell you that, not then.

And anyway, I had to admit it was true that from a distance the cops didn't seem to be doing much about any of the women who had gone missing. I mean, it had been going on for so long and there had been no progress, and people were talking; it was the focus of a bunch of media stories too.

On the other hand:

At the same time though, I was thinking of Agent Horowitz. He seemed smart, and I liked him by instinct.

And yet on the other hand again:

You were right. It had been months, years even, and no advances had been made. No killer had been caught.

And . . . what if they didn't get away this time? I mean, I couldn't bring my mom back from the dead and I couldn't get the guy who killed her, couldn't make him pay, but what if I could get *this* guy?

This guy.

This one guy.

And make him pay.

And maybe find Paris before he killed her too.

Even then I knew this was not a realistic idea.

"Plus . . . ," you said. "Don't you think that's a little suspicious? The lack of police action? I mean . . . what if the killer was a cop himself?"

"A *cop*?"

"It would add up, right?"

"I guess."

"Not only that, Julie said that Paris told her not to call the cops. Why would she do that?"

"Oh," I said. "I don't know. I'd forgotten about that."

I will give it to you: I am pretty sure you were only doing all this to distract me, to give me something to think about, rather than just uselessly worrying about Paris, but you did it *excellently*.

"Well," you continued, "what if that was because she *knew* the killer was a cop? So there would be no point calling them; she wouldn't have known which of them were in on it, maybe?"

I looked at you. "Huh. Yeah, I guess that would make sense."

"So let's do it," you said. "Let's find her." You pulled out your phone—it was an old-model iPhone; the phone of someone with money who hasn't gotten around to upgrading yet.

I was wrong in thinking that, I know that now. I didn't know it was the phone of someone with very little money at all. Someone whose dad bought it for him after he scored 1600 on his SATs. Bought it secondhand, spent days scouring eBay to get it for him.

But now I know. I know because I have spoken to your dad. A couple of times. Yeah. You didn't realize that, did you? I know a lot more about you than you think.

I don't mean this to sound sinister. I mean . . . I understand you better than I did.

Anyway.

You pulled out the phone, and you called up maps.

"This thing is too old for 4G," you said, as the screen slowly loaded. "You said this was in Bayview, right? The row of old clapboards by the sand?"

"Yeah, I think so."

You dragged the map with your finger, then used thumb and

finger to enlarge it. I had never seen anyone do that before; that's how sheltered my life was. That's how much I didn't have friends and how much the phones my dad got for me always sucked hard.

"You can just zoom it like that?" I said. "By touching? Wow."

You looked at me like I was from another planet. "You haven't seen one of these?"

"Yes! I mean, from a distance. Yeah."

"Hmm," you said. "Very Pygmalion."

"What?"

"You know, in Ovid. The guy who makes a statue of a woman, and brings it to life. But she doesn't know the language, the customs, and stuff. You're like that."

"I know the story. You're saying . . . I'm a statue woman? Learning to speak like a person?"

"You know the language already. But you haven't seen someone use a touch screen before, so it's as if you're new to the world, like her, and . . . Hmm."

"Doesn't really work, does it?"

"I admit it's a flawed analogy," you said. You smiled, and to my surprise I smiled back, though there was still an aching hole inside me where Paris had been. Where my memory of Paris still was.

"Anyway," you said. You flicked something, and the map turned from a sketch, all lines and block colors, to a satellite image.

"Whoa," I said.

"Seriously?" you asked.

"I'm a Luddite, okay?" I said. "And I'm poor and have no friends. So bite me."

You smiled again. "I love that you know the word 'Luddite.'"

"Thanks. I think you're alone in that."

"Didn't Paris love words?"

"Yes." Paris appeared between us like a ghost.

Silence.

"Sorry," you said. "Shouldn't . . . you know, mention her."

You lowered your head to your phone again, zoomed out. You held the screen up for me to see.

"What am I looking at?" I asked.

"You're looking at a straight road, with no cross streets."

"Uh-huh."

"You don't see what that means?"

I peered at it. I could see the shapes of the houses, the darkness of the beach and ocean, the street. Cars parked up and down it. Everything, even from this satellite view, looking dilapidated and sad.

"No," I said finally. "What am I supposed to be seeing?"

"You said when Paris was in the house, Julie saw a car *turn* in front of her. It woke her up with its lights. Yes?"

I took a breath, looking at the phone. I was holding it in my hand now. "But there are no cross streets," I said slowly.

"Bingo. If a car turned, then it came out of a driveway. Or a garage."

"You're thinking . . ."

"Yes."

"But how could Agent Horowitz miss this?"

"You said he was FBI, right?"

"Yeah. Or something like that."

"So he's from out of town. He wouldn't know the street."

"You're from out of town," I said. "How come you know the streets of Bayview so well?"

I asked it kind of as a joke, but you blanched a little. "I do a lot of deliveries," you said. Your tone was strange, but I didn't push you on it; I was thinking about Paris and Julie.

"I need to talk to Julie," I said.

"Yes." You took the phone back from me; put it away. "And then we need to decide what to do next. I mean, maybe she remembers what kind of car it was. And maybe . . . maybe Paris is still alive."

"You think so?"

"It's possible. No one ever finds the bodies, do they?"

"No. Well, a foot."

"Yeah. But who knows what he does with them before he kills them?"

"Thanks," I said, feeling sick. "You just made it awful again."

"Sorry. But . . . what if she's alive? Maybe we can find her together. I mean, if you want my help. If you want . . . we could try."

There you went again, using that little word. That dangerous, beautiful little word.

We.

It even clouded out my doubts—the terrible, selfish little part of me that was still thinking, *Is this because he likes Paris? Is that why he wants to save her?*

But another part of me, a voice inside me, but not THE voice, said: *No, he likes you. That's why he wants to help you.*

Anyway.

You know what? You may have planned it all along. You may have just intended it as a distraction, to get me over my grief. If so, I'm sorry. I'm sorry for all the **** it got you into. I'm sorry for everything that happened after THIS. FATAL. MOMENT. IN THE STORY.

The one where I turned to you, and I held your hand in mine, as we sat there in the baking heat by the susurrating shore, and I said,

"Deal. We'll find her together. You and me."

I AM. SO. SORRY.

INT. A TEENAGE GIRL'S BEDROOM. BUT
YOU CAN'T REALLY TELL THAT BECAUSE IT'S
PITCH-BLACK. YOU CAN'T SEE ANYTHING, IN
FACT. YOU CAN ONLY HEAR VOICES. VOICES
WITH NO BODIES. I WOULD TELL YOU
TO CLOSE YOUR EYES, BUT THEN YOU
WOULDN'T BE ABLE TO READ THIS. YOU'LL
JUST HAVE TO IMAGINE VOICES IN THE
DARKNESS.
AND THEN, NOT INCONSEQUENTIALLY, YOU
WILL GET AN IDEA OF WHAT IT IS LIKE TO
BE ME.

Oh no, wait.
Before the voices—you hear a phone being dialed, and then
a ringing tone, okay? A ringing tone in the
darkness.
Let's start again.

INT. A TEENAGE GIRL'S BEDROOM. IT IS PITCH-
BLACK. YOU HEAR A BEEPING THAT YOU SOON
IDENTIFY AS A CELL PHONE BEING DIALED. IT
RINGS.
A GIRL'S VOICE BLURRED BY TIREDNESS
ANSWERS.

ME: Julie?
JULIE: Cass? Cass, it's like two a.m.
ME: Did I wake you?

JULIE: No.

ME: I'm sorry. I've been trying you and trying you. You were out, or you weren't answering the phone or something.

JULIE: (in a small voice) I was at my mom's.

ME: Oh.

JULIE: What is it, Cass? What's up?

ME: It's the car.

JULIE: What car?

ME: The one you heard. You know, the one that woke you up? I was wondering . . . Where were you parked?

JULIE: Huh?

ME: I mean, which side of the street? And were there any cross streets?

JULIE: The right side of the street. Facing north? Toward the Cape. No cross streets.

ME: No way a car could turn onto the road?

JULIE: Um . . .

ME: I mean, a car passing you, it would have to just be going down the street, north or south? It couldn't be coming from a cross street, because there were no cross streets.

JULIE: Uh, yeah.

ME: But you said the car turned. You said a car *turned* in front of you, and it washed you with its headlights, and that's what woke you up.

JULIE: Yeah. ****** had his brights on.

ME: But it turned. Right?

JULIE: Oh . . .

ME: You see where I'm going with this? It turned, on a
street with no cross streets.

JULIE: So it must have come from a driveway. Or a
garage . . .

ME: The house she went into. It was right beside you?

JULIE: Yeah. Like twenty feet.

ME: So the car could have come from the garage.

JULIE: I guess.

ME: And something else. You said the line was bad?
Like, *shhhhing* like the ocean?

JULIE: Yeah.

ME: Or like car wheels? Like she might have been in a
car? Already?

JULIE: Oh ****.

ME: Picture something. Imagine Paris in the trunk of a
car. She has her cell in her pocket. She makes a
call. To you. That's the *shhhhing*, right? But then
the driver of the car realizes. He stops. The line
goes dead—you said that, didn't you? Then there's
a . . . what did you call it?

JULIE: (flatly) A heavy metal sound.

ME: The trunk opening.

JULIE: And then a *thunk*. And the line went dead.

ME: Yeah.
Silence.

JULIE: I need to call Agent Horowitz.

ME: Wait. What kind of car?

JULIE: Huh?

ME: The car. What was it?

JULIE: A Jeep.

ME:	Like, a 4x4? Or a Jeep, the brand?
JULIE:	The brand. I saw the logo.
ME:	A Wrangler?
JULIE:	Maybe. One of those big, fast ones. You know, with blacked-out windows? Like rappers drive.
ME:	(grateful for Dad's car magazines) An SRT8?
JULIE:	I don't know.
ME:	Air channels down the sides? Four exhausts?
JULIE:	Yeah! Yeah.
ME:	That's an SRT8. Color?
JULIE:	I don't know. It was night.
ME:	Hmm. Did you catch any of the license plate?
JULIE:	I wasn't . . . No. Wait.
ME:	(leaning forward on my bed) Yes?
JULIE:	No. Nothing. I thought . . . it's like there's something there, like something on the tip of my tongue, but I don't know what it is.
ME:	Okay.
JULIE:	Sorry.
ME:	Don't be sorry.
JULIE:	Look, Cass, I'm going to go now. I'm going to call the agent. Tell him about the car.
ME:	Don't do that.
JULIE:	What? Why?
ME:	You know people blame the cops for not finding the guy? The killer?
JULIE:	Yeah.
ME:	But what if it's not just *not finding him*? What if they *are* him?
JULIE:	The cops . . . are . . . the killer?

ME: Or a cop, I don't know. But think about it. They could suppress evidence.

JULIE: Keep it quiet. Keep their prints off stuff.

ME: Yeah.

JULIE: Jesus.

ME: Give me a couple of days. Then we'll talk to Horowitz about the car.

JULIE: Okay. You think it's him?

ME: (thinking about this) No. Not him. But could be someone else.

JULIE: I still think I should tell him about the Jeep.

ME: If he's good, he'll work it out.

JULIE: I guess.

ME: 'Night, Julie.

JULIE. 'Night, Cass.

ME: (pause)

JULIE: We'll get this ******, right? We'll get Paris back?

ME: Yes. Yes, we will.

JULIE: (sounding suddenly like a child) You promise?

ME: I promise.

CLICK. AND THE LINE GOES DEAD.

BLACKNESS.

FADE OUT.

I had no right to do that. No right to promise something I couldn't deliver.

The next day was a Monday. I had breakfast with Dad—I had nut-free toast, and he had Pop-Tarts. Dad was reading the paper.

"Oh, ****, Cass," he said suddenly.

I looked up. "What?"

"Oh, Cass, I'm sorry."

Now I knew what was in the paper. "Why?" I asked, as if I didn't know. For some reason, by some instinct, I didn't want Dad knowing about Agent Horowitz, about Julie, about any of it.

Some *helpful* instinct, as it turned out.

Dad turned the paper around. There was a photo of Paris—it must have been taken before she was ill; she looked plump and happy. Fifteen, maybe. She was standing by a pool.

"That's your friend, right? The one from the hospital?"

"Yeah," I said.

"I'm so sorry, honey. They say she's disappeared, that they think . . ." He went silent, scanning the page upside down.

Oh.

Oh ****.

"Cassandra," said Dad, and it was never a good sign when he used my full name. "Cassandra, were you hanging out with a *stripper*?"

"Um."

"Cassandra?"

"Um, yeah. But she didn't do touching, she—"

He turned the paper, showing me a picture from Paris's Instagram. It showed her with stars over her nipples, smoking.

"Are you ******* insane?" he shouted. "Oh no, wait. *Yes*! You are ****** insane! Jesus, Cass, I'm *trying* here, I'm trying to protect you, like your mom would have wanted, and you're just . . ."

"She was nice," I said quietly. "She was my friend."

Dad shook his head. He was looking at me as if I came with instructions in another language. "She was a . . . she was this"—he indicated the paper—"and look where it got her."

"You're saying girls who take their clothes off are asking to be killed?"

"That's not what I'm saying, and you know it!"

"Do I?" I said. "Do I, Dad? Because it sounds to me like you're saying that being taken by the Houdini Killer is some kind of moral punishment for being a stripper."

A long pause.

"I don't know what to do with you anymore," said Dad.

"Tell him to **** off," said the voice. "Tell him you don't give a **** what he thinks."

"Sorry, Dad," I said.

He grunted. Then there was a knock on the door. Dad went to open it.

"Hey," you said. I couldn't see you, but I recognized your voice. I went to the kitchen door, but Dad was blocking the doorway.

"Hi," said Dad. "You need something?"

"I was wondering . . . if Cass could come out."

"No," said Dad.

"Oh," you said. "Uh . . . oh."

"Have a good day," said Dad. "Shouldn't you be getting to work?"

"Yeah," you said. And Dad closed the door on you.

Sorry about that.

Dad came back to the kitchen. "No going out today, okay?"

"Okay," I said.

"I have to know you're safe, Cass."

"Yeah."

"Good."

He went upstairs and I heard the shower start. "Your own father hates you," said the voice dully.

"After six p.m.," I said automatically.

The voice shut up. Ever since I didn't cut off my toe, it had lost some of its power. It didn't push things anymore. It was more like an irritation—a wasp that circles back to your picnic table intermittently. I could mostly ignore it.

Dad came back downstairs, put on a thin jacket, and pocketed his keys from the monkey's little tray. Then he went out. "Remember: stay here," he said.

"Sure, Dad."

Ten minutes later there was another knock at the door.

"I know your dad's angry, but you want to ride to work with me?" you said. "We can talk about stuff. I have an idea I think we could—"

"Yes," I said.

I grabbed my keys and closed the door behind me.

You started the engine and pulled out, took Ocean and then Maple, driving to the center of town. As we drove, you turned to me. "Get anywhere with Julie?" you asked.

I rocked my hand; an equivocal gesture. "Maybe. She thinks it was a Jeep. One of the V8 sport models."

"An SRT8?" you asked.

I looked at you, surprised. I hadn't figured you for a car head. "Yeah. You know cars?"

You shook your head. "Nah. My dad is into them."

"Mine too." There were always magazines on our coffee table. *Muscle Car. American Auto.*

You smiled. "Something we have in common, then."

You made a couple of turns, getting closer to the center. We pulled up at a stop sign. "Could be enough," you said, almost to yourself.

"Huh?"

"The model. Gives us something to go on."

"For what?"

You did like a *bear with me* wave of your hand. "I'll tell you. I want to show you something first."

"It had better not be your genitals," I said.

You laughed, surprised. I liked to hear you laugh. Then I felt guilty because Paris was dead and here I was flirting with you. I shut up after that, and you stopped talking too—I think the same thought had crossed your mind.

Soon we had arrived at the closest thing Oakwood has to a main drag, the little grocery stores and liquor stores and toy stores. A few restaurants with outside seating.

You turned onto an alleyway, passed a bar with a neon sign showing a woman kneeling on a table, a cowboy hat on her head, swinging a lasso in one hand and holding a beer in the other. The sign was off.

Beyond the bar, there was a long, low warehouse—a redbrick building with steel roll-up doors. You parked in front of the doors and made an expansive gesture at them. "Welcome to the nerve center," you said.

Then you got out of the pickup and went to the steel door. You entered a code on a padlock; snapped it open. You rolled the door up and came back to the truck. Then you drove us both in.

"Wow," I said.

We were in a vast space; you wouldn't have known from the street how big it was. It must have covered most of the block. There was only one floor, so the ceiling was high. Corrugated-iron roof, punctuated in places by plastic windows. From these, shafts of sunlight cut down, illuminating random piles of goods, as if to highlight treasure. Motes of dust swirled in the light, little grains of darkness; inverse constellations.

And piled up, in hills, in mountains, all over the floor were bags of stuffed toys. Thousands, maybe even millions of them. Okay, not millions. But thousands.

You went to that place every day; I guess it didn't impress you anymore. But the first time I saw it . . . it was something else. It's weird: people think of the everyday world as banal, as mundane. But when you really consider it, there's so much weird and amazing stuff. For instance: an amusement park has to have a place to store its prizes.

And that place has to be *amazing*.

I walked around for a bit, just staring. There were wide walkways between the piles, so it was possible to see almost all the way to each wall; it only increased the sense of scale. It was surreal.

Warehouses are usually hard, industrial, practical places, right? This one *looked* like a warehouse—the corrugated iron, the bare brick walls. But it was full, I mean absolutely full, of soft toys. It was like something out of a fairy tale.

As I wandered, I realized the mountains were arranged by type, each towering pile of transparent bags containing a different character. There was one that was all Pokémon, another—larger—full of Angry Birds. Disney characters took up an entire wall. Minnies, Donald Ducks. Olafs. There was a whole alpine range of Beanie Babies.

"This is crazy," I said.

"It's pretty full on," you agreed.

"How do you know where everything is?"

You shrugged. "You get used to it."

"What are you getting today?"

You pulled a piece of paper out of your pocket. "Two bags medium Bugs Bunny. Three bags large Minecraft people. The kids love Minecraft. And a small bag of Mickeys."

"And you know where all of those are?"

"Yep. There. There. And there." You pointed to three corners of the warehouse. "I'll grab them in a moment. Come over here."

You led me to a small mound of stuffed dinosaurs. You pulled out a bag of them and motioned for me to sit on it. Then you sat down next to me.

"You want to show me dinosaurs?" I said.

You looked puzzled for a second. "Oh! No. But I thought of something." You pulled out your phone. "I was thinking, we could start a hash tag. #SRT8; something like that. Get people to tweet the location if they see one."

"What?"

"To find the car, you know?"

"No."

"You don't want to find it?"

"I mean, no, I have no idea what you're talking about."

"We'll get it trending," you said. "Offer a prize or something to get the ball rolling. An iPad. It doesn't matter. We can worry about making good on it later."

I looked right into your eyes. "What. Are. You. Talking. About?"

You narrowed your eyes. "Wait. You don't know Twitter?"

"Yeah. I mean, I've heard of it."

"But you haven't used it?"

"No. I look on Instagram sometimes. For, like, fashion. You know."

You glanced at my clothes, raised your eyebrows.

"Very funny," I said.

You put a hand over your heart. "Sorry. It was too easy. Okay. Listen." You took out your phone, opened the Twitter app. You showed me the timeline, the trending hashtags. "What I'm thinking is, if we get people to tweet every time they see an SRT8, and we ask them to include a location, we might start to see a pattern."

"Why would people do that?"

"That's how come the prize. We say it's a marketing thing, we pretend we work for Jeep or something. We say that every week one person who tweets that they've seen an SRT8 will win something."

"Okay . . . ," I said. "And you think this will work?"

"I have no idea. But I think it's the kind of thing the cops would never think of. They're still operating in the twentieth century."

"No. They just have systems that let them look up all the SRT8 owners in town."

"Well, okay," you said. "Point taken. But this is what *we* have. It would be better if we had a license plate, of course."

Something itched at the back of my brain.

"What is it, Cass? You look weird."

I closed my eyes. "I don't . . ."

"You thought of something?"

"Sh," I said. I had the strangest feeling. Like there was an idea curled up inside my mind and I needed to make it uncurl, open itself, like one of Dad's millipedes.

You shut up. I opened my eyes and saw the piles of toys, but I wasn't really seeing them. I was going over everything Julie had said, the whole conversation with me and Agent Horowitz. I knew there was something there. Something that made me think . . . I don't know what it made me think.

That Julie might know the license plate, without realizing she did? I didn't know why I thought that though.

"No," I said. "I can't get it. It's gone."

That feeling—of something being on the tip of my tongue, as Julie had said—had vanished.

"The license plate?"

"Yeah. It's making me think of something, but I don't know what."

"Helpful."

"Sarcasm is the lowest form of wit," I said.

"No," you said. "That's photobombing."

"What? What's photobombing?"

"I despair of you."

"Whatever."

"Anyway," you said eventually, "it could play without the license plate. We make it like one of those online treasure-hunt marketing campaigns. Pretend we're driving a Jeep SRT8 around the town. First person to spot it each day wins a prize, kind of thing. So we say that they have to tweet #SRT8 and their location. We might see a pattern. Or at least find some people who drive them."

"If you say so. The whole Twitter thing is your area."

"Or," you said, in a tentative tone—your voice a foot gingerly tapping on a frozen lake before venturing onto it. "Or . . . we could hand it over to the cops."

"You were the one who was all for investigating on our own."

"Yeah. But . . . I don't know. This feels big."

"We can't go to the cops," I said.

"You don't trust them?"

"Not that. My dad would find out. They'd tell him. They all eat at the restaurant."

"Hmm," you said. "Your dad doesn't like you hanging out with me, right?"

"My dad doesn't like a lot of stuff."

You had been playing with the bag of toys we were sitting on; you took out a stuffed T. rex and started tossing it up and down in the air, catching it by its tail. "So we do it ourselves. Run this Twitter thing. See what comes up."

"Yeah."

"Okay."

Silence. There was that moment—I know you felt it too—there was that moment where the boy and the girl realize they're sitting next to each other, alone, in a mostly dark warehouse, on a soft surface. One they could sink down into.

Together.

"Um. So which school are you going to?" I said awkwardly.

"What?"

"You said you were going to college. On a swim scholarship."

"Oh. Brown."

"*Brown*? Wow. How good a swimmer are you?"

"I'm okay. That's why I'm not around at the apartment much. I do a bunch of training, when I'm not working."

Silence.

"You?" you asked. "College, I mean?"

"I . . . I guess. I have one year of high school left."

"Sucks."

"Yeah."

Silence. You shifted a little closer to me. I felt our molecules align with each other, like when we were on the couch in the apartment, the electrons synchronizing their spins, reaching out to each other across the distance between atoms.

You looked into my eyes.

You leaned toward me, to kiss me.

And I pulled away, sharply. It was automatic. I . . . Paris had only *just* disappeared, and it felt wrong. It felt like betraying her, to be with you like that. I saw the hurt in your eyes immediately, and my heart flipped.

"I'm sorry," I said.

"No," you said. "It was . . . I shouldn't have . . ."

Your voice frayed into silence.

Unbelievably awkward silence.

Our thousandth awkward moment, give or take.

Then your radio crackled.

"714, what's your 20?" said a pissed-off sounding voice. "Where's my goddamn plush?"

"This is 714," you said, thumbing the radio. "Leaving the warehouse now."

"Good. Get to Pier Two STAT. Then I want four bags of Pokémon to Pier One."

"10-4," you said.

"Out," said the voice on the other end.

"Out," you said.

You stood up stiffly. I stood up too. "You want to come with me?" you said. "I don't want to . . . just leave you here."

"Um. Okay," I said.

Come on, Earth! Swallow me right now.

But it never does.

You pointed to the far left corner of the warehouse. "Can you grab the Bugs Bunnies? There are three piles—small, medium, large. We need medium. I'll get the rest. But I have to hurry." Your voice was flatter than usual, like you were trying not to show your feelings, trying to pave over them with smooth hardness. Concrete.

"Can't keep the kids waiting," I said jokily.

"No," you said. Still flatly.

I nodded, and started walking.

It was weird, that voice on your radio. I mean, for once a voice came from nowhere and actually helped—broke that terrible moment after you tried to kiss me and I moved away.

Has to be a first time for everything.

Here's the thing though: I wish I had let you kiss me. Part of me wanted to, I promise. Even if we were disturbed right away by the radio, I wish I had let our lips touch, wish I had not pulled away. Wish I had not caused that hurt in your eyes.

But at the same time . . . I couldn't. Not at that moment. And I was angry with the part of me that wanted me to, if I'm giving you the whole truth.

Even writing this down, I feel pretty sickened by myself.

I mean, Paris was gone, most probably dead, and I was even picturing the idea of kissing you.

Because I pictured it a lot.

Even then, just after Paris had gone missing.

Believe me, I hate myself quite a lot right now, but what can I do? I said I would tell the truth, and only the truth, so help me, God.

I offer two things in mitigation though:

1. We were only together in the first place because of her. Because I wanted to find her. I mean, that was the whole thing we were doing. The Twitter thing. Working stuff out. It was you who knew the shape of the street Julie had been on; you who worked out that the car could only have turned *out of a drive*. It was all you— the clues, they all came from you. So you and Paris, you were connected.

2. I was a teenager. Am a teenager. I figure if Paris were a couple years younger, and the situation were reversed, she would have wanted to be kissed too. If she never had been, I mean. Never kissed, I mean. She totally would. Yeah, you were the first person I kissed. Don't get a big head about it.

3. I was grieving. I was. And people's emotions do weird things when they're grieving. They want to kiss boys and stuff, and scream and shout and laugh. Or they pull away from a boy who tries to kiss them, even though they want to, even though they really want to. It's not just *feeling sad*. It's more complicated than that. Even Agent Horowitz said it.

4. The voice punished me for it. I mean, not by making me hurt myself. I'd mostly stopped doing that, now that I knew the voice *couldn't* kill my dad. Though sometimes I still cleaned my room and stuff when it told me to. Because the alternative was a lot of cursing and shouting from the voice, which was unpleasant. But . . . where was I? Oh yes. The voice did a lot of cursing and shouting after I got home that day. It was unpleasant.

5. I've gone over my two things. I KNOW.

You drove me to the pier. If it weren't for Paris being gone, it would have been as good as the first time, cruising along the beach, the hard sand under the wheels, slaloming around the groups of people. You had turned the radio on—some MOR rock ballad was playing. The windows of the truck were open, and the wind whipped my hair.

It's strange: A car on a road feels normal. A car on a beach always feels like flying. Like freedom. Even then I felt it, almost wanted to ask you if I could drive again.

You parked right by the pier and jumped down; threw the bags of toys up onto the side.

I looked at my watch. "You'd better drop me at home. Sometimes Dad comes back for lunch."

"You grounded or something?"

"It's complicated," I said.

"Sure. Okay. I get that. I get complicated."

"You do?"

"My mom died too. When I was fifteen. Me and my dad . . . Things are difficult between us."

I was staring at you.

"Oh, ****," you said. "Your mom's not dead? I thought your dad said . . . I thought it was . . . I don't know. Something else we—"

"No, she's dead," I said.

You were swallowing anxiously. "Sorry, sorry, I just . . ."

"It's cool," I said.

"I blurt stuff out," you said. "It's a curse. My voice is totally out of my control."

Oh, I thought, *you have no idea.*

"Anyway," you said. "I'll drive you home."

373

I walked into Dr. Rezwari's office and stopped. She was sitting at her desk, which was usually bare, and there was work all over it—files, sheaths of paper held together with clips. Her makeup was not applied as adroitly as usual; her lipstick was smudged and there were tracks in her eyeliner.

Her eyes were red and puffy.

"Are you all right?" I asked. She was looking at me blankly.

She did that blinking thing—I could almost see her consciousness swim up from some black depth. "I'm fine, thank you. Take a seat."

I sat down.

"The voice is still gone?" she asked.

"Yeah."

"Excellent. And how are you feeling?"

"Good," I said.

"Okay," said Dr. Rezwari. "And the medication. Any side effects?"

"No."

"No drowsiness? Lack of appetite?"

"Oh, yeah. All of that. But that's normal, right?"

"Yes. To a degree. Keep an eye on it, yes?" She moved papers around on her desk, absently.

"I will."

"Great. You're doing very well, Cassandra. I'm very pleased with your progress."

"No thanks to you." That wasn't me. That was the voice.

"Uh-huh," I said.

Dr. Rezwari rubbed at her eyes. Then she looked up at me and seemed surprised I was still there. "So . . . I'll see you next week?" she said.

"Yeah," I said. "Are you . . . um . . . can I help?"

"Excuse me?"

"You seem upset. Can I help?"

Dr. Rezwari laughed—a half-hollow, half-real laugh. "*You* want to help me? Your psychiatrist?"

"Sorry, it's stupid, I—"

"No, it's kind of you. I guess my work with you is done! The pupil has become the master. I'm fine, truly." She moved another file, randomly as far as I could see. "I just . . . something happened to one of our outpatients. Something terrible. Nothing to concern you."

"Paris?"

Her eyes sharpened. "You knew her?"

Suddenly I knew that I didn't want to talk about Paris. "Not really. We met in the courtyard. But I read in the paper . . . about . . ."

"Yes," said Dr. Rezwari. She made a sobbing sound. "Oh God. Sorry. This is so unprofessional. I was . . . I was very fond of her."

I stared at her, surprised. But yes, why not? Paris was one of those people. She didn't so much have charisma as an *aura*. To my amazement I found myself feeling a moment of connection with Dr. Rezwari. "Sorry," I said.

"Thank you. And now I must let you go, try to gather myself before my next appointment."

"Okay. See you next week."

"See you, Cassandra." She looked down at her desk and didn't look back up.

I closed the door behind me, took the corridor lined with photos of old board members and then the green stairs down to the lobby, where the bus stop was.

"Liar," said the voice. "You lied to her about everything. About your drugs. About Paris."

"Shut up. It's not six."

"Fine. But you're still a liar. And it's going to get you in trouble."

"This is it?"

"Yeah," you said. We were sitting in your pickup early in the morning, outside a liquor store. You had an hour before starting work—and every second counted. I mean, what could be happening to Paris as the hours ticked by . . . We both knew it, but neither of us said it.

You showed me the screen of your phone. I looked at it. There was a list of tweets. The pictures next to them showed a whole range of people. Young, old, white, black. I didn't know what you had done, but you had gotten a *load* of different people looking for that Jeep.

"Read it," you said.

I read.

#SRT8 Lauderdale b/t Ash and Ocean
Spotted! Bayside 8th Street #SRT8
#SRT8 @ the Laundromat on Fort in Lauderdale
#SRT8 on Mayflower Drive in Lauderdale
#Lauderdale #SRT8 #Ocean & 10th

"That's just a random sampling," you said. "Notice anything?"

"Yeah. Lauderdale."

"Hence, we are sitting here in Lauderdale."

"And we're just going to wait till we see a Jeep SRT8?" I was starting to feel less sure about this plan. "There are hardly any houses around here. It's all factories and offices and industrial buildings."

"Nevertheless," you said, "Lauderdale came up most. That means someone who owns an SRT8 either lives here or works here. Furthermore, a lot of the tweets mention Ocean Avenue. Which is why we're on Ocean Avenue."

"You're a latter-day Sherlock," I said.

"That makes you Watson."

"Fine. I'm comfortable with—"

I shut up. A black Jeep SRT8 had just turned right onto the street in front of us. It traveled north slowly. Its windows were darkened—privacy glass. *Perfect for a murderer,* I thought. *Murderers like privacy.*

"There!" I said. "There!" There was a nasty worm of a thought at the back of my mind—this could be the person who . . .

who . . .

who took Paris.

"Yep," you said. You turned the key in the ignition.

"What are you going to do?"

"I'm going to follow it, obviously." You checked the traffic and then gunned across the road to catch up with the Jeep. A guy in a BMW shook his fist at us.

"Keep two cars between us and them," I said. "I saw it in a movie."

"Yeah, I'm not going to do that," you said. "I'd just lose them. I'm not a spy."

"Okay."

We fell silent as you kept after the Jeep, turning when it turned. At one point we hit some lights and the Jeep got through just before they went red. You braked, hard. "****," you said, hitting the steering wheel with the palm of your hand.

But then the lights went green and you pulled away, and there was the SRT8, just turning left a block ahead. You accelerated—if there had been a camera, you'd have been so busted. You drove fast, turned the corner with the tires squealing. The Jeep was maybe two hundred yards ahead, just a Datsun mini-truck thing between us and it.

Then the Jeep slowed and turned into a driveway.

You slowed the pickup to a crawl and parked just down the street. I nodded at the car door and you nodded back; we both got out and walked down the street.

You took my hand. It was the first time our skin had touched. I don't know if you felt it, but I did. It was . . . it was as if there were thousands of nerve endings there, in my palm, in my fingers, that I had never known about, that had just lain dormant for my entire life. *How can I have all this skin I didn't know about?* I thought. *How can no one ever have touched it before?*

Because I had never felt anything like this before.

I swallowed.

I looked at you.

We paused at the driveway where the Jeep turned, feeling the warmth of each other's hands.

We saw the Jeep's taillights disappear behind a warehouse, which was next to a massive amount of heavy equipment—cranes, diggers, rollers. A few guys were walking around in yellow hard hats, hi-vis vests on, brown boots and jeans a kind of uniform.

But none of this was what had snagged my attention.

What had snagged my attention was:

A sign on a couple of shiny stainless-steel poles, reading:
DEVON AND SONS DEMOLITION.

"What?" you said.

"The sign. Let's say you work for a demolition firm. Think you'd find it hard to hide a body?"

"Oh."

Silence, as we both pictured Paris buried beneath the foundation of a building; her hair crushed by concrete.

Well, I did anyway. I don't know about you.

That was when the Jeep SRT8 appeared again, around the warehouse. It bounced over the rutted earth toward us, the windshield darkened so we couldn't see who was inside. We stepped back, eyes on the car.

Then another Jeep SRT8 came out behind it, black too, its windows darkened.

Then another.

And another.

"Oh," you said. "Great."

"It's a *company car*," I said, stupidly. "A company car."

A long moment of silence.

"There's a lot of stuff to demolish when the economy is down, I suppose," I said. I felt bleak. Our lead was not a lead at all. It was just a firm that owned a load of SRT8s.

"Of course," you said. "Stupid of me."

We watched the four black Jeeps drive down the road west from us, in convoy, before disappearing from view as they turned onto Ocean, toward town. Then we started walking back to the pickup.

"Well, the tweet thing worked," you said.

"Yep."

"But now we have too many SRT8s."

"So we're nowhere," I said.

"Yeah," you said. "I mean, for now."

You pressed the key fob and the pickup flashed and beeped. We opened our doors to climb in.

I put my hands against the dash. My breath was coming in gulps, violent. My heart was spinning, fast, like a blender. A blender that was turning my organs to mulch, to liquid.

I touched my cheeks. Tears were running down them; I felt like I was choking. Actually choking.

You put your hand on my shoulder. Nothing more. You didn't say anything.

"She's dead, isn't she?" I said.

"Cass . . ."

"She's dead, and we had ONE LEAD. And now . . ."

"The cops—"

"The cops know NOTHING. You said so yourself."

"Oh, Cass."

I turned away from you. Through my tears, the world on the other side of the truck window was blurred; running to the ground, melting down to nothing. I shut my eyes and closed it out.

"Cass. Cass."

I opened my eyes. We were parked on one of the streets behind the boardwalk. We were right outside a fifties motel. The Flamingo. There was a giant pink plastic flamingo outside, holding a cocktail with an umbrella in it. Three floors of rooms rose up on the other side of a thin strip of grass, pink with white balconies, like a wedding cake.

"What are we doing here?" I said.

"I want to show you something," you said.

"Don't you have to go to work?"

You shrugged. You tapped the radio on your shoulder. "I *am* at work. When there are no deliveries, I'm supposed to sort stock, tidy up the piles. That kind of ****. But they won't know."

"And if you get a call for deliveries?"

"Then I'll have to take it."

"My dad—"

"Won't be home for hours and you know it."

"He sometimes comes back for lunch."

"When was the last time?"

"About . . . Hmm. About two years ago."

"Wow," you said. "You two make me and my dad look functional."

"We live to serve," I said flatly.

You made an impatient gesture. "Anyway. I do want to show you something. Come on," you said, and you got out of the truck and walked up to the motel.

"Fine," I said, to nobody. And I followed you inside.

The lobby was arranged around a pond, a fake palm tree in the middle of it. A huddle of pink lawn flamingos gathered next to the palm tree, metal legs disappearing into the murky water. A mural of a lagoon in Florida surrounded us, lurid sunset turning the walls orange and red.

A young, bored-looking guy wearing glasses sat at the reception desk. You walked over, nodding to him.

"You got it?" he said.

"Yep." You handed him a Jiffy envelope and he slid it away, out of sight under the desk.

"Cool if we go to the roof?" you said.

"Whenever, man," said the guy behind the desk.

You nodded toward a door at the back of the lobby and then opened it for me. "Jesus," I said. "Are you a drug dealer?" I was remembering your saying that you'd made a delivery to Bayview; that this was why you knew about the cross streets.

"Not *me*. My boss."

"But . . ."

"Turns out, that's why they wanted someone with a driving license. I don't have to shell shrimp, but I do have to deliver stuff."

"But if you were caught . . ."

"I won't be. And I need the cash. It pays better than the shrimp."

"You can't need the money that badly."

You stopped and looked at me. "No? My scholarship only pays tuition and room and board."

"Your dad—"

"Lost his job like three years ago."

"Oh," I said.

"Yeah."

"So," I said. "That's what you wanted to show me? That you were dealing?"

"Actually, no."

We were climbing the stairs; we'd arrived at the top of the

building. We walked down a gloomy corridor, past a flickering green fire-exit sign, and stopped at a door that said,

POOL. OPEN 10–4 P.M., MAY TO OCT. NO NUDITY OR DIVING. NO UNACCOMPANIED CHILDREN.

You pushed open the door, and we stepped out onto the roof. Pink lounge chairs were lined up next to a surprisingly clean swimming pool, the water clear and blue under the bright sunny sky. We were three stories up; you could see over the buildings on the other side of the street to the boardwalk, and the beach beyond, the sand almost golden next to the dark navy of the ocean. A container ship crawled across the horizon.

"Weirdly beautiful, isn't it?" you said.

"Yeah."

The pool was long and oblong. To the right of it was a bar area, a tiki-style thing with a straw roof. I figured they would be big on cocktails with umbrellas in them. Next to this was a small bandstand with mike stands, amps, and instruments sitting there, as if a band had been playing them and had suddenly abandoned them for some urgent reason.

At the edges of the roof were low walls. I could see why there were NO UNACCOMPANIED CHILDREN. I could also see, by crouching, that when you were swimming you would barely see the walls—it would be as if you were swimming in the sea, nothing between you and the ocean.

You saw me crouching. "Cool, no?"

"Uh-huh."

"When you're in, it's like an infinity of water."

"Poetic."

"Yeah. Sorry."

I walked around the pool. "You come here often?"

"You picking me up?"

I raised my eyebrows. Didn't answer.

"Sorry. Yeah, I do. To swim."

"You swim here?"

You tapped your waist. "Always have swim shorts under my pants. I couldn't be a lifeguard—not enough hours. But I have to swim."

"Have to?"

"My scholarship."

I looked at the pool. Then I looked at you. "So swim."

"Now?"

"Yeah."

"Really? I don't have—"

"You just said you always do."

"Me and my big mouth. I'll swim if you swim."

I shrugged. It's like I was saying, grief takes away your inhibitions. "Okay," I said. "But you get in first. Then close your eyes."

You shook your head, but it was kind of a formality; you were taking off your shirt, your shoes. Soon you were standing there in your shorts. I couldn't help noticing the smooth ridges of your stomach. Then my eyes slid up and I saw something weird—a necklace around your neck, hanging down between your . . . between your, um, quite impressive pecs—but back to the point, the point being, it was kind of a feminine necklace. A silver chain, with a blue gemstone pendant of some kind. I thought it was odd, because it was totally the kind of thing a woman would wear.

But I didn't get to think about it for long because you smiled at me, then dived in, knifing into the water with almost no splash, coming up halfway across the pool.

"Hey, no diving," I said.

"And no nudity," you said. "So don't even think about it."

"Ha-ha. Close your eyes."

I stripped down to my underwear—of course I had to be wearing a bra that didn't match—and jumped in. The water was cold despite the warmth of the day. It sent a shiver through the core of me. I swam over to you. "Come on, then," I said. "Show me what you got."

"A race?"

"Two lengths. You and me."

"Okay . . ."

"You think you're going to destroy me? My dad was a SEAL, remember?"

"True."

We half swam, half walked to the side of the pool facing the ocean. It was a shallow pool. Then we stood and looked at each other.

"One. Two. Three."

We both threw ourselves forward. I swam as fast as I could, which was pretty fast because, well, Dad a SEAL and all that, doing the crawl, feeling the water rushing over me. When I breathed, I got a glimpse of the ocean, and you were right, it was like swimming in forever. Like there was no border between the pool and the ocean.

I also saw that, as fast as I was, you were *way* ahead. You got to the end of the pool and did one of those turns pro swimmers do, disappearing under the water and then reappearing alongside me but facing the other way, already breaking the surface with a stroke. A few seconds later I reached the end and turned to see you already back where we had started.

"Huh," I said.

You gave a sheepish smile. "I meant to go easy on you but—"

"But you can't help your brilliance?"

"I train a *lot*."

You sounded not entirely happy about this. "You don't like it?" I asked.

"It's fine. It's swimming. I don't . . . It's just something I do."

"Right."

You pulled yourself out of the pool; sat on the side and looked down at me.

"I'm staying in here," I said. "I'm in my underwear, remember?"

"How could I forget?"

"Ha-ha."

You sat there for a while, and we just didn't say anything, the sun on our skin, your legs in the water, me kind of floating there. I never knew what people meant about comfortable silences before then because silences between me and my dad were never comfortable.

A thought flashed: *Yeah, and Paris is still gone.*

It punches you like that, when you least expect it.

You kept glancing over at something—I thought maybe the bar? I thought maybe you were going to suggest that we steal a drink, which I would have been totally on board with at that point; I'd have been on board with drinking and drinking until I didn't even remember that I ever knew anyone called Paris. But eventually you levered yourself up on your hands and kind of popped into a standing position, then walked over to the bandstand.

I took a deep breath. Tried to put myself into the moment. To tell myself there was nothing I could do to find Paris right at that moment.

You came back with a ukulele and sat down again, your feet in the water. "They have, like, a Hawaiian band that plays in the evenings," you said. "It makes no sense; I mean, the decor is all Florida. But what can you do?"

"Hmm," I said. I was spaced out—the pool and the sun gleaming on it; I felt like I was dissolving. Into sparkle and blueness and the sound of lapping water, shushing and bubbling, tapping against the tiled sides.

You cradled the ukulele. I was watching you. I succeeded so totally at getting into the moment, I forgot then that there was a voice. That I had a dad. That Paris had disappeared. I was feeling the water on my skin and looking at you, at the look on your face.

The look was *love.*

I don't mean romantic love. I mean . . . the love of someone who is holding the thing they are meant to be holding. Doing the thing they are meant to be doing. It was interesting because I had not seen that look when you dived into the pool, or when you were swimming. But I saw it now, now that you had that instrument in your hands.

You ran your fingers over the frets. Then you bent your head so I couldn't see your face, and started to play. Just notes at first, then runs and arpeggios—I think that's what they're called? And scales, I guess. Then you flowed into something I recognized—the Beach Boys. "God Only Knows." You hummed along.

And here's the thing: you were amazing. Technically, of course. But also, the instrument, it was like it *breathed* with you. Like you made it live, made it want to pour out its own song. You were impressive at the pier, when you were playing what people called out, on the electric organ, but when you played that ukulele . . . it was like I was hearing your soul.

Okay, now I'm the one being poetic and sickly.

Anyway.

As you hummed, I don't know, I guess it was that faulty inhibition thing again, but I began to sing. I knew all the words. I sang the first verse, and then the chorus. You looked up at me, and I stopped, embarrassed.

You put aside the ukulele. "Hey," you said. "Don't go all shy on me. Keep singing. I like hearing your voice."

I don't like hearing my voice, I thought. I shut up.

"Oh, come on," you said. "You have a beautiful voice."

"No, I don't. I'm barely in tune."

A pause. "Yeah, okay, you don't. But I still like to hear you sing."

I made my eyes mock-wide. "Asshole! You don't think I have a beautiful voice?"

"I—I just wanted to be honest with you; I didn't want to give you some romantic bull**** and . . . ugh, I don't think before I speak sometimes. Sorry."

"It's fine. I was messing with you," I said, elbowing you.

You smiled, relieved.

"Anyway," I said, "*you're* incredible. You really should be in a band. Or, I don't know, uploading videos on YouTube." You were looking at me skeptically. "I'm serious! You have talent."

You shook your head. "Can't."

"Oh please. I saw the look on your face when you were playing. You love it."

"I do."

"So do it. Go to college or whatever, but do the music thing as well."

"You don't understand."

"Then tell me."

You took a long breath. "My mom played. She was actually kind of a star in the seventies. I mean, not a big star. But she supported Simon & Garfunkel. Kind of a guitar, singing, folk kind of thing. She gave it up, the performing, when she met my dad. He was a mechanic in a small New Jersey town. It was like the most unlikely romance, you know? Anyway. She got me into it. When she died . . . I stopped playing. At home anyway." Your hand went to your chest as you said all this, and I realized something, something about the necklace I had seen around your neck.

"That's her necklace, right?"

You looked at me, surprised. "Right."

You took your hand away, very self-consciously. Laid it on the white tiles by the pool.

"So, you stopped playing music at home because it was too painful?"

"No."

I thought for a moment. "Oh. Your dad doesn't like it? It reminds him of her, that kind of thing?"

"Uh-huh. He cleared out all the instruments. Gave them to Goodwill."

"So you swim instead?"

"Yeah."

"But you don't love swimming. You don't even like it that much."

You sighed. "No, not really."

"Come *on*," I said. "You can't let your dad take away something you love. And when he's not there . . . I mean, you could still—"

"It's not that simple."

"It *is*. Tell him how you feel. Tell him you—"

You raised a hand—like, *This conversation is over.* Then you forced a smile. "But me and you, we can come here again, if you like? I'll play, you sing. Deal?"

"Deal," I said.

Then your radio crackled. "714, come in."

"Time's up," you said. "I'll close my eyes while you get out."

I'm telling you all this, even though you were there, for two reasons.

1. The whole thing with you and swimming and music? That's going to come up again. When I see your dad, later in the story. I want you to understand it all from my point of view. I want you to see why I did the things I did. I told you: I want you to forgive me.

2. I didn't say it then; I mean I would have been too embarrassed, but that day on the roof of the Flamingo Motel . . . that was the best day of my life, since my parents took me to Disney World for my eighth birthday. I think it was the day I fell for you, properly. It was like a game of tag. You tagged me—and after that I had no choice but to follow you. Anyway. I thought I would write about it. Because it's all pretty dark from here on in.

   Hey!

   I said two reasons and I actually *gave* two reasons!

Dr. Lewis had been crying.

I was less surprised than I was by Dr. Rezwari, but still, it was pretty remarkable. I mean, he wasn't her family, he wasn't a *friend*— he was a psychologist. But four days after Paris had disappeared he was still crying.

We didn't really talk about me, we just talked about Paris, tried to convince each other she was still alive. I didn't tell him about what you and I were doing, about our private investigation. I thought he would probably tell me not to do it. Which would have been good advice.

DR. LEWIS:	And how are you? Generally?
ME:	Stuff is bad with my dad. I'm kind of grounded. Actually, I'm going to get in so much trouble for coming here this evening. If he gets back early anyway. He may not. He probably won't.
DR. LEWIS:	You still haven't told your father about coming here?
ME:	No.
DR. LEWIS:	Okay. Anyone else who is helping you?
ME:	There's a boy. When he's there, the voice goes quiet.
DR. LEWIS:	That sounds good, for you.
ME:	Yes.
DR. LEWIS:	But when he's not there . . .
THE VOICE:	Paris is dead and rotting. Fish are eating her fingers.
ME:	The voice comes back.
DR. LEWIS:	On the topic of people helping you: You're

	speaking to Dr. Rezwari? Making sure your medication dosage is correct?
ME:	Hmm.
DR. LEWIS:	She hasn't written me. I thought she might. I sent her some notes but—
ME:	You sent her *notes*?
DR. LEWIS:	Yes. Sure. Standard procedure.
ME:	****.
DR. LEWIS:	You have told her about me?
ME:	Uh, yeah. Yeah. But . . . you didn't tell her anything . . . private we have talked about?
DR. LEWIS:	About your mother?
ME:	Yeah.
DR. LEWIS:	No. The bare facts only. That we were talking.
ME:	Okay.
	Okay, okay. That wasn't so bad.
	Anyway.
	The conversation went on.
ME:	Blah.
DR. LEWIS:	Blah blah.
Etc., etc., etc.	

At the end of the half hour, I didn't stand up. "I want to stay for group," I said.

"That's not a bad idea," said Dr. Lewis. "There are a lot of people here who loved Paris. Love Paris."

"Yeah," I said, though that wasn't why I wanted to stay. I was out of leads, and Dwight was the only one who might have some more information on Paris. I wanted to grab him once group was over.

But Dwight wasn't first that day, and I worried that he wasn't going to come. Five people, maybe, turned up, poured themselves coffee into their plastic cups and then sat down on plastic chairs in the circle.

He's not coming, he's not—

But then he did. He rushed in, wearing that NJPD SOFTBALL T-shirt he was always wearing, sweat patches under the arms. His jeans had food stains on them; on his feet were old Nike sneakers. He looked stressed.

"Hey, everybody," he said. "Cass! You're staying for group today?"

"Yep," I said.

"Cool."

He sat down, and Dr. Lewis got people to talk about how they were doing. We heard about the Red Voice and how it had been very aggressive all week, had made Rasheed burn himself with cigarettes.

"My dad's voice has been bad this week too," said Dwight. "Telling me I'm worthless. Telling me I'll never amount to anything. That I don't care about . . . don't care about . . ."

"It's okay," said Dr. Lewis. "Go slow."

"That I don't care about Paris."

"We all care about Paris," said Dr. Lewis. "The voices can't change that."

"We all care. But we're not all *cops*," said Dwight.

Dr. Lewis nodded. "You feel a personal sense of responsibility."

Dwight: "**** yeah, I do! I know what people say. That we don't care about the whores, that we're not doing anything. But we have nothing. We have no clues. Nothing. ****. I shouldn't be talking about this."

"This is a confidential environment," said Dr. Lewis. "You're in the circle of trust."

"Anyway," said Dwight. "I *do* care."

"In this instance, then," said Dr. Lewis, "the voice is representing the opinion of some of the media. That the police are incompetent."

"I guess."

"So tell the voice what you would tell the media. That it doesn't understand the facts. Remind it of your schedule. You have it down to once a week, yes? The voice can talk on Fridays?"

"I did," said Dwight. "Before . . ."

"Paris," I said. I didn't mean to speak, I just did.

"Yeah. Your voice bad too?" said Dwight. His zits had come back hard, fresh new red spots over his scars.

I forced myself back into the moment. "Yeah. Before . . . before, I had a big victory." I looked out at the faces of the people. This was the first time I had spoken in group. They were looking at me with love, it seemed to me, their faces shining, some with hands clasped together. Willing me on. I smiled to myself. "The voice wanted me to cut off my toe and said it would kill my dad in the night if I didn't. I didn't. I couldn't sleep all night, but in the morning my dad was alive."

"That's amazing, Cass," said Dr. Lewis. "You didn't tell me that."

"No," I said. "I get that the voice doesn't have the power it thinks it does. But then Paris . . . and then it started being nasty again. Insulting me. Telling me—"

"That you're a nobody little ***** and everybody hates you."

That was the voice.

Obviously.

"—telling me bad things," I finished lamely.

"Anyone else?" said Dr. Lewis. "Let's talk about how Paris's disappearance has impacted our voice hearing."

Blah.

Blah.

Etc.

Here's the important part:

After the group was finished, I hung back. I was bursting with my insight; I was such an idiot. So naive. Thinking I could get Dwight to help me.

When Dwight was leaving I kind of followed outside the bowling alley to the 7-Eleven. At the coffee counter where the sugar and stuff was, I touched his arm. He had a bag slung over his shoulder.

"You're working on the Houdini Killer case, right?" I said. "With Agent Horowitz and the other guy, the fat one?"

"Cass! I shouldn't—"

"But you are?" I had told Julie not to talk to the cops, but I trusted Dwight. I had heard him talk about his voice, about the way his dad abused him. I *knew* he wasn't the Houdini Killer. I knew that. I thought I knew a lot of things.

He sighed and nodded.

"There must be something I can do."

"Leave it to the police," said Dwight. "That's what you should do."

"She could be . . . being killed. Right now."

"Or she could have run away. Gone back to New York."

"Horowitz said that too," I said. "But why would she? She left New York because her dad . . . because her dad . . ."

"I know," said Dwight. "I was in group with her, remember?"

"So what about him?" I said. "Have you checked him out?"

Dwight nodded. "Parents say they haven't seen her. And the dad has an alibi. A woman from his work who'll swear he was with her."

"You believe her?"

"It's not like a movie," said Dwight. "When people lie it's not obvious. Point is, it's a dead end. We have her photo with every police precinct on the East Coast. If she turns up, she turns up. Other than that, we have nothing. No evidence, no clues. Nothing."

"He's lying," said the voice. "He's a ******** liar. He knows something, but he's not telling."

"After six p.m.," I said quietly to the voice.

"Your voice?" said Dwight.

"Yeah. And it's saying that you're a liar. That there's something you're not telling me."

"There's an ass-load I'm not telling you! I'm a cop. This is all confidential stuff."

"It's Paris," I said. "If you know something important, I need you to tell me."

"I don't know something important."

"But you suspect something."

"No! Leave it, okay?"

"Dwight, please . . ."

"Jesus, Cass. I shouldn't even be having this conversation. And I have nothing more to tell you; nothing that will help you or Paris. I promise."

I sighed. I could sense I wasn't going to get anything more out of him voluntarily.

So I held my breath for as long as I could—I mean, literally held it in my lungs.

"Cass, you okay?"

I was, but I was hoping I looked pale. I let my eyes go droopy and slumped a little. "I get . . . low blood sugar," I said. "Would you get . . . some candy?"

"Candy?"

"Yeah. It has to be . . ." I kept my body floppy, kind of leaned on the counter, as if to hold myself up. ". . . nut free. Can you check with them?"

Dwight hesitated.

"Please?"

"Sure," he said finally. He dropped his bag on the floor by my feet and went over to the cash register. I saw him talking to the Mexican guy there, finding out what was safe.

"Quick," said the voice. "While his back is turned."

I took out my cell phone and reached down for his bag.

And there it was, inside his briefcase. A thick brown file, closed with loops of elastic:

OAKWOOD PD ACTIVE FILE LF-098

I flipped it open quickly, took as many photos as I could, turning the pages. I got maybe twenty, and then I saw Dwight coming back over—a rack of Jersey Shore car magnets was partially shielding me—and I dropped the file back into the bag and straightened up.

"Skittles," I said as he leaned against the counter and handed them over. "My . . . favorite."

The next morning I was sitting at home on my bed with my cell. I started paging through the photos of the case file. I hadn't been able to check what I was capturing—had just pointed and shot, getting as many pictures as I could. You would have been proud of me. I mean, I had to learn to use the camera function specially, practiced the previous night, taking pictures of my wall, pages from my books.

Almost immediately I stopped cold. Staring at the photo in front of me, of maybe the very first page in the case file. *I should have known*, I thought. *It should have been obvious.*

It was right there in black and white on one of the first pages:

Investigation into the disappearance of Lily Eleanor French.

Lily.

Eleanor.

Not Paris. She must have taken the name for herself, maybe when she started ... working. Because of her surname being French, maybe? Or before that, I don't know.

I remembered her saying to Shane that she was more Paris, Texas, than Paris, France, and now I thought: *not Paris at all.*

I wondered if Julie knew she was really named Lily. I figured it didn't really matter anyway. She wasn't Lily to me. She was Paris.

Minutes passed. I was still looking at the name. Somehow it struck me as the saddest thing of all, this revelation. It was like ... like an invasion of privacy. I mean, any investigation *is* an invasion of privacy. But.

So, after a few minutes of just sitting there, getting used to this new reality, I made a simple decision: I was going to un-know this information. I was going to keep thinking of her as Paris. Because that was how she wanted me to think of her.

I started going through the photos again. There was nothing else in them I didn't know already—there was no evidence at the house; no fingerprints other than Paris's; no blood. Her father's alibi, in stark print.

Mr. French was with me all night. We ate beef bourguignonne with an excellent Bordeaux.

Her mother:

I haven't seen Lily for two years, not since she moved down to that awful town of yours.

There was Julie's witness statement too, the first part of it—I hadn't managed to get any more with my phone camera. *She went into the house. After that I must have fallen asleep because when I woke up she was calling my phone . . .*

I skimmed the rest. I already knew it.

I clicked to the next picture—my wall.

I was back to the start.

I had quite literally hit a wall.

I put my phone down. I felt even more sorry for Paris. Somehow, knowing she was really Lily . . . it made her seem smaller. More exposed. Younger.

She wasn't much older than you, I reminded myself.

There was nothing in the case file, absolutely nothing. Like Dwight had said. Paris had just disappeared, and there were literally no clues to follow. I couldn't believe it. I couldn't believe I just had to . . . stop.

"You're not giving up that easily?" said the voice.

"Huh?"

"On finding her. You're not giving up, are you?"

"What do you want me to do?" I said. "The police don't know anything."

"So?"

"So a teenage girl isn't going to solve a case the police can't solve. Just . . ." I thought of Paris's body, weighed down, at the bottom of the ocean. Bloating. Hair floating. Fish swimming through her clothes.

Ugh. Stop.

"Okay, then, just let her die," said the voice.

"What do you want me to do?" I said again.

The voice fell silent for a moment. "Isn't that boy coming to pick you up? Maybe he'll have ideas."

I checked my watch. The voice was right: it was time for you to pick me up—you had your break at eleven a.m., and we'd agreed to keep looking for Paris.

"I thought you didn't like him?" I said to the voice.

"I don't."

"So aren't you going to instruct me to break up with him? To, I don't know, tell him to **** off or you will make me cut off my fingers?"

"You've made it clear you won't respond to threats like that," said the voice, in a weirdly reasonable tone.

"Right."

"Anyway, I don't need to," it said, cruel again, mocking. "You're going to mess things up yourself."

"What? Why?"

"Have you told him about me? About . . . this?"

I sat up straighter on the bed. "No."

"Well, there you go. A lie that is sure to blow up in your face. 'Oh, sorry I didn't mention that I'm a psycho.'"

"I'm not a psycho."

"Semantics."

I sighed. "Besides it's all . . . I mean . . . I shouldn't be with him anyway. It's not the right time, with Paris, and . . ."

"Love is no respecter of right times," said the voice. But not in a kind way.

"Oh, go away," I said.

And it did. I felt it go behind its curtain, and the stage of my mind was clear. I closed my eyes for a long moment. *Maybe I should tell him*, I thought.

But then he will never look at you the same way again.

Maybe I shouldn't be seeing him anyway. Maybe I'll tell him we can't be seeing each other. If my dad found out . . . If Paris . . .

Yeah, right. You tell him that. You tell him you don't want to see him.

Look. I'm capable of having a conversation with myself even without the voice.

Well.

Why start holding back now?

I went downstairs, still turning everything over. Paris, the lack of evidence, the voice, the fact that I was lying to you.

You're not lying to him; you're just not telling him something.

Yeah, right.

As I waited on the porch I felt empty; scooped out like an avocado skin. Paris was gone, and I had failed to do anything about it. I'd failed *her*. Just like I failed my mom.

A clip played over and over in my head, a YouTube video on repeat—me lying on my bed, the white noise drowning out my phone so that I couldn't hear it ringing, couldn't hear Paris calling for my help. I might as well have handed her over to the Houdini Killer myself. And now there was nothing I could do to help her, nothing I could do to help find her.

I stood there, waiting for the voice to come back again and comment. To say,

"Yes. You're worthless."

Or,

"You disgust me."

Or,

"It's your fault she's dead."

But the voice didn't say anything.

Strange.

A couple of minutes later you pulled up, one arm out the window of your pickup. You were wearing your Ray-Bans; the sun was shining brightly. There was a hummingbird hovering in the air over the rosebushes Mom planted, which had grown out of control, its red breast quivering. A few songbirds were chirping—our neighbor Mrs. Cartwright puts seed out for them.

I listened to the unchanging language of a sparrow; that same liquid phrase of notes, over and over; a musical motif that would never alter. It made me think of Philomela, and I thought, *What if that sparrow was Paris?*

I guess you probably know the story. There was a king, Tereus, and he was married to Procne. But he desired her sister, Philomela. So he raped Philomela and then, to stop her telling anyone, he cut out her tongue and imprisoned her, telling his wife that her sister was dead. But Philomela wove a tapestry depicting what had happened to her, and had it smuggled to Procne.

Procne, learning of her husband's crime, killed their son and served his flesh to her husband. Incensed with rage, Tereus pursued Procne and Philomela and tried to strangle them—but before he could, the gods turned them into birds: Procne into a nightingale, and Philomela into a swallow.

And that's why the nightingale sings "tereu, tereu, tereu," because forevermore it's accusing Tereus, naming him, exposing his hideous crime. Like Echo mocking her murderer, Pan, by singing his voice and his music back to him.

There are no nightingales in North America of course. Just ordinary thrushes.

Anyway. That was my state of mind. Standing in the yard, thinking of stories about murder and cutting out tongues, and the ghosts of women turned into birds.

Maybe she really did run away.

Maybe she did go to New York.

"And maybe I'll just never know," I said aloud. And then burst into tears.

I concentrated on the sound of the sparrow.

Cheep-*cheep*. Cheep-*cheep*.

No, I thought. *She's dead. Paris is dead.*

And what if she was in the sparrow's voice? Like Procne and

Philomela? A sparrow, instead of a nightingale or a swallow? What if she was telling me a name, telling it to me over and over, accusing someone?

Cheep-*cheep*.

It didn't sound like any name I recognized.

Or what if she was in the cranes in her bedroom, the ones she'd made with her own hands, the two hundred and sixty-one cranes—Paris gone but still there, multiple, spread across paper birds?

I shook my head.

Crazy.

"What's up with you?" you said, as you walked up.

"I was wondering what the sparrow was saying."

You listened. "I think it's saying, 'I am a sparrow,' 'I am a sparrow.' Over and over."

"Huh," I said.

"Why, what were you thinking?"

"Oh," I said. "Pretty much the same." I didn't want you to know the kind of crazy thing I was thinking. Clearly I have no such compunction now.

We went over to the pickup and got inside. "So," you said. "What did the cop say? Did you find out anything?"

"Nothing." I told you about the parents, the empty case file that gave us nothing. But you know that of course. As I spoke, you drove the F-150 into town, and to the alley where the plush warehouse was.

"What do we do now?" you said.

"I have no idea." Without warning, I started to cry again.

"Oh, Cass . . ."

You put your arms around me. They were strong, and the sound of cars passing was just a quiet shushing in the background, and I could smell you, the scent of you, and I wished that moment would never, ever end.

But it did. Those moments always do.

You pulled back, touched away a tear from my cheek with your thumb. Gently. So gently.

"But you said the cop was holding something back," you said. "That he knew something."

"Maybe."

"Then we need to find out what it is."

"Oh sure, that will be easy," I said. "We'll just make the cop tell us everything he knows, using our irresistible powers of suggestion."

"Hmm."

"Yeah, *hmm*."

You made a kind of pained shrug movement. "So we're stuck."

"Yeah."

You got out of the truck and pulled up the rolling door, then drove the pickup into the warehouse. It was a duller day; the beams of light shining down from the windows were less bright, the piles of toys lost in the gloom, as you looked deep into the warehouse. It was spookier—I could just make out the animals closest to us, their plastic eyes shining in the light from outside.

"Creepy," I said.

"Yes."

We made our way into the shadow-crossed space of the warehouse.

"What are we looking for?" I said.

"Seven mixed Disney characters, small," you said. "Two SpongeBob, medium. Three Moshi Monsters, large."

"Okay. Which way do I go?" I couldn't think of anything better to do than to help you.

You pointed to the far right corner, and I took a step—at the same time you set out in the opposite direction, so we bumped into each other; I lost my balance; my hand shot out and you grabbed my arm, put your other hand behind my back.

We stood there for a moment, our bodies touching, your hands on me, holding me.

The light shifted outside; a cloud moved away from the face of the sun, or something; and a shaft of light came down, illuminated us. We were in a glowing column, dust hanging suspended in it; I almost thought we might rise up off the ground, like people in those weird religious paintings.

You shifted forward; I shifted forward.

The electrons in our bodies reached out for each other, spinning. I felt the charge of it, you a positive and me a negative, making sparks that flew from our eyes and our fingertips to touch each other; invisible.

You lowered your face and after a moment that felt

endless

your lips met mine and we kissed, very slowly. Time ended and has never really begun again, not for me. We sank down, we knew the beam of light would hold us and keep us safe; we lay on the softness of plush toys and our tongues touched and the circuit was completed; I lit up like a million-watt bulb.

I was *shining*. Light was blazing from my every pore. My eyes were closed, and the strip lights were turning the inside of my eyelids red, everything red. That's your color, you know, the one I see and feel when I think of you. Emotions are always associated with colors, aren't they? Green with envy. Well, when you are in my head you are always there with red: sunlight, warmth, heat.

People are green with envy. Yellow with cowardice. I am red with you.

Our arms were around each other, and we were cushioned by stuffed animals. I half opened my eyes, and I saw Elmo looking back at me. It was like he was smiling at me.

I want you to know something: I have never felt safer than in that moment. I felt like a fish, like a trout in the shade of a bank, enveloped by water, lifted up by it.

The promise of buoyancy. The impossibility of falling.

Then . . .

A buzzing.

An unmistakable crackling.

"714, where the hell are those bags? Get your ass to Pier One."

My eyes snapped open. So did yours. "Unbelievable," you said.

"Yeah," I said.

You started to get up; put out your hand to catch mine and help me to my feet. "Oh well," you said. "We have all the time in the world."

I'm crying right now, just thinking about it.

There is no beam of light around me, keeping me protected.

There are only bugs, in their glowing tanks; stick insects and roaches and millipedes, crawling around with their stiff little bodies, their unloving ichor in place of blood, their clicking append-ages and hard little shells.

They're all around me, but they don't give a ****. I don't know why my dad likes them. They're creatures of coldness; no heart in them at all. Primitive things like shards of stone that move, clacking and ticking. They have no voices. They will be here when we're all dead.

I'm not proud of the next bit so I'm going to tell it quickly.

You dropped me at home and I was walking to the front door, already starting to sweat in the noonday sun, when the voice spoke.

"There is a way," it said.

"Nice to hear from you," I said without thinking. "But could you speak to me after—"

Then I stopped. I literally stopped moving, one foot up on the porch step. That hummingbird was *still* there; it was like it was frozen in time above those roses, except you could see its blurred wings beating. The sun was warm on my skin.

"Wait," I said, suddenly hearing what the voice had said, hearing it properly. "What do you mean there is a way?"

"To get Dwight to talk."

I sat down on the step. "Let me get this straight. You're helping now?"

Silence.

"Hello?" I said.

"You don't want me to help?" said the voice eventually. Its tone, its timbre, was less aggressive than usual. It sounded . . . like someone who knows they have behaved badly and is a little embarrassed, and—there's no other word for it—*apologetic*.

"Um. Yes," I said. "I guess."

"Yes, you don't want me to, or, yes, you want me to?"

"Yes, I want you to."

"Okay," said the voice. "Then listen."

I rode the bus to the police station. I didn't want to tell you what I was doing. Because I knew that you wouldn't approve. Because I knew you would tell me not to.

You would have said it was mean, and you would have been right.

So . . . I lied to you again.

Basically.

For about the millionth time, I'm sorry.

Of course, it got an awful lot worse, later. The lying, that is. Not the sorriness. The sorriness is constant, and it could not get any worse.

When I arrived at the police station I asked for Dwight.

"Dwight what?" said the woman on reception, a brassy blonde with dark roots and even darker circles under her eyes. She looked like she needed to go home and get three hours more sleep before starting work again.

"Huh?" I said.

"His last name, honey," said the woman.

"Oh. I don't know. But he's a cop. Here. His name is Dwight."

The woman tapped her long fingernails on her desk. The desk was pitted, made of cheap wood. Everything about the station was cheap. "We have two Dwights. One's in traffic. The other's in homicide."

"Homicide," I said.

She raised her eyebrows. "You sure?"

I held her gaze. "Yes."

She nodded slowly. "I'll call up. See if he's available. Your name was . . . ?"

I hadn't told her my name. "Cass," I said. "He knows me."

She dialed a number and waited while it rang. She told whoever was on the other line—Dwight, I guess—that I was there to see him. She listened for a moment, said "uh-huh", and then put down the phone.

"Third floor, right-hand side," she said. "There's an elevator just there."

I walked past a dead potted plant and got in the elevator, rode up to the third floor. I came out onto a utilitarian corridor, like you'd find in any office building, or at least any office building of a company that has seen better times. There were motivational posters on the wall—BE THE BEST YOU CAN BE. Also missing-person posters, and advertisements for charity barbecues and touch football.

I turned right and followed the corridor until I came to an open-plan office. I could see the ocean from up here—far off, a couple of recreational fishing boats. There was a haze over the water and the beach, the rides of the piers like smudged watercolor. Inside the office there were people sitting at desks, others standing and talking to each other—a whiteboard in a corner had some scribbled notes and questions on it. A few rooms with doors lined the side wall.

Dwight put his phone down, stood up from a desk, and walked over to me. "Cass," he said. His tone was . . . wary. "What are you doing here?"

"I need for you to tell me what you know," I said.

"About what?"

"About Paris. And about the cops. You went all weird when we were talking about it. I *know* there's something."

He took my arm and steered me back toward the corridor. "There isn't, Cass. Leave it, okay?"

I looked over his shoulder at the other cops working; a couple of them had turned to watch us, and this is the part I'm not proud of.

"Do they know?" I said.

He stopped, so we were standing just in and just out of the open-plan room. "Do they know what?"

"About group. About Dr. Lewis."

His eyes widened. He was looking at me like I had disappeared and some other, scarier person had been dropped down in front of him instead. Like I was an alien. "Keep your voice d—"

"Do they?"

"What do *you* think?" he hissed.

"I think they don't. Not all of them anyway. Your boss, maybe, because I guess you had to tell him. Her? Him or her. I have no idea."

"You're babbling, Cass," said the voice.

"Time to leave," said Dwight.

"No."

"What's your deal anyway?" he said. "You hardly even knew Paris. Why are you so obsessed with this?"

I took a step back, like I'd been gut-punched. "*What*? She was my friend."

He held his hands up. "Fine, fine. Just get out of here. I can't have you here."

"No," I said. "Time to tell me what you're holding back."

"Jesus, Cass! I could lose my job. I'm not being blackmailed by some teenage girl into—"

"I'm not blackmailing you," I said.

"Oh yeah, sure." His breath was bad: coffee and cigarettes. It was not helping with the nausea in the pit of my stomach, the self-hatred. But the voice was egging me on. "Look, I'm not even working the case," he said. "I don't talk to anyone about it. I don't know what they're doing. Anything I said . . . it would just be a personal hunch."

413

"Please, Dwight," I said. "Please. I'm sorry about . . . about what I said, about your colleagues. For mentioning group. But I *need* to know. I need to find Paris."

Dwight looked into my eyes for what felt like minutes.

"Cass," he said slowly. "Please understand. I cannot do what you're asking."

"But—"

He shook his head, more sad than anything else. "No buts," he said. "I'm a police officer. I'm not going to give you information. I'm not compromising our investigation, and I'm not supporting you in going on some vigilante mission of your own."

"She'd want you to help me," I said.

He flinched. "Low blow, Cassie," he said. Then he put his hands on my shoulders. "Listen. You have to drop this. Promise me you're going to drop this."

"I promise," I lied.

Dwight put his head in his hands. "****," he said. "****."

I should probably send him an apology letter too.

A picture, in my head:

Paris enters a dark house by the ocean. She thinks she's meeting some guys for a bachelor party.

Then . . . what?

Someone hits her over the back of the head? She falls, seeing stars, scuffs her hands on the linoleum floor. There is graffiti on the walls; she can smell the acrid scent of urine.

She turns; it makes fireworks of pain go off in her head. She sees a cop standing by the door, in his uniform.

Thank God, she thinks.

But then he takes a step toward her. And he smiles. And he raises the hammer again.

Why should it be a hammer? I don't know. I just get these images. I wish I didn't. I wish I could make them go away.

But we can't always make things go away.

The voice has taught me that at least.

Another picture in my head:

I'm with you, in the glow of sunset, sitting squashed together in a lifeguard stand, close to Pier Two. The lifeguard is gone, and the beach is empty apart from a few stragglers, apart from couples like us in the other stands; we were lucky to get this one, though pulling up in the company pickup probably worked pretty well to reserve it for us.

It was inevitable we'd end up here, sometime. We're both Jersey, and we follow the old paths, the old patterns. It's in our blood, like bees swarming to the same tree, year after year.

We were a boy, and a girl, and we were at the shore in the summer, and the lifeguard stand was there. Like a beacon.

The late-evening sun is hitting us horizontal, heat-lamp warm on my skin. You put your arm around me, and I feel your strength, the sheer *life* of it, buzzing, and we spark like a plug and a socket held close together, like an arc welder; the energy of it is a jolt to my heart, defib pads; ka-bam.

A seagull drifts past, eye level, on dirty white wings. Waves break whitely.

"We should do this more often," you say.

"Hmm," I say. I am merging with the sun, with the ocean, with you. I look at the white-hot disk in the sky and then my eyes put stuttering circles of light on everything—the sand, the waves, your face.

"And go on a date."

"Hmm."

"A real date, like, movie and dinner."

I frown. "I can't do that."

"You can't do a date?"

"No."

"Why not?"

"My dad," I say. "I can't go out at night."

Now it's your turn to frown. "Your dad works late almost every night."

I shake my head. "Too risky. He knows *everyone*. Someone might see us."

"*You* go out," you say. Accusation is a seam of freezing cold quartz in the rock of your voice.

A moment passes; the sun lowers one more increment; the seagull dives, splashes.

"I . . ."

"I've seen you leave. Take the bus. Last Thursday, right? You didn't get back till late."

"Um, yes," I say. *Group*, I think. But of course I can't risk you finding out about that part of me.

"So how come you can do that and you can't go on a date with me?"

"I just can't."

You shift in the seat so you're looking at me. I am very conscious of the steps leading up, white peeling paint in the sideways sun. I can hear the gulls, the ocean, cars, even, on the roads close to the pier, music. It's as if the volume has been turned up on the world. I have a brief urge to jump, to leap down to the sand below. I might break my leg. I might not. I half close my eyes instead, and the sun makes butterfly wings of my eyelashes; iridescent. Glow fills my vision like lens glare.

But this is incapable of stopping time.

I know the question that is coming.

I know it like you know the vibration in the track is a train coming, when you put coins on the rails, as a kid.

And I can't stop it anymore than I could stop a train.

"Where do you go?" you say. "Where *did* you go?"

"Nowhere."

"Nowhere?"

"Yes." I pause. "You don't need to worry. It's nothing like that." But in my head, I'm thinking: Is that true? Is that true that he doesn't have to worry? This is a question I don't even need the voice to ask me.

"I wasn't worried. I just don't get why you won't tell me."

"It's . . . personal," I say.

"I thought we were in a personal zone," you say. "Like . . . getting to know each other."

"We are," I say.

"Apart from your telling me about your life. About why you looked so gray when we first met. Why you go off mysteriously. Why your dad seems so concerned about you."

"Yes," I say, trying to lighten the mood. "Yes, apart from all that stuff."

You sigh. "So what are we supposed to do now?"

I look at the glowing ocean, the boats bobbing far out, the surf, hushing below us. "Traditionally I think the idea is to kiss."

You smile, slightly, at that at least.

"Okay," you say.

And you kiss me, and just like before, everything disappears—*flash*—like a magician's trick, the stand, the peeling steps, the susurration of the ocean, the town behind us, the calling of the gulls, everything.

There is only you, and the blackness, and the fireworks behind my eyelids, exploding across an infinite sky.

Only . . .

Is it just my imagination? Is it just retrospect, is it just what I know now that makes me think there's a hesitation, a slight pulling away? A chink of light, in the darkness, flatter and harsher than the bursting rockets of my blood vessels, something bright and cold, a lamp for examining the cracks of things, for tilting them over, and revealing their flaws.

My flaws.

But it's okay, I tell myself. *It's okay, because he's still kissing you.*

But the magic is broken. And of course, it's not like you're kissing me now.

I wish you were. I am looking at a stick insect instead. It does not seem like it wants to kiss me. And I wouldn't want it to.

I'm not that desperate.

Yet.

The next day, Julie called me. It was kind of out of the blue.

"Um . . . hi," I said.

"Hi, Cass."

Silence.

"Listen," said Julie. "You want to come over later, maybe? Just . . . I don't know. Just to talk."

I nodded, like an idiot, as if Julie could see that through the phone. "Uh, yeah, that sounds good," I said. It did actually. "What time?"

A couple of hours later I arrived at the condo. There was a police car outside, parked. Empty. I noticed it because I always noticed police cars, those days. I figured it couldn't be anything to do with Julie, I mean she couldn't be in trouble, but I quickened my pace anyway.

I rode up in the elevator and went down the corridor, then knocked on Julie and Paris's door. Julie's door, I guess I should say. Julie opened it and the first thing she said was "Sorry."

"Sorry what?" I said.

She inclined her head toward the living room. "There's a cop here," she said. "He just showed up."

"More questions?"

"No. No . . . he's the one who came. That night. When I called 911. He says he just wants to talk about Paris. He seems . . . upset almost."

"Weird," I said. Thinking: *The killer?* "Do you think he . . . I mean . . . could he be . . .?"

Julie shook her head. "No way."

"Why not?"

"You'll see."

I followed Julie into the living area. A guy in cop uniform stood up and blinked at me, as if I were brightly lit.

"Brian," he said, holding out a limp hand to shake.

"Cassie," I said.

Julie made coffee. The three of us sat there in the living area, drinking it. The others ate cookies, but I didn't of course.

"Paris made these," said Julie. "They're kind of stale."

Brian didn't complain.

For a while no one spoke. I was thinking: Julie was right. Because Brian did not seem like a killer. I mean, he had a little goatee and he kind of sniffled when he cried. He was weedy too—I couldn't see him hoisting a body over the side of a boat. Or overpowering a prostitute, for that matter.

"So, Brian," said Julie after a while, after it became clear that Brian wasn't going to break the ice. "What did you want to talk about?"

"I don't know," said Brian.

"Um. Right."

"I just . . . I wanted to talk to someone who knew her," he said.

A pause. Brian looked at me as if for help, but I didn't know what to say, didn't know how to help him because I didn't understand what he wanted.

"Why?" said Julie. "Why do you want to talk to someone who knew her?"

Brian looked down at the carpet between his feet. "Because I . . . I liked her. Loved her, I guess."

He looked up, then down again.

"Oh," said Julie.

She met my eyes, and mouthed: *What the ****?*

"I was . . . I was following you that night, you know," said Brian, looking at Julie now.

"You were *following* us?" said Julie.

421

"Yeah. I mean, following Paris. But it was usually you who drove her, right?"

"Yes," said Julie.

"Why?"

"Because of the killer! Because I was worried about her. I kept telling her, she had to be careful. But she didn't listen to me. She just laughed. She thought she was invincible." Julie turned to me. "Immortal, you know?"

"Yes," I said. I did know. I could picture her laughing.

"Well, I was the same," said Brian. "That's why I followed your car. I just . . . I just wanted to protect her."

"Yeah," said Julie. "You didn't do such a good job of that, did you?"

Brian started crying. There was no warning: tears just started leaking out of his eyes abruptly.

"Jesus ******** Christ, Brian, pull yourself together," said Julie. I was starting to see why Paris had liked her. She was tough.

"Sorry," said Brian.

Julie flinched. "No. I apologize. There was no need to snap at you." I could hear her mom in her voice; it's weird how people can do that, kind of scold themselves—it's wired into them from childhood, I think. "It's just . . . *everyone* was in love with Paris."

It was my turn to flinch. That was me, wasn't it? I was just like everyone else. I didn't mean anything to Paris. I was just one of the people, the little people who—

"So," said Julie, interrupting my thoughts. "You were there, already, when I dialed 911. Right?"

"Uh-huh," said Brian. "When dispatch put the call through, I was already on the scene. I just had to drive up. That's how come I was so fast."

"You were there already," I said. "So you could have killed her." It was *such* a lame thing to say. So direct and unsubtle. But this is real life, where you don't have time to think through everything you say before you say it. This isn't some Nancy Drew story. That much is going to become rapidly obvious.

"I loved her!" said Brian. "She was everything to me. And what are you thinking anyway? That I, like, murdered her in the house and then somehow hid her body and got back to my *police* car, and then drove up?"

Put like that, it did sound kind of dumb.

"I mean, how does that even work?" he continued. "We searched that house. What would I have done with the body?"

"Maybe you hid her in the trunk," I said, without much conviction.

"Of my squad car? Yeah."

We sat there in silence for a moment.

"How did you meet her anyway?" I asked.

Brian blushed.

"Oh," I said, figuring out right away what the blush meant.

"Yeah," said Brian. "It was a party. She . . . did her thing."

"She took her clothes off," said Julie, with a little acid in her voice.

"But . . . it was more than that," said Brian. "I mean, for me. She was . . . she was an incredible person. That sounds cheesy. But . . . she was, like, lit up, you know? Like neon."

"I know," I said.

"Yeah," said Julie.

There was another long moment where no one said anything. I got the sense Julie would very much have liked Brian to leave the apartment but was too polite to say so.

"Okay," I said finally. "So assuming you're telling the truth, Brian, who do you think did kill Paris?"

"Why?" he said. "Because you're going to solve the case? Like some Nancy Drew ****?"

"Maybe," I said.

He stared at me for a moment, the smile slowly dying from his lips. "You're serious?"

"What are we going to do? Just *forget* about her?" I said.

Brian turned to Julie. "You're involved in this?"

Julie shook her head.

Oh great, thanks, Julie.

"You should leave it to the agents," said Brian to me. "That guy Horowitz is good. He blew my timeline in, like, a day. Confronted me about it. I mean, he *knew* I got there too fast. I had to tell him . . . what I just told you."

"But he doesn't know who the killer is," I said.

"He doesn't talk much. But I think he has a theory. I think he maybe has a suspect."

"You think?"

"Yeah."

"You don't know?"

"No."

"And you don't know who this suspect might be?"

The most fractional hesitation. "No."

"Then we'll keep looking," I said.

"I would say that it's dangerous and that you totally should not do that," said Brian. "But I don't think it would make much difference, would it?"

"No."

He sighed. "Okay. What's your next move?"

I shook my head. I had no clue. "You have any ideas?" I said.

"You're . . . what? You're recruiting me to your little Nancy Drew gang?"

"Will you stop talking about Nancy Drew?" I said.

"And it's not a gang," said Julie. She cut me a look, a sort of angry look. Like she didn't like me wanting to find the killer.

"Anyway," said Brian to me. "You want me to *help* you? This is crazy. I'm a *cop*."

"Exactly."

He sighed again. "I'm not going to help you get yourself killed."

Another awkward, quiet moment.

"Hey, Cass," said the voice.

Oh, yes. Just what I needed. *Come back after—* I started saying, silently, inside my head.

"No, wait," said the voice. "Ask him why he thinks Horowitz has a theory."

"What?" I said. I realized I had said this out loud when I saw the others looking at me. "I mean . . . ," I said to them, ". . . what am I supposed to do, abandon my friend?"

Brian shrugged.

"He *hesitated*," continued the voice. "He hesitated when you asked if he knew who the suspect was."

I rewound my mental tape. The voice was right.

You're helping me now? I asked, silently this time.

"I'm not allowed to help you?" said the voice.

No, of course. Of course you can.

"Good. So ask him."

"Why do you think Horowitz has a theory?" I asked.

"I don't know, he doesn't talk much, he just—"

"No. I don't mean, what makes him have this theory? I mean, what makes *you* think that he has a theory?"

"Oh." Brian thought for a moment. I could see that he was weighing up the risks of talking to me. He seemed uncomfortable with the whole situation actually, and I figured that was good for me. It might make him talk, just to get out of there. "It was something he said about an alibi."

"Which was?"

Brian looked at Julie for help, but she wouldn't meet his eye. He looked back at me. "The dad, okay? Horowitz doesn't like his alibi. Plus . . . the phone call. To Julie. Paris's phone call, after she disappeared."

I thought for a second. "Because she told Julie not to call the cops?"

"Yeah. Why do that? Unless maybe you know the person who has grabbed you."

Julie was frowning. "So, what, her dad who lives in New York just happens to come down to Oakwood and orders a stripper and thinks, ****, it's my daughter, so he kills her?"

Brian shrugged. "I guess not. But maybe the dad knows she's a stripper. Comes down and hires her, to confront her about it. And things go wrong. Get violent."

A pause.

It seemed plausible, I had to admit.

"But his work colleague said he was with her that night."

Brian's mouth was open. "You know about that? How?"

I shrugged. "I know a lot of things." This was basically straight fronting—there was a lot I didn't know—but Brian looked impressed, and that was enough for me.

"Yeah, well, Horowitz said anyone could say that. No real way to verify, unless they went to a restaurant or something, which they didn't."

I stood up, my head spinning.

Paris's dad.

Maybe not the Houdini Killer at all.

Maybe her own dad.

"See?" said the voice. "Now you're getting somewhere."

Say you're a father, and you abused your daughter in some way when she was growing up.

You're not a nice man.

Then one day you hear that she's doing sex stuff for money, down in New Jersey, where you pay for her to attend college.

Say you're a psychopath, maybe.

1. You travel down to Oakwood.
2. You have your daughter's card, or her cam website, or something. You use these to e-mail, using a new account you have created. You say it's for a party.
3. You make the appointment at a deserted house. Maybe you have searched through foreclosure records.
4. Your daughter arrives. You fight. You push her, maybe, and she falls, hits her head on a step. She is out; you think maybe she's even dead. You put her in the trunk of your car, but you don't realize that she has her cell, that she is going to call her friend Julie.
5. Though, as it turns out, your daughter does not name you anyway.
6. And she isn't dead. But you kill her. You do kill her. Later. So that she can't talk.
7. And you tell some girl from your office to say that you were at home all night.
8. *And she does.*
9. And the police have to accept your alibi.
10. Except that there is one policeman who *is* suspicious. Agent Horowitz.
11. And there is me.
12. And I'm coming for you.

Or say something else.

Say you're a cop and you're in love with Paris. Say you follow her and Julie to a party where she's going to be stripping.

Say that suddenly you can't take it anymore, the idea of her exposing herself to other men; you wait till she leaves and you grab her—I mean, Julie's timeline is shaky; she said herself she fell asleep—and:

1. You kill her, you strangle her, I don't know, or you think you kill her anyway and
2. You put her in the trunk of your car and
3. She calls Julie but doesn't give your name because you're a cop and
4. You dispose of her body after you respond to the 911 call and
5. You lie to the annoying girl looking into Paris's death and you tell her that the father did it.

Or it's neither of those things.

It's the serial killer, and he's someone else entirely. Someone who drives a Jeep SRT8.

Or Paris ran away and isn't dead at all.

I'm nearly at the point where I lost you—where I threw you away.

I've been putting it off.

But I can't put it off any longer.

When you came back from work I was waiting up in my room. Shane was already sitting in one of the deck chairs—you flung yourself down into the other one and Shane handed you a beer.

I went downstairs and out into the yard.

"Hey," I said.

"Hey," you said, because our relationship CONTINUED TO BE SCRIPTED BY THE GREAT PLAYWRIGHTS.

"You okay?" you said.

"Yep," I said, in AN EXCHANGE TO RIVAL MARLOWE.

Shane raised his beer. "Hey, Cass," he said.

"Hey, Shane."

Shane started to stand. "Here, take my chair," he said. "I'll sit on the ground."

You raised your eyebrows. "You say that to all the girls?"

"Whatever," said Shane. "I'm the one being gentlemanly and offering my chair. I don't see you getting off your butt."

"Touché," you said.

"What?" said Shane.

"Never mind."

Shane gestured at the chair. "Cass, sit."

"No, it's cool," I said.

"You leaving?" you said.

"Actually, no . . . I was kind of hoping I could speak to you alone for a moment," I said to you.

Shane raised his hands and opened his eyes wide, doing an exaggerated cluing-in gesture. "Oh hey, I don't want to get in the way," he said. "I might hit the bar. Get a drink there, maybe play some pool."

"You don't have to—" I began, but my tone must not have been convincing because he laughed and did a big sweeping bow, then walked off down the street, giggling to himself.

"Childish," you said as Shane disappeared, but there was indulgence in your voice.

"He's sweet," I said. "Dumb, but sweet."

"Yeah," you said.

"Yeah."

→ THAT ONE COURTESY OF SHAKESPEARE ←

Anyway.

We sat on the chairs.

"What's up?" you said.

"I miss Paris," I said. I kind of blurted it out. Always smooth, me. You put your arm around me. "I know," you said. "I know and—"

"No, you don't," I said, pulling away. "I want her back. I never had a friend like her. What if I never have a friend like her again?"

You looked slightly hurt by that. "You will," you said.

I shrugged. "Anyway . . . so I met this cop, Brian, and he said that they think it's Paris's dad. Well, he didn't say that exactly. But it's obvious that—"

"Wait," you said. "You met a cop? Where?"

"Julie's. But I also took a look at the case file, the other day. See, I kind of know this other policeman named Dwight, he's a . . . um . . . a friend of my dad's, and I—"

You held up a hand. "Whoa, slow down," you said. "You're talking to cops now?"

"Yes. No. I mean, he was just at Julie's place. The second cop. But what he said . . . about Paris's dad. I wondered . . ." I paused, looked into your eyes. "I wondered if you would drive me to New York. To see Paris's dad."

"Jesus, Cass." You shook your head. "That would be a very stupid thing to do."

"Excuse me?" I was glaring at you.

You swallowed. "That came out wrong. But . . . that's a super dangerous idea, Cass. What if . . . I mean . . . what if he did kill her, and you just go and confront him? What if he gets violent?"

I hadn't really thought of that possibility.

"Um," I said. "I don't know."

"You have to be more careful," you said. I could see from your gestures and your face that you were really worried; even though I was pissed with you at that moment, there was a warm feeling right inside me about that. "I mean, Cass, I can see why your dad worries about you so much."

The warm feeling turned cold—hard-pack snow, balling in my chest.

I stared at him. "Are you serious?"

"What? What?"

"You talk to my dad about me?"

You raised your hands. "No! Well, he spoke to me once. Said you were vulnerable. I think it was supposed to be a warning, that kind of thing."

"I can't believe you're chatting to my dad about how weak I am."

"That's not—"

"And now!" I shouted. "And now, to make things worse, you're taking his *side*? ********. You're supposed to be on *my side*."

"Whoa, Cass. There are no sides."

"There are sides. And I want you on mine. On Paris's."

You moved your hands in a placating gesture. "You've got me, Cass," you said. "I'm totally here. On your side." You moved toward me, put those same hands on my hips. "One hundred percent. Always. But I am not driving you to New York to see Paris's dad."

I felt the ice core melt a little. I felt the heat of your fingers, that electric power again, like I could charge myself just from contact

434

with you, like energy would surge into my every nerve ending just from your touch.

"You're really on my side?" I said.

"Yep."

I sighed. "Well, okay, then."

"And no trip to New York? At least till we know more?"

I loved that "we." "Yeah, okay."

You kissed my forehead. Fireworks went off in my head; Roman candles spun, throwing off sparks, hissing, blazing stars into the blackness behind my eyelids, my closed eyes, waiting for—

You pulled away.

Oh, okay. We were in the yard. That was why. I remembered; I saw the trees, the flowers, the thrush landing on the thin branch of a bush. You weren't going to kiss me where my dad might come home and see. I got it. I got it, but I still wanted you to.

But then you smiled and handed me a beer. Our fingers touched—blazing sparks flew, invisibly.

"I don't drink," I said. I knew the voice would punish me if I drank the beer, even with the progress I'd made. I handed back the can.

"Oh," you said. "That's cool. Straight edge, huh?"

"Something like that," I said.

"You want to come up to the apartment?" you said.

"What, now?"

"Uh, yeah."

"My dad might come back," I said.

"He's on a late night, right?"

"Yes."

"And you said he hasn't come back early on a late night for, what, a year?"

"Yes."

"So I think you're safe."

"Okay," I said. "We can talk about what to do. About finding Paris."

"Sure," you said.

But we both knew that wasn't going to happen.

I followed you up the steps and into the apartment. The place was still a dump—still the empty pizza cartons, the takeout boxes, the bottles of Coke. Still clothes hanging from every available surface, discarded menus, dust.

"You should fire your housekeeper," I said.

"*You're* our housekeeper, in theory anyway."

"Yeah. And I've been terrible. You should fire me."

You laughed, and then space compressed between us, some kind of freak twist of physics, and we were standing very close together. The kitchen fell away from around us, the dirt and detritus; there was only the evening light from the windows, slanting through the shutters, and the buzzing circuit formed when our hands touched.

White noise roared in my head, blocking out every other sound. You tuned the radio of my mind to a dead channel, switched off my thoughts.

It was amazing.

I shut my eyes, and we closed together neatly, like we were hinged, and you kissed me.

It felt like it lasted forever, that kiss. Like not only the kitchen fell away but the whole universe, and we were floating in a deep black abyss, where only the contact between us meant anything at all.

I don't want to do that kind of line, like you read in books. The ones where it says, "He took off my top," or that kind of thing. Because the undercurrent, the suggestion, becomes that you pushed me in some way, "only wanted one thing," you get the idea. And anyway it wouldn't be true. And it implies some kind of linearity when all I can say with confidence is that there was a moment when both our tops were on and then they were both off, and I was in my bra, which had strawberries on it, embarrassingly.

Our bodies touched. Hands moved. Fingers were outlined with electricity, dancing with it, St. Elmo's fire; I felt like we were phosphorescent.

I half opened my eyes, and saw your hair, haloed with light. A blade of sunshine reached us from between the shutters, so sharp it looked like it would cut straight through us.

I closed my eyes again.

My head filled with static.

%%%%%%%%%%%%%%%%%%%%%%%%%%%%%%%%%%%
%%%%%%%%%%%%%%%%%%%%%%%%%%%%%%%%%%%
%%%%%%%%%%%%%%%%%%%%%%%%%%%%%%%%%%%
%%%%%%%%%%%%%%%%%%%%%%%%%%%%%%%%%%%
%%%%%%%%%%%%%%%%%%%%%%%%%%%%%%%%%%%
%%%%%%%%%%%%%%%%%%%%%%%%%%%%%%%%%%%
%%%%%%%%%%%%%%%%%%%%%%

"CASS?"

Huh?

"CASS."

I opened my eyes, blinking, turning, already knowing. Already shrinking back.

And there was Dad, standing in the doorway. A dark figure against the reddish evening sunlight.

"I ran into Shane on the boardwalk," he said. His voice was horribly, horribly calm. "He told me you were home. But you weren't in the house."

Silence.

"You put your shirt on and come with me right now, Cass," he said.

His voice was cold. Cold and merciless as the sea.

I hauled on my T-shirt and as I passed Dad, he grabbed my upper arm, and pretty much pulled me down the steps.

"Dad, you're hurting me," I said.

He ignored me.

He dragged me all the way to the house and then pushed me away from him when we got to the den; hard. My leg slammed into the coffee table—I don't think he meant for that to happen, but it sent a shock of pain up my hip. I stood very still, trembling.

"Again, Cass?" he said. His voice still had that quiet, dangerous tone. "I thought I made myself very clear."

"Sorry, Dad," I said.

"*Sorry*? *Sorry*? You know who called me today, Cass? You know why I left the restaurant early?"

I looked at him, puzzled.

"A *cop*, Cass. A ******* cop. Said you went to the police station? Something about harassing an officer of the law. Seemed to think you might get yourself into trouble."

"I—"

"You're not a ******* detective, Cass! I don't know what goddamn books you've been reading, but you can't solve this **** on your own and then get a ******* medal from the mayor, okay? What the ****, Cass?"

Silence.

"She was my friend," I said eventually.

"She? Who the— Wait. You mean the ******* whore?"

"Paris."

"*Paris*. Jesus H. ******* Christ. I knew that girl was trouble when I saw her at the hospital."

"She's probably dead," I said.

"YES, AND YOU'RE NOT! Not yet anyway."

"I'm not going to die."

"You sure about that? You're sick, Cass. You're sick, and you shouldn't be running around playing Sherlock."

I didn't say anything.

"I can't believe anything that comes out of your mouth, can I?" he said. "My own daughter."

"Yes, you can."

"Like when you said you wouldn't hang out with that boy? I *told* you about him. He's a college freshman, Cass."

"He's not. He's starting in the fall."

"And have you even told him about your problem?" he said. "I'm thinking of his protection too here. I mean, does he know? About the voice?"

Me (in a low voice): No.

"And you don't think that's unwise? You don't think that's dangerous? You're hooking up with this boy, or whatever you call it, and he doesn't even know you're mentally ill."

"I'm not mentally ill," I said.

"Sure," said Dad. "You're perfectly fine." He scrubbed his face with his hands, scoured it. "I don't know what you're trying to do to me, Cass," he said. "It's like you're doing this **** deliberately."

"I don't mean to—"

"It's like you *want* to break this family apart. What's left of it anyway."

I started to cry then. My arm and my leg were stinging; my eyes were prickling, like I'd rubbed salt in them. "I don't . . . I . . . That's not . . ." I took a breath. "What do you want from me?"

"I want you to keep away from that boy. I want you to stay in the house when I'm out. Keep meeting Dr. Rezwari. Keep taking your meds. Will you do those things, Cassie?"

440

I did not see the trap coming.

Stupid me.

"Yes, yes, yes, yes," I said. "Yes, I'll do those things."

He took a step forward, fast as a snake, and I staggered back, thought he was about to hit me, went down on the coffee table—luckily it was wood, not glass, but my butt hit it hard, and I skinned the backs of my calves; my hands went behind me to try to stop my fall, and my right hand struck the side of the table, twisting my wrist.

Silence.

Silence.

Silence.

Something had sucked all the air out of the house; we were standing in a vacuum, in absolute stillness.

"Jesus, Cass," he said. "Are you okay?"

"I thought . . ."

He must have seen it in my eyes. "Jesus, Cass." He took a step forward and reached down for my hand, then helped me up. "I wasn't going to *hurt* you."

"I . . ."

He put his head in his hands. "I don't know how to deal with this ****. I really don't. I don't know how to deal with your lies."

"What?"

"You said you're taking your meds?"

Now I saw the trap. Oh no. But what could I do?

"Uh . . . yes."

"Liar," he said quietly.

He went out of the room.

When he came back in, he was carrying my nightstand in one hand—you remember when I said he would carry full trash cans to the street? He had my nightstand in one hand, and he swung up his other hand to catch the front of it, then he upturned it, so that the drawers fell out in a *shwoosh* and hit the floor.

Blister packs of drugs spilled all over the carpet.

For the longest time we both just stood there looking at the drugs on the floor.

"Dad, I can explain, I—"

"No," said Dad. "Not now."

I remembered Dr. Lewis, telling me to speak to Dr. Rezwari. To follow her instructions. And I had lied to her instead. Stupid, stupid, stupid.

"I've been good, Dad, I've been hearing the voice but it's *helping* me now, it's not hurting me anymore. I've—"

"It's *helping* you?" he said. "The invisible voice in your head is *helping* you?"

"Yes."

He sighed. "Tomorrow morning, we're going to see the doctor. And you're going to do whatever she says, okay?"

"Okay."

"And that boy. This is because of him, isn't it? Not taking your meds?"

"What? No."

"Of course it is. You think because you've got a crush, you don't need the drugs anymore. But you're *hearing voices*, Cass."

"One voice."

He glared at me. "Yeah, like that makes a difference. Anyway, he's out of here. He can find somewhere else to live."

"Dad! You can't kick him out."

"Yes, I can."

THE VOICE: "Yes, he can."

"Whatever."

I sat down heavily on the couch. I wanted time to rewind, so I could leave the apartment before Dad got home. But then

I guess the cop would still have called him. Would it have been Brian? I guessed so. ******* Brian. Selling me out to my dad.

"But he's . . . he makes me feel . . ."

Dad kicked over the coffee table; it flipped with a crash. "I don't give a ******** **** how he makes you feel, Cass."

I told you: my dad's anger, it swims under the surface, and you don't see it, but then it bursts up like a killer whale flinging itself into the air, gleaming blackly.

"He makes the voice go away," I said eventually.

"The *drugs* make the voice go away. He's out of here."

"No!"

"Yes. Because I . . . I cannot. Lose. My. Daughter. Too."

"You're not losing me!"

"Oh yeah?" He kicked the pile of drugs so that blister packs skittered over the floor, loose pills, the meds jumbling together.

THE VOICE: "He's right. You're already lost. You're a slut. That's why this is happening."

I put my head in my hands. "I hate you," I said, to both of them.

Dad shrugged.

"He's just a *boy*," I said. "He doesn't have anywhere else to stay. He's just—"

Dad closed the distance between us and leaned in close, the anger seeming to bake off him, shimmer in the air, like desert heat. "He's *eighteen*," he said. "He's a man. And you're a girl, with a ******* mental illness, which you have not even told him about so that he can make a responsible decision, and which you're NOT TAKING YOUR DRUGS FOR. Seriously, Cass, I don't know what else to do here. You're giving me no choice. I've tried setting rules, and you've broken them, over and over."

444

I felt like I didn't know who he was anymore. Punishing you for *my* mistake. "If Mom were here, she would—"

"Don't you dare talk about your mother," said Dad, practically spitting the words. "If it weren't for you, she wouldn't—"

Then he stopped.

He held himself very still, his eyes strange and wide, shocked by his own words. He actually took a step backward, like he was trying to physically reverse from what he had just said.

And something in me snapped.

I mean, those things happened at the same time. Dad started saying that sentence, and something in me snapped. But I can't put them side by side on the page.

Anyway.

I have learned that when people snap, it can be very quick.

"If it weren't for me, she wouldn't be dead, right?" I said. "That's what you were saying."

"No. No . . . I . . ."

"That's what you were going to say. That it's my fault she's dead."

"What? N-n-no," he stammered. "****, Cass. I was going to say—"

"But it's WHAT YOU THINK," I shouted. "It's what you think, so why don't you say it?"

"What do I think? What are you talking about?"

"You think because I moved her, she died. Because I lifted her head."

Silence.

"I don't think that."

"Yeah? Then why did you wait so long before saying anything?"

"I don't think that, Cass."

"Oh please," I said. "It was a head injury. You don't move

445

someone with a head injury. EVERYONE KNOWS THAT. That's why you hate me so much."

"I don't hate you," he said wearily.

"You do."

"Cass, seriously, I'm warning you—"

"YOU HATE ME AND I DESERVE IT."

"I don't—"

"It was my fault. Admit it. It was—"

And then it was his turn to snap. I said that it can happen very suddenly.

"I don't ******* know, Cass!" he shouted. "I don't know. One of us was there and one of wasn't, okay?"

"What are you saying? You're saying because I was there and you weren't, that's why she died? Right?"

"I don't know what I'm saying," he said.

We looked at each other.

"Go to your room, Cass," he said.

And then he walked out.

Here are some things that happened after that:

1. I had to go and see Dr. Rezwari, and she went kind of ape**** by her standards, which actually just means that she raised her voice a tiny bit, and she asked me a load of questions and said that I had "taken my treatment into my own hands" and it was incredibly dangerous.

2. She made me stay in the hospital for two days. They gave me drugs; they made me take part in group and make a jewelry box out of wood. I don't have any jewelry, but whatever.

3. The voice went away.

4. Paris and her dad and the whole alibi thing went to the back of my mind.

5. Dad kicked you and Shane out. Made up some bull**** about needing the apartment for a relative who was coming to stay.

6. I broke your heart.

7. I don't know if I broke your heart. That might be overdramatic. I hurt you though. I know that.

Actually, with Dr. Rezwari, it wasn't too bad.

After the initial blowup, she kind of softened. I went to see her at the end of my two days in the hospital, sitting at her weirdly blank desk, and she smiled at me.

"How are you feeling, Cassie?" she asked.

"Oh, super," I said.

"You don't like the drugs?"

"No."

She sighed. "I've spoken to Dr. Lewis. On the phone." She indicated the phone on her desk, as if I needed to have the concept explained to me. Illustrated. She steepled her fingers. "He tells me you have made some breakthroughs, in dealing with the voice."

"Uh, yes, I guess."

"However . . . he was surprised to learn that you had made a decision *on your own* to stop your medication."

I stiffened.

"I mean, Cassie . . . I'm trying to help you here. He wrote me, did you know that? To tell me that the two of you were meeting."

I looked down at the floor. "Um, yeah, he mentioned it."

"And you didn't think you might therefore be able to talk to me about it? To discuss it? And to talk about your drugs? I was waiting to see if you would bring it up, and you never did."

"I don't know."

She made an exasperated sound. "Listen, Cassie . . . I want you to tell me how you feel about the drugs you're taking."

"What?"

"Please. Indulge me. Tell me honestly. You can look at me too. I won't bite."

I met her eyes. They were open, interested—clear. "I . . . I hate

them. They make me too tired and I can't think properly and . . .
they make me *not me.*"

"And you believe you function better without them?"

"Yes."

"Your father believes otherwise."

"He's just pissed because I met a boy."

"Hmm," said Dr. Rezwari.

A pause.

"Look . . . You have to work with me, Cassie. Has it occurred to
you that these drugs, paroxetine especially, have withdrawal effects?
That stopping abruptly may have been extremely dangerous?"

"Uh . . . no."

"Evidently not. And has it occurred to you, too, that you never
actually *told me* you didn't like taking them?"

Oh.

No, it hadn't occurred to me.

"Okay, so. Let's start over. I'm Dr. Rezwari. And you are?"

"What?"

"You are . . . ?"

"Cassie."

She smiled, and reached out to shake my hand. "Nice to meet
you, Cassie."

"Uh . . . Nice to meet you too," I said. My head was all fuzzy.

"You hear voices. You are currently pursuing a therapeutic
approach to dealing with those voices, under the care of Dr. Lewis."

"Yes . . ."

"And this has led to your being able to"—she flipped open the
single note pad on her desk, lined up neatly with the edge—
"schedule times when the voice can speak to you? Challenge the
voice's power?"

"Yeah."

"That's good. Very good. And you are currently supposed to be taking risperidone and paroxetine?"

"Yes, you prescribed them to me."

"I know that." Another sigh. "So here's the thing, Cassie. I'm not some monster. I don't live to turn you into a robot. I want you to be a fulfilled, absorbed, contented person. But you're also someone who *hears voices*. That can be very dangerous. For you and, frankly, for other people. Do you see that?"

"I don't know. Maybe." I mean, the voice had done some ****ed-up stuff to me. And had wanted me to hurt other people too. "But I wouldn't hurt him. The boy. My dad thinks I might, but I would never do that."

"I believe that you believe that. Nevertheless, we have a duty to protect you, and to protect others. Do you agree?"

"Yes . . ."

"*Having said that*, I am aware of the progress being made by people like Dr. Lewis. There have been some promising studies. So—"

I opened my mouth and stared at her. "I can stop the—"

She raised her finger. "Wait. We are taking this one step at a time. I want regular meetings with you and Dr. Lewis. I want to involve your father. No, listen, don't look at me like that; you're under eighteen. And I want, for now, to keep you on risperidone, albeit a slightly lower dose. I also feel that long term you will truly benefit from the medication. You are at major risk of depression otherwise. But . . ."

"Yes?"

"But I'm prepared, *if* I'm satisfied with what I see, to look at your drug regimen with you. To empower you, in your own recovery and ongoing . . . you know . . . life."

I smiled—it was funny, to see an adult, a psychiatrist at that, struggle for the word they were looking for.

Dr. Rezwari laughed. "Brain not quite operating on full power today. Anyway. Does that sound good to you?"

I was still a little in shock. "Yeah," I said. "Yeah, that sounds good."

"This is with the condition that you continue taking the drugs—no, wait—that you continue taking them *for now*. Until we can *all* make a proper appraisal. Together. Is that okay?"

I took a breath. "Yeah, okay."

She smiled and smoothed her dress. It looked expensive—Chanel, maybe? "Now, you have never taken me up on my offer of a book, to borrow. But I always see you looking at them. Please, take one when you leave."

"I don't . . ."

"Really, any book. Any book you like."

"Okay . . ."

I stood and glanced down the shelves. A name popped out at me: Haruki Murakami. I loved the one Jane had given me. It was weird, but amazing. This one was called *A Wild Sheep Chase*. I pulled it from the shelf—it shushed against the book next to it, a soft, velvety sound. "Can I take this one?"

"Of course. Murakami. Good choice."

"Thanks."

"You're welcome. Now get out of here. There's lasagna in the cafeteria, and if I'm late it'll all be gone."

So, not too bad, huh?

I started taking the slightly lower dose. I had a meeting with Dr. Rezwari and Dr. Lewis. They argued a bit but it was obvious they respected each other; everything was hunky-dory. The voice came back, not so bad as before, but I could deal with it. I had the tools now.

Dad wasn't speaking to me, but I'd caught him looking at me like he was about to speak. We'd even, like, half smiled at each other when passing in the house.

Stupidly, I allowed myself to believe that things were getting better.

I don't remember the specifics of my life after that point, for a while anyway. I was all over the place, honestly.

Oh, some days passed.

I don't really remember them.

I don't remember what happened.

But I remember the next big thing.

And it was the next thing that led to me hurting you.

The next big thing:

It was Thursday. Group day. Group evening. You know what I mean.

I sat up in my room until Dad had gone to work, then I went downstairs and out into the yard. I was hoping you would still be at work. But I timed it badly, or you came back early, I don't know. Maybe all the concession stands had tons of stuffed animals and you got to go home.

Anyway: you were just walking from your pickup. Shane was in a bar somewhere, presumably—drinking with the other life-guards.

****, I thought, when I stepped out into the yard and you turned and saw me.

"Hey!" you said, running over. "Are you okay? Jesus, Cass. You went with your dad and then you just disappeared, for like three days . . . I thought maybe . . . I mean . . . did he hurt you?"

"No. Yes. No. I just . . . went to stay with a relative for a while."

You looked stricken. "I'm so sorry, Cass. I didn't know . . . I didn't realize . . . how angry he was."

"Yeah," I said.

"He's throwing me out, you know that?" You sounded incredulous. "I have till the end of the week to find somewhere else."

"I know," I said. "I'm sorry. Really." I started to cry, despite the drugs that Dr. Rezwari had reintroduced fogging up the window of my world again, making everything soft and blurred.

"But we can still see each other, right?" you said. "I mean, when he's at work—I can pick you up, we can go to the pool . . . or to the warehouse . . ."

I nodded. "Uh-huh." *Please don't remember what day it is. Please don't ask where I'm going.*

You smiled. "Good. Good." Then you seemed to realize that I was leaving, that I had been crossing the yard when you got back. "You going out? You need a lift?"

"Um. No. Thanks."

"Where are you going?" you asked. Fake-casual.

"Um," I said. Even at this point, after your declaration of 100 percent, I was afraid to tell you how messed up I really was.

I'm still afraid, to be honest. I'm afraid you're reading this and resolving to run as far from me as you can go, to Mexico, to the South Pole, to anyplace but Oakwood and any girl but me. Still, I have to try, don't I? I mean, you're 100 percent on my side, or you were, when you told me that. But I'm 100 percent on your side too. And I need you to know it.

Anyway.

You nodded. Nodded in this really unsurprised way, like, "I thought so." You closed your eyes and breathed out, long and hard.

Which was maybe the moment at which *my* heart broke a little, though I don't expect much sympathy from you. I don't deserve much.

"Sorry," I said.

You didn't say anything.

Your radio crackled.

"714? Sorry, we actually need you again, if you're still sober enough to drive. Dippin' Dots emergency."

You glared at the radio.

"You'd better get to work," I said.

You saluted sarcastically like I was an Army officer commanding you and half smiled, though I could still see the hurt and confusion in your eyes, which broke my heart into even smaller pieces, and then you got in the F-150 and drove away.

I walked to the bus.

How could I have known that you would tell your boss you'd had a couple of beers already?

How could I have known you would follow me?

What comes after, you already know. Part of it, at least. The part I wanted you to see.

I went to group at the bowling alley. You don't need to know what we talked about; it was more of the same stuff. Voices. Aggression. Accommodation. Dr. Lewis asked how we were, and he made me talk first, so of course he'd spoken to Dr. Rezwari, so I had to humiliate myself by talking about the bomb I had placed under myself by lying to her, by lying to my dad, and all the fallout, the dirty ash fallout, coating everything, the drugs, the suspicion in my dad's eyes always now, the guilt.

The stupidity of it.

You'd have thought I'd have learned my lesson about lies, right?

DR. LEWIS: It sounds like Dr. Rezwari has your best interests at heart.

ME: Maybe. But I don't feel like *I* do.

GROUP: (faint laughter)

ME: I break everything.

DR. LEWIS: Now, that's not true.

THE VOICE: No, that's true.

Then at the end, I hung back. I hung back because I wanted to leave with Dwight—I wanted to ask him if he'd told on me to my dad.

So we came out onto the street together.

And that was when I saw you, in your truck, across the street. A little farther down, south toward Hudson; I registered you in my peripheral vision, kept my eyes rigidly forward, like I hadn't seen you, like I had no idea.

It was as if the atmosphere got cold all of a sudden, like Dwight and I had stepped into a current of air, one of those weird eddies you get in the ocean, snaking barrels of iciness, boring through air, though, instead of water.

I shivered.

And I want you to know, I want you to know right now, that I wasn't thinking clearly. I was back on the drugs, smaller doses, but still—I was still looking at the world through plate glass, separated from it; held at bay.

"Take Dwight's hand," said the voice.

"No," I said. "Oh, and come back after six."

"Okay, then tell the boy all about me," said the voice. "About group."

Only seconds had passed. You were still in your truck, still watching. I saw, from the corner of my eye, you moving, saw the truck door click open. You were coming over.

****.

"Do it now," said the voice. "Trust me."

"*Trust* you?"

"What?" said Dwight.

"Voice," I said. "Give me a moment."

Dwight nodded. We stood still on the sidewalk. In the cold air, under the merciless stars.

"Better hurt him than tell him the truth," said the voice. "Tell him the truth and he'll pity you. Hurt him and he'll only hate you."

You were stepping out of your truck. Looking left and right. Getting ready to cross the street. The light of the 7-Eleven sign was on your face; a sickly halo.

The voice sighed. "Bitch. Or crazy person. You decide."

Huh.

A cog turned over in my mind; a ball bearing was released, rolled down a track, flipped a switch. I thought of the hospital. The way the cab drivers looked at me on the days when Dad paid for a cab to bring me home. The paramedics in the ambulance, the warmth that went out of them when I told them the drugs I was prescribed; radiators clicking off.

This is sick, I said, inside my head now.

At the same time I was thinking: *This could work. He doesn't know what Dwight looks like. He thinks the cop I spoke to was a friend of Dad's.*

"It's necessary," said the voice. "Or do you want to tell him you've been lying to him? Your dad's right. You have to think of *his* protection. People close to you die. Think of your mom. Think of Paris."

A dry click from my heart; sound of a revolver clicking to an empty chamber.

Me: *don't say that.*

Voice: "It's true and you know it."

Me: (nothing. Just the roar of the ocean, when you put your head underwater, filling my eardrums, inside me.)

So I did it. Because I was too . . . too selfish and horrible to risk telling you the truth, because I preferred to create a lie rather than to see the look in your eye when I told you I was a voice hearer, because I didn't want you to be afraid of me, because I thought I might die if I saw fear in you; but if I saw pain, that would only be what I expected, because I expected to hurt people, it was in my nature, and because I AM A TERRIBLE PERSON.

You were halfway across the street. I know this all sounds slow, but it was fast; as fast as thought, as fast as film, *tick tick tick*, twenty-four frames a second.

The voice went silent. Maybe you were too close now, muting it, your force field doming over me, where I stood with Dwight, embracing me.

Not for long.

I grabbed Dwight's hand. He turned to me, surprised.

I didn't need the voice to tell me what to do next. I didn't need the voice to say: kiss him.

I just kissed him.

I leaned up, grabbed the hair at the back of his head, kicked one heel up, like an old starlet. Kissed Dwight hard on the mouth. He was too shocked to pull away; he didn't exactly kiss me back either, but I didn't need him to; you were still twenty feet away, maybe more.

I pressed myself against him.

Finally pulled away.

"What was that, Cass?" Dwight asked.

"A thank-you," I said. "For helping. With Paris." I saw his face flicker; two images superimposed—guilt, I thought, for a flash, and then a strange smile. Probably it was him who called my dad. But that wasn't what I was concentrating on.

What I was concentrating on was turning, turning to see you.

You had stopped in the middle of the street.

Cars were passing you, horns blaring, lights flashing. But you were motionless, a still point in a world of noise and brightness.

I let my mouth fall open. I let Dwight's hand fall from mine.

You were in a trance, almost. You looked at me, like, "Why?"

I shrugged.

And it was like that broke the spell. You turned, and held up your hand, and an SUV stopped, a Cadillac, gleaming in the artificial light, and you walked back to your truck.

Which was what I wanted, of course.

Which was what the voice wanted.

Which was part of me.

So why was I crying?

I dialed Dad's cell number. After a few rings he answered—I could hear the bubbling of voices in the background, the scrape of knives, the chinking of glasses. "Yeah?" he said.

"Hi," I said coldly.

"You okay, Cass?"

"No I'm not *okay*. What do you think?"

Silence.

"So what did you call me for?"

A pause.

"Listen, Dad."

"Yes?"

"You don't have to worry about 'that boy' anymore. And I kind of hate you right now. Just so you know."

The line went dead. He had hung up.

I'm so sorry.

I walked all the way home.

It took hours.

It took hours, but I felt like I deserved the punishment. I didn't even care if Dad got back before me; he might want me to take buses because of the killer, but I could give a **** what he wanted.

You were sitting on the grass of the yard. Of course you were.

Not on a deck chair, but right on the ground; it must have been damp—there was a storm supposed to be coming and the air was thick with moisture—but still you were sitting there. Like you had just run out of kinetic energy, as you crossed from the sidewalk, like your mind had been so blank that you had just dropped, like a puppet let go by its master.

****, I thought.

You looked up. Your eyes were red.

The moon rotated a thousand times around the earth, in its cold black vacuum. The stars wheeled around us for aeons; the universe was born and died, and was born again, and fast-forwarded from the big bang to a night in Jersey, in the twenty-first century, the crickets buzzing in the undergrowth.

"Who was that guy, Cass?" you said.

I wanted to be able to fly. I wanted to be a bird. I wanted to step forward into wings, unfolding from my back, the softness of feathers, and step again up into the air this time, pinioned on those wings, strong, pressing down on the suddenly viscous air, and spiral up, away from you, through the window of my room.

Or away. Away into the sky, like I had dreamed about, drifting into the piled black clouds of the horizon, the dull light of the moon. Float, forever.

But my feet were concrete, bolted to the ground.

"I'm sorry," I said, the words glass in my throat.

"I said who is he."

I shook my head. "No one."

You kept your eyes on mine. Your expression was horribly, horribly calm. "Seriously, Cass?" you said.

"What do you want from me?" I said, trying to keep the shaking out of my vocal cords, the tears, the ocean of tears that would come spilling out if I let it, break over the sea defenses, wash everything away, the sidewalk the grass the bushes the crickets.

"How about the truth?" you said.

"I can't do that," I said.

You nodded very slowly. "In that case, I'd like you to get out of my sight." You didn't say it like in a movie. Not dramatically. You said it smooth and frictionless as marble. No intonation at all, no rise and fall. Stone.

"Okay," I said.

And I did.

When I got to my room I lay facedown on the bed, pressing the duvet into my face, wrapping myself in it.

What do I do now? I thought. *What am I supposed to do now?* I felt like a clockwork toy with a broken spring, like a puppet with wood where a heart should be. No Paris. No you.

No way to get you back either. Not without telling you the truth, telling you everything, and the dead would talk through the tongues of birds, I mean really talk, before I was going to do that.

"Find Paris, then," said the voice.

Yes, I thought. *Yes*. It was something to cling onto. A piece of driftwood, floating on the open ocean, after a wreck.

But no. I'd had a warning, hadn't I? Dad had told me, the police were onto me. They didn't want me interfering. They didn't want me getting myself killed.

"So be careful," said the voice. "Don't let him know you're still after him."

"Shut up," I said.

"I'm trying to help."

"So help by shutting up. I don't want to hear from you right now."

I wanted to be sharp, so I was glad Dr. Rezwari had lowered my dose a little. It wasn't great, as far as alertness went, but it would have to do. I wasn't about to get myself locked up again.

I rolled over on the bed and realized I had no idea *how* to find Paris. How to find the killer.

"Call Agent Horowitz," said the voice. "Ask about Paris's dad. The alibi. Find out what he's doing."

"He'll tell my dad. He'll . . . I don't know. Give me an official warning or something. And anyway, what if Horowitz is the killer? We still think it might be a cop. Say he decides I'm poking my nose in, and that I would be better off . . . dead?"

"Fine," said the voice. "So don't take any risks. Let the killer go. Just like the guy who smashed your mom's head in."

"**** you. Don't use Mom."

"Also, you know how the killer is out there somewhere, out there in this town, maybe even torturing Paris right now?"

Me: (through gritted teeth) "We don't know there's a killer. Paris might have just left town. Split."

"You believe that?"

Me: silence.

"Just saying," said the voice. "He's not going to just go away, is he?"

"So?"

"So the only way to really make yourself safe . . . to make any girl in this town safe ... is to get the killer. To put him behind bars. Or in the ground."

I pursed my lips.

There was a logic in that.

SEE? NOT THINKING CLEARLY.

"Anyway," said the voice. "Horowitz hasn't been in town long enough to be the killer."

Huh.

Well, that was true.

"So," said the voice. "Now that lover boy is gone, what do you have to lose?"

Nothing.

Nothing, I realized.

I had nothing to lose.

"I'm not doing anything till the boys are gone. They're still in the apartment. We only just ... broke up. It's too soon. When they've gone ... Then I start again."

"Okay, but Paris could still be alive. She could be in a basement right now, fighting for her—"

"Shut up."

And, miracle of miracles, the voice did.

But just then Dad shouted up from downstairs. "Cass! The boys are moving out tonight. Ahead of schedule. I don't know what **** you pulled, but it worked. Your one? Skinny kid? He looked an awful lot like he'd been crying."

I didn't say anything.

"Well ... You wanna talk to me about it, you can." A cough. Embarrassed. A pause. "So anyway, I want you with me on cleaning duty tomorrow. Got new guys coming in on Saturday."

"Whatever," I shouted down.

"You want me to come up there?" he shouted back menacingly.

I seethed. "No," I called. "No."

"Then be ready to clean tomorrow. Eight sharp. And don't go anywhere till then. I'm going back to the restaurant—we have an inspection tomorrow. I want you in that room and nowhere else."

Again, I didn't say anything. After a while I heard him walk back from the stairwell to his study.

**** *you, Dad*, I thought.

"So," said the voice. "No calling Horowitz tomorrow, if we're cleaning with your dad."

"No," I said. "****."

"We'll have that apartment sparkling in no time," said the voice. "Might finish up early. After all, I made you do all that practice."

"Ha-ha," I said.

It sounded hollow.

As hollow as my life had become.

As hollow as your eyes, when I didn't tell you the truth.

I wrote you a note.

It was a short one. It said:

The truth is that I hear a voice that isn't there and I go to a group to talk about it and that guy you saw me with was Dwight, the cop I talked about, who goes to group too. I'm not interested in him. I just kissed him so you wouldn't know I was crazy.

I want you.

Only you.

I folded it up.

I had no intention of giving it to you.

But better late than never, right?

It was when I was cleaning your room that I found it.

It was on the floor just under your nightstand—you must have knocked it off in the night or something and not realized in the morning. You had other things on your mind of course. The necklace, with its little blue pendant. Your mom's necklace, the one you usually wore. I wouldn't have seen it if I hadn't been on my knees, with the handheld vacuum cleaner.

I picked it up and held it in my hand for a moment. The metal of the thin chain was cold and silky against my skin, like water. I closed my hand around it, then I put it on. It made me feel closer to you, though I didn't deserve to. Then I kept cleaning. I got the dust balls from under the bed, picked up a couple of books you had left behind. Your Ovid, your *Middlemarch*. I loved that you had a copy of *Middlemarch*.

Then, dusting the top of the wardrobe, I found a small instrument—a banjo, I think. Or a ukulele. I remembered you playing me a Beach Boys song by that pool on the roof. It felt like the last time I was happy. Maybe the last time I would ever be happy. I figured you had brought it with you and forgotten about it, up there on the wardrobe.

Before I left your bedroom—well, not your bedroom anymore—I took off the necklace. I showed Dad the necklace and the banjo in the den. "He left these," I said.

He nodded. "I'll call him. Tell him to come pick them up."

But it wasn't you who came for them.

You know that already of course.

I woke up early. Sun was streaming through the window, sharp, rhomboid.

"Is it over?" said the voice.

"One more thing," I said.

I put the note I had written you in my pocket and left the house—Dad was at work—and walked down the street to the beach. Then I went right up to the water. The sun was hard and flat on the waves, the ocean made of beaten metal.

I took the note out of my pocket; it felt toxic against my skin. I didn't want it anymore. It's stupid, but I didn't want it in the house *at all*. I didn't really understand why I had written it even. I felt like . . . like the truth was a poison that might hurt me, like it was bad luck, an evil talisman. Like you might find it and hate me more than you already did, or fear me, which would be worse. (I wanted you to hate me. I wanted not to see you recoil from me. Can you understand that? I guess I will find out soon. It's nearly time to send this.)

Anyway, the note. It felt like:

An exposure.

A curse.

Superstitiously, I thought if I could just get rid of the note, then I would free myself, I would be safe.

STUPIDEST THOUGHT EVER.

Anyway, I slowly and deliberately tore the paper into strips and ribbons, then I threw them one by one into the ocean. The breeze caught them and one or two fluttered back onto the sand but most landed in the water. A gull thought it was food and swooped down, pecking at the red paper, but then realized its mistake and wheeled into the sky again, crying.

Torn clouds drifted overhead.

"Okay," I said, when the last shred of paper was gone. "It's over."

I felt disassociated from the world, like my body was one of those robot limb things that scientists move by remote control. Everything was removed from me. The cell phone felt like an alien weight in my hand. I suppose I was in shock, again.

You killed your mother and you just broke his heart. Everything you touch turns to ****.

That wasn't the voice speaking. It was my conscience. Which was worse.

Then the stuff with your dad happened. Another time I covered myself with glory.

That was sarcasm, of course.

It was him who came for your stuff.

He drove over the next day from your little town twenty miles inland. I guess you had sent him instead—you hated me so much you didn't want to risk seeing me. I didn't blame you.

Your dad turned up in a beat-up Honda when my dad was out. When I saw that car, I realized right away that I had gotten it wrong about you and your iPhone; I mean, I had gotten the wrong idea about the background to your life. Other people's lives are like stage sets, aren't they? Which is to say, there are a couple of things in the foreground—items that set the scene, appearance, accent, and stuff—but most of it we fill in with our imaginations, assuming the backdrop, the rest of the picture.

Your going to Brown, your swimming . . . I guess it had all read middle class to me. But then that car rolled out, and your dad levered himself out of it, sweating, his back stooped and his arms covered in what looked like prison tattoos, and I saw I had gotten it all wrong. His radio was blaring—country music faded out, and then an announcer came on, talking about a storm system that was on its way.

"Come for the stuff," he drawled. "The stuff my son left behind."

I nodded. "I'll get it."

I went into the house and picked up the necklace and banjo. Or ukulele, or whatever. You must know—just fill in whatever is right.

Outside, I handed the necklace over first. Your dad's eyes gleamed briefly when he saw it, as if someone had passed the beam of a torch over a dark pond. His chest expanded, like he was drawing in air to soothe a pain inside him. Then he put it in his pocket.

I held out the banjo/ukulele. (Delete as appropriate.)

"Nope," he said.

"Um . . . sorry?"

"Ain't his. He don't play."

He turned around and spat as he did so, opened the door of the car. I wondered if you'd said anything about me to him, if he was pissed off with me. His whole attitude pissed *me* off anyway, even though I wasn't in a position to be judging anyone else, and I guess that's why I didn't keep my mouth shut.

"He does," I said.

Your dad turned. "Wassat?"

"He does play," I said. "He plays beautifully."

Your dad shook his head. "Stopped when his mom died."

I glared at him. His whole stance and the set of his eyes—everything about him was signaling belligerence, and usually I would have backed down, done anything to remove myself from the situation. But I didn't. Maybe it was the influence of the voice.

"You mean you wanted him to stop?" I said.

"What?"

"Maybe it reminds you of your wife when he plays. But what about what *he* wants?"

Your dad's expression had changed to incredulity. "What the **** are you talking about? Who the **** are you?"

Okay. So you hadn't told him about us.

"Wait," he said. "Are you guys together?"

"Not anymore," said the voice. "She **** on his heart."

"Um . . . ," I said.

Your dad spat again. "Told him to keep away from girls," he said.

"He's eighteen. He can do what he wants."

A short bark of a laugh. "Trainin' comes first," he said.

"Swimming training."

"Yep."

"Oh come on, I was just—"

473

"Distraction," he said, talking over me. "You're a distraction."

"Was."

"Was? What?"

"Was a distraction. We broke up."

"You can say that again." That from the voice.

"Good," said your dad. "Maybe that'll make him focus. I timed him the other day, and his ass was a second down on the hundred meters."

"What are you, his trainer?" I really don't know what had gotten into me. A voice, maybe. Animating my vocal cords. Speaking for me.

"Yep," said your dad flatly. "You know he's been selected for National team trials?"

I stared at him. "Are you serious?"

"As a heart attack. So that's why swimmin' comes first. Now I'm going. I hope that's okay, princess?" He began to turn away from me.

"He doesn't even *like* swimming," I said, lamely. I was angry— with myself as much as anything. I wasn't really in control of what was coming out of my mouth.

Your dad shook his head. "What?"

"He doesn't like it, but he does it, instead of music. Because of you."

You dad rolled his eyes. "We all have to do things we don't like. Boy has to learn that."

"He should be making music. You should see how happy he is when he plays."

He shrugged. "Ain't none of your business," he said. Then he got in the car and slammed the door.

I said,

"Wait—" but the revving of the engine drowned out my voice.

The car peeled away, black smoke billowing from the exhaust. I realized I was still holding the banjo/ukulele. Your dad had never taken it—he was so sure it wasn't yours. He was so sure you didn't like to play anymore. Maybe I shouldn't have told him you did, maybe I shouldn't have exposed you like that, I don't know. He just made me angry, and I know it sounds weird when I'm the one who broke you, but I wanted to protect you too. I wanted you to be happy.

I *still* want you to be happy.

INT. AN APARTMENT ABOVE A GARAGE. A
TEENAGE GIRL IS SITTING ON A BED THAT USED
TO BELONG TO HER . . .
HER WHAT, ACTUALLY?
BOYFRIEND?
FRIEND?
HER FRIEND. LET'S GO WITH FRIEND.
SO . . .
A TEENAGE GIRL IS SITTING ON A BED THAT
USED TO BELONG TO HER FRIEND. SHE LOOKS
LIKE SHE HAS BEEN CRYING. IT'S LATE; THE
MOON IS SHINING IN THROUGH THE WINDOW.
VERY FAINTLY, WE CAN HEAR THE OCEAN IN
THE DISTANCE.

THE GIRL:	You here?
A VOICE WE CANNOT SEE:	Always.
THE GIRL:	You have any suggestions for what to do now?
THE VOICE:	Yes.
THE GIRL:	Like?
THE VOICE:	The house. You haven't been to the house.
THE GIRL:	Which house?
THE VOICE:	Which house do you think?

The house Julie had driven to.

That house.

I had never been there.

I had only pictured it, in my mind, shown myself terrible movies. A hand raising a hammer. Paris's dad, waiting to ambush her. His hands around her neck. The bare walls, bare except for graffiti. Curse words on white plaster.

I had seen the outside, on Street View on your phone. The clapboards, the damp.

But something had kept me away. Some force field. Some uncrossable barrier of pain.

Well.

Maybe it was time to let the pain back in.

The next day Dad had to go back to work, even though what he really wanted to do was stand guard over me, make sure I stayed grounded. "House arrest" might be a more accurate term. But he couldn't keep it up. He couldn't avoid the restaurant anymore.

He *did* lock the door so I couldn't get out.

But I had pretty much always been able to climb out my bedroom window, down the apple tree in the front yard. I opened the window, grabbed a thin branch to steady myself, and jumped down onto the joint with a thicker branch, then shinned down to the ground.

There was a chill in the air. The sky was gray and dirty as a sidewalk, mist rising off the water. Over the ocean, I could see dark clouds. Fall was just around the corner, but it wasn't usually this cold in the morning. There was something coming. A storm.

I almost wanted it to come. To wash away the town, wipe it clean. Leave it sparkling, the streets empty, like a mind with no memories, all the dog walkers gone, the kids building sand castles, the joggers, the old people driving their mobility scooters.

All gone. The sidewalks shining.

I shook away the fantasy.

I knew where the house was of course—even if I hadn't remembered the address, it was in the notes I had photographed while Dwight was getting me candy.

I rode the bus—I needed to get the 9 and then the 7, to the north side of the boardwalk. I tried to switch off and just watch stuff go by. A T-Mobile ad. A L'Oréal billboard. An Arby's. A load of kids following an adult wearing a yellow vest; kids on some kind of trip. A couple of bums drinking from paper bags, outside a Blockbuster that had closed down years before, a big crack in its window.

The town was still busy, but it was winding down a bit. There were fewer people on the streets, fewer tourists. It's funny how we still call them tourists. I mean they're not on some grand tour, taking in the art and landscape of France and Italy. They're getting drunk in a crappy town in New Jersey, and throwing up on amusement park rides.

I watched men, in particular. I felt like the Houdini Killer could be any one of the guys passing on the main road: the businessmen in suits, the frazzled-looking guy in the Cure T-shirt, the IT geek with the non-ironic glasses.

The 9 stopped at the central bus station in town and I got off. The doors slid shut behind me with a hiss; a predator closing its mouth. The little square was busy with kids arriving on buses from New York City. A cold breeze was now blowing, and I saw people shivering in their T-shirts, underdressed for Jersey with a storm coming.

I just hoped it wasn't going to rain till the evening. I was not dressed for rain. I was not dressed for anything much. I have told you already that getting clothes right is a difficult thing for me.

I didn't even realize I was just around the corner from the plush warehouse until I saw your Ford F-150 turn the corner in front of me. It was unmistakable—white, with the Piers logo on the side, and of course your face, your beautiful face, behind the wheel.

You didn't see me; you kept on driving toward the warehouse.

On an impulse, I started running. I don't know why. I don't know what I thought I was going to achieve. It had something to do with talking to your dad, I think, that new insight I had into your life. I wished you'd told me about him. About . . . where you came from.

I don't know.

I just wanted you to know I was sorry.

About everything.

And that you . . . I guess I wanted you to know that you could be whoever you wanted to be. I know, I know. The arrogance of it. Like I was a counselor or something.

Which brings me full circle back to the sorry thing.

Anyway.

I veered around the corner, nearly knocked over an old woman pushing a Wonder Wheeler beach cart. I jumped some cardboard boxes that had been left out behind a Chinese restaurant, pounded down the street in my Converses, feeling the hardness of the concrete below my feet.

You were just pulling up outside the warehouse doors when I came running up, panting. You saw me, frowned, and put the pickup back in gear. You looked down as you started turning the Ford, to leave again. The afternoon sun caught the windows of the office block across the street, fired them like lava flow.

Suddenly I couldn't let you go, not without speaking to you one more time anyway.

I sprinted around to the front of the truck, banged my hands down on the hood as the big Ford began to lurch forward. I saw your lips mouth a curse, and the pickup juddered to a stop. You opened the door.

"Cass, get out of the way," you said.

"No. I just want to—"

"I don't care."

You started to close the door again, and I started to cry. My eyes were burning; I felt like I was choking. I felt like the anger on your face was the worst thing I had seen.

"Please," I said. "Please. Just one minute."

The scene in front of me blurred with tears—the truck, the

street, the windows of apartments, the blocks of the air-conditioning units. I heard rather than saw your door open again, and then you were standing in front of me.

"What, Cass? What do you want?"

"I just want to tell you that I'm sorry."

You spread your hands, like, whatever. "Fine. Can I go now?"

"I saw your dad," I said.

Silence.

"He said you were training for the National team," I said.

A shrug. "Just tryouts."

"Still. You never told me that."

"There's a lot you don't know about me, Cass."

I could hear the bitterness in your voice. I really didn't know what I thought I was doing, what it was going to change.

"But I wanted to say . . . ," I said. "I wanted to say . . . you don't have to do what he wants you to do. I mean, you don't have to live his dream. You could be a musician. You don't even like sw—"

"What are you talking about?"

"Music! Your passion! I tried to give your dad your banjo or whatever it was and he wouldn't even—"

"My banjo? I don't have a banjo."

"Ukelele, then."

"I don't have a ukulele either."

"But . . . ," I said. "It was on top of the wardrobe."

"Cass, I don't have a uke or a banjo, and I didn't leave anything on the wardrobe. Just my necklace." You touched your chest. "Which . . . um . . . thank you for finding."

"Oh," I said. An image came to me as a sudden flash—the hipster kid who had stayed in the apartment last summer. The one with the beard and the super-tight jeans. He was just the kind of guy who would have played a ukulele. Or a banjo. "But the swimming, you don't have to—"

You shook your head sadly. "Cass, you don't understand *anything*. You think my dad *made* me stop playing music? I'm my own ******* person, Cass. I can make my own decisions. I *chose* to stop playing, at home anyway. Because I could see how much it hurt him. Don't you see? I *chose*."

"Oh," I said again. I sounded so dumb. "But you could go to music school, you don't have to take the swimming scholarship, you could—"

You laughed, a hollow, bitter laugh that reminded me unpleasantly of my dad. "Colleges give sports scholarships," you said. "That's just the way it is. People watch *American Idol*, and they think there's money in music, but they're not even being *logical*. I mean, most of the contestants *don't win*. That's the whole thing. No one makes money from music. Hardly anyone anyway. I wanted to go to college. My dad couldn't pay. So I took a swim scholarship."

"But you're so talented."

Another laugh. "I passed a dude busking on the street yesterday, playing sax. He was, like, one of the best players I've ever heard. And he was *busking*, Cass. People don't want to pay for music. But people will pay for sports." You shrugged.

I looked down at my dirty Converses. I felt like such an idiot. I had shouted at your dad and for what? For no reason at all.

"Anyway, what about you?" you said.

"What?"

"You, lecturing me about doing what my *dad* wants. What about you?"

"I don't . . ."

"You think I'm stupid? Your dad busts us and you disappear for *three whole days*, and then suddenly you're with some guy on the street? And you want me to believe you didn't see me before you kissed him? I saw you notice me. My truck. I don't even know what you're doing. But you're ****** with my mind, whatever it is. And you're not even doing it for your own reasons—me, I have a feeling you're doing it because of your dad, because of whatever messed-up thing is going on between the two of you. It's not even *you* pushing me away. It's him. I think that's the hardest thing to forgive." You climbed into the truck. "I hope for your sake you sort your **** out."

It wasn't him, not really. It was me. You know that now.

"I'm so sorry," I said. "I'm so sorry." I was crying again; I felt like there was a heat behind my eyes that I had to get out.

You were half in the truck, one leg inside it, the other out. Something about your stance softened then. "Listen, Cass. If you didn't do anything with that guy, not really . . . You could tell me. If your dad is . . . I don't know. If he's hurting you, or threatening you or something . . . I could help you. We could face it *together*. But you have to be honest with me."

I was wrong.

That was the moment when my heart broke.

"My dad isn't threatening me," I said. Which was true. Kind of. "He has never hurt me. Not once."

"Then what?" you said. "What are you afraid of?"

"I'm not afraid of you. I just cheated on you."

"I don't believe you."

I shrugged. "I've known him longer than you. Sometimes we hook up. It doesn't mean anything. It's just sex."

I used the word deliberately. I wanted its hardness.

You stared at me, like I was someone you didn't know anymore. The sun caught on the hood of the Ford and flashed white, blinding

483

me for a second. I couldn't see your face. I couldn't see you at all. It was like the light was washing you out of existence, washing you out of my life.

"Also," I said, every word feeling like a heavy stone that I was having to lift out of my mouth, with my tongue, so heavy, so hard to say. "Also he kisses better than you. Is that good enough for you?"

I turned around and walked away. I didn't look back. A moment later I heard the engine of the truck start again. And you drove out of my life.

Please come back?

I mean, I *want* you back.

I was stupid. I know that now.

But I didn't do the thing they said I did.

I swear.

I changed to the 7 bus.

I mean, what else was I going to do?

I rode for fifteen minutes. Something like that. Finally I got off, which was a relief because there was a creepy mustachioed guy in a shiny plastic jacket who was checking me out the whole time, thinking he was being subtle. I was like four blocks away. I walked and turned, following the little map I had drawn, after looking up the place on Google Maps on Dad's computer in his study.

The same computer I'm sitting at right now. With the insects around me. Appropriate, I guess. Being surrounded by lowly little insects.

Am I overdoing it with the self-flagellation? I think maybe yes. I'll stop now. I mean, either you're going to forgive me or not.

It was weird, walking the north side of town. The buildings got dirtier, and more run-down, as you walked. Once past the piers, the poverty and dilapidation set in and everything seemed to slump. Like a time-lapse movie of the aftertimes—once nuclear war has come or a virus or whatever—the whole town slowly rotting, falling into the sand and the marsh, once all the people are dead and no longer caring for it.

That was the kind of very cheerful thought I was having.

Anyway.

For a while, I walked on the beach, listening to the gulls, breathing in the ocean air. Then I turned up, past the tufted dunes, to the streets. This was Bayview, the part where Paris had gone missing. I was walking the street closest to the beach; there were swirls of sand on the cracked concrete, abstract shapes, as if the wind was trying to write something, to pass on some message that no one could understand.

I kept walking. I was on the block now, maybe a hundred yards from the house—I glanced at my hand-drawn map again. Yes. Nearly there.

And . . .

And just then a black Jeep came driving toward me, down the perpendicular street to the one I was on, slowing as it reached the junction with the beach road.

A Jeep SRT8. Like the one Julie had seen turning in front of her.

I shrank back, spinning the other way, as if I had just been curious about which way this street went, and now I was returning to the beach—north, away from town. I walked quickly, until I was a little sheltered behind a row of crappy cars, Civics and Daewoos mostly, and some rusted old American sedans—Chevys and Fords. The crappy cars of Bayview. Rusted by the ocean. Local cars.

The SRT8 was not rusted, that was clear. Even from the brief glimpse I had gotten, I had seen that it was shiny. Gleaming like something built for evil. Some black tank from some private army.

I leaned against a car and took out my phone as if it had just rung; I don't really know what I thought I was doing. Trying to act inconspicuous, I guess, since my pulse was an engine, two stroke, rattling in my veins. I held the phone to my ear and kind of half turned around, and that was when I saw the car turn, leaving the stop sign where it had been pulled up. Onto the beach road. The road where Paris had gone missing.

KRS1-GH7 said the license plate.

I felt the breath catch in my throat.

Why?

What did that mean to me?

"The song," said the voice. "The song that Julie had stuck in her head."

"What?"

"The *song*," said the voice.

"What song? When?"

"When you went to the apartment the day after . . . you know. When Julie was telling Horowitz what happened."

I thought back to the conversation with Julie. What was the song she'd had in her head? An earworm—that was what people called it, wasn't it? It had been triggered by seeing Brian's cop car turning up . . .

That was it. "Woop, woop, it's the sound of da police . . . woop, woop, it's the sound of da police . . ."

It was a stupidly catchy song. And now it was going around in my head, again and again. Impossible to make it stop, once you thought of it. I was only half-aware of it though; it was playing in the background of my thoughts.

Oh, I thought.

Oh, ****.

I should have gotten it quicker. I mean, old-school hip-hop was my thing. Before the voice anyway, it was my thing. Because of Travis and the other kids who used to hang out at the restaurant.

"KRS1," I said, to the voice. "That's what Julie saw. That license plate. That's what put the song in her head."

"Yes," said the voice.

Julie had been pissed with herself; guilty about the earworm, I remembered. She thought it was bad that when Paris was being . . . whatever happened to her . . . that she had this old rap song going around in her mind. "Woop, woop, it's the sound of da police." She had thought it was random, had been angry with her own distracted mind, the disrespect of it.

But it hadn't been random. When I asked her about the license plate, what was it she said? That there was something "on the tip of her tongue." Something bothering her. But she didn't know what it was. Except that her subconscious knew. Her subconscious knew what she had seen, what the link was.

KRS-One, the rapper from the nineties. Whose biggest hit was a song called . . . yes . . . "The Sound of da Police."

****, it was so clear now. Julie had seen the Jeep driving away, and on some level, she had registered the license plate.

KRS1-GH7.

And seeing that—that coincidental conjunction of numbers and letters—followed by the sound of an *actual* police siren, had got KRS-One's most famous song playing on her mental stereo.

Holy ****. This was the car Julie had seen. This was the actual car.

Without any moment in between, any transition, at least that I was aware of, I was running, following the car.

"It's turning," said the voice.

"I see that," I said.

Sure enough, the black car was pulling into the driveway of a house just in front of me. My scribbled map was in my inner eye, like a pilot's heads-up display, superimposed on the real street, and I realized that this house, this place where the black Jeep was parking, was maybe two or three houses south of the one Paris had gone into.

And so already I was thinking . . . I was thinking, *It's just a neighbor . . .*

But it was like that thought was a thorn I wanted to pull out, something I wanted gone; I still moved, I was still running, the main control for my mind had been wrested from me, the copilot had taken over, and wanted to see who was in that Jeep.

I mean, I'd told Dwight about the SRT8. And he would have passed on the information, and the police would be looking into it. Horowitz probably, and his team. But they were looking in the wrong place, weren't they? Checking out the demolition company, probably running the backgrounds of every employee, when they weren't investigating Paris's dad.

"It's just a neighbor," said the voice. "Julie saw the car turn because they were leaving the house. That's all."

"Shut up," I said.

I got to the driveway as a woman got out of the driver's seat of the car.

"A woman," said the voice.

"I can see that," I said. I stopped, out of breath. I wasn't used to exercise.

The woman was staring at me. I'm not good at judging the age of adults. I guess she was in her thirties? No makeup, hair pulled back. Tight yoga leggings and a zipped-up body warmer. I assumed she had been at the gym. She looked hard. Wiry. Like she spent too much time there.

"You think this is the killer?" said the voice. "Really?"

I scanned from her to the car. There was no one else in it.

"Uh . . . can I help you?" she said. Blond eyebrows tight together. Concerned.

"I . . ."

"Yes?"

I breathed deep. I suddenly felt like this was a big mistake. A feeling that was familiar to me.

"Is your husband home?" I said. I had seen the ring on her finger.

"No, I'm afraid not. Do you . . . I mean . . . what do you want him for?" Worry in her voice now. *Is this girl having an affair with my husband?* I bet that's what she was thinking.

Come on, Cassie, come on.

"I, uh, my dad owns Donato's. The pizza place? Your husband left his business card in our prize drawing? Raffle, you know? It's a big prize. A vacation to Italy. I . . . My dad sent me to tell him."

"Oh." Still suspicious. But curious too. "Italy, huh?"

"Yeah. It's a vacation for two."

"Well, he's working in Dubai. He's in construction project management."

I nodded. "We called his phone. I figure that's why it wouldn't go through."

The woman examined me. "You're shivering."

I glanced down. There were goose bumps on my bare arms.

"You should get inside," said the woman. "Storm's coming." She wasn't inviting me into her house. That much was obvious. It was clapboard, but from what I'd seen on Street View, better maintained than the one Paris had gone into. Clean paintwork, no peeling—a new mailbox bolted to a post. Little round trees by the door.

I looked up. The sky was a bruise now, thin sickly bars of light showing through clouds that were almost black. Pressing down. The air was frigid on my skin. How had I not noticed? I'd been running, I guessed. But also I was in my head, thinking of Paris. Always thinking of Paris.

And how all hope was gone now.

Almost all hope.

"How long has he been in Dubai?" I said. "I mean, I'm trying to figure when he put his card in the jar."

"Four months," said the woman.

Nope.

That was it.

All hope gone.

"He wasn't here when Paris . . . disappeared," said the voice.

"I know that, genius," I said.

"What?" said the woman.

"Nothing," I said. "Sorry. I'm sorry I came. I'll go now." I started to walk away, down the street, toward the house, the one where . . . the one where . . . I could feel it pulling me, could feel its painful gravity.

"What about the vacation?" she said to my departing back.

"Can only give it to him," I said. "Call us when he gets back."

I kept walking.

"Wait," said the woman. "Wait. His business card would have his work address. How did you find us?"

I ignored her. I ignored her and kept walking. I heard her go into the house. Maybe she was going to call the cops. Maybe she didn't believe my story.

I didn't care.

The license plate was a dead end, and that just left the Houdini Killer and Paris's dad and there was nothing a seventeen-year-old girl from Jersey could do about either of those.

I didn't care about anything anymore.

We're coming to the part when I died, now.

I know, spoiler alert.

But I'm writing this, aren't I?

So maybe that's spoiler number two.

The woman was gone now, forgotten.

The wind was up, whipping from the ocean, leaving a thin layer of freezing water on my skin, but it was okay, I deserved it.

I took maybe ten more steps, and I was right outside the house. Wooden numbers, one of them with screws missing and tilted on its side, were screwed to the wall.

3151.

The number I had written down.

3151 Seafront Drive.

I would like to say the house loomed or crouched there, or something that might make it seem evil. But it was just a one-story clapboard house, on a seen-better-days street near the ocean. But where the neighbors had gentrified, here the neglect was obvious. Everything was dirty or worn or peeling or all three. The front yard was overgrown with weeds. There was a little driveway, and the house had windows and a door and all the stuff you would expect. There was a satellite dish on the roof.

Even now, there was a police tape across the door. But I could see that it was standing open. "Ajar"—the word popped into my head. There was a discordant ringing in my head too, a sickly resonance. Spray painted on the front of the house were the words SICK ****.

Kids, I realized. Kids had tagged the place, and broken in. Probably they went in there at night, with a Ouija board. Got stoned, drank 40s. I don't know. Dared one another, maybe. It was the kind of thing kids did.

I stood there, looking at the open door. I took a step forward, and stopped.

See, I had imagined her death so many times. I had played scenes in my head, little snippets of film, of video. I had run it through, over and over, different permutations, different scenarios.

A hammer a knife a rope a gun a bat a chain a—

But in my imagination, the house was always vague, always diaphanous, a construct of clouds and smoke. And the actors on that stage, Paris and her dad, were not much more solid, their mass leached by the blurred background, the whole thing barely coalescing in my mind, before dissolving into nothing.

It was never very *real*, even though I tortured myself with it.

And if I went in there?

If I went in there, I wouldn't find any clues. I was starting to realize that now. I was not Sherlock Holmes, as Dad had said. I wasn't going to uncover some link to the killer that the crime-scene technicians had somehow missed; I mean, real life just doesn't work like that.

I'd known one thing, had worked out one thing, which was that a car turned in front of Julie and so must have come from a drive on the street, and it turned out that, yes, it had, it had come from the neighbors, where an uptight gym-bunny wife whose husband was in Dubai had been driving out to the store or the yoga class or whatever.

It was *nothing*.

And if I went into that house, I would find nothing.

I would just know where she died; I would have a stage for my worst imaginings, a stage with depth and width and heft and presence. A stage that would make the scenes on it more real.

I remember being asked if I wanted to see my mom when she was dead. In the funeral home, I mean. And I said yes, because I thought that was what I was supposed to say; I thought I was supposed to say good-bye; I thought my dad would be hurt if I didn't.

But she was a waxwork doll; she was empty; she was nothing

but skin and makeup that she wouldn't have chosen herself; and I wish, wish, wish that I had never seen her like that. I wish I had said no.

Standing outside the house where Paris died, I took a deep breath.

Then I turned, and walked away.

I wasn't going to go in there.

It was as I neared the next house on the street that I saw it.

A narrow gap ran down the side of the house. There was a rusting old bike propped there, between the wall of the house and a wooden fence; a couple of trash cans, one fallen over.

And beyond, in the gray pre-storm light, a sliver of a pier, just a narrow one it seemed like, visible through the thin opening. A rickety old thing, collapsing at the end into the ocean, green with seaweed.

I didn't think; I just turned and headed down, past the side of the house, and then I was on a path that ran the length of the backyard. Similar paths came from the other houses and it seemed like at some point the pier must have served the row, a shared resource, for people to moor their boats.

Now, it teetered into the ocean drunkenly, on sea-slimed pillars, many of its boards broken like smashed teeth. I gazed at it. The water was high; coming up almost to the backyard. Above and around me and out over the ocean, merging with it, indistinguishable from it at the horizon, the sky was a boiling mass of darkness now, tinged with white. To the south, I could see rain slanting down on the water, turning it from smooth glassy expanses and waves to a lo-res pattern of gray dots—blurred; pixelated.

And there was the old pier, jutting out into the water like a gesture, like an invitation.

Paris died here.

It wasn't the voice. It was a conviction, deep inside me. I could see her, being dragged down the backyard from the house, then along the pier, screaming maybe, or maybe unconscious. Feet trailing. Hands under her arms. Pulled like a slack puppet down the length of the wooden jetty, *bump, bump, bump,* her feet over the joints, to the end. Weighed down with rocks. With chains. I don't know.

And pushed into the ocean.

My body was moving now with no control, no input from me, and I was out over the churning water before I really did any thinking at all, over the chop and swell of it, the inky darkness.

The planks were slippery. I walked carefully, gingerly, finding what purchase I could among the seaweed, slicked by the water, which was rising up in a spray all around me, a rain that came from below.

And then the rain came from above.

Just like that:

No warning, no *boom* of thunder, just one moment no rain and the next the skies opened like the jaws of those grabbers you see in movies at garbage heaps, dumping the contents of all those roiling clouds on the ocean, on the pier, on me.

It was almost full dark, the sun gone; you would barely know it was day.

Instantly I was soaked to the skin. The rain was colossal, unbelievable, not single discrete points falling through the air but simply a wall of water, everywhere. Then there did come a flash, shocking white light, illuminating the world—I saw the pier in X-ray relief, the house to my right, a skeleton structure, pale in the darkness; even the grass behind me and the grains of the wood under my feet, the eyes, the whorls, all flooded with light, monochrome.

And—

Black again.

One,

Two,

Three,

Four—

Boom.

The thunder didn't roll over me, like people say, it detonated around me, seeming to come from just outside my ears, punching me, shivering my foot on the slippery pier, making me lunge forward to keep my balance, shaking now with cold too, the water plastering the clothes to my skin.

"Well, this was a smart move," said the voice.

I ignored it. I kept on moving, slowly, treading oh so carefully, the soles of my Converses sliding on the treacherous surface. The ocean boiled beneath me, frothing, leaping, as if excited to finally let go of everything it was pretending to be. As if letting out the predator within.

One plank.

Two planks.

Three planks.

I did it like that, three at a time, counting again and again.

FLASH.

The whole world lit up, full black and white, contrast whacked up to maximum, and then went black again, and three seconds later, the explosion of thunder shook my eardrums again.

I kept going.

One plank.

Two planks.

Three and then I was there. Waves were crashing into the woodwork below me now.

I was at the end of the pier, or at least the end of the walkable pier, because the rest was in the ocean, bare struts, the walkway that was held up by them long since fallen into the water and washed away.

I looked down into the shifting murk. Water was still falling from the sky, baptismal, epic in its scale, the day pretty much

midnight black now, lightning occasionally floodlighting everything, this whole stage for . . . what?

What was I doing here?

"A very good question," said the voice.

And then I saw it.

I looked down, and there in the water was a white shape, and I
leaned closer. My toes were over the edge of the wooden structure,
and for a second I thought of Paris standing at the edge of the
pier, just before your truck arrived below, and how she thought
we were playing Dare, how she thought the game was to get close to
the edge, to play with death, and I'm seeing Paris in my mind's eye,
losing her balance, nearly falling and then—

FLASH.

I was seeing Paris below me. Her face, looking up at me through
the water, it was her body down there, floating, I knew it; her
hair was billowing around her face, haloing it, her beautiful
black hair framing her skin, the paleness of it, spreading around
her, and her eyes were looking up at me but seeing nothing.

Boom.

I was so startled—though not afraid, never afraid of Paris—that
I took a step back, and the plank cracked beneath my foot, and then
the whole thing must have been rotten because the next one along
broke too, and then there was a creaking that I heard even over the
thunder that was just echoing out of the sky, fading, and the pier fell
away beneath me, and I was weightless, just for a moment.

Then

    I

        fell.

And as I fell, I twisted, or something, I had no sense of the
orientation of my own body or what had collapsed, whether it was

just part of the pier or all of it, or even if I was facing down or up, and anyway the important thing is my head smashed against some object, hard, I mean smashed hard and the thing was hard too, and stars burst out of the storm-curtained sky, where there was nothing but rain clouds, and I blacked out.

And then I was in the freezing water, plunging under, feeling it enveloping my body and head, my eyes half-open so the world was suddenly darkness and bubbles.

I tried to swim up to the surface, but I was too weak, and my head was nothing but agony now, a sensation in place of an object, a sensation of gripping, vice-like pain.

My eyes were still open though, so I could see up through the thin layer of water that was going to drown me—it doesn't take much water to drown you—and I could see that the clouds had tattered, just for a second, the wind whipping open a vortex in the sky, exposing for a moment the glow of the half moon and the icy sparkle of the stars.

I looked around me. Half the pier was gone, and I was in deep water. I turned toward the beach. But it wasn't a beach.

Why didn't I check when I started?

Behind me, the ocean smashed into a tumble of rocks, which lay between me and the yards of the houses, a barrier of rubble.

I dived down, looking for Paris, eyes open and searching through the murk, but I couldn't see her, and I couldn't hold my breath either, and I had to push myself back up to the surface.

How was I going to climb out over those rocks?

I had no idea. But I had to try.

I kicked toward them and my head ripped open and light flooded in, or lightning flashed, or both, I don't know, and for a second I may have blacked out again; my mouth and nose were underwater, breathing in water, then I lifted myself up, coughing, spluttering. My arms were lead; my legs were marble.

I felt stickiness, a sting, on my forehead, and I raised my hand and touched it to my head—big mistake, I went under, a wave hitting me, and for a moment was in the blackness again before I desperately trod water, got my head above water.

And big mistake too, because I realized I was wounded. Whatever had struck my head, whatever I had struck my head on, had hurt me badly.

I managed a couple more strokes, but I saw straightaway, even from this distance, the steepness, the angle and smoothness of the rocks between me and the shore; there was no way I was climbing them.

"Swim south," said the voice. "To the main beach."

Four blocks, I thought. I couldn't even talk out loud, I was so cold, and my head was a bass drum going *bang, bang, bang*; what an irony, when your voice can speak and you can't. *I can't make four blocks.*

"The rocks might end before that," said the voice.

Can't do it, I thought.

And then, cold as the ocean surrounding me, I realized something.

I was going to die.

I was going to die right here.

It had always been waiting for me, this time this place, and now it was here.

I tried, Paris, I thought.

I was so very cold. My whole body was shaking.

For a moment I thought about your swim training, about how you had been trying out for Nationals, and I imagined you surging strongly through the water toward me, knifing through it, swimming the crawl, to take me under the arms and hold me up. Or my dad, I mean he was a Navy SEAL, maybe he would be there suddenly in the water, maybe he had followed me in some way and he would—

But this is not that kind of story, and this is not a movie, and you weren't there.

My dad wasn't there.

"It's okay," said a voice in my ear, a quiet voice, thrumming muted through viscous water.

But not *the* voice.

No.

Paris's voice.

"It's okay," said Paris again. "It's okay; you did try—you did."

I looked for her, treading water, turning to see her in the pale light, but I couldn't. Even now there was a cold, rational part of me that thought she had never been there, that I had imagined her face in the water, the hair framing it.

"You did try. You did."

At first it sounded like an echo, Paris's voice repeating itself, but then I heard it, a soft burr, a hitch, in the throat of the speaker, a sound I knew so well. It was a different voice.

Mom?

"Yes, honey, I'm here. Oh honey, I'm so sorry."

For what?

"Dying. Leaving you."

Not your fault. Those men. Just wish . . . just wish we could find them . . . wish we could make them pay.

"Oh baby. Don't you know? Don't you know by now? Haven't you learned anything?"

Her voice getting quieter; departing. Leaving me.

What? What? What should I have learned?

"It's not for us to find people. Or to make them pay. You take revenge, all you do is throw away your soul. Sometimes things happen that you can't control. Sometimes we lose things we can't get back. And there are some things we just can't ever know."

But—

A whisper now, nothing more:

"I'm sorry, Cass."

Then gone.

Nothing but cold, blank water, all around me, and I saw that I had sunk under it, had gone below the surface, and I hadn't even registered. The water was dark around me; I wasn't even sure which way was up.

Then the clouds parted, and I realized I was looking right at the surface, was seeing the storm-lit sky through maybe a foot of seawater. There was a break in the darkness, and the stars were shining through, thousands of them, millions.

I fixed on the stars.

Eternity, and a couple of minutes, passed.

Pressure tightened around my head; my chest was burning. And I kept on looking up through the water, as slowly, slowly, the stars began to go out, one by one. And then my heart did what it had been practicing for in the moment between every one of its millions of beats and, at last, stopped.

I died.

I mean, I guess I can't prove that I did. But I *know*.

My heart was still. There had been pain in my chest, but now it was gone, suddenly.

Everything was pitch-black, and I had the sense that I was unraveling, a mummy with its bandages spiraling off it, crumbling into darkness and dust, disintegrating.

The blackness opened its vast mouth and—

"Excuse me, but are you *fucking* kidding me?" said the voice, from the darkness. I opened my eyes. The sky was dim light, above, through murky water.

What? I thought, and I was kind of reeling in shock, I've tried to echo it by putting in the swearword when normally I star it out, to try to give you an idea of how that voice poked sharply through the darkness, how loud and intense it was, but I don't know, it's not something I can really convey.

"Is that all you've got?" said the voice. "Are you ******* serious? You're just going to give up and DIE? You ******* coward. You weak ******* *****. Enough of this ****, Cass. Go. There's a rope right next to you, can't you feel it touching your shoulder? It's a tether rope, hanging from the pier. Grab it and haul your *** out of this water. Right now."

Leave me alone, I thought.

I closed my eyes again.

For just a fraction of an instant, I thought about giving up, giving in, to the black. Forgetting. Forgetting Paris being gone and Mom and all of it. But then the voice said this:

"After all your weak-*** whining, THIS is how you're going to let it end? You've got this. You're in control now. You can still make things right. Haul your *** out of this water and go and get him, and tell him you're sorry. Are you really going to let him go?"

Confused, I thought of you.

Let him go? I wasn't meaning to—

"Come on," said the voice. "Get up there. Breathe. Get him back."

He won't want me back, I thought.

"Well, if you die, he won't have much choice," said the voice.

Huh.

"For him," the voice continued, "it'll be like you when your mom died. When Paris disappeared. You'll be gone, and there'll be nothing he can do about it. But if you fight . . ."

If I fight, I thought, *then I can at least give him the choice.*

But the sky was so far above, and I was so tired.

"Look," said the voice, almost reluctantly. "It's not your fault, what happened to your mom. Or Paris. How were you supposed to save them? But if you breathe in this water and die right here, then what happens to him, how he feels about it, will be absolutely, entirely your fault. One hundred percent."

It was that 100 percent that got me, just like the voice knew it would. Your words, in the apartment.

I thought about how you'd always been there for me, always tried to help me, even when I hurt you. At least, I figured, I ought to try to be there for you too.

Oh screw it, I thought.

I could feel rope, rough against the skin of my arm. I twisted in the water and there it was, simultaneously friction-heavy and slimy, and I turned my head up and saw it rising into light. I seized it with my hands, my fingers wrapping around the rope almost without my asking them to.

They closed around its clammy surface; it was as taut as a cable, almost resonating with the pull of the pier above and some weight below—a boat, long-since sunk?

Whatever: it was a rope hanging from the pier and I was going to climb up it.

I was going to live. And I was going to ask you to forgive me.

I wasn't going to be competing in Nationals. I wasn't a Navy SEAL, but my dad taught me to swim when I was three years old, and I could do our house to the end of the boardwalk when I was seven, and I was *not* going to die in the ocean.

Slowly, hand over hand, I pulled myself up and out of the water—my head broke free and I took a long, rasping, hitching breath. It was half-ocean, that breath, and I coughed as the acrid cold water hit my throat, but there was air too, and it filled my lungs. I felt instantly less like I was going to burst, less like a balloon on the verge of popping.

Greedily, I gulped down air, felt it filling my lungs, wheezing. I had never been so hyperaware of my chest, my diaphragm and bronchioles, the simple mechanics of being alive. The stuff I took for granted.

For a long time, I just breathed in and out, relishing it, enjoying it. I couldn't tell what was rain falling on me and what was sea spray, whipped by the wind from the waves. It was still dark, and then FLASH, everything was lit.

I glanced all around, getting my bearings in the light of the lightning.

Good news: whatever happened when I fell, whether a few planks had broken or the end of the pier had collapsed or what, there was still some of the structure remaining, a dark frame against the darker sky, rising up like a promise.

Bad news:

It was high.

For a moment, I just clung to the rope, in the cold, cold ocean, gazing at the far-off safety of the pier, mind spinning.

Gym ropes was the absurd phrase that kept repeating in my head, like a prayer, like something to hold on to.

Gym ropes.

I was looking up at the impossible five feet between the surface of the water and the top of the pier, the rope glistening, leading up to the wooden bollard it was tied to above, and I was thinking about gym ropes and how in gym class I had never been able to climb them.

"But in gym class you weren't in danger of drowning," said the voice. "You've got this. It's going to hurt, but you've got this."

I sighed. Fine.

I reached up my other hand and grabbed the rope a little higher up—then I pulled my body out of the cold water. My arms burned; my fingers were numb from the cold.

Other arm.

Other arm.

My muscles *screamed* at me. Maybe I was screaming too, out loud, I don't know. But the air was beginning to warm my skin, I was starting to feel less like I might shiver out my teeth.

"Not far now," said the voice. "Not ****** far now."

510

Dear Manager,

I am writing to you because I am interested in the position of teller at your South Side branch. I am a good team player with

Sorry, Dad came in.

So.

Where was I?

Oh yes, I was climbing the rope.

My legs were out of the water; I could feel the moist air on my skin; my clothes were plastered to my body. I wrapped my feet around the rope, chafing my ankles—one of my Converses had come off and was sinking to the bottom of the Atlantic, where I would have been if not for the voice.

"Two feet now," said the voice. And it was true; the pier, what was left of it, was just above. "Come on, you ******."

But I couldn't. My arms wouldn't work. It was like something had been cut between my head and the muscles. Snipped.

"********, come on," said the voice. "You can ****** do it. You can do it. You can do it. You can do it."

"I can't."

"Yes, you can. You can do anything. We can do anything. Come on."

"Okay," I said. I was just pain, all over. My head, my arms, my throat where the cold water had burned it.

And then suddenly there was more strength flowing into my arms; that's what it felt like, hot liquid flowing; lava.

"We're ****** doing this," said the voice. "We're not ****** dying in the ******* ocean."

One arm went up; the fingers were gone, I mean I didn't feel them anymore, but somehow they gripped onto the rope and . . . and then slid . . . but then they caught, found purchase, and again that's what it felt like—

—like I had to *buy* every inch, pay dearly for it. But I was moving again, moving up the rope, even if I felt something tear in my shoulder, and in my forearm. Something detaching from the bone, a tendon maybe, I didn't know.

Then.

Then a miracle. I was by the side of the pier, hooking my knee over it, and then I fell, hard, and sprawled on the wooden top.

Tears filled my eyes, blinding me, as if the water was still trying to get me, as if the ocean had gotten in behind my eyes, as if it didn't want to let me go.

Let me go, I thought.

"No, I'm staying with you," said the voice.

"Not you," I said.

"Oh," said the voice. "Well, then move. You keep still, you're going to die of hypothermia."

"Okay."

I could see the knots in the wood of the pier below me. I pushed myself up onto my hands and knees. Rain no longer seemed to be falling, and the sky was lightening, a fast wind somewhere far above scouring the clouds, scrubbing them away, so that it almost seemed like the daytime that it really was.

Ridiculously, I began to crawl. I didn't have the strength to stand. I crawled along, and splinters from the wood cut into my hands, and I was glad because it meant I was alive; we can only be hurt when our hearts are beating.

I don't know how long I crawled along the pier for. A ray of sunshine illuminated my hands. I was shivering so hard my teeth were rattling. I didn't realize that was a thing; I thought it was made up, for stories.

Then I heard footsteps, and a black boot stopped in front of me.

I looked up. A policeman stood there in his uniform, looking down at me with a worry that didn't seem totally about my safety, the concern you see in the eyes of someone who thinks you might be crazy. He had a mustache, but a trendy hipster one, not an old-guy one. He was maybe thirty.

"You fall in, ma'am?" he said.

"Yes," I said. My voice came out tattered, like there were knives in my throat that had cut it into ribbons. "I thought I saw Paris in there, and I leaned down . . . to . . . look. And I fell in, and she wasn't there."

A pause.

"Right, ma'am. Come on. Let's see if we can help you up. Aaron, you got the blankets?"

He pulled me to my feet.

"You're lucky. Neighbor called. Said there was a girl—"

But after that I don't remember anything.

After that, it's not even black. It's just nothingness.

Until . . .

INT. A HOSPITAL. DAY. A TEENAGE GIRL IS
LYING ON A BED. THERE ARE FLOWERS ON
A NIGHTSTAND NEXT TO HER. HER FATHER
IS STANDING BY THE BED, HOLDING HER
HAND, HE HAS BEEN HOLDING IT FOR HALF
AN HOUR; HE DOESN'T WANT TO LET
IT GO.
THE GIRL BEGINS TO CRY. SHE CRIES LIKE IT'S
NOT OKAY. BUT IT IS; IT'S JUST SAD. THAT'S THE
THING ABOUT LIFE. SOMETIMES IT'S SAD, AND
YOU DON'T GET TO KNOW STUFF, BUT YOU JUST
HAVE TO ACCEPT IT.

AND CLING TO THE PEOPLE WHO ARE LEFT.

MINUTES PASS.

HER FATHER: I'm proud of you, Cass.
THE GIRL: Thanks, Dad.

He steps away. He brushes at his eyes.

THE GIRL: Don't.
HER FATHER : Don't what?
THE GIRL: Don't take your hand away. I like it when
               you stroke my hair the way you used to.
               When I was little.

He doesn't. He doesn't take his hand away. He doesn't take
his hand away for the longest time.

"You're sure about this?" I said.

"I'm sure," said Julie. She was pale, had a hand on my arm, but she was wearing a faint smile.

The Ferris wheel clunked to a stop, swung back and forth for a moment, a pendulum in the night air. The breeze that drifted past us was full of seawater, fizzing with it—the sky around us so dense you could have held it in your hands. Strings of light snaked out from the blaze of brightness below us, a glittering, phosphorescent bacterial culture, shimmering with neon, every color that forms the light we see, blinding.

Julie looked down. Breeze ruffled her hair, and the sun glinted on the metal bars of the seats. "Remember Paris saying she wanted to wrap her arms around the little people down there?" she said.

"Yeah," I said.

"To protect them."

I nodded.

There were words in the air between us, the ocean air, that did not need to be spoken: *we couldn't protect her.*

We didn't *know* she was dead. I mean, we knew. But we didn't know for sure. We still talked to Agent Horowitz, me more than Julie, I'll admit. I tried not to call him too often, knew that it annoyed him, but it seemed like he had resigned himself to it, like he understood that I was never going to stop.

Progress was slow. They had Paris's father's license plate; they could prove that his car, at least, traveled from New York down to Oakwood the day before Paris disappeared. But he was saying he'd lent the car out to a friend, and at the moment it was stalemate. There was still no actual physical evidence. It might even have been the Houdini Killer. Hell, Paris's dad might have been the Houdini Killer, though it seemed unlikely, what with him living in New York, and as far as I could tell from Agent Horowitz, who was understandably reluctant to share too much, they hadn't caught his plate on other occasions.

So.

Run away? I was pretty sure not.

Father killed her? Probably.

Houdini Killer? Maybe.

Dead?

Definitely.

And would I ever have closure, would I ever know for certain, would anyone ever pay for it?

Most likely not.

But Julie and I could still do this. Could still finish something, at least.

Julie took a deep breath. "We can't protect any of those people." They moved, below us, so many of them, bacteria under a microscope. "We can't protect anyone."

"No," I said. "But that's okay. It's okay."

Julie looked at me, surprised.

"We can't keep anyone safe," I said. "So we just have to cling onto people when we can."

A moment of silence.

Then Julie smiled.

And took my hand.

"You got the bags?" I said.

"Yep."

Julie lifted the bags; they were just plastic shopping bags from a 7-Eleven. She held the first out to me, and I took one of the handles too, so we were holding it together, then we stood. The car of the wheel hung suspended in space and time.

"Now?"

"Now."

We tipped the bag over the side of the car. Then we did the second bag. Someone gasped in one of the cars below us. The cranes spilled, fluttering, all the colors of the lights below, falling in spirals, catching on the air, twisting. Sharp angles of their wings and beaks. Two hundred and sixty-one of them, paper birds, a confetti of birds, drifting down through the night air, spreading as they fell, caught in eddies and currents, caught on the struts of the wheel, landing inside cars.

I thought of Julie saying that Paris loved everyone, of Paris saying that she would embrace the town if she could.

Good-bye, Paris, I said silently in my head. I kept my eyes on the falling birds as long as I could, the cranes, which she had folded with her own hands, all of them.

I watched them fall, slowly, spiraling. Blue and yellow and red and pink. I remembered lying in bed, half-asleep, thinking of the place where birds live, above the town, as a kind of heaven, and that was the idea of course, to drop her from here, to put her in a kind of heaven.

It was like her soul had been divided into two hundred and sixty-one pieces, and now it was scattering over the glow of the town, over the brightness, spreading Paris all over, brightly colored pieces of her. Pan tore Echo into scraps, but the gods did the same to her voice, to her soul, made it everywhere and in fragments, so that she would never die, and now we had done the same for Paris, thrown her into the wind and the darkness and the glow of the town, the brightness, like Echo's voice flung into the rocks and the trees and the mountains, Procne in the song of the nightingale, ringing out her accusation but also her voice and her soul, singing that there was a part of her that would never be killed, as long as she was remembered, and in the same way Paris would always be around, because of the cranes, if we came up here, to the top of the wheel and the place where the town was laid out below us like a city of light, shining in the darkness, glowing, the hope of the resurrection.

"****," said Julie. "Some of them are stuck in the bag."

She reached in to pull them out, to dislodge them, and the wheel jolted into motion and we stumbled into each other, stupidly put our arms out to clutch each other, toppled over.

Julie screamed as we fell, but then the car was just moving slowly around and we weren't dropping down to the ground below, plummeting; we just fell on our asses on the cold, hard floor of the car.

"Ow," said Julie.

"Double ow," I said.

Quickly we scrabbled in the bag, yanked out the remaining cranes, threw them over the side—saw them whipped away by a sudden wind that had struck up.

Julie got up first and pulled me to my feet. Her hand went to her backside, and she made a disgusted face. "I have gum on my butt," she said.

And then I was laughing, and she was laughing, and we laughed so hard, we laughed until we cried.

And that's it.

But listen.

This is the important thing. When I fell into the water, the ocean got behind my eyes, and you . . . I feel like you have done the same.

You're behind my eyes; you're under my skin. The smell of your hair is in the cavities of my body, coursing in my veins. I can't get rid of it. And you were 100 percent there for me, I see that now, you were on my side—hell, even when I kissed Dwight you were still worried that my dad was forcing me into breaking up with you, that he was abusing me in some way . . . I mean, he wasn't, not really, but you still *cared*. You still wanted to help me.

You're on my team. You were, I mean. I never really had that before, not at school, not anywhere, my mom and dad just, but that's their job, right? I'm rambling. What I mean is: you are kind of amazing. I don't really deserve you, but I'd like to try to repay you if I can.

I'd like to be on your team.

100 percent.

So . . . meet me? When you have read this? At Pirate Golf, on Pier One, on Friday at five p.m.?

I know what you're thinking. You're thinking, *Why would I forgive this girl when she hurt me like that?* You're thinking, *Why would I want to see her again, after her dad kicked me out, said he didn't want me seeing her? Not to mention that she hears a voice.* And I understand that, I do. But I have some things to tell you, some things that might make you feel better.

I don't know. I don't want to pressure you.

But.

First: I like you. I like you a lot. And believe it or not, everything I did to hurt you, I really did, in a ******-up way, because I was trying to keep you safe. Truly. Okay, that's a lie. It's also because I was

520

embarrassed, by the voice, all that stuff. But . . . at least I'm honest, right? I mean, I am *now*. You don't need me to protect you, but I swear I will always try to.

Second . . .

It's about my dad. And about me.

After I got out of the hospital, Dad drove me home. We went silently into the house. We both knew things were going to be hard. There was going to be a lot of media intrusion. I was going to have to talk to Dr. Rezwari and Dr. Lewis. Work out where to go with my treatment.

I told Dad that in the hospital. I explained to him about the voice support group; I said how much it had helped me, how Dr. Rezwari was willing to try a collaborative approach. I told him how the *voice* helped me, when I was in the ocean, helped me to have the strength to climb. He didn't say anything, but he did nod, which I took as a positive sign.

Anyway.

We went into the den. I had been told to get lots of rest. Dad led me to the couch and sat me down and then sat down beside me.

"Is there anything I can do for you?" he said. He looked gray; he had lost so much weight. The stress had taken such a toll on him, I could see that now.

"Yes," I said.

"What? Food? Coffee?"

"You can forgive me," I said.

Dad frowned. It accentuated his new wrinkles, and I felt another stab of guilt. His muscled, tattooed arms were less muscled now.

But I was sick of feeling guilty.

I had had enough of feeling guilty.

"What?" he said.

"I want you to forgive me for . . . for . . ." I started to cry.

"Pull yourself to-*******-gether," said the voice, but I didn't mind, it was okay, that was just how the voice talked; I knew that now. Also it was quiet these days, not the loud voice it had been—more like a whisper in my ear. Almost as if it was the wind speaking, like I could ignore it easily if I wanted to.

"For what?" said Dad.

"For killing Mom," I said all in a rush.

"Oh," said Dad.

Silence hung between us like string drawn tight; a humming kind of silence—a bird hanging on the air, wings beating, or one of Dad's insects moving its legs together so fast you can't see them.

"Yeah," I said.

"Cass," said Dad slowly. "I don't think you killed your mom."

"You do," I said.

"You may think that. I don't."

I continued to cry; I felt better and worse at the same time. "I moved her head," I said. "I moved her head, and she had a head injury and—"

"She was already dead," said Dad, a strange expression on his face. "Didn't you . . . didn't you know?"

"What?"

"She was already dead, Cass. The doctors were very precise on that point." I was staring at him. I saw that his eyes were red, but there was such love in them—do you understand? Such love and such softness, it was like I had broken through some hard shell on the outside of him, some exoskeleton, and suddenly he was the flesh of the bug beneath, naked.

"What?" I said again, dumbly.

"She was already dead when you lifted her head, or at least there was no possibility of recovery. The doctors had no doubt. No doubt at all. The blow. It . . . it . . . it destroyed the cerebral cortex, pretty much. That's the part that does all the thinking. All the being."

"But I . . . you let . . . why didn't you . . ."

"Why didn't I tell you? It was an upsetting detail. I didn't think . . ."

"But when we argued," I said. "When you dumped out my pills, you said—"

"I was angry, Cass. I felt like I couldn't trust you. Like you were going behind my back again and again, and I didn't know how to get through to you and I just . . . snapped. I couldn't control it. And I was . . . I am . . . I was angry with myself, for not being there when she died. For the fact that it was you. That I wasn't there for her."

Snapping. It happens in a moment, it happens suddenly.

I knew that feeling. I knew what it was like.

"So you don't . . . you don't blame me?"

"Cass," he said, very softly, but then he fell silent.

"Yes?"

"Cass, I don't blame you. I blame myself, for not being there to stop it. You . . . I'm only grateful to you."

"*Grateful*? Why?"

He moved closer to me, put his arm around me. "You know what I tell myself? In the dark, at night. I tell myself . . ."

"Yeah?"

"I tell myself that the last thing she saw, the last thing she knew, was you reaching down to hold her. You, kneeling to pick her up. You. She loved you so much, you can't imagine. One day you'll get it, when you have kids, I guess. You were the universe to her, and all the stars in it. So I picture her looking at you, having you as her last sight in the world, your face, and then the darkness inside me goes away."

Oh.

I'll skip the next bit. There was a *lot* of crying. You don't need to see that.

But there was something else important.

After all the hugging was done, the hugging and the crying, I kind of coughed, like you do when there's something hard to say and you don't want to say it but at the same time you know you have to.

Cough.

"Dad," I said. "I'm not going to stop seeing that boy. I mean, I don't know if he will forgive me now, but I'm going to write him, and you can't stop me."

"Cass . . ."

"No. I'm not a little girl anymore." And that was true. Something had changed in me when I climbed that rope. I could feel it.

"I know that, and—"

"I swear to God, Dad, if you stand in my way, I will leave this house and you will never see me again."

He sighed.

A long silence.

"I don't want to stand in your way."

"So you won't stop me seeing him?"

Another silence.

"If you follow your doctor's orders," he said eventually, "if you—"

"Sure," I said. "I'll see her *and* Dr. Lewis, and we'll work it out together, I promise."

"Yes, yes," said Dad. "Him too. But fine. If you do all that, then I'm not going to stand in your way." He made a lame effort at a smile.

"Seriously? You're . . . you're fine with this? With me writing to him?"

"I wouldn't say I'm fine with it, but I can live with it." He stood up. "But I would say, Cass . . ." He looked pained. "I would say it's not me you need to convince. I don't know what you did to that boy, but last time I saw him he did *not* look happy."

"I know," I said.

Dad stood there for a moment, awkwardly. Then he let out a long breath. "Oh, **** it," he said. "If you write to him, tell him I'm sorry too."

Oh, and, ****, I'm running out of time now, but I'm aware, okay? I'm aware of what my dad said.

It is you I need to convince.

It is you I need to apologize to.

So . . . Here's the thing. I've learned stuff. I'm no longer the same person I was.

For example: I have learned that some people come into our lives, and then are gone. And that part of the thing, part of life, is to accept that fact, to accept that they're gone.

But there's something else too: and that's realizing that a part of them will *never* be gone. We think of lives as stopping, suddenly. But they don't. They are like waves, like ripples, like echoes that continue to resonate from their point of origin, out into the world. There was an Italian scientist named Marconi who said that sound waves, once generated, reverberate through the universe forever. Like, you could stand on Jupiter with a powerful-enough micro-phone and you'd hear conversations I had with my mom, with Paris.

I mean, he was wrong, sure. But I love the idea. It's like Echo, but real. Voices outlasting their owners.

And, of course, and more simply, I can just remember those voices, and that keeps them with me. Remember their lives. Remember their words. The time my mom carried me home from the store, just because she said I'd soon be too heavy to do it. The time Paris won that Elmo, with her terrible fishing.

But.

But there are also, of course, people you don't have to just remember, because they're still around.

And I guess that's the other thing I have learned. There are people who come into our lives, and then are gone. But there are *also* people who come into our lives and who *we need to hang on to.*

I have lost so many people. Friends, my mom, Paris. But there is one person I lost, and can maybe get back.

You.

I don't want to let you go. I need you, 100 percent on my side.

But here's the thing: I'm 100 percent on your side too. I mean, I'm not claiming I'm ever going to be the best girlfriend in the world. But I *know* you. I knew you the first time I saw you, in your muscles, in your smile. And I think you know me. And I think we could be something special.

And I will never, ever let you down.

Again.

I mean, I'll never let you down *again.*

Ahem.

So, more important, I'm also sorry, okay? I need to finish this and hit Send—otherwise you're not going to have time to read it before Friday—but I'm sorry.

I'm sorry for making you think that I was with someone else, if you ever did believe that, I don't know. If you didn't, then I'm sorry for making you think I was a total ***** who wanted to **** with your mind.

I'm sorry for shouting at your dad. I'm sorry for not under-standing, about your mom, about the music, about the swimming.

Though I hope that even if you do take the swim scholarship, you keep playing music.

It would be a shame if you stopped.

I'm sorry for everything the voice made me do.

And I would like another chance.

Oh.

Oh, I should tell you about the voice too, I mean, hell, maybe even if you forgive me you won't want to take me back because of the voice, because you don't want a crazy girlfriend. I would understand that, I would.

But here's the thing—I'm *not* crazy.

Something bad happened to me; I saw my mom die, and then when I found the foot on the beach, something went wrong, the needle skipped on the record in my brain—or substitute that with some more relevant modern analogy, I guess—and I started hearing a voice. But it was a *coping mechanism*. It took my hatred for myself and insulated me from it. Placed it outside myself.

And then, when I learned how to deal with it, how to act toward it, how to give it a schedule, limits, it started to help me.

I'm not crazy. I'm really not. I got hurt; I developed a scar; and now the scar is healing. I see Dr. Rezwari and Dr. Lewis together now, and I'm doing well. Dr. Rezwari has helped me to see that I maybe fixated on Paris a bit, obsessed about her disappearance as a distraction from thinking about my guilt over my mom. I mean, Dwight was right: I hardly even knew her. Which is not to say that I didn't like her.

I don't take the risperidone at all anymore. The paroxetine, I still take. Dr. Rezwari was right about antidepressants, as it turns out: they just make everything a little bit easier, for now anyway. The plan is that, at some point, I can slowly ease off them—NOT just stop taking them right away, because both Rezwari and Lewis have helped me to see that dropping my drugs instantly might not have been the best decision I ever made. I mean, I went after a serial killer. I knowingly ate a chocolate bar that could contain nuts; I pretended to be with Dwight, to get rid of you so that I didn't have to tell you the truth.

I was not, let's say, strictly rational.

But anyway, the antidepressants are it for now—most of it's using the techniques Dr. Lewis has taught me. I've got one more year of school, and I'm going to make it count, go to college, study Classics. I'd like to anyway.

And the truth is, I hardly hear the voice anymore. And when I do, it's helpful, it's nice . . . Well, okay, not *nice*. But it's like my friend now, it points out things that I might have missed, it gives me clues, it gives me cues. It's *useful*.

And it really is no more than a whisper, it's so quiet, and it's hardly ever there.

What else?

I joined Julie's roller derby team. I suck at it, but it's fun, and I like feeling part of the group. A group that doesn't involve people talking about their invisible voices. Though I still go to that group anyway. How long I'll be able to hang out with Julie for, I don't know. I want to go to college, and I think I'd like to leave Oakwood to do it. But for now it's good, I mean she's good, I mean she's my friend and that's good.

It's nice to have a friend. That sounds like the lamest, most bland thing anyone has ever said, but it's true.

And anyway:

This is who I am.

So.

So I lost myself for a long time, and I did some terrible things to you and told you some terrible lies. But this is me now, okay? This is my real voice, my one true voice, which I am sending to you through the ether, over the wires and the wireless, so that you can hear it.

I'm like Echo, speaking to you when you can't see me, I'm like the voice that came to whisper to me and insulted me and made me hurt myself but in the end, right at the very end, became my friend.

But now I want to be a real girl, not just a voice, I want my body back, and I want you to be the one to hold it; I want to hear my name on your lips.

I want you to be the one to whisper to me.

SEND.

Author's Note

I have only heard voices once. I was babysitting at a house where I would often spend the night if the parents were going to be out late. The children were asleep, the parents were still out, and I was lying in bed, and I could hear people, in the room, discussing me. Discussing me in very cold, contemptuous tones. "Look at him. What an idiot. He can't even see us." It was so profoundly disturbing—a precisely accurate term in this case—that it bubbled up years later in this book.

I can only imagine though what it would be like to hear voices more often. And that's what I have tried to do in *Whisper to Me*—to imagine it, and imagine how it could be conquered.

Because these kinds of illnesses—or traumas—*can* be conquered. That's something I don't have to imagine, since for a number of reasons and in a number of ways I have had close and direct experience of mental illness for a large part of my life. And I know, for an absolute fact, that people can get better. Things can get better. Life can get better.

Estimates vary, but statistics reported by the Mental Health Foundation put the proportion of teenagers suffering from some kind of mental problem at around 10 percent. It's not unusual, it doesn't make you weird—it's very common. And it is extremely important to know, if you happen to be one of those teenagers, that help is available—and it works.

Never listen to any kind of voice inside you that says things will not get better.

Things can get better, and with help, they will.

In the United States:

National Alliance on Mental Illness (www.nami.org)
The Hearing Voices Network USA (www.hearingvoicesusa.org)

In the United Kingdom:

MIND (www.mind.org.uk)
Hearing Voices Network (www.hearing-voices.org)

The techniques used by Dr. Lewis in this fictional work are similar to those employed by the Hearing Voices Network, a support organization inspired by the academic research of Professor Marius Romme and Sandra Escher. They have coauthored several fascinating books on the subject, including the seminal *Accepting Voices*.

In real life, as in the novel, there is some tension between this approach—which stresses the roots in trauma for much voice hearing and the practical tools that can be employed to deal with it—and the psychiatric one. However, this is *Cassie*'s story: it isn't intended to present my or anyone else's view on that debate, and

I hope that it gives as balanced a perspective as possible. It also goes without saying that Cassie, Dr. Lewis, Dr. Rezwari, and all the characters in this book are figments of my imagination and any resemblance to any actual person, living or dead, is entirely coincidental.

Acknowledgments

I am deeply grateful to psychiatrist Dr. Martine Lamy, MD, PhD, and psychologist Dr. Michelle Madore, PhD, for their assistance in reading an earlier draft of this book and making comments. Any errors that remain are, of course, mine and mine alone.

My wife, Hannah; my editors, Cindy Loh and Rebecca McNally; and my faithful Second Reader, Will Hill, all made invaluable suggestions that helped me in the shaping of this story. It was a hard one to marshal, and without all of them it would be a mess. Thank you.